MICHAEL VEY

THE PARASITE

BOOK EIGHT

MICHAEL VEY

THE PARASITE

BOOK EIGHT

RICHARD PAUL EVANS

MERCURY INK

SIMON PULSE

NEW YORK   LONDON   TORONTO   SYDNEY   NEW DELHI

This book is a work of fiction. Any references to historical events, real people, or real
places are used fictitiously. Other names, characters, places, and events are products
of the author's imagination, and any resemblance to actual events or places or persons,
living or dead, is entirely coincidental.

SIMON PULSE / MERCURY INK
An imprint of Simon & Schuster Children's Publishing Division
1230 Avenue of the Americas, New York, NY 10020
First Simon Pulse/Mercury Ink hardcover edition September 2022
Text copyright © 2022 by Richard Paul Evans
Jacket illustration copyright © 2022 by Owen Richardson
All rights reserved, including the right of reproduction in whole or in part in any form.
Simon Pulse and colophon are registered trademarks of Simon & Schuster, Inc.
Mercury Ink is a trademark of Mercury Radio Arts, Inc.
For information about special discounts for bulk purchases, please contact
Simon & Schuster Special Sales at 1-866-506-1949 or business@simonandschuster.com.
The Simon & Schuster Speakers Bureau can bring authors to your live event.
For more information or to book an event contact the Simon & Schuster Speakers
Bureau at 1-866-248-3049 or visit our website at www.simonspeakers.com.
Jacket designed by Tiara Iandiorio
Interior designed by Mike Rosamilia
The text of this book was set in Berling LT Std.
Manufactured in the United States of America
2 4 6 8 10 9 7 5 3 1
Library of Congress Control Number 2022936946
ISBN 978-1-6659-1952-4 (hc)
ISBN 978-1-6659-1954-8 (ebook)

To Glenn Beck. Thank you for believing in Michael Vey from the very beginning.

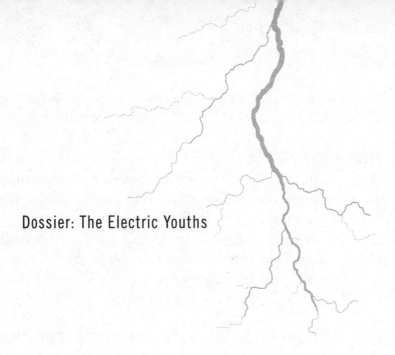

Dossier: The Electric Youths

Michael Vey

Power: Ability to shock people through direct contact or conduction. Can also absorb other electric children's powers.

Michael is the most powerful of all the electric children and leader of the Electroclan. He is currently studying international business at Boise State University as he prepares to someday take over as CEO of the Veytric Corporation (the former Elgen Corporation) from his father. Michael and Taylor are boyfriend–girlfriend. Many Tuvaluans still think of Michael as the lightning god Uira te Atua.

Ostin Liss

Power: Not an electric child.

Ostin is very intelligent, with an IQ of 155, which puts him at the same level as the average Nobel Prize winner. He is one of the original three members of the Electroclan and Michael's best friend.

He is currently enrolled in advanced courses in math and physics at Caltech in Pasadena, California. McKenna is still his girlfriend.

Taylor Ridley

Power: Ability to scramble the electric synapses in the brain, causing temporary confusion. She can also read people's minds, but only when touching them.

Taylor is Tara's identical twin sister, and is one of the original three founding members of the Electroclan. She is also Michael's girlfriend. She and Michael discovered each other's powers at Meridian High School, which they were both attending. Taylor and her twin, Tara, are roommates and psychology majors at Arizona State University in Phoenix. In addition to Taylor's ability to scramble and read minds, a new power has begun to emerge. She dreams of events before they happen.

Abigail

Power: Ability to temporarily stop pain by electrically stimulating certain parts of the brain. She must be touching the person to do so.

Along with Ian and McKenna, Abigail was held captive by the Elgen for many years because she refused to follow Hatch. She joined the Electroclan after escaping from the Elgen Academy's prison, known as Purgatory. She is currently studying to become a CRNA at Texas Christian University in Fort Worth, Texas.

Bryan

Power: The ability to create highly focused electricity that allows him to cut through objects.

Bryan is one of Hatch's Glows, and one of two Glows still loyal to the former Elgen. Since the fall of the Elgen, Bryan's whereabouts are unknown. He is believed to be with Kylee.

Cassy

Power: An extremely powerful electric, Cassy has the ability to freeze muscles from a distance of more than two kilometers. She also has the ability to cause mass heart attacks.

Cassy was rescued by the voice before the Elgen knew of her existence. She was raised and trained in Switzerland by the voice. She is currently working with Dr. Coonradt in Switzerland as a liaison between Veytric and the EU. She fell in love with Michael while battling the Elgen in Taiwan.

Grace

Power: Grace acts as a "human flash drive" and is able to transfer and store large amounts of electronic data.

Grace was living with the Elgen but joined the Electroclan when they defeated Hatch at the Elgen Academy. She worked with the resistance but had not been on any missions with the Electroclan. After the fall of the Elgen she went to work with Carl Vey and Veytric.

Ian

Power: Ability to see through electrolocation, which is the same way sharks and eels see through muddy or murky water.

Along with McKenna and Abigail, Ian was held captive by the Elgen for many years because he refused to follow Hatch. He joined the Electroclan after escaping from the Elgen Academy's prison. He is currently leading an oceanic exploration team hunting for sunken treasure and shipwrecks. He has been featured on the History Channel and the Discovery Channel. He is currently working with famed producer Tim Horejs on a documentary called Atlantis Uncovered.

Jack

Power: Not an electric child.

Jack spends a lot of time in the gym and is very strong. He is also excellent with cars. Originally one of Michael's bullies, he joined the Electroclan after Michael bribed him to help Michael rescue his mother from Dr. Hatch. He has been hired by the Veytric Corporation (the former Elgen Corporation) as the assistant head of security. He is currently stationed in South America. The distance has caused a rift between him and Abigail, who is currently studying at Texas Christian University in Fort Worth, Texas.

Kylee

Power: Born with the ability to create electromagnetic power, she is basically a human magnet.

One of Hatch's Glows, she spends most of her time shopping. Kylee and Bryan are the only Glows who remained loyal to Hatch after the battle of Hades. Along with Bryan, she is currently a fugitive. Whereabouts unknown.

McKenna

Power: Ability to create light and heat. She can heat herself to more than three thousand kelvins.

Along with Ian and Abigail, McKenna was held captive by the Elgen for many years because she refused to follow Hatch. She joined the Electroclan after escaping from the Elgen Academy's prison, known as Purgatory. McKenna is studying thermal engineering at Stanford University. McKenna and Ostin are still a "unit," as Ostin calls it.

Nichelle

Power: Nichelle acts as an electrical ground and can both detect and drain the powers of the other electric children. She can also enhance their powers, though not nearly as much as Tessa can.

Nichelle was Hatch's main source of power over the rest of the electric children until he abandoned her during the battle at the Elgen Academy. Although everyone was nervous about it, the Electroclan recruited her to join them on their mission to save Jade Dragon, and she has become a loyal Electroclan member. She is currently living in Spokane, Washington, where she attends Gonzaga University.

Quentin

Power: Ability to create isolated electromagnetic pulses, which lets him take out all electrical devices within twenty yards.

Quentin is the president of Hatch's Glows. Before his defection, he was regarded by the Elgen as the second-in-command, just below Hatch. He is now a member of the Electroclan. After the fall of the Elgen, he moved to Florida, where he started several businesses, including a popular dance club called Q.

Tanner

Power: Ability to interfere with airplanes' electrical navigation systems and cause them to malfunction and crash. His powers are so advanced that he can do this from the ground.

After years of mistreatment by the Elgen, Tanner was rescued by the Electroclan from the Peruvian Starxource plant and was subsequently staying with the resistance so he had a chance to recover. Tanner died in the battle of Hades. There is a monument to him, and other fallen heroes, on the north end of the island.

Tara

Power: Tara's abilities are similar to her twin sister's in that she can disrupt normal electronic brain functions. Through years of practicing and refining her powers, Tara has learned to focus on specific parts of the brain in order to create emotions such as fear or joy.

Tara is Taylor's twin (they were adopted by different families after they were born) and lived with Hatch and the Elgen since she was six years old. Tara is now Taylor's roommate at Arizona State University. Like her sister, she is studying psychology.

Tessa

Power: Tessa's abilities are the opposite of Nichelle's main power—Tessa is able to enhance the powers of the other electric children.

Tessa escaped from the Elgen at the Starxource plant in Peru and lived in the Amazon jungle for six months with an indigenous tribe called the Amacarra. She joined the Electroclan after the tribe rescued Michael from the Elgen and brought them together. She is currently just enjoying her life, painting and working on a book about her adventures in the jungle living with the Amacarra tribe.

Torstyn

Power: One of the more lethal of the electric children, Torstyn can create microwaves.

Torstyn is one of Hatch's Glows and was instrumental to the Elgen in building the Peruvian Starxource plant. He is Quentin's right-hand man. He was always a thrill-seeker and extremist and, with only his powers, would hunt anacondas and jaguars in the jungles of Peru. After the end of the Elgen, he moved to Florida with Quentin, but his need for danger pushed him into undesirable company.

Wade

Power: Not an electric child.

Wade was Jack's best friend and joined the Electroclan at the same time he did. Wade was killed in the jungles of Peru when he was surprised by an Elgen guard. Jack commissioned a monument for his friend, which was erected in the jungle at the place where Wade fell. Though the site is difficult to get to, Jack visits the monument every year to lay flowers.

Zeus

Power: Ability to "throw" electricity from his body.

Zeus (real name Frank) was kidnapped by the Elgen as a young child and lived for many years as one of Hatch's Glows. He joined the Electroclan when they escaped from the Elgen Academy. Zeus is currently trying to decide what he wants to do with his life and is in no particular hurry to find out.

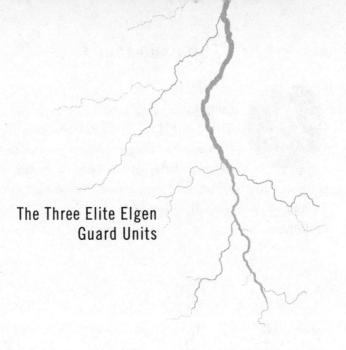

The Three Elite Elgen
Guard Units

Chasqui

Translated from the ancient Quechuan dialect, the word *"chasqui"* means "messenger of light." The Chasqui are a special Elgen military order in Peru. Their roles are specifically connected to the Peruvian Starxource plant in Puerto Maldonado. Like the other elite Elgen units, they operate independently of the Elgen command.

Domguard

Also known as the "Order of the Amber Tunic." The Domguard are a very powerful and secretive global force. They operate more as a cult than a corporate security force. Their intense, esoteric beliefs and their worship of the electric children make them the most dangerous of the Elite Guard.

 **Lung Li**

The Lung Li (literally translated from Mandarin Chinese as "dragon power") is a special Chinese Elgen military order. Their activities are limited to countries in the Eastern Hemisphere, including China, Singapore, Taiwan, Korea, Japan, Vietnam, Cambodia, Thailand, and the Philippines.

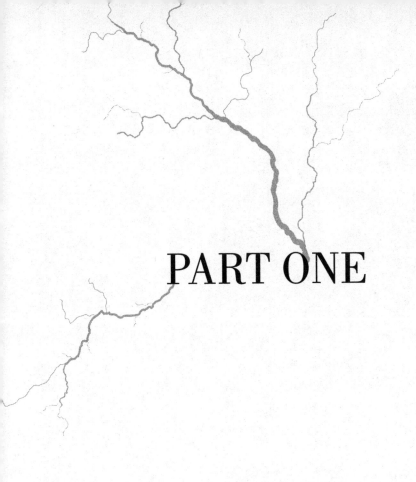

PART ONE

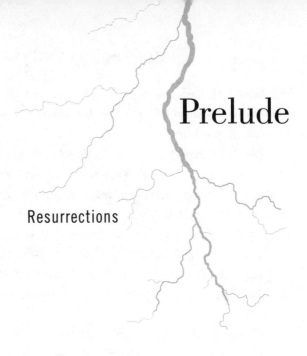

Prelude

Resurrections

**Chasqui Elgen Guard Headquarters, Peru
(Three Years Earlier)**

"Your Eminence, we've just received an intelligence."

"Intelligence," the Chasqui sovereign repeated without looking up. "Why must they call it that? What is this *intelligence*, Lieutenant?"

"Admiral-General Hatch is dead."

Eli Amash, the Chasqui's sovereign leader, looked up from the maps he was studying. "Are you certain?"

"An agent on Funafuti radioed the message during the night."

Amash pounded his fist down onto his desk. "The Domguard beat us to him. I didn't expect them to make their move so soon."

"It wasn't the Domguard, Your Eminence. It was Michael Vey."

The sovereign looked at him quizzically. "Michael Vey is dead."

"That is what we believed, Your Eminence. But Vey is alive."

"That's impossible, Lieutenant. I saw him die. He was struck by lightning on the Hades radio tower just before that explosion decimated the island. Even if he survived the lightning and the explosion, he couldn't have survived the fall from the tower. It was more than two hundred feet high."

"We can't explain it, Your Eminence. But we have confirmed it was Vey. We have multiple eyewitness reports, and one of our agents sent a digital video before he was captured by the Tuvaluan rebels. I have seen it myself. It is Vey. Only, his power has grown."

The Chasqui sovereign considered the report. "Perhaps being struck by lightning added to Vey's power. What of Tuvalu?"

"The Tuvaluans have regained control of their country. They have overthrown the remaining Elgen forces and freed their prime minister."

"Where are the Elgen boats?"

"All were sunk except for the *Edison*, which was out to sea when the insurrection began. We do not know the status of the *Joule*."

"And where are Hatch's electric children?"

"Also unknown, Your Eminence."

The sovereign tapped his pen on his desk as he thought over his next move.

". . . There's more, Your Eminence. We have discovered the identity of the voice."

"Yes?"

"The voice is scientist Dr. Coonradt, the inventor of the MEI."

"Coonradt was also believed dead. . . ."

"And he was working with Carl Vey."

"Another dead man. Remarkable. The resistance was far more clever than we believed. Let us hope that Hatch stays dead. What of Hatch's EGGs? Have they tried to take control of the Elgen?"

"No. Except for Welch, they are all in the custody of the Tuvaluans. We could free them."

"No. Let the Tuvaluans deal with them and save us the trouble."

"What are your orders, Your Eminence?"

"Send out forces to raid all South American Starxource plants. Secure all computers and files—then bring the Elgen soldiers and scientists to the compound in Puerto."

"What if they won't come?"

"Then eliminate them. Anyone not with us is against us." He scratched his chin. "One more thing. I want you to bring me two Glows: the one they call Grace and the one they call Taylor. Grace has access to all the information the Elgen hold, every hidden account, the name of every official Hatch bribed or threatened along the way. She knows everything."

"Do we know her whereabouts?"

"The last we knew, she was with the voice."

"And the other Glow? What is her benefit to us?"

"The Glow Taylor has powers she does not yet fully understand or comprehend."

"What kind of powers?"

"She can see the future. Grace knows everything that has happened in the past, but Taylor knows what will happen in the future. But we must hurry. With Hatch gone, the Domguard will immediately start hunting the Glows, so they can worship them in their twisted rituals." He breathed out slowly. "I think I would like to know more about Michael Vey."

"I will see to it, Your Eminence. Should we prepare to capture all the Glows?"

"In time. Right now, just bring me Taylor and Grace. Whoever captures Grace will rule the empire the Elgen built. But whoever captures Taylor will rule the world."

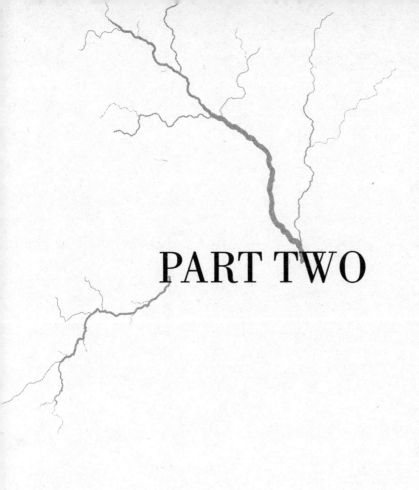

PART TWO

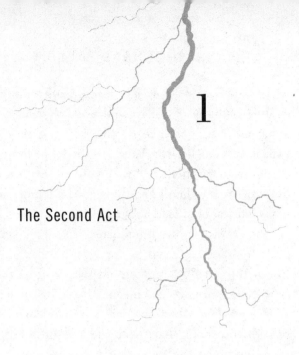

1

The Second Act

My life is snoring.
Everything's boring.

Tuesday, April 16 (My Birthday)

My name is Michael Vey. It's been a few years since I've written anything about my life. Really, there hasn't been a whole lot to write about. At least not anything you'd want to read. That's because the last three years have been what most people consider normal—and by "normal," I mean not being tied up and fed to rats or being hunted by a homicidal maniac who bought a cannibal fork so he could celebrate his victory over us by eating me.

I'm in my second semester of my junior year of college, working toward a business management degree. Even that sounds boring. I scribbled that rhyme—technically a couplet—as I counted down the minutes until class was over. Other than our upcoming Electroclan reunion, there's nothing in my life that vaguely excites me right now.

The thing is, in a life like mine, normal doesn't feel *normal*. I hear these college students around me talk about what they want to do with their lives. I've already faced death, brought down a dictator, captured billions of dollars, and saved the world from Elgen tyranny. What am I supposed to do for a second act? I mean, what other college student has the Tuvaluan medal of honor and is also on the Peruvian government's Most-Wanted Terrorists list? (I'm still on it. You can see it online.) The thing is, easy living makes for boring reading. Who wants to read about someone's normal day?

Since I last wrote, I graduated from high school, started college at Boise State, and went fishing with my dad in Alaska. Actually, the fishing thing had its moment. My dad and I were fishing for salmon at Mendenhall Lake in Juneau. After an hour we still hadn't caught anything when I had an idea. I put my hand into the water and pulsed. You should have seen the fish jump out of the water. Six of them jumped into the boat. It was crazy. A thirty-inch king salmon smacked me in the face. Another landed in my dad's lap. My dad hinted that it took the fun out of fishing, but really, how much fun is fishing anyway? Sitting around in a boat holding a stick? Besides, I don't think catching fish was really what was on his mind. I think he just wanted to spend time with me. After him being gone for eight years, we had a lot to catch up on.

Which leads me to another thought. The last time I wrote, I had just found out that my father was alive, something I learned just as General-Admiral-President-Doctor Hatch—whatever he was calling himself back then—was about to kill him. I'm grateful he's back, but it's changed things. To be honest, reconnecting with my father was harder than I thought it would be. A lot harder. First, deep inside, I think I still have some resentment for what his "death" put my mother and me through. I'm not saying he didn't do the right thing in faking his death. We were all in real danger, and faking his death was probably the only way my father could have kept us all from really dying.

Second, for all those years, my mother and I were all we had, so there's a special bond there. It's not like I have an Oedipus complex or anything. I just still feel intensely protective of her. That's why I risked my life rescuing her from the Elgen. People say things like "I'd take a bullet for you," but I really did. That's something few people will ever experience. I feel guilty saying this, but, in all honesty, it felt a little like my father was crashing the party. But I'm working through this. At least I'm trying. Maybe I need a therapist.

Having a father around isn't the only major change I'm dealing with. We now live in a mansion in the same neighborhood where I went to my first real party—the one where I knocked Corky over. It still doesn't feel real. Maybe it's imposter syndrome.

I think my dad bought the mansion because he was trying to make up for all my mother and I had gone without, but my mom really didn't want a house that big. "It's just more to clean," she says. So, we got house cleaners. But I think there's more to it. We had lived in little apartments for so long, it's what we were used to. In our apartment I couldn't sneeze without my mother asking me if I was coming down with something. Now I could scream in my room and no one would hear me. Like in outer space.

Taylor and I are still together—at least emotionally. I'm here in Boise, and she's studying psychology at ASU in Phoenix, Arizona.

Taylor and her twin sister, Tara, are roommates. I don't know what Tara's majoring in. Maybe psychology as well, but more likely partying. I love Tara, but talk about head games. One time, she made everyone think she was Ostin. I suspected something, so I said, "Ostin, explain again the Dyson sphere." Tara just looked at me, then said, "I'm not feeling like it," which, frankly, was more revealing than her not knowing what a Dyson sphere was. The one thing Ostin is never *not* in the mood for—besides eating—is explaining something.

Case in point. I once asked him a complex geometry question. I was doing homework late at night, and he was watching TV. He answered the question correctly. When I said thank you, he didn't answer. When I checked on him, he was asleep.

I'm not really sure where Jack and Abi are. At least relationally. Physically, Jack went to Italy for a year to train with Veytric Security and then was re-stationed in Brazil. It's his job to watch over all the South American Starxource plants. The Peruvian Starxource plant in the jungle we destroyed was never rebuilt. A new one was constructed closer to Lima, which made more sense.

The first time Jack went back to Peru, he called me and we reminisced about the old days, like when Zeus saved us all by setting off the sprinkler system, killing the rats and almost himself in the process. Jack said it was a head trip going back, like a soldier returning to an old war zone. He even went back to the spot where Wade was killed. I don't think Jack will ever get over that. None of us will, but no one was as affected as Jack.

Jack wanted Abi to go with him to Italy, then South America, but she didn't. She had her own dreams. I think that's what started the rift between them. I don't blame Abi for not going. She wanted to go into the field of medicine. She started in nursing. She's exactly the kind of nurse I'd want—especially since she can take away pain without drugs. Then she decided to get her doctorate as a nurse anesthetist at Texas Christian University in Fort Worth. That way she can take away pain without always suffering herself.

Then, there's Ostin. Ostin's studying at Caltech. If you don't know where Caltech is, don't worry, you're not going there. It's one of those schools where you have to have a 4.17 grade point average to get in. I didn't even know that grade point averages went that high. That means if you have a straight-A GPA, you're way below average.

Of course, Ostin is anything but average. His SAT was 1600, which is perfect. To put that into perspective, more than two million students take the test each year. Less than five hundred people get a perfect score. That's like half of a percent of a percent of a percent. Ostin didn't just get a perfect score—he finished the test in less than an hour. The SAT is supposed to take three hours and fifteen minutes with breaks. He answered the last question at forty-seven minutes, twelve seconds. He timed it. Of course he did.

I don't know why I thought everything would be easy after defeating the Elgen—as if I thought the world was peaceful except for them.

It's not. It never has been. There will always be monsters and bullies. Big countries bully little countries. Countries bully citizens. Citizens bully each other. Maybe if people were more kind, countries would be too.

After all we experienced, it's no surprise that I have some PTSD. I've heard it said that soldiers can leave the war but the war doesn't always leave them. I get it. Sometimes I wake in the night screaming.

A few years ago, I woke screaming, and my mother came in to check on me. I was still asleep and I thought she was an Elgen guard. I shocked her so badly, she lost consciousness. It could have been much worse. I could have electrocuted her. I lock my door now.

Like I said, things have been pretty predictable and dull, and the only thing I was really looking forward to was our upcoming Electroclan reunion. And that's when my story got interesting again.

I was hoping for something exciting to come along. I guess I should be more careful of what I wish for.

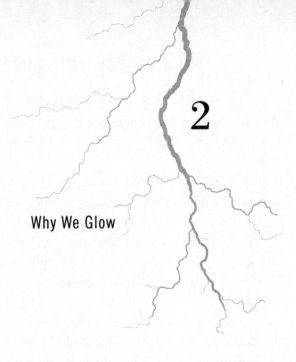

2

Why We Glow

I was walking to the student union building to get some lunch when my phone rang. The ringtone was the sound of dueling light sabers. I let Ostin pick his own ringtone.

"I know why you glow," Ostin said before I could speak.

Classic Ostin. Normal people start phone calls with a question, like "How are you?" or "Whassup?" or, considering the day, "Happy birthday, man." Not Ostin. He always started calls with a declaration, like, "Tesla was definitely smarter than Edison," or "Dark matter accounts for eighty-five percent of the matter in the universe." Or, in this case, "I know why you glow."

But then, Ostin's not exactly normal. I don't mean that as an insult. Actually, it's a compliment. What makes Ostin *abnormal* is precisely what I admire most about him. Normal people don't change the world.

"That's what you're studying at school? Why we glow?"

"No. I was doing my own research and figured that out on my own."

I'm guessing that Ostin's the only student at Caltech who creates his own homework, because he didn't have enough already. He once told me that he resented sleeping because it took away from his study time. (He also told me that he loved to sleep because it was like death without the commitment.)

"So why do we glow?" I asked.

"The same reason the *Aequorea victoria* species of jellyfish glows. It has a fluorescent protein that generates bioluminescence. But there's more."

Of course there is.

"I figured out that if I were to place a single protein on an aluminum electrode and expose it to ultraviolet light, it would create a nanoscale electric current. So here's my idea. Imagine merging a sentient organism with nanoscale technology. Totally Borg."

"I have no idea what you just said. Speak like a normal human."

"Which part didn't you understand?"

"Pretty much all of it. Actually, all of it."

"Let me put it this way. We could take a small piece of a jellyfish and use it as a battery to run small devices."

I just shook my head. Ostin would probably win a Nobel Prize for something he did for fun. "You did all that research, and it had nothing to do with your studies?"

"It's my extracurricular activity. All schools have extracurricular activities."

"That usually means a fraternity or sports," I said. "Or pranks."

"We've got pranks. Caltechians are famous for their pranks. In fact, pranks are encouraged by the administration. As long as property isn't damaged, no laws are broken, and no one gets hurt."

"What kind of pranks?"

"Creative ones, of course. One year a group of Caltechians showed up in Boston on registration day and handed out free MIT T-shirts. The back of the shirts read, Because Not Everyone Can Go to Caltech."

I laughed. "That's funny."

"Another time, they hacked into the scoreboard during the Rose Bowl and changed the teams, from UCLA versus Illinois, to Caltech thirty-eight, MIT nine, which is probably the only way Caltech would win the Rose Bowl."

"That's the *only* way Caltech would get into the Rose Bowl," I said. "Does Caltech even have a football team?"

"They did, but they shut it down thirty years ago. We were the Beavers."

I couldn't tell if he was joking, even though he never joked. "The Beavers?"

"Yeah."

"Not even 'the fighting Beavers'?"

"Nope. Just Beavers."

"Fierce," I said. I actually expected something like the Caltech Technicians or the Killer Droids. "Were they any good?"

"I don't think they would have shut the program down if they were any good."

"Of course not."

"But *if* they ever brought football back and if they made it to the Rose Bowl . . ."

". . . Two majorly unlikely 'ifs,'" I said.

"I know, but if it happened, I have an idea for an awesome prank."

"Again, not going to happen, but tell me about it."

"I'm going to figure out a way to project a hologram of a flying saucer right above the field."

"That would be cool until someone has a heart attack or gets trampled in the panic."

"Why would someone have a heart attack or panic?"

"Because it's a UFO . . ."

Ostin didn't respond.

". . . and they were terrified."

Still nothing.

"It would be like Orson Welles's *War of the Worlds* broadcast."

"That made broadcast history. I could make history."

"You already made history when you helped bring down the Elgen. Maybe you should just stick to your studies."

"Too boring." Only Ostin could go to the toughest school in the world and be bored.

"I still think you should have just taken the job with Veytric. You could learn on the job with some of the top scientists in the world."

"I know. But it's like those high school football players going straight to the pros. Sometimes it's best to finish school."

"Wisely said. So whassup?"

"I just finished my *final* final." He sounded sad about this. I'm sure he was.

"How did you . . . ?" I stopped myself. Stupid question. "Perfect score?"

"Yeah. I found a mistake the professor made on the test. I showed him."

"I'm guessing he probably wasn't too happy about that."

"He wasn't. How did you know that?"

That was just so Ostin. He could recite pi to a hundred thousand digits but couldn't understand why showing up his professor might make his professor mad.

"So what are you going to do with all your free time? Besides study jellyfish and hologram projection."

"I've been doing some sightseeing. You know Caltech is in Pasadena. It's less than a mile from the old Elgen Academy."

The mere mention of the place made me feel nauseous. Home of Cell 25.

"I was thinking of going back to visit. For old times' sake."

"That's like Custer going back to Little Bighorn," I said.

"No. Custer died. We didn't."

"We came close enough," I said. "Besides, I'd rather not remember that. I hear it's a private school now."

"It is. I wonder what they did with Cell 25."

"It's probably just a storage closet now. When is your flight home?"

"Tomorrow. Six twenty-nine p.m. Unless it's late. Delta flight 1275."

"That's precise. When does McKenna get into town?"

"Thursday, four fifty-five p.m. United flight 2274. What about Taylor?"

"Tara and Taylor get in tomorrow afternoon. They're flying in on the company Learjet."

"The company jets are sweet," Ostin said.

"I try to forget Hatch used to tool around in those. Do you need a ride home from the airport?"

"No, my parents are picking me up. Then we're going straight to dinner. Dorothy's worried that once McKenna gets here, she'll never see me." (Ostin had taken to calling his mother by her first name.)

"She's a little possessive of you."

"I just hope she doesn't make a Welcome Home sign with a balloon arch she wants me to walk through. It's so embarrassing." He changed the subject. "We've got to do PizzaMax. For old times' sake."

"I heard they might be closing."

"What? Kill me now."

"Won't do that."

"Then I'll buy it."

"Maybe it's just a rumor. Give me a call when you get home."

"Before you hang up, happy birthday. I have a present for you."

"Is it a Caltech sweatshirt?" I asked.

"How did you know that?"

"Lucky guess. I'll wear it on the Boise campus. Impress people."

"I'll see you tomorrow," he said.

"See you, Liss." We hung up. "Go, Beavers."

The student union was always crowded. Or maybe it just felt that way because I was always alone. Nothing makes you feel lonely like a crowd.

I got a bowl of rice noodles with spicy pork, and a slice of pizza, then sat down to eat. I spent a lot of time alone at school. Sometimes I felt like an invisible man walking through a campus of people who didn't know me and had no idea what I'd been through. Think of it this way—what if you were a soldier and you'd escaped from a POW camp where you'd been tortured and beaten on a regular basis. Then you got home and you heard someone say, "I broke a nail today. Life is so hard."

That's what my life felt like every day, which led to this observation. *The more insignificant someone's life is, the more they try to make insignificant things seem big.* Just human nature, I guess.

I was halfway through my meal when my phone rang again. It was Taylor. Her ringtone was an oldie she also programmed herself—"Take My Breath Away." No explanation needed.

I missed her. We were in an awkward place, where we were too young to commit to something permanent, but after what we'd been through, I knew she was the one I wanted to spend the rest of my life with.

Taylor wasn't as lonely as I was, since she was with her twin sister, Tara. They had a lot of missed time to make up for. Today was Taylor and Tara's birthday as well.

"Happy birthday, gorgeous," I said.

"Happy birthday to you, handsome electric man. What are you doing?"

"Eating lunch."

"With who?"

"Just me."

"That makes me sad. You're eating alone on your birthday?"

"I eat alone every day."

"You should find some friends."

"I have all the friends I need. I just hung up with Ostin."

"What's he up to?"

"The usual brain games. He just gets smarter."

"He'd lose his mind here. You'll never believe how stupid some of these students are. Today, in my astronomy class, one girl asked why meteors always fell into craters."

"Was she serious?"

"As serious as a brain aneurysm. And last week, in my social psychology class, we had a pop quiz. There were twenty true-or-false questions. One of the students got every one of them wrong. I mean, he could have guessed and gotten at least half of them right. The professor was so amazed that he bought the student a cup of coffee."

"That's a special kind of stupid," I said.

"Stupid is what stupid does," she said.

"You mean like live in a different city than my girlfriend?"

She sighed. "I miss you, Michael. But I'll see you tomorrow."

"A temporary reprieve."

"Yeah, but right now I'll take every minute with you I can. Are your parents doing something for your birthday?"

"My mother made me waffles for breakfast. Like always."

"She'll never change."

"I hope not. How about you?"

"We're celebrating tomorrow. My mom's making a cake for Tara and me." She lightly groaned. "Tara's calling. I'd better take it. I sent her on an errand, and she's probably lost. I'll see you tomorrow. Bye, love."

"Bye." I hung up my phone. Having Taylor back was really the only birthday present I wanted.

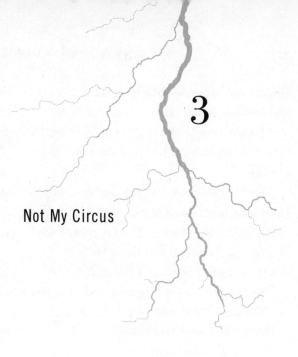

3

Not My Circus

I finished my lunch, then grabbed my backpack and walked across campus to my car. As I was crossing the parking lot, my thoughts were disrupted by the sound of two people arguing. About twenty yards in front of me a man and a woman were standing between two cars, the woman with her back to me. The fight sounded pretty heated, so I looked away. *Not my circus, not my monkeys.*

When I was parallel to them, I glanced over. The woman was petite with long brunette hair. She was clearly the student of the two. She wore glasses and had a backpack over one shoulder. The guy was tall and bald, with an anchor beard and mustache. He looked like he was a bodybuilder, with a thick upper body and narrow waist.

I soon realized that it wasn't an argument but an attack. The dude, who was like twice her size, was red in the face from yelling at her.

Suddenly he grabbed her by the hair and slammed her head

against the truck with a loud bang. She dropped her backpack and grabbed her head.

"Please stop," she said, her voice trembling. Her head was down, cowering from him, her hair covering her face. "I was only trying to explain—"

"Don't talk back to me!" he shouted. Before she could say anything else, he clocked her on the side of the head. Her glasses flew off as she fell to the ground. She lay there, blindly groping for her glasses. She found them and put them back on.

Dude, leave her alone, I thought.

"Are you sorry yet?" he shouted. "Or you still got excuses?"

"I'm sorry," she said.

He kicked her. "You sure?"

"Yes. I'm really sorry."

That's enough, I thought. I set my backpack on the ground, then walked back toward them. Like I said, the guy was big, like football-lineman big. He kind of reminded me of an Elgen guard without the uniform and weapons. Not that he intimidated me. It had been a long time since anyone had scared me. Swallowing lightning will do that.

"Hey," I shouted at him. "Leave her alone."

The guy turned toward me. His eyes looked crazy. "What did you say?"

"I'll speak slower so you can understand, moron. I said, leave. Her. Alone."

"And you think you're going to make me?"

"If that's what you want," I said. "Probably not your best option." I looked down at the woman. "Let me help you."

There was fear in her eyes, but she didn't say anything. She probably just thought that I could only make things worse for her. This guy was going to pound me into the asphalt, then punish her more because I intervened.

"You don't need to be afraid," I said. "I can handle this." I looked up at the raging dude. I was twitching because of my Tourette's. Any kind of excitement set off my tics.

His eyes narrowed. "Are you winking at me, you fairy?"

If he was trying to make me angrier, he just did. I looked into his face. "Dude, you're really ugly up close. Is that a mustache, or did you braid your nose hair?"

His face turned red.

"I'm giving you one last chance to walk away," I said.

His expression turned from homicidal maniac to slightly amused. "You're giving *me* a chance?" He raised his fist. "I'm going to—"

"Too late," I said. I stretched out my hand and pulsed. The sound of arcing electricity crackled in the air as the force of my pulse slammed him so hard against the car behind him that its alarm went off. He fell to the ground just a few feet from the woman. He was still twitching uncontrollably when I offered the woman my hand.

She just looked at me. After what I'd just done, she was probably afraid to touch me. Up close, I noticed that she already had a black eye—which she had tried to cover up with makeup—and her arm had large bruises on it. This obviously wasn't the first time this guy had used her as his punching bag.

"Let me help you up," I said. "I promise it won't hurt."

She cautiously gave me her hand, and I helped her to her feet. I glanced over at the guy, who had now crawled onto his knees and was trying to stand, his legs still shaky. You would think that after a shock like that he'd stay down, but I'd only made him angrier. Like Tasing a bull. (You can see that online. Spoiler alert: bulls don't like being Tased.)

Jack used to say . . . *Don't injure what you can't kill.* The thing is, I had enough electricity in me to kill about anything. I had to cut way back on my pulse not to seriously hurt him. Like they said on that *Star Trek* show, set phasers to stun. I wasn't as electric as I'd been in Tuvalu, after the explosion—most of that had worn off—but I was definitely more electric than I'd been before Tuvalu.

I looked around to see if anyone was watching. Then I asked the woman, "Is this your truck?"

"It's his. He was picking me up from class."

"I can give you a ride somewhere."

She glanced back at the man. He was now back on his feet, leaning against his truck.

"You're not going anywhere," the man said to her, pointing his index finger at the woman. "And you, twitchy . . ."

This dude had obviously missed science class, because he said that while he was leaning against his truck.

"You want to see who's twitchy?" I put my hand on the truck and pulsed, adding a little more juice this time. The jolt again knocked him off his feet. He groaned out as he hit the asphalt. He was twitching again.

"Just a minute," I said to the woman. I walked over and took a knee next to the guy. "Okay, dude. It's clear you're not the sharpest tool in the shed, even though you are a tool." I put my hand on his shoulder and continued shocking him with a lesser but constant pulse. His muscles seized as he shook beneath my electricity.

"I'm taking this woman someplace far away from you. I know you can't stand right now, but when you can, if you come after her, you won't stand again for a very, very long time. Do you understand what I'm saying?"

He was unable to communicate except with his eyes, which were wide with confusion and maybe a little fear.

"Sorry." I stopped pulsing. "It's hard to speak with all that voltage pulsing through your body. Do you understand?"

"Yeah."

"I was kind of hoping you'd put up more of a fight. Few things are more satisfying than giving a bully what they deserve. Just look it up on the internet. That kind of thing gets millions of views.

"Maybe we should have filmed all this so the whole world could see the coward you really are. Tough guy like you hitting a woman that's half your size. Even you have to admit how pathetic that is. Don't you?"

He just looked at me.

"I asked you a question, bonehead." I pulsed again.

He was clearly a narcissist, so I knew that having to do what I said was killing him. At least metaphorically, which was better than being killed by my electricity. I pulsed harder and he shouted out, "Yes."

"Shock treatment's a pretty effective training tool. Especially for dumb animals. Just remember what I said. You stay on the ground until we're gone. If not, we're going to start this all over for real. Understood?"

"Yes, sir."

"Good boy." He groaned when I took my hand off him. I slapped him on his head, then stood and walked back to the woman, who had been watching quizzically. She was dark featured, with pretty but sad eyes, swollen from crying.

"Come on," I said. "I'm parked over there."

After we'd walked a few steps, the woman asked, "What did you do to him?"

"I Tased him."

"You don't have a Taser."

I already had an excuse handy. "I know, it's something experimental. It doesn't need wires. I work for an electrical appliance invention company."

"I could use one of those."

"Or a new boyfriend," I said.

"He's my husband."

I looked at her. "I'm sorry."

We stopped in front of my car. She looked at it for a moment, then said, "This is your car?"

I nodded. "Yes."

"It looks like a race car."

"It's an Aspark Owl. It's an electric sports car."

"You must be very rich. How much did it cost?"

"A lot." I opened the door for her, which lifted like a bird's wing. The interior of the car looked more like a jet cockpit than a roadster. "Get in."

She sat back in the bucket seat, and I closed the door after her. Then I walked around to my side of the car.

I was used to this kind of response to my car. The Aspark Owl is one of the coolest cars in the world. It's super low to the ground, only thirty-nine inches high, which means you have to slide down into it.

It didn't just look fast. It had the fastest acceleration of any car in the world, zero mph to sixty mph in 1.72 seconds. Faster than a Porsche, Ferrari, Lamborghini. All of them. That's, like, rocket-sled fast. (Actually, it's not. Ostin let me know that a rocket sled can accelerate and travel at speeds in excess of Mach 5, more than ten times that fast.)

Still, my car was pretty fast. It can hit its top speed of two hundred fifty miles per hour in less than ten seconds. Not surprisingly, it's also one of the most expensive cars in the world, costing more than three million dollars. That's Rolls-Royce–Bugatti Veyron territory.

I know that's a ridiculous amount of coin to spend on a car, but we didn't pay that much. In fact, we didn't pay anything at all. It was something my father worked out. He was partnering with the company who made the car, designing custom Starxource charging stations, and the car I was driving was part of the package. My father gave it to me for my eighteenth birthday. If he was trying to make up for a lot of missed birthdays—mission accomplished.

If I was trying to avoid attention, it really wasn't the thing to drive. At almost every intersection I stopped at, someone rolled down their window to ask what it was. Sometimes I'd find people taking selfies next to it.

One time Taylor and I were getting some lunch at a café when I heard a man bragging to the waitress, pointing to my car in the parking lot. I think she surprised the guy when she asked for a ride.

"I wonder how he's going to get out of that," Taylor said.

To our surprise the guy looked at the waitress and said, "Sure, why not?"

Taylor and I just looked at each other. "This is going to be interesting."

A few minutes later they walked out to my car. Taylor and I followed ten yards behind them. I was holding my key fob in my pocket. When he was close enough to touch my car, I set off the alarm. It let out a piercing siren, and the man jumped back. The waitress shouted over the wail, "Why don't you shut it off?"

I walked past them, shut off the alarm, and opened the door for Taylor.

"Because it's not really his car," I said.

The man turned beet red. The waitress glared at him, then walked back to the restaurant, while the guy shuffled off to his own car, which was something like an old Ford Pinto. I kind of felt bad for him.

"I feel like I'm in a spaceship," the woman said to me, looking around the car.

"Pretty close," I said, rolling down my window. "What's your name?"

"Alexis."

I shook her hand. "I'm Michael." I pushed a button to engage my car. When I looked up, her husband's truck was driving toward us. "Your husband's going to ram us."

"He has anger issues."

"Apparently." I put my hand out the window, hoping I could pull a Quentin and short out his electrical system. He was still a hundred feet from us when I sent a massive lightning ball toward the truck. It exploded against the truck's grill, and the sound of the roaring engine stopped, though the truck continued rolling toward us.

"Don't do it, man. You can't afford the repair bill."

He was a road-rage-fueled parking-lot kamikaze.

He kept coming.

"Sit back," I said to the woman.

By the time his truck hit us, it had lost most of its power but was still moving fast enough to cave in the front side of my car. My beautiful car. It was like slashing a Picasso. Also, the airbags deployed, which, if you've never felt that, roughly feels like being hit in the face with a punching bag at two hundred miles an hour.

As the airbag deflated, I looked out the window. I couldn't see the dude's face since his airbags had inflated as well, but now I was really mad. Sparking mad, I called it, which means electricity was arcing between my fingers. I hid my hands from the woman so it wouldn't scare her. "Are you okay?" I asked her.

"I think so. I'm so sorry."

"It's not you," I said.

I got out of the car. As I walked around the back side of the truck, crazy man threw open his door and hopped out like he was entering a fighting cage, ready for round two, or three—whatever round we were on by that point. His nose was bleeding, from the truck's airbag.

"You just crashed into my car," I said. I pulsed so hard, it knocked him off his feet. He fell back to the asphalt, smacking his head hard enough that I could hear it. I was still holding back, though it took practically all the restraint I could muster. If I hadn't stopped his car, he could have seriously hurt us. I wanted to fry the guy. Instead, I took out my cell phone and dialed 911.

"Nine-one-one. What's your emergency?"

"I'd like to report a car accident and an assault."

"What is your name?"

"Michael Vey."

"Thank you, Michael. What is your phone number and location?"

I gave the operator my details.

"We're on the north end of the east parking lot at Boise State."

"We will have emergency vehicles there shortly. Is anyone injured?"

"Not seriously," I said.

"Tell me what happened."

"The driver of the truck beat up his wife, then rammed my car after I offered her a ride home."

"Where is the driver now?"

I glanced down at the man. "He seems to be knocked unconscious from the collision."

"Is he carrying a weapon?"

"I don't know. I haven't seen one."

"I'm going to keep you on the line. If he comes to, do not engage him."

"I'm going to give the phone to his wife so she can tell you everything that happened. She's a bit shaken up."

I didn't wait to see if the operator was okay with that. I wanted to stay close to the man before he could try anything else. And her question about the weapon had made me wonder. I could stop a bullet, but it had been a while.

I opened the passenger-side door of my car and handed the woman my phone. "It's nine-one-one. I told them they should talk to you."

She took the phone from me. "Hello."

I walked back to the guy. His eyelids were flickering a little and he was lightly moaning but was still unable to move.

"You really are a dumb animal. I thought I was pretty clear about you staying away from her, and then you come right back at us. By the way, it's a four-million-dollar car, dork." I held my hand out before him, with my fingers spread. Electricity sparked between them.

"The police will be here soon, but since you have such a poor memory, I'm giving you a warning you can take with you just in case you decide to take out your anger on your wife." I put my hand around his neck. My fingers sizzled against his flesh. He yelped with pain.

"That's a reminder. Next time, I won't hold back. Do you understand?"

His voice was slurred. "Yes, sir."

"I don't believe you. Are you sure this time?"

"Yes, sir."

"Stay on the ground."

As I stood, I saw a campus patrol car driving toward us. I waved it over. Then I stepped out near the road to talk with the officer. He shut off his car and got out.

"What happened?"

"This man was beating up his wife. I was going to give her a ride home, so he rammed my car."

He looked over at the man, then my car. "What kind of a car is that?"

"It's an Aspark Owl."

"I've never seen anything like that. What did that set you back?"

"Too much."

He pushed. "Really, what's the price tag? Out the door."

It bothered me that he was focusing on my car in the middle of a crime scene. "Three and a half," I said.

"Three hundred and fifty thousand," he said incredulously. I didn't correct him. "Either you have a rich daddy or you run a drug cartel."

"Something like that," I said, hoping he was done and ready to arrest this guy.

He looked over the damage of my car. "Airbags deployed. Still, doesn't look like he was going too fast."

"He started out fast. I think his truck stalled before he hit us."

". . . Or his brain kicked in and he hit the brake." He looked back toward the truck. "No skid marks. You were lucky. Where's his wife?"

"That's her in my car. She's talking to nine-one-one."

Just then another campus patrol car pulled up, followed by a Boise police car and a paramedics vehicle. The paramedics stopped next to the truck, and a man and a woman got out. One of the paramedics crouched down next to the man while the Boise police officers walked over to Alexis, who set my phone on the dashboard, then lifted the door. They talked to her for a moment. Then she got out of my car.

The Boise police officers walked over to the dude on the ground. I could see him pointing at the burn on his neck, then point to me. The police ordered him to his feet and had him stand up against his truck with his legs spread as one of the officers frisked him for weapons. He found a knife, then handcuffed him.

The older of the two officers walked over to me. He was short and plump and wore a dark blue uniform with a Boise sheriff deputy badge. The hair at his temples was gray.

"I'm Officer Larkin," he said. "Is this your car?"

"Yes, sir."

"You drive an Aspark Owl?"

"I'm impressed," I said. "I've never met anyone who knew what it was."

"I'm a car nut. Japanese produced, fastest acceleration of any car in the world, gas or electric. I didn't know there was one in Idaho." He looked back at me. "Are you the one who called nine-one-one?"

"Yes, sir."

"What's your name?"

"Michael Vey."

He wrote something on his notepad, then looked back up. "How do you know these people?"

"I don't. I was walking to my car when I saw the guy hit her."

"And then what happened?"

"I told him to leave her alone. He didn't like that, so he came after me."

"Then what happened?"

"I punched him. In self-defense."

"You punched him?"

"Yes, sir."

He glanced at the man, then looked back at me. "And that worked?"

"I'm stronger than I look."

He still looked skeptical. "Apparently." He pointed at Alexis. "You're sure you don't know this woman?"

"Like I said, until an hour ago, I'd never met either of them."

"Sorry, I had to ask. Sometimes we get these love triangles. It complicates things."

"This isn't one of them. I have a girlfriend."

"And you aren't carrying a weapon?"

"No, sir."

"Not even a Taser?"

It wasn't the first time a police officer had asked that. The first time had been in middle school after I'd shocked a kid when he had shoved me into a garbage can. My mother and I had had to move after that. The question triggered me a little. "No, sir."

He still looked skeptical.

I raised my arms. "You want to search me?"

"No. He just said you Tased him."

"He's probably just dazed from the airbag. Or embarrassed that someone smaller than him knocked him down."

The officer nodded. "Probably. That would be humiliating for a tough guy like him. Not the first time I've seen that."

As he wrote on his pad, I asked, "Do you know an officer named Charles Ridley? He used to be with the Boise police department."

The officer looked back up at me. "Chuck Ridley? Everyone knows Chuck. He left the force a few years back to work in the private sector. How do you know Chuck?"

"I'm dating his daughter."

He grinned. "You're dating Blasting Cap Chuck's daughter? Good luck with that."

Blasting Cap? I had never heard the nickname.

The officer handed me a clipboard with a form on it. "If you don't mind signing that, we'll be done here."

I looked over the report, then signed it and handed it back to him. "What happens to gorilla-man?"

"Assault and battery. Damage to your car. He'll spend some time in jail. Tell Ridley hi from Officer Gordito. He'll know who I am."

"I will."

"Have a good day," he said.

After the officer left, Alexis walked over to me. "The police want me to go down to the station to file a report, so I guess I'll go with them."

"All right," I said. "Good luck."

"Thank you for everything. I'm sorry about your car. Buck's a mess."

Buck. The vermin had a name. "You know you can do better," I said.

"I know. And I'm leaving him. Sometimes we get tangled up in things we didn't plan to." She smiled sadly. "Just like you did, right? I'm sorry for all this, but thank you for saving me."

"You're safe," I said. "That's what matters."

She handed me a piece of paper. "That's my phone number, if you ever want to hang out or get a coffee. I'd love to see you again."

"Thank you. That would be nice. . . ."

She just looked at me. "But . . ."

"I have a girlfriend."

"Of course you do," she said. "The good ones always do." She leaned forward and kissed me on the cheek. "Lucky girl." She turned and walked to the police car.

4

Pasta Puttanesca

The police were going to call a tow truck for my car, but the damage was mostly cosmetic, so I just drove it home. I parked in the garage, then walked in through the kitchen. My mother was standing at the stove, stirring something. A pungent aroma filled the air. She smiled when she saw me. "Hi, Michael."

"That smells good. Italian?"

"Italian. I wanted to make something special for your birthday, so I'm trying something new they had on TV. Pasta puttanesca. It has anchovies, so we'll see."

"I like anchovies," I said. "Sometimes."

My mother smiled. "Like I said, we'll see. How was school?"

"School was tolerable. After school, not so great."

She set the spoon down on a ceramic spoon holder. "Did something happen?"

"I was walking to my car when I saw a guy beating up his wife. I stopped him."

"That was heroic of you. Are you okay?"

"I'm fine. My car's not."

"What happened?"

"I was going to give her a ride home, so her husband rammed me with his truck."

"He rammed your car?"

"Yeah. Fortunately, I was able to stall his truck before he hit us. That slowed him down, but not enough. He smashed in my front end. Go see for yourself." I opened the garage door. My mother walked over and looked out.

"Oh no." She turned to me. "Were you hurt?"

"Not really. I tweaked my neck a little. I'm mostly just mad."

"Did you call the police?"

"Yeah. They handcuffed the guy and took him away. I think they thought he was high on something, since he kept telling them that I had magical powers like Harry Potter."

My mother sighed a little. "Did anyone else see?"

It surprised me that, after what we'd been through, she still worried about that. It's not like it mattered anymore, since there were no Elgen left to hunt us.

"The woman saw. She was cool about it. She asked what I had done to her husband, then just let it go."

My mother shook her head. "Well, I'm glad you helped that woman. You might have saved her life."

"I don't understand why people marry so poorly."

"If you can figure that out, you could write a bestselling book. By the way, your dad will be home tonight." She stopped. "That was a bad segue. I didn't mean anything by that."

I grinned.

"He's got the company jet. He says they'll be landing at about five, so we'll eat dinner when he gets home. When do Ostin and Taylor get in?"

"Not until tomorrow afternoon."

"Oh good. Should we have them over for dinner tomorrow?"

"We can't tomorrow. Taylor's mother already invited me over for Taylor's birthday, and the Lisses are doing their own thing. You know how they are with Ostin."

She smiled. "I know. Dorothy's a helicopter mother if I ever knew one. Remember how she used to make Ostin wear a football helmet at his clogging lessons?" She laughed. "It still makes me chuckle."

I had almost forgotten that there had once been a spongy-soft, over-sheltered version of Ostin. He went from tap-shoe clogging to fighting Elgen bad guys in the jungle, saving my neck a few times in the process. "I think he's changed the most out of all of us."

"You've changed a bit yourself," she said. "Is everyone coming to the party?"

"Almost. We're still waiting to hear from Jack, Abi, and Torstyn."

"Is Cassy coming?"

"No. She said she can't make it. She's caught up in something with the EU."

"That's too bad." She put the lid back over the boiling sauce. "Cassy has a crush on you, you know."

I frowned. "I know. Taylor knows too. The mind-reading thing makes a relationship tricky."

My mother smiled. "Trust me, we women don't have to be able to read minds to figure some things out."

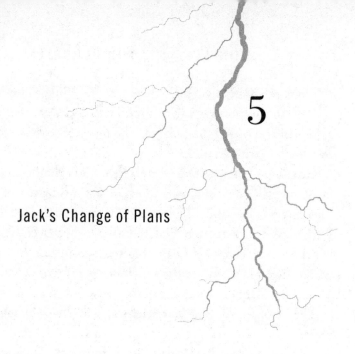

5

Jack's Change of Plans

When I got to my room, I called Taylor and told her about the accident. She hesitated for a moment before asking, "Are you okay?"

"I'm fine. The car's not."

"This happened just after we spoke?"

"About a half hour after. I was walking to the parking lot when I came across this guy beating his wife. So I stopped him, then offered her a ride home. The guy wasn't happy with that, so he rammed us with his truck."

"That's who she was . . . ," she said to herself.

"That's who *who* was?"

"Sorry, nothing. I'm happy you're okay, but sad about your car. Not exactly a great birthday. First, you eat lunch alone, then someone rams your car."

"I had waffles," I said. "And I helped someone. I could do worse."

"I'm being selfish. I was looking forward to driving around Boise with my boyfriend in one of the coolest cars in the world. I guess we'll just have to hang out and whatever. . . ."

I smiled. "In the meantime, I'd better get some homework done."

"If you must. Ciao, *bello*."

"Ciao."

Three hours later I was lying back on my bed, reading from my international business textbook on my tablet, when my mother paged me over my room's intercom.

"Michael, Dad's here. Dinner's on the table in five."

"Be right down."

I finished the chapter, then put down my tablet and went downstairs. My parents were already seated at the table. My father was wearing a crisp white shirt with a crimson silk tie. He looked stressed, but he smiled when he saw me.

"Happy birthday, son."

"Thanks." He definitely looked stressed.

"You're okay?"

"I'm good." I sat down at the table. "You saw my car."

He nodded. "Not the greatest birthday present. Your mother told me what happened. What did the police say?"

"Not much. They asked a few questions, then gave me a report for the insurance."

"The guy went to jail?"

"I think so. He was in handcuffs."

He still looked anxious. I don't think it was just the car.

"Let's eat before the pasta gets any colder," my mother said. "It's puttanesca."

"Sorry, honey," my father said, his voice low. He took off his tie. "Thank you for making such a nice meal. It smells delicious."

"It smells like anchovies," she said. I couldn't tell if she was explaining or apologizing.

After a few bites, my father said, "This is delicious. You are a culinary artist, my dear."

My mother smiled. "My pleasure."

"This is good," I said. "Thank you."

"You're welcome."

My father turned back to me. "Scott, our pilot, told me he'll be picking up Taylor and Tara in Phoenix tomorrow. They should be back here by three."

"That's what Taylor said. Thanks for letting us use the jet. It's been at least two years since we've all seen each other."

"Julie must be so happy to have the girls come home," my mother said.

"Ecstatic," I said. "Can I borrow your car to pick them up?"

"Of course."

"With all your friends in town, you're going to need a car," my father said. "I'll have Marius pick you up a rental car in the morning so you can cart your friends around. Electric, of course. I'll see if they have a Tesla Y. We can lease."

"Thanks." I took a few bites of pasta, which, in spite of my mother's apprehensions, was good, anchovies and all. "I'm really excited to see everyone again. It's been too long."

My father looked at me with a flat expression. "Speaking of which, I have some bad news. Jack won't be able to make it."

This was bad news. Jack was one of the people I was most excited to see.

"He told me he was coming."

"I know. It's not his fault. We have a problem at the Peruvian Starxource plant, so I had him lead a team down there to check things out."

"What happened?" I asked.

"Someone broke in. Some things were stolen."

"What kind of things?"

"The MEIs," he said. "To begin with."

"Oh my," my mother said.

"How do you break into a Starxource plant?" I asked.

He looked at me. "You should know."

"I do know. We couldn't have done it without our powers."

"Unfortunately, our security isn't as intense as the former

occupants. We generally try not to shoot people."

"That's too bad," I said. "I mean about Jack. I've really missed him. I haven't seen him since he left for Italy."

"I'll make it up to him. And you."

"Did he tell Abigail?"

"I don't know."

"I'll let everyone know."

My mother walked over to the counter, lit the candles on a cake, and brought it over.

"Happy birthday," she said. "Should we sing?"

"No, I'm good. But thank you."

"We have a present for you," my father said.

"The Owl was present enough for a few lifetimes."

"Well, this isn't another Owl, but it goes with your Owl." He handed me a package from under the table. "It's from your mother and me."

I unwrapped the package. It contained a pair of dark brown leather driving gloves.

I tried one on. "These are cool."

"They're Italian," my father said. "They're made of lambskin, which is why they're so soft. And this kind of goes with it." He handed me another box. Inside was a pair of sunglasses.

"These are cool too."

"Wiley X," he said. "They're military grade. It's what NATO equips their soldiers with. I thought it was fitting, since you are a warrior."

I liked that. "Thanks." I turned to my mother. "And thank you for everything. These things, the waffles, and dinner."

"The anchovies," she said, smiling.

At around ten o'clock Taylor called again to say good night. Talking three times in one day was unusual, but it was our birthdays, and since she was coming home, we had a lot to talk about.

"So, you'll pick us up at the airport. Then we'll go to my house for our birthday dinner."

"That's the plan. Did you find out if Abi is coming for sure?"

"She just RSVP'd. I was worried that she might bail on us. She and Jack aren't doing well. Maybe it will be good for them to see each other with us all there."

"Jack isn't coming," I said.

She thought he was. "Is it because of Abi?"

"No. My dad just told me that the company needed him to lead a security team to Peru."

She didn't speak for a moment, then said, "Maybe it's for the better. Long-distance romances are hard. Long distance is the *wrong* distance."

"Tell me about it," I said. "I can't believe that I finally get to see you tomorrow."

"I've been counting the hours. I love you."

"I love you too. Good night."

We hung up, and I rolled back in bed. I really couldn't wait to see her. I just wished Jack would be here too.

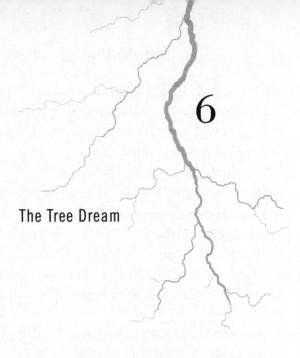

6

The Tree Dream

That night I had the dream again. It was the fifth time I'd had the same dream in the last month. The *tree* dream, I called it. I'm not sure where it came from, but it reminded me of an experience I had in the jungle when Tessa, Jaime, and I were fleeing the Elgen.

We were hiking through the Amazon jungle when we came across an odd-looking tree.

"It's called the sandbox tree," Jaime said. "But sometimes it's called a dynamite tree."

"Why do they call it that?"

"You don't want to stick around and find out."

The tree was tall, more than a hundred feet high, its crown towering above the jungle canopy. Its trunk was covered with thorns, and small fruit hung from its boughs like miniature pumpkins. I asked Jaime if the fruit was edible.

He answered in his usual droll tone, "Only if you like to eat poison, *señor*." He grinned, then said, "These fruits are dangerous in other ways. They are like small bombs. When the fruit is mature, they will explode and shoot out their seeds."

"A lot of plants shoot out their seeds," I said.

"Yes, Señor Mike, but not at two hundred forty-one kilometers per hour. That's enough to kill a man. I've seen dead monkeys on the ground near these trees."

"Don't want to be a dead monkey," I said to myself. We left the tree alone. At the time I didn't think much more about it, really. I had more terrifying things on my mind, like the Elgen guards who were hunting us. The tree was just another thing on a long list of things in the jungle with the potential to kill me. I had completely forgotten about it until last month when I had the tree dream.

When I told Taylor about my dream, she acted a little strange about it. When I asked her why, she didn't answer immediately. Then she said it might be a good thing. She read somewhere that trees in dreams represent our personal journey of growth or a great new opportunity coming our way.

My dream didn't feel anything like that. It felt like a nightmare. In this dream, I was standing in a large garden with trees of all kinds around me. Then I noticed a tree unlike the others. It was growing fast enough that I could see it grow. It was small at first, not much bigger than a thistle. It could have been easily plucked from its roots. But since it was so small, no one else really paid it any attention.

It continued to grow rapidly. Soon, it was too deep to uproot. That's when people started to notice the tree. Many of them admired it. Some praised all the fruit growing on it. Only a few noticed, or cared, that it was choking out the other trees in the garden. Soon, its shadow eclipsed a large part of the garden, darkening it in shade. Then it was discovered that even though the tree's fruit was plentiful and looked delicious, it was poisonous. Even the sap of the tree caused blistering of the skin and blindness if it touched the eyes.

By the time the people of the garden realized the danger the tree posed, it was too late to stop it. The tree continued to grow until it covered the whole garden, killing all the trees around it. Even the grass in the garden bent toward the tree. The garden was no longer the same. The tree controlled everything.

Then, one night, a storm blew over the garden, carrying with it heavy dark clouds and lightning. A powerful bolt of lightning struck the tree, exploding it into thousands of splinters.

The next morning when the people came to the garden, they found the once great tree strewn around the garden, pieces of it still burning. The people just went about their business as if nothing had happened.

I went back to check on the tree. The splintered trunk was still smoldering from the lightning strike. But when I looked closer, there were three new green shoots growing from the base of the trunk.

Every time I had this dream, I woke panting and soaked with sweat.

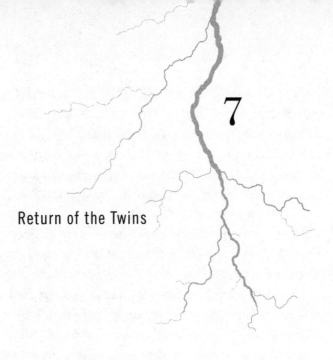

7

Return of the Twins

I woke the next morning drenched in sweat once more. I pulled off my wet T-shirt and shorts and took a shower, pushing the dream from my mind.

As I was getting dressed, my phone rang. It was Marius, my father's assistant.

"Mr. Michael, sir, I have your rental car ready. It is a metallic-blue Tesla model Y, as your father requested. I hope that is satisfactory."

It was hard not to like Marius. He was cheerful and efficient. "That's great, Marius. Thank you."

"My pleasure. I will personally deliver your car in two hours. I will be picking up your Owl to take to the repair shop the manufacturer recommended in Las Vegas."

"You're driving my car to Vegas?"

"No, sir. It will be carried on the back of a truck. We would not want to put that many miles on your odometer. Also, I confirmed with our pilots that the flight with Taylor and Tara will be here on time."

"Thank you," I said again. "I'll see you in a couple of hours."

Marius arrived when he said he would. He parked the rental Tesla in front of the house, then guided the tow truck into my driveway. I opened the garage door, then walked out and handed him the keys to the Owl.

"Here you go, Marius."

"Thank you, sir. And here are the keys to the rental car. Also, I hope it is okay, but I bought a box of chocolates for Taylor for when you pick her up today. A late birthday present. They are in the glove box."

"Thank you. She'll love that."

"My pleasure, sir."

Like I said, he was hard not to like. I left for the airport a couple of hours later. I was waiting when Taylor came walking out from behind the airport baggage claim. I saw her before she saw me. I waved to her. "Taylor. Over here."

A big smile crossed her face. "Michael!" She ran to me. It had been more than three months since I'd seen her in real life. As always, she looked even more beautiful than I remembered. She practically tackled me, pressing her lips against mine. I pushed her back.

"Nice try, Tara."

Tara grinned. "Wow, you really could tell."

"You don't kiss like Taylor."

She leaned into me. "But it was nice, right?"

"No comment."

Taylor walked up behind her. I'm still amazed at how much the two of them look alike. Especially after not seeing her for months.

"So, which of us is the better kisser?" Taylor asked.

"You, of course."

"Right answer if you ever wanted me to kiss you again." We kissed. It was definitely her.

"I think you guys are having too much fun at ASU," I said.

"Party central, baby," Tara said.

"For one of us it is," Taylor said. "The other one actually studies." She turned back to me. "I've missed you so much. I hate this separation."

"Me too," I said.

"By the way," Taylor said, "pay up, sister."

"Pay up?" I said. "Wait, you made a bet with her?"

"Yep," Taylor said. "Twenty bucks that you'd know the difference between our kisses."

"I still don't get how you could tell," Tara said. "Biologically, we have the exact same lips. Maybe it's just because I'm so much better at it. . . ."

"That's not true," Taylor said.

The truth was, Tara always chewed Clove gum, and Taylor hated it. I could not only smell it on her breath, but I could taste it in her mouth. Of course, it was just a matter of time before Taylor read my mind and found that out.

"There you go." Tara handed Taylor a twenty-dollar bill.

"Thank you," Taylor said.

"No, thank *you*," Tara said. "I got you to let me kiss your boyfriend for just twenty dollars. Who's the loser now?" She suddenly turned herself into a clown.

Taylor rebooted her. Tara turned back into herself.

"Stop that," Tara said. "You know I hate it when you do that."

"That's why I do it. And you know clowns freak me out." Taylor turned back to me. "Where were we? Oh, yeah." We kissed again. "I was saying that I hate being so far away from you."

"Arizona's not so far."

"Any distance from you is far."

"I just threw up in my mouth," Tara said.

"C'mon, let's go," I said. I took Taylor's bag and led them out to the parking terrace.

"It's good being back home," Taylor said. "You know, I don't even know where my home is since my parents moved."

"I know where it is," I said. "It's not far from mine."

"Your home is a mansion," Taylor said.

"Almost." Our new home was even larger than Mitchell's, which we'd hidden in from the Elgen. I remember thinking that his garage was larger than our whole apartment.

"Yours isn't exactly small," I said.

"After living in a dorm for the last year, I'm good with anything. My mother said our new place is two and a half times bigger than our last home." Taylor's last home had been a small, faded tan-painted rambler with pink flamingos and a small grove of aspen in the front yard.

"At least that," I said. "Spoils of war."

"Thank you, Dr. Hatch."

"Did you really just say that?" I said.

After my father took over the Elgen Corporation, he paid out a sizable compensation to everyone who had risked their lives in the fight. That included Taylor's parents and the Lisses. Each of them received more than five million dollars. It was enough money to dramatically change all their lives.

In addition, the Ridleys and Mr. Liss had gone to work for Veytric, Julie in corporate travel, Chuck Ridley in local security, and Mr. Liss managed the new Starxource plant facility in Boise, which wasn't that far of a stretch from what any of them had already been doing in their previous employment.

I opened the back of the Tesla rental car and put in their bags, while Taylor hopped into the passenger side and Tara got into the back.

I got into and started the car. Before I pulled out, I remembered Marius's gift. "Wait. Marius left you something." I reached over and opened the glove box. I took out the wrapped box and handed it to her.

"What's this?"

"Expensive chocolates."

"Marius got these for me?"

"He remembered it was your birthday."

"Did he remember it was mine?" Tara said.

"He is so thoughtful," Taylor said. She opened the box. "My favorite hand-dipped chocolates."

"I hope you plan to share," Tara said.

"Of course I do." She lifted the lid, then tilted the box to me. "Have one."

"Thank you." I took out a caramel.

She then handed the box back to Tara, then took one herself.

As we were driving away from the airport, Taylor said, "I'm so sorry about your car."

"Still, it's better that my car got hit than that woman."

"You're such a good guy, Vey," Taylor said.

"Tay showed me a picture of your car," Tara said. "It's totally cool. Wasn't it like three or four million dollars?"

"If we'd had to buy it, it would have been. It was part of a deal with Veytric and the car maker."

"Taylor said you can run it from your own electricity."

"My dad had his engineers customize it by wiring the stick shift to a capacitor and battery charger, so I can charge the car just by pulsing on the stick shift. The knob is made of pure silver."

"At that price it should be gold."

"Silver's better. It's the most conductive metal on the planet."

"Your car cost more than my parents' new house," Taylor said.

"But it doesn't have a pool."

"We have a pool?"

I looked over. "A nice one."

Taylor smiled. "We have a pool."

Taylor's parents' new home was in a new Meridian subdivision, only a couple of miles from where my parents now lived. The Ridleys had moved into the home just three months earlier. The home was a two-story, French château design with a stone-and-stucco facade with cobalt-blue shutters. There was a balcony extending out over the front stone portico, with French double doors and an intricate wrought-iron railing. Like Julie Ridley said, it was easily double the size of her last home, though it looked even bigger, especially with the steep pitch of the roof and the three-car garage.

As I pulled up to the home, Taylor clapped her hands. "Shut up. That's my home?"

"I told you it was big."

"It's French provincial," Tara said. "Classic."

"It's really beautiful," Taylor said. "I can't believe that's my house."

The house had a cobblestone driveway lined with terra-cotta pots with kumquat plants growing from them. While their last home's garage barely fit one car, this new one would easily fit three cars and still have room in back for Mr. Ridley's workshop.

I pulled the Tesla up the circular driveway. Taylor's mom was standing near the front door trimming back a rosebush. As I entered the driveway, she set down her garden scissors.

"There's Mom," Taylor said.

I parked near the front door and rolled down the window. "Hi, Julie. I've brought you something."

Her smile broadened. "Thank you for picking them up, Michael."

Mrs. Ridley and I had gotten closer over the last year. I had seen more of Taylor's mom than she had.

Taylor jumped out of the car and hugged her mother. Tara did as well, though it wasn't quite the same. After Tuvalu, Tara and Taylor had never separated. Taylor's parents, especially her mother, did their best to make Tara feel like she was part of the family. She even told Tara to call her "Mom," but I think Tara was still getting used to the idea of having a family.

"Are Todd and Tom here?" Taylor asked.

"Yes. They just ran to the store. Why don't you girls put your things in your rooms, then come down for dinner."

"Where are our rooms?"

"Of course. I'll show you."

We followed her into the house. There was a large foyer with an ornate crystal chandelier above a curved stairway. I carried Taylor's bag upstairs.

"Tara, we thought we'd give you the first room, but you two can switch if you like. The rooms are the same size. The furniture is about the same too. We kept with the French theme."

"This is beautiful," Tara said. "Thank you." She set her suitcase on the bed. It was queen-sized and new, with a carved wooden headboard and a lush floral duvet.

"It's pretty," Taylor said. "Are you good with this?"

"Of course," Tara said.

"I hoped you would like it," Julie said. "I figured you'd probably want to decorate your rooms yourselves, so I just did the bare minimum."

We walked to the next bedroom. Other than the bed being positioned against the opposite wall, it was pretty much the same as Tara's room. Both rooms had large, curtained windows that overlooked the front of the house.

"This is beautiful," Taylor said. She turned back to her mom. "Who would have thought we would ever live in a house like this?"

Julie smiled. "I certainly didn't."

I set Taylor's suitcase near her bed.

"The dresser is empty. We just put your things from the old house in the closet."

"Thank you, Mom," Taylor said.

"You're welcome, dear."

"Thank you, Mrs. Ridley," Tara said.

Mrs. Ridley looked at her. "Tara, please call me 'Mom.' Or even 'Julie.'"

"Sorry. It's just habit."

Julie walked over and hugged her. "I'm just grateful to have you as my daughter. More than you could ever know."

Tara's eyes moistened a little. "Thank you."

"All right, I'll let you two get settled. Dinner will be ready in about a half hour."

Julie left the room.

"See you in a minute," Tara said. "I'm going to unpack." She walked back to her own room.

Taylor sat down on her bed. She motioned for me to join her.

"What do you think?" I asked, sitting next to her on the bed.

"It's incredible." She smiled at me. "Isn't fate a strange thing?"

"How so?"

"We wouldn't be here if I hadn't seen you shock Jack, Mitchell, and Wade that day."

The mention of Wade made me sad. . . . "And maybe Wade would still be alive."

She frowned. "There will always be that."

I lay back on the bed as Taylor unpacked her suitcase into her drawers.

"Fate is a strange thing," I said.

8

The Quarterback Fumble

Ahalf hour later the three of us walked downstairs. Taylor's two brothers were standing near the dining room table. I had only met them once before, and then it was only briefly. Both were tall with curly blond hair. No one would ever guess them to be Taylor's brothers, since they didn't look at all like her, which wasn't surprising, since Taylor was adopted.

"Brothers!" Taylor shouted, running to them. Her oldest brother, Todd, was six years older than her. Her other brother, Tom, was four years older. Every one of the children in Taylor's family had a name that started with a *T*. I'm not sure why, since neither of her parents' names started with a *T*. Even more unlikely was that Tara's name started with a *T* as well, and they weren't even adopted together.

"Let me get this right," Todd said, glancing back and forth between the two girls. "You're Taylor?"

"Idiot," Taylor said, grinning. "You don't recognize your own sister?"

"Not since you sprouted a twin."

"Sprouted?" Taylor said.

Tara said, "So, I'm Tara. The *sprout*."

"Just kidding," Todd said, hugging her. After they parted, he said, "Maybe you should, like, wear name tags. At least for the next few days."

"Or we could write an *X* on Taylor's hand with a Sharpie," Tom suggested.

"Tom, Tom, Tom," Taylor said. "All this time and you're still such a dork." They hugged.

"And who is this dude?" Tom asked, looking at me.

Taylor shook her head. "You know Michael."

"Oh, it's Michael. You just have so many boyfriends."

"Dork," Taylor said again.

"Tom," I said, shaking his hand. Then I turned to Todd. "It's been a while."

"Too long."

"How's work?" I asked.

Todd was the assistant manager of a Coeur d'Alene hotel in northern Idaho.

"It's good. Busy. Travel season is starting to ramp up. What are you up to?"

"School. I'm at Boise State working toward an MBA."

Taylor's brothers had been out of state during the Elgen battle, and the Ridleys had decided not to share any of it with them, so they had no idea about the Elgen, or what Taylor and I had been through together.

"Then working for Daddy?" Tom said.

"That was rude," Taylor said.

"It's okay," I said. "I don't usually call him 'Daddy,' but yes, I plan on working with my father at Veytric."

Todd looked at me with a peculiar expression. "So, I hear you're pretty tough."

I thought it was an odd thing for him to say. "Where'd you hear that?"

"Taylor. My dad."

"I never said that," Taylor said. "Quit bugging him."

"I'm just welcoming him to the family. You wouldn't understand; it's male bonding." He turned back to me. "I think we should have an arm wrestle."

"I'd rather not," I said. I think both of Taylor's brothers had a lot of their father's tough-guy cop personality. *Blasting Cap Chuck.*

"I think someone's a little bit chicken," Tom said.

"Michael, chicken?" Tara said. "You don't know him."

"Looks like you have a fan," Todd said.

"Leave him alone," Taylor said more firmly. "He's not chicken. He's courageous in places you don't have places."

"Whatever that means," Tom said.

"Nope," Todd said. "He's a chicken. Grade A, free-range poultry."

"Yep, that's what I am," I said. "I just don't want to be humiliated by you."

"Well, you're going to be. That's how we roll here. You don't have a choice."

"There's always a choice," I said.

"C'mon, Vey," Tom said. "Show us what you got."

"All right," Taylor said angrily. "Show him what you can do."

"Not a good idea," I said. "I'm not going to . . ." I took her hand so she could read my mind. *Sizzle him like bacon.*

"Do it," she said out loud.

"Do what?" Todd asked. "Cry in front of your girlfriend?"

"Definitely do it," she said.

"All right," I said. "Have it your way." I sat down at the kitchen table.

Taylor must have had a sudden change of heart. Either she didn't want me electrocuting her brother or maybe she just realized that shocking her brother would require a whole lot of explanation. "You're right," she said. "Not a good idea."

"You think?" Todd mocked. "I'll try not to break his arm."

"That would be good," I said.

"Wait," she said. "Corky."

I looked at her quizzically. "What?"

"Remember Corky? At that party a million years ago."

I nodded. Corky had challenged me to a fight in front of a large group of people. Instead of shocking him—or getting beaten up—Taylor had rebooted him just as I'd plowed into him, knocking him over.

Todd sat down across from me, and he and I clenched hands. He was about two inches taller than me, and his arm was longer.

"Let's make this interesting." I said to Todd. "I win, you buy Taylor and me dinner."

"Okay, so when I win, you buy Tom and me a steak dinner. And trust me, we've got big appetites."

"Superfluous," I said. "Do you want to count to three?"

"I will," Tom said.

I took a deep breath. If he had asked a couple of years earlier, after all our battles, I would have easily crushed him without any powers. Now this just seemed childish. "Let's do this."

Todd looked into my eyes as he pushed himself against the table, trying to gain an unfair advantage. I just looked at him with a half-bored expression. "Taylor and I like sushi," I said.

"On three," Tom said. "One, two, . . ."

Todd's eyes suddenly went blank.

". . . Three!"

I slammed Todd's hand down onto the table so hard, it knocked an empty glass over.

"Holy crap," Todd said, lifting his hand and rubbing it.

"Dude, you just got owned. You didn't even look like you were trying," Tom said, which could have applied to either of us. He looked at me and fake clapped. "Well done, Vey."

"I wasn't ready," Todd said.

"Wasn't ready?" Tom said. "I gave you a count, man."

"I want a rematch."

I breathed out. "All right," I said. "Double or nothing."

He looked worried. "Whatever."

I looked at Taylor. "You got this," she said.

"All right. This time, wait until I'm ready," Todd said to Tom.

Tom rolled his eyes. "Okay. Are you ready?"

"Yes."

"On three. One, two . . ."

Todd jumped the gun. He stood, pressing his weight into me. I don't know what Taylor was doing, but she never rebooted him. I instinctively pulsed. Todd shouted out as I again slammed his hand to the table, though I'm sure it wasn't the table that hurt him this time.

"You shocked me!" Todd said.

"How did I shock you?" I asked.

"I don't know. You got a Taser in your pocket."

"You're saying that electricity from a Taser traveled all the way up through my body, and you're the one that got shocked? Sorry, but Tasers don't work that way. The only way you could be shocked is if I were holding the Taser wires in my hand, in which case, we'd both be shocked."

"He's right," Mr. Ridley said, walking into the room. "I think you need to accept that he's just a lot stronger than you."

"But I felt it. . . ."

"You just hit your funny bone," Mr. Ridley said.

I looked at Mr. Ridley, and he winked. "You could always try again," he said.

"I can't afford it," Todd replied.

"How about you, Tom?" I said. "You feeling strong?"

"No, I'm good," he said.

Julie walked into the room. She opened the oven, then brought out a roasting pan and set it on the counter. "Chuck, will you carve the roast?"

"On it," he said.

"Everyone, sit down, please," Mrs. Ridley said. "Let's eat."

"It smells delicious," Taylor said.

"French dip," Mrs. Ridley said. "Mashed potatoes and gravy, green beans, and salad."

"My favorite meal," Taylor said.

"And one of mine," Tara said.

"That's the idea. We're celebrating both of you."

Mr. Ridley said grace; then we passed the food around.

We had been eating for a while when Taylor said, "Someone hit Michael's car."

"The Owl?" Mr. Ridley asked.

"Yeah."

"You call your car the Owl?" Todd said.

"No," I said. "The manufacturer did."

He glanced at Tom. "What, it has feathers?"

"Why are you being such a jerk?" Taylor said.

"He's still mad that Michael crushed him," Tom said.

"I'll crush you," Todd said.

"Boys," Mrs. Ridley said. "Behave."

Taylor held up her phone with a picture of my car. "This is Michael's car," she said. "It's called an Aspark Owl."

"Holy crap," Tom said. "That's your car?"

I nodded. "That's the Owl."

"It will do zero to sixty in one-point-seven seconds," Taylor said. I was impressed that she knew that.

I was waiting for the question that invariably followed. I wasn't disappointed.

"How much did that set you back?" Todd asked.

"About two hundred years of your salary," Taylor said.

"How bad is it?" Mrs. Ridley asked. "The damage."

"It's dented in the front," I said.

"In an intersection?" Mr. Ridley asked.

"No. It happened in a parking lot."

"Someone backed into you?"

"No. This guy intentionally crashed into me."

"What did you do to deserve that?" Tom asked.

"I was giving the guy's wife a ride home."

"And you just admitted that in front of Taylor? Dude, you've got stones."

"In the head," Todd said.

"He was helping her," Taylor said. "The woman's husband was beating her."

"I met a friend of yours," I said to Mr. Ridley. "Officer Larkin."

"We called him '*Gordito*.' It means 'the little chubby one.'"

"He had a nickname for you too," I said. "He called you 'Blasting Cap.'"

Mr. Ridley looked embarrassed. "Yeah. They called me that."

"Because he was so powerful," Tom said.

"Because he had a reputation for blowing up," Mrs. Ridley said. She winked at her husband.

Mr. Ridley shrugged. "It's true."

"Taylor and I did something really crazy," Tara said.

"Do tell," Tom said.

"So, there's a guy at school who was hitting on Taylor."

"We don't need to talk about this, Tara," Taylor said.

"I mean, Taylor's taken, right? But this guy won't give up. He's kind of a big deal in his own mind. Actually, a lot of people's minds, since he's the starting quarterback at ASU."

Taylor shook her head. "Really, Tara?"

"You didn't tell me about this," I said.

"I was going to tell Michael myself," Taylor said.

"So, anyway, this guy's used to girls falling all over him. So he's really mad. So he told some of the other players that Taylor was . . ."

"What did he say?" I asked.

"You can stop now, Tara," Taylor said.

"You don't stop a story midway," Todd said.

"Well, we took care of him. They were playing the Arizona Wildcats, not an important game, just bragging rights, so the first three times they hiked the ball, I made the football look like a rattlesnake. He fumbled three times in the first quarter. The coach pulled him."

Todd said, "What do you mean, you made the ball look like a rattlesnake?"

Taylor glared at her.

"I mean . . ."

I wondered how she was going to get herself out of that one. Suddenly, both brothers looked like they'd just woken up from a nap. Taylor had rebooted them.

"What were we talking about?" Todd asked.

"Michael's car," Taylor said. "Someone crashed into it."

"That's right," Tom said, still looking confused.

Taylor turned to Tara. "You're welcome. Now keep it shut."

"Sorry. I forgot."

"Forgot what?" Todd asked.

"You wouldn't understand," Taylor said.

Everyone went back to eating.

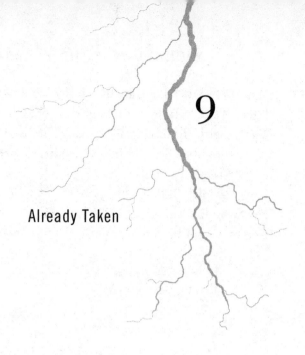

9

Already Taken

After dinner Mrs. Ridley brought out a chocolate birthday cake that had both Taylor's and Tara's names written on it in frosting. They blew out the candles together; then Mrs. Ridley cut up the cake. Afterward we all just sat around the table and talked, catching up on each other's lives. Tara excused herself first; then Taylor and I went up to her room a half hour later.

"I'm sorry about that quarterback thing. I was going to tell you."

"I'm not surprised he came on to you. I live in fear that you're going to find someone else."

"You have nothing to fear. Where in the world would I find someone like you?" She frowned. "I still feel bad about what we did to that guy. We might have ruined his life."

"You mean, what Tara did."

"I could have stopped her."

"It's not your job to police her. Besides, it sounds like he needed a little humbling. And it's better than me going down there and taking care of the guy myself."

"You wouldn't . . ."

"You really think I wouldn't?"

"Yeah. You definitely would."

"I'm a little protective of you."

"Not so little," she said, taking my hand. "You always have been protective of me." She suddenly looked into my eyes. "Someone asked you out yesterday. She was very pretty."

"No one asked me out."

"She asked if you wanted to get a coffee. She handed you a piece of paper with her phone number. She was really into you."

The mention of the note sparked my memory. "Oh, you mean the woman I was going to drive home before her husband crashed into me. You saw that?"

"And you told her . . ." A big smile crossed her lips. "I like that. And she was right, it's no surprise you're taken."

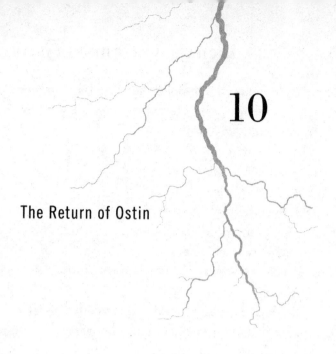

10

The Return of Ostin

A few minutes later my phone dinged with a text. I glanced down at it.

"Who's that?" Taylor asked.

"Ostin."

"Is he back?"

"He should be." I read the messages.

Ostin

Back in Idaho. With parents.

Me

When can we get together?

Ostin

Lunch tomorrow?

Me

I've got Taylor. She'll be excited to see you.

Ostin

Likewise. How about PizzaMax?

"Is PizzaMax okay for lunch tomorrow?" I asked Taylor.
"Of course."

Me

PizzaMax it is.

"I'm surprised he didn't come straight over," Taylor said.
"I'm not. He's in Dorothy's custody."
Taylor laughed. "That's a good description. I just feel bad for
McKenna. Dorothy acts like a jealous girlfriend around her. Could
you imagine having Dorothy as a mother-in-law?"
"If I were McKenna, I'd probably set her on fire. You could just
reboot her every time she annoyed you."
"Which would be every five seconds," Taylor said. "I'd probably
break her brain."
I grinned. "Probably."

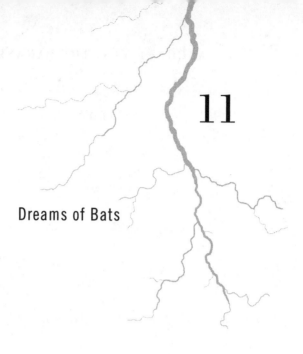

11

Dreams of Bats

It was a little past midnight when Taylor walked me out to my car.

"Can I ask you something?" she said.

"Of course."

"Are you still having that dream? The one about the tree."

"I had it again last night."

Taylor frowned. "I need to tell you something." She looked nervous to tell me. "I had the same dream."

"When?"

"It was before you told me about it." She looked me in the eyes. "Why would we have the same dream?"

I shook my head. "I rarely even remember my dreams."

"Do you remember when I had that dream in Taiwan and I saw everything that happened, right down to Cassy freezing everyone?"

I nodded.

"It's like that, but it's happening more and more often. And they're coming true. Like, a week ago, I had a dream that that woman asked you out after someone crashed into your car. I woke shaking. I didn't know if you were hurt or not.

"Then two nights ago, I had one where I saw Grace. She was in a bed, but not in a hospital. She was just lying there, her eyes wide open, but lifeless. I don't think she was dead."

"That one's not coming true," I said. "Grace is fine. She works with my father, I think I'd know if something was wrong."

"I hope so. Last night, I had a new one. I was locked behind bars, with bats flying all around me. There was bat poop on everything. I woke screaming."

"Bats?"

Taylor nodded. "Bats."

"Why didn't you tell me about these dreams before?"

"I guess I'm still just processing it all. I keep hoping that it's just my imagination, but then . . ."

"Yes?"

"Then they come true." She breathed out slowly. "At least this bat thing won't be true. It's too bizarre. Do you think these dreams could have something to do with my electric power?"

"It's possible. Maybe your electricity is making your synapses fire too much while you sleep."

Taylor suddenly smiled. "You sounded just like Ostin."

"I was trying," I said, smiling. "I bet Ostin could figure this out."

"I just wish they would stop."

I held her for a moment more; then we kissed good night and I drove home, thinking about her dreams. I hoped they weren't all true.

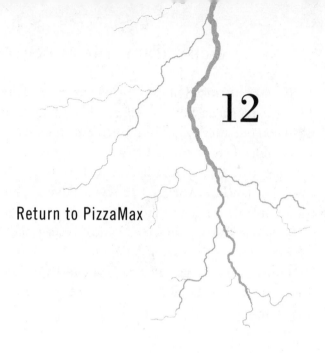

12

Return to PizzaMax

Back when Taylor's mother, Julie, was a travel agent, she told Taylor that people who travel together form a special bond. I'd say that people who face death together do even more so. The experiences we had as the Electroclan were as intense as you could have. We were more than fellow travelers; we were survivors.

I drove to Taylor's about an hour before noon. Mrs. Ridley answered the door. She was wearing a light jacket and had her purse over her shoulder. She was standing next to Tara.

"Good morning, Michael."

"Good morning, Julie. Hi, Tara. What are you ladies up to this morning?"

"Mom and I are going shopping," Tara said.

"A little one-on-one girl time," Julie said.

"Sorry I'm bailing on lunch," Tara said. "But . . . it's shopping."

"Have fun," I said.

"Oh, we will," Tara said. "We're *shopping.*"

Taylor walked down the stairs behind them. She was wearing a robin's-egg-blue sweater over a T-shirt and blue jeans. "Good morning, handsome," she said. She reached the foyer and we kissed.

"Well, we're off," Julie said. "You two have fun." The two of them walked out.

"You weren't invited?" I asked.

"No. I think it freaked my mom out a little when Tara called her 'Mrs. Ridley' yesterday. She's trying to build their relationship."

We got into the car. About a mile from her home, we stopped at a bakery to place an order for two trays of chocolate éclairs, Ostin's favorite pastry, then drove over to pick up Ostin.

Ostin lived in the same apartment he had always lived in—in the same apartment building where my mother and I had lived. Even though the Lisses had been given the same compensation as the Ridleys, they hadn't moved. In fact, it didn't look like they had done anything with the money. They drove the same old cars, wore the same clothes. Ostin told me the only thing that was different about his family was the massive new television in their living room and the fact that his parents ate out more often at nicer restaurants. And they went on three cruises a year instead of just one. Dorothy was made for the cruise life—nonstop meals, shuffleboard, and free entertainment.

The money would have come in handy for Ostin's college, but with all the scholarships he was offered, they didn't have to pay any of it anyway.

Ostin was waiting for us in the apartment's parking lot as we drove in, his hands deep in his pockets. As usual, he was lost in thought, and he didn't even notice us until I stopped the car about six feet in front of him and rolled down the window. "Ostin, brother!"

"Michael!" I got out, and we man hugged. He looked back at the Tesla. "I didn't recognize your car. Where's the Owl?"

"It was in an accident."

"You crashed it?"

"No. I'll tell you about it at lunch."

Taylor got out of the car too. "Hi, Ostin."

"Hello, beautiful Taylor."

Taylor smiled. McKenna had obviously been coaching him on his people skills. Then Ostin put out his fist to Taylor. "Bones."

"Still don't do that," Taylor said. "But it's good to see you." She leaned forward and kissed him on the cheek.

"You too," he said awkwardly.

We all got into the car, Ostin in the back, and drove to PizzaMax. It was crowded, as usual, which made me doubt the rumor of them closing down. There were four metal benches in the waiting area, all of them filled except one. The cheerful plinking of a player piano reverberated throughout the restaurant.

"Let's sit down," Taylor said, motioning to the vacant bench. We were walking toward it when a well-fed dude ran past us and sat down in the middle, taking the whole bench for himself. He had a smug, victorious look on his face, as if he'd snuck past us at some imaginary finish line.

"We were about to sit there," Taylor said.

"Sorry, babe. First come, first serve."

Taylor's face screwed up. "Did you really just call me 'babe'?"

"But you can sit here with me if you want. There's room for two."

"Barely," Ostin said. "But then you'd probably touch. And you look kind of sweaty. She'd have to go home and wash her clothes."

The man glared at Ostin. The thing is, Ostin wasn't trying to be mean. He was just accurately describing the situation.

"Yeah, I'll pass," Taylor said.

I glanced over at her. "I got this."

I walked over next to the bench and put my hand on the back of it, then pulsed. He was surprisingly agile for his size. He popped off the bench like a waffle from a toaster.

"Change your mind?" I asked.

"Something shocked me," he said, looking back at the bench.

I looked around it. "I don't see an outlet."

Taylor cocked her head. "Maybe you should try it again."

He reached out and touched the bench, cautiously like he was checking something to see if it was hot. Nothing. Then he sat down. I waited a few seconds before I pulsed again. This time he landed on his knees. "It shocked me again."

"That's so strange. Maybe we'll try it."

"You can have it," he said. "You'll see."

We all sat down. The guy just stared at us, waiting for something to happen. After a few minutes he walked out of the restaurant.

"That was justice," Ostin said.

"No," Taylor replied. "It was Michael."

Ostin turned to me. "So what happened to your car?"

"Yesterday, just after I talked to you, I was walking through the parking lot when I noticed a guy hitting his wife. Huge dude. All muscle."

"I can see where this is going," Ostin said.

"I thought I did too. I took the guy down, then offered his wife a ride away from him. But after we got into my car, her crazy husband rammed us with his truck."

"That's like breaking a Ming vase," Ostin said. "Did you fry him?"

"I wanted to. But I held it together and called the police."

"That must have been tough. I mean, not doing it yourself."

"It was harder than you could imagine." I smiled. "It's good to be back here. The old PizzaMax."

"I miss it," Ostin said.

"How often do you eat here?" Taylor asked.

"Not often," I said.

Even though I still lived in Boise, it had been more than a year since I'd been to PizzaMax. I don't know why. Maybe it was a psychological thing, and it felt wrong or unfair coming here without my friends.

About ten minutes later, the host sat us in the same part of the restaurant where Ostin, my mother, and I had sat the night my mother was kidnapped. The host handed us menus even though none of us needed them.

"I'm ordering the Kitchen Sink," Ostin said.

The Kitchen Sink was exactly what it sounded like—a fourteen-inch pizza with everything on it.

"You know it has anchovies," Taylor said.

"You say that like it's a bad thing," Ostin said.

"What's wrong with anchovies?" I asked.

Taylor grimaced. "No offense, but they taste like overly salted fish that were left out in the sun for a month."

"If it's overly salted, then you can leave it out," Ostin said. "Salt, or sodium chloride, is a natural preservative that keeps meat from spoiling by drawing out the moisture in—"

I cut in before Taylor lost her mind. "I'm going to have the Hawaiian calzone, extra pineapple, no anchovies. How about you, Taylor?"

"I'll have the Margherita," she said.

"Did you know that Margherita pizza was the first pizza ever made?" Ostin said, not finished talking from the first time. "It was invented by a Neapolitan chef as a special meal for the Italian princess Margherita. He was trying to come up with something that had the colors of the new Italian republic, so he chose the white of mozzarella cheese, the red of tomato sauce, and a sprig of basil for green."

Taylor nodded. "Yes, I knew that. When does McKenna get in?"

He glanced down at his watch. "Four hours, twenty-one minutes, eight seconds."

"That was . . . precise."

"I've been counting down the minutes until I get to see her. It's like Christmas. Without the fruitcake."

Taylor smiled. "That may be the most romantic thing you've ever said."

After the waitress took our order, Ostin said, "Michael, are you still having that dream? The one with the tree suckers."

I glanced over at Taylor. "Yes. I had it last night."

"What's a tree sucker?" Taylor asked.

"Tendrils growing up from the trunk are called tree suckers."

"That's a stupid name," Taylor said.

"I didn't make it up."

"What do you think my dream means?" I asked Ostin.

"The first part of the dream is easy. The tree represents the Elgen threat growing throughout the world. The lightning, of course, was the Electroclan. We struck the tree and brought it down."

"Then what about the tree . . . *suckers?*" Taylor asked.

"Maybe it means that something is going to take the Elgen's place. It's like the mythical Hydra. You cut off one head, and three more grow back."

"You think we didn't really end the Elgen?" Taylor asked.

"We did," I said. "Hatch was the head of that snake, and he's gone. The guards are in jail or dead; we took over all their Starxource plants and all their money. And we have the *Joule.* How could the Elgen still exist?"

"No doubt Hatch stashed away billions of dollars in offshore accounts," Ostin said. "In Switzerland, or the Cayman Islands."

"Taylor had the tree dream too."

Ostin turned to her. "You had the same dream?"

She nodded. "The exact same one."

"That would make sense."

"Why is that?" Taylor asked.

"We know that Michael can absorb other electrics' powers for a while. He must have absorbed yours. At least enough to have the dream. That would also prove that your dreams are being caused by your electric power."

"But we haven't even been together," Taylor said.

"No," Ostin said, looking deep in thought. "But you've talked on the phone. Cell phones transmit through radio frequency, which are just electromagnetic fields. That's how Michael absorbs power."

Taylor breathed out. "Enough of dreams," she said. "We need to get ready for the reunion." She opened her purse and brought out a piece of paper. She unfolded it on the table, then smoothed it down with one hand. The paper had an ASU logo printed on it with a picture of a Sun Devil.

"Let's go down the guest list." She put a pen to the paper. "There's the five of us, including McKenna and Tara." She put a check by our names. "Then Zeus will be here; he's driving up tomorrow from Las Vegas. He says he'll pick up Tessa."

"That's seven," Ostin said.

"Are those two still together?" I asked.

"You never know," Taylor said. "McKenna arrives in a few hours; Ian and Abi arrive tomorrow. Abi is flying in at around three thirty, Ian a half hour before that. Nichelle is driving down with her boyfriend; they'll be here tonight as well."

"Nichelle has a boyfriend?" I asked.

Taylor nodded. "He's a Nonel."

"Are we allowing outsiders?" Ostin asked.

"It's not fair if we don't," Taylor said. "Ostin has McKenna; Jack has Abi. At least we think he does." She smiled and looked at me. "And you have me."

I smiled back and took her hand.

"What about Cassy?" Ostin asked. "Is she coming?"

I watched for Taylor's reaction. The last time she and Cassy spoke, it wasn't especially friendly. She accused Cassy of flirting with me, which she was.

"Cassy can't get out of work," she said dismissively. She moved her pen down the paper.

"Quentin will be here tomorrow morning," I said. "What about Grace?"

Taylor shrugged lightly. "I don't know. I was hoping that you had talked to her. I've texted her, but she still hasn't responded."

"She won't need a hotel or a ride, so she's probably thinking that she'll just show up. I'll ask my dad what's going on with her."

"What about Torstyn?" Taylor asked. "My texts to him didn't go through."

"Quentin's still working on Torstyn," I said. "But he says it's not likely he'll come. Torstyn's not doing well."

"Doing well with what?"

"Everything," I said. "Adjusting to his new life."

Taylor looked down a moment, then said, "This is going to sound weird, but a few nights ago, I was lying in bed thinking about the time we were in that prison in Peru, when I realized that I actually miss the old days."

"You mean the Dr. Hatch days," Ostin said.

Taylor sighed. "I said it would sound weird. They were filled with horror and danger, but we were also together. We were close."

"It's really not that surprising," Ostin said. "It's common for soldiers to come home and feel displaced. I mean, look at us. We were fighting to save the world. Now we're fighting for a grade."

"When did you ever fight for a grade?" Taylor asked.

"Not literally, but you get the idea."

"I'm fighting for a grade," I said.

"You know," Ostin said, "after World War II, research showed that the British were actually less happy in peacetime than they'd been during the war. The feeling of comradery and unity overshadowed their fear and suffering."

"Is there anything you don't know?" I asked.

"A lot of things."

"Like what?"

"I don't know what I don't know."

"That's a reasonable answer," I said. "What else?"

"I don't know why McKenna likes me so much."

"That's a mystery too," Taylor said.

I think anyone else would have been offended, but Ostin just nodded.

". . . I also don't know how long a proton can exist, or why, in quantum physics, particles can be in two places at the same time, but objects in our world can't. And is the universe infinite or just really big?"

"That makes my head hurt," Taylor said.

"Is there anything else you don't know?" I asked.

"Yeah. Whatever happened to Bryan and Kylee?"

13

Dark Thoughts and a Hatch Cutout

We took a really long lunch. We had a lot to catch up on, and it was good to be together, even though Ostin kept checking his watch. After lunch, we drove by a party store to pick up some banners and things for the reunion. Ostin told us that he had something there to pick up as well. He had ordered a life-size cutout of Dr. Hatch. I thought it was pretty funny, but Taylor didn't think so.

"Where did you even get a picture of Hatch?" Taylor asked.

"Off the old Elgen corporate page."

Ostin picked it up anyway. He had already paid for it and thought it might be fun for Zeus to shoot lightning at.

We dropped Ostin off at his apartment; then Taylor and I went to the mall. She wanted to pick up a gift for my parents.

"You don't need to get them anything," I said. "You're the present."

"I know. It's just nice." She bought some scented bath salts and lavender room spray for my mother and a key-lime-scented candle for my father. Then we stopped at a kiosk and bought some flowers, a large bouquet of red tulips with purple irises.

"You know, the prevalent theme here is scent," I said.

"I know," Taylor said. "Everything smells happy."

I smiled. "How does something *smell* happy?"

"Scents are the best ways to make you feel happy. It's because smells bypass the brain's thalamus and go straight to the olfactory bulb, which is connected to the amygdala and the hippocampus."

"You sound like Ostin," I said.

"Should I be flattered or insulted?"

"Choose one, but hurry, or we'll be late for dinner."

"Now *you* sound like Ostin," Taylor said.

Just then her phone dinged with a text.

"Who's that?" I asked.

"It's Grace. She says she can't make it to the reunion."

I looked over. "Did she say why?"

"No."

"That's strange. I'll ask my father if he knows what's going on."

My home was only ten minutes from the mall. My parents were standing in the doorway as we pulled in. I parked the rental car in the driveway and grabbed the bag of gifts, while Taylor got the flowers, and then we both got out.

"Oh, Taylor," my mother said. "It's so good to see you."

Taylor handed the flowers to my mother. "I brought these for you."

"They're beautiful. I love tulips. I have such happy memories of them."

Taylor glanced over at me, with an *I told you so* look.

"Thank you." She hugged Taylor. "I'm going to put them in water."

As she walked inside, my father put out his hand. "It's good to see you, Taylor."

The moment they touched, Taylor tensed up. She looked as if she'd just been told that someone close to her had died, which, of course, made me wonder if someone close to her had died.

My father looked at her quizzically, then asked, "How's school, Taylor?"

"It's great," she said, a little too enthusiastically. "I room with Tara, so we've had a lot of time to catch up. And you can't beat the weather."

"No, it's nice down there. What's the temperature these days?"

They were talking weather. Now I was certain that my father had noticed something was up with Taylor.

"It got up to eighty-nine degrees last week."

"Our low last week was thirty-seven," my father said. "At night. Sixty-five during the day."

"I'll take Phoenix," Taylor said. "At least for three of the seasons."

"Summers in Phoenix can be a bit much," my father agreed. "They always have some news segment where they fry an egg on the sidewalk."

"I've felt like that egg." She reached into her bag. "Speaking of melting, I brought you something." She handed him the gift. "A candle."

My father smiled as he took it. "Thank you. Key-lime scented. Nice."

"What is that?" my mother asked, walking back out of the house.

"Taylor got me a candle. Key lime."

"You love key lime."

"I got you something else," Taylor said to my mother. She handed her the other gift bag. "It's just some things from Bath and Body Works."

"Flowers *and* this. You really didn't need to do this. It's your birthday, not ours."

"It's nothing," Taylor said.

"Well," my father said. "We'd better be off or we'll be late for our reservation."

Taylor glanced over at me but just as quickly turned away. I could see dread in her eyes. Whatever she had seen in my father's mind was serious.

We walked over to my father's car, an aqua-color Bentley

Mulliner. He opened the door for my mother, then walked around to his own door.

"Hey, Dad, I think I'll drive separately so I can take Taylor straight home. It's on the way."

"That's fine," he said. "Do you know the way to the restaurant?"

"It's in my phone."

"Great. We'll see you there."

As soon as we were in my car, I turned to Taylor. "What did you see?"

She looked at me with sad eyes. "I'll tell you later."

The way she said that made me even more anxious. "How bad is it?"

Taylor's voice came with an edge. "I'll tell you later."

We met my parents at a downtown steak house called Chandlers. It was pretty fancy. We started off with a half dozen oysters on the half shell. I ordered the Wagyu burger with candied spiced bacon and a lobster bisque. Taylor got the veal piccata with a mascarpone polenta soufflé, and a wilted spinach salad. For dessert we got the butterscotch crème brûlée and a chocolate torte.

What a different life I was living now. When it was just my mom and me, a celebration meant waffles and whipped cream. Now I was eating rich foods I couldn't pronounce. Still, I preferred the simple food I grew up on. Maybe that's true of everyone. I suppose that's why they call it comfort food.

The dinner conversation was light, almost forced at times. My father left the table twice to take phone calls, and throughout dinner it was mostly my mother talking. I think she sensed there was something wrong. She usually did.

I noticed my father glance over at Taylor a couple of times with an anxious look on his face. Taylor pretended like nothing was wrong, which wasn't something she was good at.

"So, are you excited for your reunion tomorrow?" my mother asked.

Taylor nodded. "It's going to be so great seeing everyone again. I've really missed McKenna and Abi. But I think I'm most curious about Nichelle. I can't wait to meet her boyfriend. I picture someone who looks like Edward Scissorhands."

We all laughed.

My mother asked, "How's Ostin doing in school?"

I grinned. "I can't believe you asked that. It's like sending a fish to swimming lessons."

"That's a good metaphor."

"He's bored at Caltech. In his spare time he's working on an organic battery made from a single cell from a jellyfish. It would be the world's smallest battery."

"What would it run?"

"Nanotechnology," my father said, finally speaking up. "Micro-bots." He turned to me. "I really wish he would just come work for us. He would be such an asset to our team."

"I told him that. Maybe you could talk him into it when you see him."

"Maybe I will."

After dinner, my father asked if we would drive my mother home since he unexpectedly needed to run in to the office. I told him I would, even though I was dying to hear what Taylor had seen and this just prolonged my agony. As we pulled into the driveway, my mother said to Taylor, "It's so good to see you. Thank you again for the lovely gifts."

"It's my pleasure."

She looked at Taylor thoughtfully for a moment as if she was going to say something, then changed her mind. "Give your parents my best."

"I will. Thank you."

She turned to me. "I'll probably be asleep when you get back. Good night."

"Night, Mom."

After I had pulled out of the driveway, I turned to Taylor. "What did you see in my father's mind?"

She took a deep breath. "It was awful. And bizarre." She turned to me. "It was exactly like my dream. I saw Grace. She was in a coma or something. The weirdest part was, she was in one of those hospital beds with railings, and she had all these machines around her, but she wasn't in a hospital. And there's more. Jack isn't just on a mission. He's missing. Your father thinks he might be dead."

I felt sick to my stomach. "This can't wait. We need to go talk to my father. I'm going to call Ostin. He should come with us."

"He's with McKenna."

"Good. She should be there too."

14

Expected and Unexpected

McKenna and Ostin were waiting at the front curb outside the Veytric building when Taylor and I arrived. They got out of their car as we pulled up.

In spite of the circumstances, it was good seeing McKenna again. She was holding Ostin's hand and smiling sweetly. It was hard to believe that the first time I met her was in a prison cell at the bottom of the Elgen Academy.

"McKenna!" Taylor shouted, hugging her. "I've missed you!"

"It's been way too long," McKenna replied. She turned to me. "And you too, Michael." We hugged. "I've missed you."

"I've missed you too," I said. "How have you been?"

"I'm good. School is good."

Most people who want to learn more about themselves take psychology or read a self-help book. McKenna studied thermal engineering.

"What's going on here?" Ostin asked. "What's so urgent?"

"Taylor saw some things in my father's mind that are . . ."

". . . Disturbing," Taylor said.

"What kind of things?" McKenna asked.

"It's best we talk to my father about it. It has to do with Jack and Grace."

McKenna's expression changed. "Has something happened to them?"

"We don't know. That's why I wanted you two here when we talked to him."

"Let's go," Ostin said.

Other than at the Elgen Academy in Pasadena, the Elgen had worked almost exclusively from their fleet of ships, hiding in international waters to avoid government intervention. After my father took control of the company, he purchased a twelve-story office building in downtown Boise to house the international company.

I let everyone in, then walked to the alarm pad and silenced it. I called my father from the building's lobby.

"Dad, it's Michael. We need to talk."

"I was expecting you. Who's with you?"

"Taylor, Ostin, and McKenna."

"I'm in my office. Come on up."

We rode the elevator up to the twelfth floor. We stepped out onto a marble floor, to see my father unlocking the glass door that led into the twelfth-floor lobby. During the day, the floor held about fifty employees and was a hive of activity. I had never been to the office at night, and it was quiet and dark. My father opened the door for us. He looked anxious.

"Hi," he said. The word sounded more like a sigh than a greeting. "Let's go to my office."

We followed him down a long, wide hallway covered with pictures of Starxource plants around the world. My father's office was luxurious, with a wide view of the city. He motioned for us to sit around a round, elegant table of polished burled walnut.

After we were all seated, I asked, "Why were you expecting us?"

"After what Taylor saw, I guessed you'd have some questions. I know I would." My father turned to Taylor. "What do you want to know?"

"Is Jack dead?"

All of us froze as we awaited his answer. My cheek started twitching.

My father frowned, then said simply, "We don't know."

"What do you know?" I asked.

"Our Starxource plant outside Lima was attacked and plundered."

"Attacked by who?"

"That's the question. The group that attacked us was not only well armed, but they knew exactly what they were looking for. They kidnapped seven guards and stole six MEI machines. Then they let loose close to a half million electrified rats. They burned more than twelve hundred hectares of jungle."

"What would they want with the MEIs?"

"We don't know. But the possibilities are disturbing." My father scratched his head. "The next day we sent a team down to investigate what happened. They disappeared without a trace."

"And Jack was with them?" I asked.

"No. After we lost them, we sent a second team down to find the first team. I asked Jack to lead that team, since he knew the most about the Elgen."

"But the Elgen don't exist anymore," McKenna said.

My father shook his head. "I wish that were true. Hatch doesn't exist anymore. The former Elgen Corporation is now controlled by us. But there were powerful cells of Elgen guard that remained. Sometimes after you cut off the head, the body keeps living."

"Like a chicken," Ostin said.

My father glanced at Ostin but didn't say anything.

"Where did Jack and his team disappear?" I asked.

My father walked over to a large world map on the wall. It was huge, from floor to ceiling. He pointed to a spot on the map. "The last contact we had with them was here, just east of the plant."

"Does Abi know this?" Taylor asked.

"Abi knows that Jack's on a mission, but she doesn't know that we've lost contact with him."

"I need to tell her," Taylor said.

"Not yet," my dad said. "It will only complicate things."

"If Jack's missing, we need to go after him," I said.

"Jack wouldn't leave any of us," McKenna said.

"*Nemo resideo*," Ostin said. "No one left behind. That was always his motto."

My dad frowned. "We've sent two teams down so far; both of them disappeared. We don't know what we're dealing with."

"We're not abandoning him," I said.

"We're not *abandoning* anyone," my father said. "We're just being smart. We've already lost a security team; we don't want to lose anyone else. As we speak, our Alpha Team is on its way down to Peru. Alpha Team is composed of elite military soldiers who were trained for this kind of search and rescue."

"I still don't get it," I said. "Who would attack a Starxource plant?"

"At first we thought the attacks might have been done by holdouts from the Shining Path terrorists, seeking revenge against the Elgen, or maybe even a drug cartel trying to extort from us. But then something else happened that changed our minds."

He raked his hand back through his hair. "I want to show you something." He walked over to his computer and typed into it. A moment later a paused video showed up on the massive monitor behind his desk. The words on it said the date and time.

CONFIDENTIAL

MARCH 17 / 12:35 A.M.

VRAEM

My father pushed a button, and suddenly the image changed to a view of a clear nighttime sky. A bright, red-orange light flowed and swirled in the air, like floating lava. It was mesmerizing to look at.

"What is that?" I asked.

"It's beautiful," Taylor said.

My father glanced over at her, then rubbed his chin. "During the Gulf War, the retreating Iraqi forces lit the oil wells on fire. The gas burned thousands of feet high. Some soldiers who witnessed it at night said it was beautiful." He frowned. "It might be beautiful to look at, but it's catastrophic."

"What is it?" I asked again.

He turned to me. "Michael, you've seen something like this before."

The remembrance sent chills through my body. "The rat bowl."

"Yes." My dad slowly breathed out. "That's what you're looking at."

"But it's in the air. Flying rats?"

"In a manner of speaking."

"Chiropterans," Ostin said.

My father nodded slowly. "Exactly."

"What are chiropterans?" Taylor asked.

"Bats," Ostin said.

"More specifically, Mexican free-tailed bats," my father said. "We've recovered some of their carcasses."

My eyes were still glued to the screen. "Why are they glowing?"

"The same reason the Starxource rats do. They were electrified."

"Why would someone do that?"

"We have our theories. The most likely one is that someone has weaponized the bats."

"What do you mean?" McKenna asked.

"During World War II, a dental surgeon from Pennsylvania was visiting the Carlsbad Caverns in southern New Mexico. There were millions of bats in the caves. The floors were littered with bones inches thick. He learned that the bats emerged for a few hours after sunset but always returned to roost before the sun came up. He had a bizarre but brilliant idea. What would happen if the bats all had small incendiary devices attached to them and you dropped a few thousand of them above a city?

"At the time, we were at war with Japan, and back then, the Japanese cities were mostly built of paper and wood, so they would go up in flames."

"How could a bat carry a bomb?" Taylor asked. "They're tiny."

"That was the challenge, of course. But it only takes a small spark to start a massive wildfire. It's all a matter of when the fire is discovered and if it's stopped before it spreads. Bats are small and they nest in places humans don't usually go, like belfries and attics and the tops of buildings. By the time the fire they started was detected, it would already be spreading."

"What kind of bomb did they attach to the bats?" Ostin asked.

"At first, they started with white phosphorus. Then another scientist joined the team. He had just invented something a bit more potent. Napalm."

"Like they used in Vietnam," Ostin said.

My father nodded. "Think of the advantage these electrified bats would have over that World War II technology. They don't have to carry anything, so they could fly farther and faster, they wouldn't need to set off the incendiary bomb at the exact time, and there's no chance of a fire pod malfunctioning."

"It would be thousands of times more efficient," Ostin said.

"And the old technology was already effective enough to cause severe damage. When the army was preparing to test the idea, a few of the bats that had been outfitted with the fire pods escaped. Just three bats burned down the entire compound.

"Imagine if a million bats had been let loose above a large city. They figured the destruction would be more potent than dropping a thousand tons of bombs. Whoever electrified these bats has created a weapon of mass destruction."

"There's still a problem with their plan," Ostin said. "The primary reason the Elgen used rats was because they bred quickly. Bats reproduce slower. Much slower."

"True," my father said. "But the other side of that coin is that rats have a short life span of just a few years. Some species of bats live up to forty years. That's almost twenty times longer than a rat. That's why there's so many bats in the world. Bat species make up about one-quarter of all mammal species on earth.

"They're also much more mobile. A rat rarely travels more than a dozen miles from its home in its lifetime. The Mexican free-tailed bat is the world's fastest mammal. It can fly up to one hundred miles per hour, and some bats can cover a range of more than two hundred miles in a single night. These bats have already burned down several thousand jungle acres."

"What would they gain by burning down a jungle?" I asked.

"Little. Unless they were using it as an example. During the Mexican drug wars, the cartels would sometimes wipe out innocent neighborhoods just to intimidate the government and municipal police into staying away from them. The Elgen might be doing the same."

"The Elgen?" Taylor said. "You think the Elgen are behind this?"

"A remnant of them," my father said. "We shouldn't have been surprised that the Elgen didn't just vanish. When the DEA and Mexican marines arrested El Chapo, the billionaire drug lord of the Sinaloa cartel, the flow of drugs didn't slow at all. In fact, it increased. The competition for the drug business spread out to a half dozen smaller cartels.

"When you conquered Hatch and the Elgen guard in Tuvalu, there were still the Elite Guard units, the Chasqui, the Lung Li, and the Domguard. They were in other parts of the world, and their organizations were still very much connected to the Elgen system Hatch had created.

"On top of that, Hatch managed to stash away billions of dollars in gold and gems and secret accounts. We've been working with Grace to track it all, but we've only scratched the surface.

"What we've discovered is that these organizations only appeared to be on the same team. They operated independently of Hatch's Elgen guard. They even handled their own finances and investments."

"Investments?" I said.

"Organized crime always has legitimate investments. Real estate, stocks, businesses. And, at the core, that's what these Elgen guard units were—organized crime. Each of the Elite Guard organizations was independently wealthy, and all of them were waiting for Hatch to fail.

"We managed to infiltrate one of the Domguard pods. They were already preparing to take down Hatch. They were far more extreme than Hatch ever was."

"How can you be more extreme than Hatch?" Taylor said. "He bought a cannibal fork so he could eat Michael."

"I know," my father said softly. "The Domguard were more of a cult than a secret service. They had their own rituals. They worshipped the electric children as something more than human."

"You mean . . . gods?" Taylor asked.

"Yes. And the future of the world. They believed the Elgen, or their version of it, would someday fill the world. They saw the electric children as part of a long-awaited fulfillment of prophecy."

"But when we took Hatch down," I said, "didn't they see that their belief system was messed up?"

"You would think," my father said. "But that's not the way psychology works. Almost all cults have doomsday prophecies. That's how they attract followers. It's a fascinating phenomenon. Let's say a cult leader says that doomsday is coming on January first of the next year. It creates intensity among the members. They start preparing for the end of the world. They start selling or giving away everything they own, or they incur debts they think they'll never have to repay. Then, when the day comes and nothing happens, instead of leaving the cult, they actually become *more* committed. It happens when the lie becomes more tolerable than the truth."

"That's bizarre," Taylor said.

"You could say that," my father said.

"Aren't you studying psychology?" Ostin said.

"I'm not you," she replied.

"The truth is, the different Elgen Elite Guard units acted more like street gangs than allies. They each had their own territory, and if it was violated, they would react with violence.

"For instance, about six years ago, the Domguard started recruiting guards in Singapore, which the Lung Li had already claimed as territory. A group of Lung Li guards stormed the hotel where the Domguard were staying and machine-gunned them all. It was just like a drug hit. A week later, the Domguard responded by detonating a bomb in the Lung Li headquarters.

"Hatch only intervened when he realized that the groups had

become more concerned with their internal battles and competition than growing his army. He held a summit, bringing in the leaders of each of the groups. He made them sign an agreement binding them to specific territories. But it was already too late; the damage was done. They were sworn enemies. Which, as you know, wasn't necessarily something Hatch would have discouraged. One of the ways he kept power was to keep his subordinates fighting each other. That way he didn't have to fear that they might join together against him. Divide and conquer was always Hatch's game plan."

"That's true," Ostin said. "Even with the Glows."

"We knew that the Elite Guard were working toward overthrowing Hatch; it just wasn't the time. But now that Hatch is gone, it's a free-for-all."

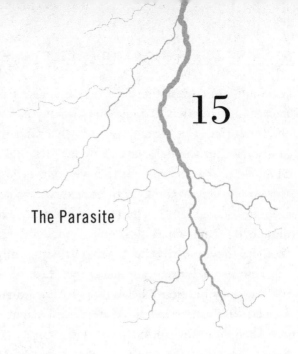

15

The Parasite

"Then, is it the Domguard that are making the electric bats?" Taylor asked.

My father shook his head. "It's not likely. South America is Chasqui territory."

"Maybe they wanted to attack the Chasqui before the Chasqui attacked them," I said. "A preemptive strike."

Ostin said, "The whole bat thing doesn't fit the Domguard's modus operandi."

"Their what?" Taylor asked.

"Their way of doing things. The Domguard are about order and discipline. Randomly burning villages isn't their way. That seems like something the Chasqui would do."

"Ostin's right," my father said. "The Chasqui are about chaos. They want to burn the world down, then rise from the ashes. The best way to understand the Chasqui is to think of them as a parasite.

'Chasqui' isn't even their real name. Their true name is a secret known only to a few. It's just one of many names they've used over the centuries. The earliest record we found of them was as the Hashishans, or the Assassins, in Syria. After being put down by the Mongols, they were thought to have gone extinct. They didn't; they were just hiding, waiting for their next reincarnation.

"They showed up, briefly, in the eighteenth century in the Bavarian illuminati. That's where they refined their strategy for survival. From then on, they survived as sleeper cells within other groups, surviving off them like a parasite, advancing their host only so far as to further their own cause. Some believe they came to America, where they merged with various secret societies, including the Ku Klux Klan.

"Then, midway through the last century, they re-emerged in South America with the Shining Path rebels, a Maoist terrorist group. We believe that's where they first came in contact with the Elgen, who were recruiting the Shining Path rebels as Elgen guards—the same way the Kuomintang soldiers were recruited by drug traffickers after losing the war in China."

My father turned to Ostin. "I'm sure Ostin has heard of the matapalo tree."

Ostin nodded. "The strangler fig. Genus *Ficus*. It has an interesting survival strategy."

"Exactly," my father said. "It's a good example of what we are dealing with."

"More trees," Taylor said.

"The 'matapalos' is the name given to the tree by the Amazon natives. It means 'tree killers.' In the deep Amazon jungle, competition to survive is fierce. But the matapalos has found a way to not only survive but flourish. In fact, the more competition it has, the better.

"The matapalo doesn't grow like other trees, fighting its way up from the crowded soil. Instead, it starts its life in the tops of the trees, where birds and monkeys leave its seeds in their droppings. It finds safety in another's tree bark or crevices, where it has sunshine and protection.

"Once it has taken hold, it grows quickly. The matapalos stretches its branches up toward more light, capturing more energy, while at the same time sending its roots down the tree, enveloping the host tree until it reaches the ground. Once it does, it sucks up all the nutrients from the soil and grows even faster, taking the nutrients from the tree it's living off. So, as it grows stronger, the host grows weaker until it dies."

"That's sad," McKenna said.

My father said, "The matapalos is the perfect metaphor for the Chasqui. They infiltrate other organizations until they grow so powerful that they take them over. That's why they were attracted to the Elgen. It had money and power and something the entire world needed: electricity.

"Their plan was to grow quietly inside the Elgen until the Elgen had reached its full potential; then they would secretly take over power. They already had two members on the Elgen's highest counsel."

"The EGGs," Ostin said.

"The reality is, it doesn't matter what group the Chasqui attach themselves to, or what name they're existing under. They'll embrace any cause if it gives them the power to grow their own cause."

"And what's that cause?" I asked.

"World domination."

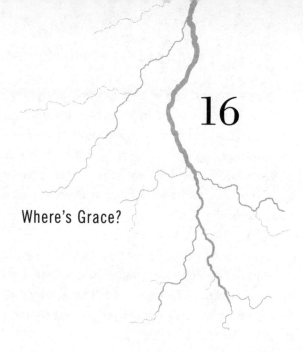

16

Where's Grace?

"**W**hat about Grace?" I asked.

I could see the weight the question carried by my father's countenance. He breathed out slowly. "Are you sure you want to know?"

"Of course we do. She's one of us."

"We need to know," Taylor said.

My father looked around at us, then said, "To explain, I'll need to show you something. Come with me."

We walked out of his office back to the elevator. My father used a magnetic key to take us to the tenth floor. We walked out of the elevator and down a hallway to where an armed guard stood in front of a metal door. He stepped aside at my father's approach.

"Sir."

"Unlock the door, please."

The guard looked us over, then took a card from his pocket and waved it over a control panel near the door. A series of green LEDs flashed on the panel. My father stepped forward and put his finger on the panel, and the door slid open. My father turned to us. "Before you enter, I need to warn you, what you're going to see won't be easy."

I stepped inside the room, followed by Taylor, McKenna, and Ostin, then my father. The guard shut the door behind us. The room was dimly lit with an amber light on the far side of the room. My father pressed another button, and the light slowly increased, growing in illumination like the morning dawn. Taylor gasped.

A row of six graphite-black computer mainframes hung from the ceiling like stalactites, with lights flashing in syncopation. In front of the computers was a hospital bed with Grace lying on it. It was just as Taylor had seen in her dream—and in my father's mind—the bed surrounded by hospital machinery with PICC lines and monitors running to her body. A heart monitor beeped with each beat of her heart.

"Grace!" Taylor shouted. She ran to the bed. The rest of us followed her over.

Grace's eyes were closed and her body was still. Her skin was a pasty white.

"My dream was true," Taylor said.

She put her hand on Grace's head and closed her eyes, trying to read her mind. She spun back to my father. "She doesn't have any thoughts. What have you done to her?"

"We haven't done anything to her," my father said defensively, "except keep her alive. This is what she chose."

Tears welled up in Taylor's eyes. "Is she in a coma?"

"I suppose you could call it that."

"What does that mean?" I said to my father. "Why isn't she in a hospital?"

My father looked at me calmly. "It's not what you think, Michael. Don't forget, I ran a hospital. That's how this whole mess began. Grace isn't in a hospital because she wouldn't let us take her."

"What do you mean she wouldn't let you?" Taylor said. "She's in a coma. She's completely helpless."

"She's not as helpless as you think. Grace had a unique ability.

She was able to absorb the electrical data within a computer. It wasn't flashy like most of your gifts, but it was just as valuable in its own way. At first, her most important contribution to our war with the Elgen was to provide us with all the information she carried. But she wanted to do more.

"Grace didn't just download files like a flash drive, as we originally believed. The data actually entered her consciousness. She could put her hand on a computer, then tell us, from memory, what was on it, as if her brain stored the information like a computer." My father breathed out slowly. "She started wondering if her consciousness could flow both ways."

"What do you mean?" I asked.

"She knew that data from a computer could enter her consciousness. But what if *her* consciousness could enter a computer?" My father raked his hand back over his hair again. "Do you realize the ramifications of this? If her consciousness could enter a computer, she could know the whole of human knowledge. She might even become immortal. It was a frightening reality.

"Ever since humankind conceived of AI—artificial intelligence— we have feared its potential. Grace wondered if she could become that consciousness.

"When she told me her idea, I told her no. It was too dangerous, for her and the world. But she didn't give it up. Without telling any- one else her plan, she convinced several of the scientists to help her create a more direct connection to our mainframe—one that was physically connected to her body. That's what those wires coming from her head are." My father shook his head. "They did it. She was sitting at her desk; then, in a moment, she left."

"What do you mean, 'left'?" McKenna asked.

"Just that. Grace's consciousness left her body. Her heart contin- ued to beat, and her brain waves remained, so she wasn't dead, but the consciousness we know as Grace was gone.

"Our first concern was her physical welfare. We called in medical specialists from all around the world, neuroscientists, brain surgeons. They were all baffled. Of course, they had never seen anything like it. Just trying to explain her electric gift was overwhelming for most of them. Some of them flat-out wouldn't believe it. The only advice they gave us was to hook up this life support system, since her body still needed nourishment to survive."

"How long has she been this way?" I asked.

"Four months."

"But she responded to one of my texts," Taylor said. "She said she couldn't make it to the reunion."

"It must have been someone else with her phone," I said.

"You're not understanding me," my father said, his expression growing even more intense. "Grace isn't *dead*. Her consciousness just changed realms." He looked at me. "Michael, after you were struck by lightning, where did you go?"

I shook my head. "I can't really explain. It was like a dream. A sort of . . . limbo."

"But you kept trying to come back to us."

I nodded. "It took me a while to figure out how to re-manifest in this realm."

"We believe that's what happened to Grace. At first, we didn't even know she still existed. After several months, a team of doctors advised that we shut off her life support. We all came together and turned it off."

Taylor angrily asked, "You would just shut off her life support? You would kill her?"

"Of course not," my father shot back. "You think I didn't care about her? I've spent more time with Grace than any of you have. We spent years together combing through all the Elgen data. We became close friends. I admired her. She was quiet and sweet, which is surprising for someone who was raised by a sadistic tyrant.

"But Grace was in what doctors call a persistent vegetative state. It's one step above being brain dead. Turning off the machine was about respect for who she is—or was. If it was me, that's what I would have wanted. To shut off the machines was to let her die with dignity."

Taylor lowered her head. "I'm sorry."

My father paused. "I wept when Grace's heartbeat stopped. But then the machine turned back on.

"The doctor overseeing her transition thought that something was wrong with the machine. He tried to shut it off again, but again it turned itself back on. Then a message came on this screen right here. You can still see it."

My father walked over to a computer monitor near Grace's body. On it was a page of dialogue.

"This was the first time she spoke to us. She was learning to communicate." My father pointed to the first line.

LEAVE IT

"Grace wrote that?"

"There's no other explanation."

"What's all this other writing?" Ostin asked.

"These are all the times she's reached out to us from the cyber world. We've kept a log of everything she's written."

"This is unbelievable," Ostin said. "She could be the most powerful person in the world. If you can still call her a person."

"Of course she's a person," Taylor said angrily. "She's Grace."

"If she's moved her consciousness into the cyber world, she is much more than a person. She's omniscient," Ostin said. "Like a god."

"She's not a god," Taylor said.

"The Tuvaluans still think Michael's a god," Ostin said. "*Uira te Atua.* So do the Domguard."

"The Domguard worship anything that sparks," Taylor said sardonically. "And Grace isn't a god. She's our friend."

"Well, our friend is somewhere in the cyber verse," Ostin said. He went back to reading the other messages Grace had sent.

I THINK, THEREFORE I AM

"Descartes. Brilliant. She's telling us that her consciousness is intact."

"Or she's telling herself," I said.

"Exactly."

THE TRUE SELF IS THE REASON OR THE
INTELLECT THAT CONSTITUTES THEIR SOUL

"She's quoting Plato," Ostin said. "Just as you said, Michael, she's trying to define her own existence."

"That's the conclusion we came to as well," my father said. "This is uncharted territory for the human race. I suppose the real wild card is her memory. Does she remember who we are, and will we still matter to her?"

"And what about her emotions? Fear, excitement, sadness," Ostin said. "Will they still exist in a cyber intellect?"

"And love," Taylor said.

"If not, she could become very, very dangerous," Ostin said.

"How dangerous?" I asked.

"A weapon of mass destruction," Ostin said.

My father nodded. "She would have unfathomable power. Imagine if someone had access to every computer, every electrical machine, every electrical communication device. All that power with unlimited knowledge. In one thought, she could stop every device that's connected to the internet or a computer. Or launch nuclear missiles. She could kill the world."

"Omnipotent, omniscient, omnipresent," Ostin said. "God."

"Quit saying that," Taylor said.

I turned to my dad. "If she knows everything, then it's possible that she knows where Jack is."

"It's possible. The problem is trying to communicate with her, and her trying to communicate back to us. So far, everything has come from her trying to give us clues. She hasn't really answered any of our questions yet. Except one, which was a little vague." He turned to Taylor. "And there's your text message. Did you text her back?"

"I told her that we'd miss her, but she didn't respond."

"Do something for me," my father said. "Do you have your phone?"

Taylor lifted it.

"May I see the text?"

Taylor unlocked her phone and handed it to my dad.

"Do you mind if I write her something?" he asked.

"No."

He typed:

Grace, are you there?

For a moment we all looked at the screen, hoping for a response. Nothing came. After a few minutes I said, "You said she had answered one of your questions."

He pointed back to the computer screen again. "I asked her where she was. This is what she wrote back."

UNKNOWN

Taylor walked over to Grace's body and took her hand. She leaned close and said softly, "Grace, if you can hear me, please come back to us."

Nothing.

After a moment of silence my father said, "So that's where things stand with Jack and Grace. I know you're worried about your friends. So are we. Please just give us a chance to see what we can do to get Jack back safe. As far as Grace, it's completely up to her."

"If Jack is in danger, who would be better to help him than us?" I asked.

"Which is exactly what the Chasqui might be anticipating. This could be a trap. The Elgen spent more than a decade gathering you all. The Chasqui might see the opportunity to do the same thing in just one day."

"We've escaped traps before," I said. "Then why not send us?"

My father's eyes locked on mine. "Because I finally have my son back. Do you think I want to risk losing you again? Do you have any idea how terrifying it was to follow you the first time you battled the Elgen?"

It hadn't occurred to me that his reason was personal.

"I know I can't stop you from doing what you think is right. I just ask that you give us a chance to save Jack without risking your lives again."

I glanced over at everyone. Taylor nodded lightly.

"All right," I said. "Just keep us informed of what's going on. We'll decide when it's time. And when that time comes, we'll expect you to help us."

"Fair enough," my father said. He glanced down at his watch. "It's after midnight. You all have a big day tomorrow. You'd better get some rest."

"All right," I said. I walked over to Grace. At least she looked peaceful, as if she were asleep. I leaned over and kissed her on the forehead. "Come home, Grace."

At that moment there was a slight irregularity to the heart monitor. I don't know if it meant anything. Maybe it was just a coincidence.

Taylor squeezed Grace's hand again, then took mine. "Let's go."

As we walked out of the building, Taylor said, "First Jack. Now Grace."

"It almost feels like it used to," Ostin said. "The bad old days."

"What are we going to do about Jack?" McKenna asked.

"We'll give them some time to rescue him," I said. "Then we go. No man left behind."

"I don't think I can keep this from Abi," Taylor said, shaking her head.

As we walked out to our cars, Ostin said to me, "There's one thing about all this talk of the Chasqui, Domguard, and Lung Li."

"What's that?"

"It explains the tree dream."

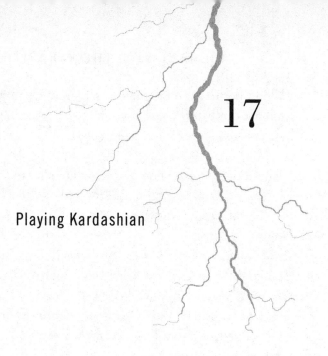

17

Playing Kardashian

Friday, April 19

I woke the next morning with my face ticking. I felt like I hadn't slept all night. As much as I hated that recurring tree dream, I would have preferred it to what had now occupied my mind. My heart was filled with dread.

Not only did I have tics, but my chest felt heavy. What my father had showed us weighed on my heart like a sack of concrete. Hearing that Jack had disappeared was bad enough. But seeing Grace's frozen body had sickened me.

For months I had been looking forward to the reunion. Now I wished it wasn't happening. I didn't think I could hide everything that was churning inside me, especially with my Tourette's.

I grabbed my phone off the nightstand and called Taylor. She answered with a soft, "Hi."

"Are you okay?" I asked, already knowing the answer.

"Not really. I could barely sleep last night. I kept thinking of Jack being locked up somewhere."

"I couldn't sleep either. And then Grace . . ."

". . . And Grace. I had the worst nightmare about her. Her eyes opened, and she looked at me and said, 'Help.'" Taylor groaned. "Yesterday, Tara kept saying that she was going to talk Grace into coming."

"Then she doesn't know."

"Of course not."

"I forget that she can't read minds like you."

"It's a good thing. If she could, my thoughts would have been screaming all night. I don't think I can keep this from everyone."

"You're going to have to. At least for now."

"I know what your dad said, but we've never just sat back and waited for others to tell us what to do."

"We did with the voice. And it never led us astray. The only difference now is, we know who the voice is."

"You're right," she said softly.

"It's just for a little while. If they don't find him soon, we go."

"Who do you mean by 'we'?"

"The Electroclan. At least, whoever wants to help."

"So, what do we do in the meantime?"

"We act like nothing's wrong."

"I don't do that well."

"Me neither. I'm ticking like crazy. I might as well have a blinking neon sign on my head with the words 'stressed out of my brain.'"

"I'm sorry. At least we're together for this." She sighed. "McKenna texted earlier. Do you want to get lunch with her and Ostin?"

"Yes. When?"

"They want to meet a little before noon."

"All right. Is Tara coming?"

"Tara's still sleeping. She went out dancing last night."

"She went alone?"

"She's never alone. Guys are always fighting over her."

"Of course, she's beautiful."

"Thank you," Taylor said. "But she's got one up on me. If the fish aren't biting, she just changes the lure."

"You mean, she changes how people see her."

"Once, she went to a fraternity party as Kim Kardashian. The place went mad."

"How did she get out of that?"

"She went into the restroom, then came out as herself. Everyone was so confused. People were literally lined up outside the bathroom to see her.

"The funny part is, people took pictures of her before she changed back, but on camera she just looks like herself, so all these people who posted pictures of themselves with Kim Kardashian just got mocked."

"You're having a very different college experience than I am."

"I know."

"I'll pick you up at eleven thirty."

"Bye, boyfriend."

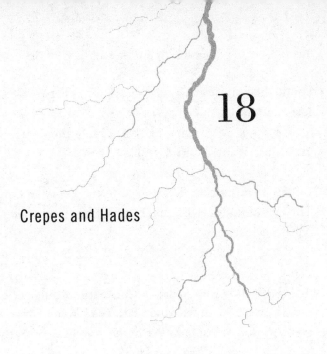

18

Crepes and Hades

We met Ostin and McKenna at a place called Brittany Crepes, which you might think was named after the owner, but you'd be wrong. Brittany is the region in France where crepes came from. The restaurant was in Eagle, Idaho, just a few miles from Meridian.

Taylor, Ostin, and McKenna all ordered the Romantique crepe, which had white chocolate, fresh strawberries, and strawberry syrup. I wasn't in the mood for sweet, so I got a savory crepe—the Versailles, with brie cheese, prosciutto, tomatoes, and herbes de Provence.

The crepes were good, but our mood was grim. It was like eating lunch at a funeral. There wasn't just an elephant in the room; there was a whole herd of them.

"What are we going to do?" McKenna asked. "We can't abandon Jack."

"No one's abandoning him," I said. "But we've got to be smart about this. My father might be right. What if it's a trap? We could lose more of us."

"Or all of us," Ostin said. "Not to mention, we're still on the Peruvian Most-Wanted Terrorists list."

"I thought your dad was taking care of that," Taylor said.

"He's working on it," I said. "But the Peruvian bureaucracy is slow. They wouldn't even consider it until he threatened to raise the price on their electricity."

"Maybe he should just cut it off," Taylor said. "See how they like that."

"He wouldn't do that," I said. "People would suffer."

"So if we go down there, are they going to sic the army on us again?" McKenna asked. "We barely got away from them last time."

"That's when Wade was killed," Ostin said.

"Yeah, we know that," Taylor said.

"They won't come after us if they don't know we're there," I said. "It's easier for us to get in on a private jet."

"I just don't know how we're not going to tell everyone at the party." Taylor exhaled. "I wish the party had been last week."

"Speaking of which, do you guys need any help for tonight?" McKenna asked.

"We've got it handled. After lunch we're going to the bakery to pick up the éclairs, and then to the trophy store, for our awards."

"Éclairs?" Ostin said.

"We got them for you," I said.

"You're giving out awards?" McKenna asked.

"They're just for fun," Taylor said.

"McKenna should get one for being the hottest," Ostin said. "Literally. And euphemistically."

McKenna looked happy. "Thank you."

"That's the idea," Taylor said.

"What time should we be at the restaurant?" McKenna asked.

"We told everyone five, but we'll be there an hour early to meet with the DJ and make sure everything's ready."

"We'll come early too," McKenna said. "Just in case you need help." She turned to Ostin. "We don't really have anything else today, do we?"

Ostin shook his head. "Nope."

"We'll be there around four." We were quiet for a moment; then McKenna asked, "How long do we give them?"

"To set up?" Taylor asked.

"To rescue Jack."

I exhaled slowly. "I think we'll see as we go along. Either Alpha Team rescues him or they can't find him."

"Or they disappear as well," Ostin said. "That could happen."

"Then what do we do?" Taylor asked. "What if it's all just a big trap?"

I set down my fork. "Then it's Hades all over."

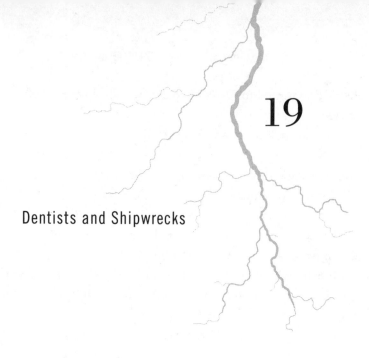

19

Dentists and Shipwrecks

For the party, Taylor and I had reserved a restaurant called Barbacoa, a Spanish word that, Ostin pointed out, is the root of the English word "barbecue." It was one of our favorite restaurants, not just in Idaho but in the world.

The party was scheduled to begin at five, but since everyone was arriving at different times, we had arranged to have the dinner served buffet style. When we got there, the staff was filling the tables with food. There were appetizers and hors d'oeuvres, a table of salads and two tables of main courses, including king crab legs, steak, and roast beef.

There was one table filled with desserts, including cotton candy lanterns, cheesecake lollipops, and a chocolate fountain. We set the éclairs at the end of the table. As a joke, Taylor set a sign next to them that read, OSTIN ONLY.

"This is glorious," Ostin said, watching the chocolate fountain. "I could bathe in that."

McKenna smiled. "I'd join you."

Taylor and I were walking over to check out the stage when someone shouted, "Did I hear there was free food?" Zeus walked into the room.

"Lightning man!" I shouted.

"Michael, my man!"

We man hugged.

"How are you?" I asked.

"Mr. Vey, if I were any better, I'd be you. And what are you up to? Besides the gorgeous Taylor Ridley. You two still bookends?"

"We're still together," Taylor said, hugging him. "I just can't shake him."

"Thanks," I said. "I'm just doing school. What are you up to?"

"Oh, you know . . . still trying to figure out what to do with the rest of my life, which is code for 'playing.' I can't believe how long it's been. Who ever thought we'd be back here together, all respectable and crap?"

"I don't know about the *respectable* part," I said.

"You have 'respectable' written all over you, Mr. Vey. Someday you'll own Elgen Inc."

"Veytric Inc.," I said.

"See, it already has your name." He smiled. "I see Ostin and McKenna. Who else is coming?"

"Almost everyone. We're missing a few. Cassy and Torstyn . . ."

"You know Cassy, she's in her own high-power world. But what's up with Torstyn?"

"I'm not sure. Quentin's got the scoop on that."

"Jack's not coming either," Taylor said.

"No Jack? Really?"

"He's in Peru on Elgen . . ." I caught myself. "Corporation business."

"That's too bad. Abi must be really upset about that. Speaking of which, where is she?"

"She's coming," Taylor said. "Her flight must have been late."

"I'll keep my eye out. So Cassy, Torstyn, and Jack are AWOL."

". . . And Grace," Taylor said.

Zeus looked the most surprised by this. "Grace, too? I thought she was a given. I mean, she lives here, right? Doesn't she work like a mile from here?"

"She had something come up," Taylor said.

His brow furrowed. "That doesn't sound like Grace at all. What could be more important than this?"

"I think she's going through some stuff," I said.

"What kind of stuff?"

"Personal stuff." I felt like a liar, even if it was technically true.

"All the more reason to be here. As long as I'm here, I'm going to talk to her."

I tried to change the subject. "I thought you'd be coming here with Tessa."

"I was going to pick her up at the airport, but as usual, we got in a fight and she decided to take an Uber instead. So here I am. Tessa-less."

At that moment I felt a sudden surge of power. Electricity shot from Zeus's hand to a light socket, and my fingers started sparking. Tessa was in the building.

"Speaking of the devil. Looks like she's here," Zeus said.

". . . Who's here?" Tessa said. "Hi, Taylor. Michael."

"I always know when you're around," I said.

"I know. You get all . . . sparky."

"You don't get all sparky when I come around," Taylor said.

"No, you have a different effect."

Taylor smiled.

"Hi, Tessa," Zeus said.

"We'll talk later," she said curtly.

"What's up with you guys?" Taylor asked.

Tessa said, "We're just fighting."

"Not at my party. This is a no-fighting, all-love affair."

"All right." Tessa leaned forward and kissed Zeus on the cheek. "It's good to see you. Even if you are an idiot."

"Thanks," Zeus said. "I feel so much better."

Ostin and McKenna walked up. Ostin was holding a plate with a couple of éclairs.

"Ostin, my man," Zeus said.

"Zeus," Ostin said.

"McKenna, you're smoking hot as usual," Zeus said.

"As usual," she said. It was an inside joke between them ever since she accidentally burned him. Zeus glanced back and forth between them. "So you guys are also still a set."

"Still are," McKenna said. "Always will be."

Zeus said to Ostin, "You're definitely a genius if you can keep this one."

"I am a genius," Ostin said matter-of-factly.

"Hi, you guys," Tessa said.

"Hi, Tess," McKenna said. They hugged. For a moment McKenna flashed brightly.

"Sorry," Tessa said. "I'm just all fired up."

"Me too," McKenna said.

"So, Ostin man," Zeus said. "What are you up to?"

"Postdoctoral-level math," he said. "Advanced physics."

Zeus laughed. "Mr. Literal. Don't change, brother. Never change."

"I hope he doesn't," McKenna said.

"That looks delicious, Ostin," Tessa said.

"Éclairs." He held up his plate. "Did you know that the word 'éclair' in French means 'lightning'?"

"Then it's my kind of dessert," Zeus said.

"They called the pastries that because people love them so much, they eat them as fast as lightning. Which would be physically impossible since—"

"You can always count on Ostin for the lowdown," Zeus said.

Behind us a female voice said, "Hi, guys."

We all turned around. It took me a moment to realize it was Nichelle. She didn't look at all like she used to. Her hair wasn't dyed anymore but was its natural auburn color, nicely trimmed and carefully styled. She was wearing a surprisingly conventional outfit. I always thought she was cute, at least after she stopped trying to kill us, but now she looked pretty.

She was holding a man's hand. He looked more like someone's father than Edward Scissorhands. He was gangly, tall, and slightly balding. He wore a yellow cardigan, loafers, and thick prescription glasses. He looked older than Nichelle by at least a decade.

Nichelle smiled. "It's me. Nichelle."

"It took me a second," I said. "You look . . ."

"Respectable? I know, I changed a little."

"You've changed a lot," Ostin said.

"Haven't we all?" Taylor said.

"That's for sure." I turned to her date. "And your friend . . ."

"This is Corbin, my boyfriend." Nichelle turned to him. "Corbin, this is my friend Michael. He's the reason we're here. And by 'here' I really mean 'alive.'"

"That's a bit much," I said.

"No," Zeus said. "It's accurate, *Uira te Atua.*"

Corbin looked confused by the conversation. Still, he reached out his hand. "Hi, Michael. It's nice to meet you. I've heard so much about you."

I wondered how much Nichelle had really told him about me, or us, or what we'd been through.

"I hope that's good," I said, furtively glancing over at Nichelle. She winked at me.

Nichelle continued with the introductions. "And this is Michael's girlfriend, Taylor; Zeus; Tessa; McKenna; and Ostin. My family."

I loved that she called us that. Everyone exchanged the usual pleasantries. It was a little surreal seeing Nichelle with someone so normal. Like Taylor, I'd expected Nichelle to show up with someone edgier—someone with a colored mohawk and a safety pin through his nose.

"What do you do?" I asked.

"I'm a dentist. I have a family practice in Spokane."

"A dentist?" I looked at Nichelle. "Wow, that's . . . unexpected."

She grinned. "Yet, kind of perfect, right? We both deal in pain."

Everyone laughed except Corbin, who still looked confused. He adjusted his glasses. "For the record, I try not to hurt my patients."

"So you say," Nichelle said.

"Where did you two meet?" Taylor asked.

"In his dental chair. I needed a dentist," Nichelle said. She turned to him, then said sweetly, "I guess in more ways than one."

Corbin smiled. "I'll say. She had some fairly serious gingivitis, not to mention two amalgam restorations."

"They really don't want to know this," Nichelle said.

This was definitely not the Nichelle I'd met in Purgatory—proof that people can change.

"How about you, Michael?" Corbin asked. "What do you do?

"I'm at Boise State. I'm working on an MBA."

"That's great. So, Nichelle told me that you have a unique talent."

I looked at Nichelle. "Did she?"

"Sorry," she said. "It just kind of came out."

"Can you really shock people?"

"Only if I rub my feet on the carpet."

"Oh," Corbin said. "She made it sound like it was more than that."

I winked at Nichelle. "She's got a dry sense of humor."

"Dry as toast," he said.

Taylor took my arm. "Almost everyone's here; maybe you should go onstage and say 'Hi' or something."

In the center of the room there was a small platform for the DJ. As I walked over, the DJ stopped the song he was playing and handed me his microphone.

"Hey, everyone. Welcome. We're glad you've all made it safe. There's a lot of food."

"Too much," Taylor said.

"No such thing," Ostin said.

"My point being, eat a lot. We're glad you're here." I handed the microphone back to the DJ, and he started a new song. "Electric Avenue."

Taylor and Tessa were now talking, so I walked over to the food table. I was looking over the buffet when someone said, "Hello, handsome."

It was Cassy. Her short blond hair was tucked back behind her ears. She looked more European than American, which I suppose she was. She was also even prettier than I remembered.

"Cassy. Our Swiss Miss."

"Don't call me that," she said. "It makes me sound like powdered cocoa."

"You say that like it's a bad thing."

She smiled. "Well, it is sweet."

"I didn't think you were coming."

"Neither did I. I had some high-level EU meetings in Brussels, but at the last minute I decided to ditch my plans and just come."

"I'm glad you did."

She looked at me intently. "Are you?"

"Of course I am. How have you been?"

"I'm good. I'm running the Veytric office in Geneva with Dr. Coonradt. Dealing with all that EU regulation. And someday you'll be my boss. How about you?"

"Nothing that exciting. I'm still home. I'm taking business classes at Boise State. It's pretty boring."

"Not like the old days of hunting Elgen."

"I think we were the ones being hunted."

"How quickly I forget," she said. "So, I'm in town for a few days. I was wondering if we could get together while I'm here."

"I'd love to. I'm sure Taylor would too."

". . . I meant just the two of us."

I paused. "That's probably not a good idea."

She frowned. "Then you and Taylor are still a thing?"

"We're still a thing." There was some awkwardness. "How about you. Dating anyone?"

"No. I mean, it's not like I have trouble getting boys."

"No. You could stop hearts without your powers."

She smiled coyly. "Thank you. That's sweet."

"There must be a million guys . . ."

"Don't do that, please."

I stopped talking.

"Like I said, I don't have a problem finding guys. I can't tell you how many guys have asked me out in the last month. I was invited by a Saudi prince to his palace." She breathed out. "The thing is, we're not like other people, Michael. We were raised in a different world. It's hard to find someone who could understand what we've been through. Or who we are."

"Nichelle found someone."

She glanced over at Nichelle and her boyfriend. "Yeah, I saw them when I came in. I didn't recognize her."

"I didn't either. Not at first. They seem happy."

"Maybe," Cassy said. "But then, Nichelle's different from us."

"How's that?"

"For starters, she can't kill her boyfriend with a thought."

"That's dark."

She glanced back over at them, then said, "We'll see how that works out."

Just then Taylor walked up. She looked uneasy. "Hi, Cassy."

"Hi, Taylor," Cassy said. There was definite tension.

"I didn't think you were coming."

"Neither did I. I changed my plans."

I noticed that they didn't hug or even touch. Cassy kept her distance. I guessed she didn't want Taylor to read her mind.

"We're glad you came. How are things in Switzerland?"

"Good. I'm doing a lot of skiing when I'm not working."

Taylor took my hand. It seemed a little obvious. "Do you have anyone?"

"No. Still just playing around. Michael says you guys are doing well."

"We are."

For a moment they just looked at each other until it became awkward.

"Well, I guess I'll go mingle," Cassy said. She turned to me. "Bye, Michael."

"See you, Cass."

She walked away. I turned back to Taylor. "You're not mad. . . ."

"No, I just wish you didn't think she was so beautiful."

"I'm sorry."

She sighed. "I'm going to see what's taking Abi."

After she left, I walked back over to Ostin, McKenna, and Ian. Ian had walked in during my introduction.

"Michael man!"

"Hey, Ian," I said, hugging him. "It's so good to see you."

"Not as good as it is to see you."

"I was afraid he wasn't going to make it," McKenna said. "Spending all that time at sea."

"I know," Ian said. "So many shipwrecks, so little time."

"I thought you would have found them all by now," Nichelle said, walking up to him. She was holding Corbin's hand.

"Is that you, Nichelle?"

"In the tattooed flesh."

"Girl, you have changed. You even got some tattoos removed."

"How do you know that?" Corbin asked. "They're under her clothes."

"Who are you?" Ian asked.

"This is my boyfriend," Nichelle said. "Corbin. He's a dentist."

"Nice to meet you, dentist-guy," Ian said.

Corbin looked annoyed.

"How many years until you've found them all?" Nichelle asked.

"I could never find them all. There are more than two million recorded shipwrecks. I'm just looking for the most important ones."

"And by 'important' you mean the ones carrying the most gold?"

He grinned. "No. Some just have historical value."

"I'm just glad you took a break from sailoring and came to see your old friends," I said.

"Are you kidding? I wouldn't miss it. Being back with my friends. Best day of the past year."

"That's saying something," Ostin said. "Considering your find of the *Merchant Royal*."

Ian smiled. "You read about that, huh? That was a good one."

"I follow your exploits," Ostin said. "I read about it in *Nat Geo*."

"What's the *Merchant Royal*?" McKenna asked.

"The *Merchant Royal* was a seventeenth-century English merchant ship," Ostin said. "She was carrying a hundred thousand pounds of gold when she went down off Land's End in Cornwall County, England."

"A hundred thousand *pounds* of gold?" Nichelle said. "That's like fifty tons. That would be worth billions."

"I was referring to the British pound," Ostin said. "Currency, not weight. It's roughly worth about forty-two million dollars, give or take a few million."

"Oh, is that all?" Nichelle said sarcastically.

Ian shrugged. "You know what they say. A million here, a million there, pretty soon you're talking about real money." He grinned. "Check this out." Ian brought out a silver coin and handed it to Nichelle. "That's a piece of eight."

"No way, dude," Ostin said. "You have one of those?"

"I've got more than one. So you know what it is."

"Is there anything he doesn't know?" McKenna said.

"The piece of eight was the first international currency," Ostin said. "The Spanish dollar, or '*peso fuerte,*' is where the Mexicans got the word 'peso.' That coin you're holding is at least four hundred years old."

Nichelle looked it over. "So cool." She handed it back.

"No, keep it. I brought it for you. I brought one for everyone." He reached into his pocket and brought out a handful of coins. He gave one to Ostin, Zeus, and McKenna.

"Thanks, man," Zeus said.

"This is awesome," McKenna said.

"Nothing's too good for my posse." He handed me two coins. "One for Taylor, one for you."

"Thanks," I said. "This is really cool. I'll put it on my shelf next to my cannibal fork."

"You still got that?"

"The one Hatch was going to eat me with."

"You're not being literal," Corbin said.

"Oh, he is," Ian said. "This dude planned on eating Michael. Michael ate him instead."

"Not being literal about that," I said.

"If you don't mind me asking," Nichelle said, "what's your take of the loot?"

"About forty percent."

"Forty percent of forty-two million dollars? That's more than sixteen million dollars. You are so stinking rich."

"It's really just the sport of the thing," Ian said.

"You're a professional treasure hunter?" Corbin asked, trying to catch up on the conversation.

Ian looked a little perplexed by the question. "No, I'm more of a ship hunter. The treasure's just a fringe benefit."

"I'd say sixteen million dollars is more than a fringe benefit," Corbin said.

Ian shrugged. "Whatever. I just give most of it away, anyway."

"How do you go about finding a shipwreck?" Corbin asked.

"It starts on land with a lot of homework. I spend days in the archives section of libraries studying rare books, old documents, and maps. Based on what I find, I make a plan; then I go out and look."

Corbin's brow fell. "What do you mean, *look*?"

None of us knew how much Corbin knew about us, or how much Nichelle wanted him to know, but based on his tattoo comment, he clearly didn't know much about Ian. To Ian, everyone was naked.

"Special equipment," Ian said. "I sit at the bottom of the ship and watch. It's like watching the Discovery Channel, but even better since it's real time. Have you ever seen a shark eat a shark? Or a giant squid attack a whale? Or how about an underwater river?"

"An underwater river?" McKenna said. "How exactly does that work?"

"In Mexico there's a freshwater river that flows under the ocean. It even has waterfalls and trees on its bank."

"What kind of technology are you using to see all that?" Corbin asked.

"Highly sophisticated technology."

"Oh, really?" Nichelle said. "I don't think I'd call it . . . *sophisticated*. More like *churlish*. Or, what about 'clown-like'?"

"Thanks, Nichelle," he said. "You still got it."

"What's the most surprising thing you've seen underwater?" McKenna asked.

"An alien city."

We couldn't tell if he was kidding or not.

Ostin asked, "Are you being serious?"

Ian burst out laughing. "Relax, I'm just kidding, guys. The most *surprising* thing I've seen? Maybe the pyramid of Yonaguni, Japan. It's under twenty-five meters of water. It looks identical to the pyramids in Mexico or Guatemala. I think it's just fascinating that there are pyramids all around the world even though these cultures had no contact with each other."

"Maybe there are aliens," Zeus said, walking into the conversation. "It wouldn't surprise me. What do you think, Ostin?"

"Never say never," Ostin said.

"Hey, Ian," Zeus said.

They hugged. "Hey, brother."

"What's your next expedition?" I asked.

"You know my dream is still to find the lost city of Atlantis," he said. "But *National Geographic* has just commissioned my company to look for the *Flor de la Mar*. It sank around 1511 near the Strait of Malacca and may be the richest vessel ever lost at sea. It's believed to hold a treasure of diamonds and gold worth more than two billion dollars."

"Then you can retire," Nichelle said.

"Are you kidding? I'm having fun."

Zeus said, "Hey, there's Taylor."

"It's not Taylor; it's Tara," McKenna said.

"Yep," Tara said, walking up to them. "The evil twin." She hugged Zeus. "How is my favorite Greek god?"

Zeus smiled. "I'm great. What are you up to?"

"Right now I'm running back to the house, since I forgot the reunion T-shirts."

"We get T-shirts?" Ian asked.

"Yeah, they're cool. They say 'Electroclan' in lightning bolts. Nichelle designed them."

"Thank you, Nichelle," McKenna said.

Nichelle looked happy. "I had fun designing them."

"Do you need some help?" Zeus asked.

"No, thank you. It's just one box. I'll be right back." Tara turned to me. "Michael, Taylor needs to talk to you. She's out in the hall."

"Got it." I held one of the piece-of-eight coins. "Thanks for these, Ian. Real treasure."

"You are welcome, my friend."

I walked to the door, excited to show Taylor what Ian had given us. Instead, I put the coins into my pocket. Taylor looked really upset.

"What's wrong?"

"Abi's missing."

"She missed her flight?"

"No, she's *missing*. She's disappeared."

Just then someone said, "Hey, lovebirds. Am I interrupting something?"

I turned to see Quentin walking toward us. He wore a tan leather jacket, designer jeans, and tall heeled, python-skin boots. He always dressed like a movie star.

"Sorry," Taylor said, wiping her eyes. "Just some drama."

"Drama," Quentin said, shaking his head. "I never get enough of that." He kissed Taylor on the cheeks, then turned to me. "Bro, it's been too long." We hugged.

"It's been way too long," I said.

"Did you bring the Owl? I didn't see it out there."

"No. It's being fixed."

"Fixed? You crashed it? That's like dropping a Ming vase."

"No, someone crashed into me."

"Someone else dropped the vase, then. I hope they have good insurance."

"Not likely. It's a long story. I'll tell it to you later."

"All right, but you owe me a drive." He looked toward the door. "Is everyone inside?"

"Just about," I said. "Did you ever hear from Torstyn?"

"Yeah. No surprise, he's not going to make it. I'll catch you up on him later." He looked over at Taylor, then back at me. "I'll leave you. It looks like you two have things to talk about."

"We'll just be a minute," Taylor said. "Thank you."

"Is your twin here?" he asked.

"She ran home for a second, but she'll be right back."

Quentin smiled. "All right, then. Great seeing you both. See you in a few."

After Quentin left, I asked Taylor. "What do you mean, she's *missing*?"

"She left her dorm with her luggage, but she never got on the plane."

"How do you know this?"

"The Veytric car service said she never arrived. The driver had a friend at the ticket gate who confirmed that she never boarded the flight in Dallas."

"Did you call her?"

"At least a dozen times. Her phone goes directly to voicemail. Then I called her roommates. One of them saw her leaving with a group of kids. She didn't recognize any of them."

"I'm sure there's an explanation," I said. "Maybe she changed her mind, because of the thing with Jack."

"Abi would never do that." Taylor's eyes welled up. "Why is all this happening right now?"

I put my arms around her. "I don't know. Maybe the battle never really stopped. We just did."

20

An Unexpected Text

"So what do we do now?" Taylor asked.

"I need to think. Give me a minute."

Taylor took a deep breath, wiped her eyes, then said, "All right. I'll keep the party going. We've still got the awards to give out."

"I'll be right in."

Taylor walked back to the party room. Less than a minute after she was gone, Quentin came out of the room. "So, what's going on, boss?"

"You know, same old."

Quentin looked at me skeptically. "C'mon, buddy. We've been to hell and back together. I know when something's not right."

"That's all I need," I said. "Another mind reader."

"Well, I'm not a mind reader, and I'm not psychic. I just pay attention. You tic a lot when you're really worried about something. So what is it, boss? What's troubling you?"

I exhaled. "All right. But we need to keep it between us for right now."

"I'm with you."

"Some bad things are happening. Jack is missing."

"I thought he was in Peru with the corporation." Quentin always called the company "the corporation," which started back when he was with the Elgen.

"He was. He went down to investigate some missing security personnel, and then he and his team disappeared."

Quentin's expression turned hard. "Then why are we still here? We should be on a plane to South America."

"My father's already sent a team of soldiers down."

"Do they have any idea who took them?"

"Just guesses."

He thought for a moment, then said, "This isn't the corporation's problem. It's ours. And we're wasting time."

"We're all on the same team," I said. "But we might have another problem. Taylor just told me that Abi's disappeared. That's what we were talking about when you walked in."

"Wow. When were you going to tell everyone?"

"When I had to."

"You need to tell them before they all leave."

"I know."

Quentin patted me on the back. "I know you'll do the right thing. You always do. Just know I'm ready to go." He grinned lightly. "Besides, I could use some excitement."

Quentin went back to the party. He stopped and held the door for Taylor as she walked out. Quentin hugged her, then walked in.

"He knows," Taylor said.

I nodded. "I told him. He knew something was wrong."

"What did he say?"

"He asked why we were still here."

"He's right, you know," Taylor said. She sighed. "Let's just go ahead with the awards."

"Is Tara back?"

"No. But it's rush hour. She's probably stuck in traffic."

"Where are the trophies?"

"I left them in the car."

"I'll get them."

I walked out to our car for the box of trophies. As I was walking back in, I noticed a car that looked like Taylor's mother's car—the one Tara was driving. I wondered how we hadn't seen her return. I walked back into the room. Taylor was writing on a pad of paper.

"Are you ready?" I asked.

"Yes, go on up. I'll be right there."

I set the box of trophies down next to the lectern, then lifted the microphone. The DJ shut off the music.

"All right, everyone. Let's gather in."

Everyone moved in together. Only Cassy was standing alone. When I looked at her, she cocked her head, her eyes set on mine.

"You have no idea how good it is to see you all. It's been too long."

"You know it, brother," Zeus shouted.

"So, we have some awards to hand out tonight."

Taylor walked up onto the stage and stood next to me.

"My lovely assistant, Taylor, will be announcing the winners."

"Thank you, Michael," she said. She took one of the trophies from the box. The statues looked a little bit like Oscars, though the figurine held a lightning bolt, instead of a sword.

"The first award goes to . . ." I turned to the DJ. "Could we have a drumroll?"

"No problem."

He pushed a button, and there was the sound of a pre-recorded drumroll.

". . . the person most likely to find the lost city of Atlantis . . ."

"Ian," everyone shouted before I could announce his name.

"Yes, it's Ian."

"Thank you, thank you," Ian said, walking up to the stage.

I handed him the statue and the microphone. He looked over the statue, then at Taylor and me.

"Thank you, Taylor. Michael." He clutched the statue to his chest, then turned to the group, speaking in mock drama. "I saw my first shipwreck on the way to Tuvalu. I wondered then if it might be my last. Thank you to the Electroclan, and especially Michael, for seeing that it wasn't. I'd like to thank the people who sunk their ship so I could win this prestigious award. And, of course, I'd like to thank the academy."

"Which academy?" Zeus said. "The Elgen Academy?"

Ian grinned. "Yes, the Elgen Academy. Especially Dr. Hatch, who, for reasons beyond his control, couldn't be here tonight."

Everyone laughed.

"Most of all, I'd like to thank Poseidon, who buried Atlantis just so I could find it. Thank you all."

Everyone clapped. Ian raised both hands above his head, then handed me back the microphone and left the stage. The DJ, catching the spirit of it all, played some Academy Award stage exit music.

"All right. That was . . . something. Our next award is . . ." I tipped the microphone toward Taylor. She leaned into it.

"The next award goes to the person who has changed the most." She looked at me. "Michael?"

"The person who has changed the most—other than Dr. Hatch—I think we can all agree is Nichelle."

Everyone clapped as Nichelle walked up to the stage. She kissed me on the cheek, which was kind of proof of the award in itself, then took the trophy from Taylor. She had a broad smile on her face as she looked out at everyone.

"You know, I never thought I'd ever get an award in my life. Any kind of award. Even a participation trophy, since I've never really participated in anything." She laughed; then her voice became more sincere. "I know these awards are just for fun, but . . ." Tears welled up in her eyes. "It means something to me. Until you all came along, I had no one in my life. No one to love. No one loved me. Especially me. I'm sorry for the pain I've caused all of you. The regret I feel for hurting my friends still hurts." Nichelle wiped her eyes.

Taylor put her arm around her.

"You believed in me when I didn't even believe in me." She took a deep breath. "I wish Jack and Abi and Torstyn and Grace were here. Because we're a family, and it's the only family I've ever had.

"We should hold get-togethers more often, because I miss you all more than I can say. And thank you, Corbin, for caring for me and putting up with me. I must drive you crazy with the way I talk about these people all the time, but I hope you can see why. They're my family. And I love them all very, very much."

For just an instant the whole room was silent, and I actually saw Zeus wipe a tear from his eye. Then it erupted in applause. Ian shouted, "Yeah, Nichelle!"

"We love you too, Nichelle," McKenna said.

Quentin lifted a glass to toast. "To family!" Then he said, looking at me, "And family is always there when you need them."

Quentin's toast was answered by a chorus of, "To family."

Nichelle hugged Taylor, then handed her the microphone and stepped down from the stage. Taylor again wiped her eyes, then said, "We feel the same way, Nichelle. We love you."

Nichelle mouthed back, "I love you."

Corbin put his arm around her.

Taylor breathed out heavily. "Okay. That was awesome. Fortunately, I had some tissue."

I took her hand. She turned to me. "Do you want to do this one?"

"No, you're doing great."

"Okay, the next award goes to the person most likely to rule the world after Hatch. Of course, this goes to . . . Quentin."

The DJ played the Tears for Fears song "Everybody Wants to Rule the World."

Quentin laughed as he walked up and took the trophy. "These are nice," he said. "Well done. I too would like to thank the Electroclan and the academy and, of course, Dr. Hatch, for his most important achievement of his life . . . dying."

Everyone laughed.

"You should thank Michael for that," Zeus said.

"Indeed," he said. "I'd just like to—"

Just then all our phones began to ding. It sounded like a bell choir.

"I was saying, I'd just like to remind you to silence your phones, lol. . . ."

I wondered who would be texting all of us.

"Michael. Look at this," Taylor said, holding up her phone.

save jack taylor now

Zeus held up his phone. "Who's Jack Taylor?"

"I think it means Jack *and* Taylor," Ostin said. "Two people."

"I don't need saving," Taylor said.

"Why would Jack need saving?" Tessa asked.

"Who sent this?" Nichelle asked. "How did they get all our numbers?"

"Wait," I said. "Where's Tara?"

Taylor blanched. "She should have been back by now." She dialed Tara. Everyone watched as she stood there.

I stepped closer to see her screen. "No answer?"

Taylor shook her head. She dialed again. Still nothing.

"Oh no," I said.

"What?"

"There's a car like your mother's in the parking lot."

Taylor ran out of the room. I ran out after her. When I got there, Taylor was standing next to her mother's car, the one Tara had driven to the party. The driver's door was open.

"No . . . ," Taylor said, her voice heavy with fear.

"There's got to be an explanation," I said.

Ostin, McKenna, and Zeus walked out behind us.

"They have surveillance cameras out here," Ostin said. "Let's go see what happened."

We went back inside the restaurant. There was a long line of guests waiting to get in. Taylor marched past them to the hostess. "Do you have parking lot surveillance cameras?"

The woman glanced over. "Yes. I'm helping someone. I'll be right with you."

"This is an emergency. We need to see your recordings. Now."

"I'll have to call the owner to get his permission."

"We don't have time for that," I said.

"Sorry, but it's either that or the police . . ."

Taylor rebooted the woman. When she came to, she looked confused. "May I help you?"

"You were taking us to view the security video."

"Oh." She still looked confused. She said to another woman who was near the front. "Riley, will you take the desk for a minute?"

"Sure."

She turned back to us. "This way, please."

Taylor, McKenna, Ostin, and I followed her past the front desk, through a door, and down a short corridor to the restaurant's back office. There was a single oak desk with a large computer screen divided between four different cameras. On one of the screens we could see Julie's car.

"What are you looking for?" the woman asked.

"That screen right there," Taylor said. "We need to see it about . . ."

"Forty-seven minutes ago," Ostin said. "That's when Tara left the party. More or less."

"Let's see." The woman sat down at the desk. She put her hand on the DVR's dial and shuttled the video back until the car's door shut.

"Right there," Taylor said.

We watched Tara as she walked out to the car.

The woman looked back at Taylor. "Isn't that you?"

"It's my twin sister. Keep going."

The woman manually advanced the screen. Tara had just gotten into the car when a white van pulled up in front of the car, obscuring our view of her. It was there for less than a minute before it drove off again. The car door was open and Tara was gone.

"They took her," I said.

Taylor started to cry.

"Go back to the video of the van," Ostin said.

The woman shuttled the video back. Ostin stepped closer to the screen. "Do you mind if I try?"

"Go ahead." She stepped back from the desk.

Ostin shuttled the video back and forth, looking for any identifying feature. He took out his phone and took a picture of the screen. "I'll study it."

"Do I need to call the police?" the woman asked.

"No," Taylor said. She rebooted her again.

The woman looked down, then back up at us. "I'm sorry, what are we . . . ?"

"We're done here," I said. "Thank you."

"Anytime," she said, though I'm sure she had no idea of what had just happened.

"We need to put out an AMBER Alert," Taylor said.

"She's too old for that," Ostin said. "They'll do a missing-persons alert."

Taylor lifted her phone and dialed it. When someone answered, she said, "Dad. Someone's kidnapped Tara. We have the video. We don't know who. Can we put out some kind of alert? . . . All right. I'll see you in a minute." She turned to us. "My dad's on his way here. He still has friends who can help, but he needs more information before he can order an alert."

"All right," I said. "Let's get everyone together. We've got to act now."

21

The Party's Over

After we were back in the room, I excused the DJ, then locked the door after him.

"What's going on?" Cassy asked.

"... And did you find out who sent this text message?" Nichelle asked.

I breathed out slowly. "We think it's Grace."

Everyone looked even more confused.

"Grace?" Zeus said.

"It couldn't be," Nichelle said. "I have a brand-new phone number. No one knows it. I barely know it."

"Obviously someone does," Zeus said.

"What did that mean, 'save Jack Taylor,'" Tessa asked.

"There's something I need to tell you," I said.

I glanced over at Quentin. He was just quietly watching, his arms crossed at his chest. He nodded lightly. Everyone else looked at me expectantly.

"You know that Jack isn't here because he went on a mission for the corporation. What you don't know is that he and his team disappeared. We believe they've all been abducted."

The room went silent.

"Why didn't you just tell us to begin with?" Nichelle asked.

"The corporation asked us to keep it quiet for now. They've already sent another team to rescue them."

"Why didn't they send us?" Zeus asked.

"They didn't want to put us back in danger. They were afraid someone was setting a trap for us."

"Wait, wait, wait," Cassy said. "I'm totally lost. Start from the beginning. Who is setting a trap for us? Where is Jack, and why would Grace send us this message?"

"Why isn't Grace here?" Tessa asked.

Everyone just stood there looking at me for an explanation. Taylor said to me, "I guess the party's over."

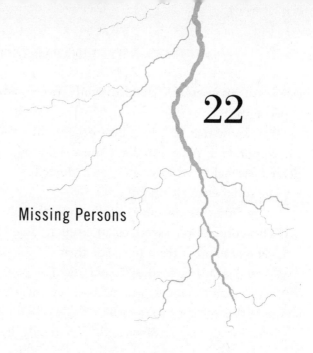

22

Missing Persons

"**W**hat I'm about to tell you is confidential." I looked at Nichelle. "For our ears only."

Nichelle looked at me quizzically. "And?"

I glanced over at her boyfriend.

"Oh, you mean Corbin. Right." She turned to him. "I'm sorry, honey. Do you mind?"

He looked around at all of us, then said, "No, I'm good. I'll be at the bar."

"Thank you."

He kissed her on the cheek and walked out.

After he was gone, I said, "All right, Cassy's right. I should just start from the beginning. Last night my father told us that someone had attacked the Peruvian Starxource plant. The corporation sent a security team down to investigate, and they disappeared. So they sent a second team down, this one led by Jack. Three days ago, they also disappeared."

"What do you mean, 'disappeared'?" Cassy asked.

"We believe he's been abducted," I said.

"Who would do that?" Tessa asked. "The Elgen?"

"What Elgen?" Nichelle said. "Last I checked, we'd destroyed them in Tuvalu."

"That's not completely true," I said. "When we brought down Hatch and his guards, there were still three groups of Elite Guards in other parts of the world."

"The Chasqui, the Lung Li, and the Domguard," Quentin said.

"Exactly," I said.

"Nichelle and I have met their leaders. Scary dudes. Hatch didn't even trust them."

"If he didn't trust them, why did he have them?" Taylor asked.

"It was like Hitler and his Brownshirts," Ostin said. "He used them to gain power. But the moment he didn't need them, he turned on them. *Nacht der langen Messer.* The Night of the Long Knives."

"It was just like that," Quentin said. "Except, they were planning to take Hatch out first, then deal with each other later. It was a last-man-standing sort of deal. Winner takes all."

"And by 'all' he means 'the world,'" Nichelle said. "Like Quentin said, I've met them too. Nasty people. And that's coming from me. The queen of nasty."

"You're not nasty anymore," McKenna said softly.

"Thank you," Nichelle said.

"If the attacks were in Peru, it's got to be the Chasqui," Quentin said. "That's their turf. It's where they keep their army."

"That's what we think as well," I said.

"I still don't get it," Tessa said. "Why are we hearing this from Grace? And why isn't she here?"

"That's a little more complicated," I said.

"That's *a lot* more complicated," Taylor corrected.

"Then let's get complicated," Cassy said.

"We don't really know where Grace is," I said. "But we know where her body is. . . ."

"Her body?" Nichelle said.

"Now I'm more confused," Cassy said.

"May I explain?" Ostin asked.

"Please," I said.

"Use simple words," Tessa said.

"I can do that," Ostin said. "You all know Grace's power. She could connect with a computer and bring in all of its information. She decided to see if she could reverse that. She wanted to actually go into a computer."

"That's just freaky," Zeus said.

"So she succeeded," Cassy said. "That's how she's reached us."

"It would appear so," I said.

"So, where's her body?" Nichelle asked.

"It's at the corporate office. After she left her body, they put her on life support."

"Is she coming back?" Zeus asked.

"We have no idea."

"This day just keeps getting more bizarre," Tessa said.

"And now Tara's gone," Taylor said. "And Abi."

"Wait," McKenna said. "What happened to Abi?"

If there was someone everyone loved, it was Abigail. She and McKenna were especially close.

"We're not sure," I said.

"Abi was supposed to be here," Taylor said. "She left her dorm, but she never got on the plane."

McKenna looked panicked. "How long have you known this?"

"I just found out," Taylor said. "I was trying to find her just before we started the awards."

"We've lost Jack, Abi, Torstyn, *and* Tara," Nichelle said.

"Torstyn's a different matter," Quentin said. "He lost himself."

"Okay," Nichelle said. "Then we've lost three of us."

"We're being hunted again," Tessa said. "Just like before."

"Maybe," I said.

"So, what do we do?" Nichelle asked.

"We save our friends," Zeus said.

"I'm not waiting here for them to pick us all off one by one," Tessa said. "Been there, done that."

"We should try to save Tara first," Taylor said. "She might still be in Idaho."

"Taylor's right," I said. "But we need to make sure we don't lose any more of us. No one leaves without a partner. Nichelle, you and Corbin match up with someone with assault powers. If we split up in twos, we could cover a lot of ground."

"They're probably going to fly her out," Taylor said. "We should go straight to the airport."

"Which airport?" I said. "They're not going to fly commercial." I turned to Ostin. "How many possible airstrips are there in this area for a private jet?"

"A lot. There's Boise Airport, Friedman Memorial Airport near Sun Valley, Magic Valley Regional in Twin Falls, and McCall Municipal Airport in McCall. Then there are the abandoned airports—Boise Air Park, Bradley Field, Floating Feather Airport, Glider Air Park, Green Meadow Airport, and Walker Field. I don't know how many of their landing strips are still usable."

"That's way too many," I said.

"Someone would definitely notice if a jet suddenly landed on an abandoned airfield," Quentin said. "I don't think they'd risk it."

"He's right," Ostin said. "Most of those old airstrips are surrounded by suburbs by now."

"Then we stick with the major airports," I said. "Ostin, if you were kidnapping someone, what would you do?"

"I'd fly a private jet out of Boise. With all the traffic, it's the least likely to be noticed."

"How do we find their jet?"

"It's about range," Ostin said. "It would probably be a jet that can fly direct to Peru. Most of the Elgen's fleet were Learjets and Gulfstreams. The maximum range of a Lear is only seventeen hundred miles, but the Gulfstream can go intercontinental. It can cover seven thousand seven hundred and sixty-seven miles."

"Far enough for Peru?" I asked.

"Far enough for Argentina."

"We need to check with the airport to see if there are any private jets flying to Peru," Taylor said.

"That won't work," Ostin said. "Private jets aren't required to file a flight plan."

"Then we'll check out every plane that can make the trip," I said. "The Elgen aren't going to make stops along the way. It's too risky. Ian, you come with us to the Boise Airport.

"Quentin, would you take charge of putting together a search plan for everyone else? Ostin will send you a list of airports and a picture of the van."

"On it, boss."

"All right. Let's go."

As we walked out to my car, Chuck Ridley's car squealed into the parking lot. Taylor waved him over. He pulled up next to us with his window rolled down. "What's going on?"

"Tara's been kidnapped. There's video footage inside showing the van that took her."

"I've got to see that."

"I can show him," McKenna said.

"Where are you going?" he asked me.

"We're searching the airports," I said. "We think they're going to try to fly her out."

"You think *who* will?"

"Whoever took her," Taylor said. "We've got to go."

As we drove out of the parking lot, Ostin said, "I sent the picture of the van to Quentin and Mr. Ridley."

"Tell Quentin to call if they find anything," I said.

"On it."

Ostin showed his phone screen to Ian. "This is a Gulfstream jet. That's basically the size of what we're looking for."

"It would be hard to miss that," he said.

"Drive fast," Taylor said. "They've got a big head start on us."

"I wish I had my Owl."

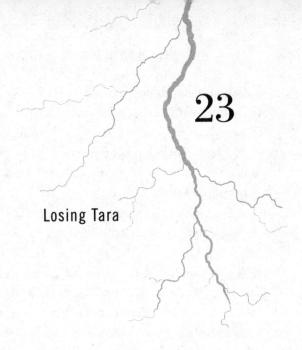

23

Losing Tara

"**Y**ou know, part of Grace's text is good news," Ostin said.

"How is any of that good news?" Taylor asked.

"It means that Grace remembers who we are and she's still on our side. That's good news."

"Ostin's right," I said. "I wonder if she can help us. Would someone text a reply to her and ask if she knows where Jack is?"

"I got it," Ian said.

After a few minutes Ian said, "Nothing."

I knew where the private jets came in, since Veytric kept their two jets at the airport. The airport was fenced in, and we drove another half mile before we came to the Million Air building, which was the airport's only public fixed-base operator.

"See anything?" I asked Ian.

"Nothing yet."

I pulled into the Million Air driveway. "I'm going inside to ask."

"We'll come with you," Taylor said.

"It's been one hour and twenty-six minutes since Tara's abduction," Ostin said. "For reference purposes."

"Could they be in the air that fast?" Taylor asked.

"It's possible," I said.

We walked inside the small, private terminal. Even though their front door was unlocked and the lights were all on, the place looked deserted. There wasn't anyone at the flight counter.

"There's a woman in back," Ian said. "She's watching TV."

I walked up to the counter and pushed the doorbell-like button. A moment later a woman walked out of a door behind the counter. She was about my mother's age. She wore glasses and a navy and baby-blue flight attendant uniform. She looked annoyed, like we had disturbed something.

"May I help you?" she asked curtly.

"Have you had any jets fly out of here in the last hour?" I asked.

"Are you one of our clients?"

"No, we're looking for someone."

"If you're not a client, I can't help you."

"My sister has been kidnapped," Taylor said. "We need to know if she's on a flight."

"If someone was kidnapped, you should notify the police."

"We have," I said. "They're on their way."

"Wait," Ian said. "There's a jet taxiing. It's about to take off."

The woman followed Ian's gaze, which led to the wall. "How can you see that?"

Ian walked to the wall and put his hand on it. "Tara's there."

"Is this a joke?" the woman said.

"She's not moving."

"You need to stop that plane now," Taylor said.

"You're kidding, right?"

"Do I look like I'm kidding? Hurry."

She just smirked at us. "You want me to believe that your friend here can look through a wall and see someone inside a plane? I don't think so. You need to leave."

Taylor turned to Ian. "What color underwear is this lady wearing?"

"Red panties, black bra."

The woman looked stunned.

"He can see through things," Taylor said. "Even your clothes."

This only made the woman angrier. "Out of the building. Now."

I could see the anger building up inside Taylor as well. I put my hand on her arm. "Taylor, call your dad. See what he can do."

Taylor took out her phone and dialed.

I said to the woman, "Please, you have to stop that plane."

She crossed her arms over her chest. "I don't have to do anything. Besides, I couldn't if I wanted to. This is a private terminal. These are private airplanes. I'm not air traffic control; I don't have any power over them."

"Then call air traffic control," I said.

"Not going to happen."

Ostin asked, "Do you know where that jet is going?"

"No. These are private jets. They don't have to file a flight plan with us."

Taylor stepped up to the woman and asked more forcefully, "Do you know where they're going?"

The woman's jaw tightened. "You're in my personal space."

"Look," Taylor said, stepping back. "I understand, as a professional, you're just doing your job. But I'm not asking you as a professional. I'm asking you as a decent human. My sister is on that plane. This is a matter of life and death. Do you know where it's going?"

The woman glared at her, then said, "As a *decent human*, my obligation is to our clients."

Taylor squinted, and the woman let out a small gasp. Then Taylor grabbed her arm. "Do you know where that plane is going?" The woman said nothing, but Taylor turned back to us. "They filled up with fuel yesterday. A crew member said they were flying to Peru."

"Lima?" Ostin asked.

Taylor looked at the woman. "Where in Peru?"

The frightened woman still didn't speak.

Taylor said, "The man said something about Puerto Maldonado."

"That's not good," I said. I called Quentin. He answered on the first ring.

"Did you find her?"

"Ian saw her in a plane," I said. "Just before they took off. Where is the Chasqui HQ?"

"We think they took over what was left of the first Peruvian Starxource plant after we destroyed it. It's in the Amazon jungle near a town called Puerto Maldonado."

"That's where the plane was headed," I said.

The woman pulled her arm away from Taylor. "You need to leave before I call security."

"We're leaving," I said.

"Thanks for all your help," Taylor said sarcastically. "By the way, I don't blame your husband for leaving. You're just a mean old woman."

The woman looked stunned. "How did you know he left me?"

"Lucky guess," Taylor said. "Just like your underwear."

After we were all in the car, I called my father. "Tara's been taken."

"Chuck told me," he said. "Gather everyone at the office. We're on our way."

I hung up, then said to Ostin, "Have everyone meet us downtown at the corporate office as soon as possible."

"On it," Ostin said.

I took off in the car. Taylor started to cry. "What if we don't find her?"

"We'll find her," I said. "I promise."

I hated making promises that were really just hopes.

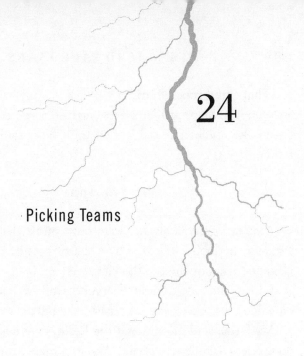

24

Picking Teams

Zeus, Cassy, and Nichelle were already inside the lobby of the Veytric building when we arrived. The only lights on were the brass wall sconces, so it was dark enough that a passerby could have seen everyone's glow. I looked around to see who hadn't arrived yet. Ostin guessed my thoughts.

"We're still missing McKenna, Tessa, and Quentin."

"We'll wait until they get here," I said.

As we stood there, Cassy walked up to Taylor and hugged her. "I'm really sorry about Tara. We'll find her."

Taylor wiped her eyes. "Thank you."

Cassy looked into her eyes. "I mean it."

"I know you do."

"Where's Corbin?" I asked Nichelle.

"He went back to the hotel."

"Probably for the best," I said.

"He figured it would be."

Quentin, McKenna, and Tessa arrived a few minutes after us. No one spoke much. The sadness on their faces said it all. I texted my father.

We're here

Almost immediately the loud buzz of an electronic lock echoed through the lobby, followed by a sharp metallic click, unlocking the glass door that opened to the elevators.

I held the door while everyone walked inside. All ten of us crowded into one elevator. I pushed the button for the twelfth floor.

My father and mother and the Ridleys were waiting for us as the door opened. Julie was crying. The two men wore grave expressions. Julie hugged Taylor as she got out of the elevator.

"I'm so sorry, honey."

Taylor cried into her mother's shoulder.

My father said, "Let's meet in the conference room."

We followed my dad down the hall to the glass double doors of a large conference room. He opened both doors, then gestured for us to enter. "Please, everyone, take a seat."

We sat down in the black leather seats that surrounded the polished mahogany table. The setting lent a stark formality to the gathering. Taylor and her mother were the last to enter. Even though I had kept a seat for Taylor, she sat down at the opposite end of the table next to her mother.

After everyone was seated, my father said, "I understand that you've all been briefed on Jack and Grace. I can answer more questions about that later, but right now Tara's abduction is our most time-sensitive issue." He looked around the table. "Just to be clear, our first priority is to make sure that we don't lose anyone else."

"I've already told everyone to stay in pairs," I said.

"Good. We don't know the full extent of this attack or how many operatives the Chasqui have here."

"Then it is the Chasqui," Quentin said.

"It would appear so," my father said.

"Have you heard from the last team you sent to Peru?" I asked.

My father nodded. "Alpha Team reported to us this afternoon. There has been no sign of activity from the Chasqui. They seem to have accomplished their objective and left."

"Then maybe they were just after Jack after all," Nichelle said.

"Maybe." My father exhaled. "I just learned that Abigail may also be missing. Michael, could you catch us up on Abi and your hunt for Tara? I want to make sure we're all on the same page."

I stood, leaning against the table. "Tonight, about an hour after the party started, we found out that Abi had left her dorm for the airport but, for reasons we don't know, never made it. Taylor has talked to her roommates, and they saw her leave for her car with her suitcase.

"Her car is still in the dorm parking lot. She's also not answering her phone, which, as you all know, is highly unusual for Abi. We believe that she could also have been kidnapped. It was about a half hour later that Tara was taken." I looked around the room. "I think it's clear that we are being hunted again.

"As soon as we realized that Tara was missing, we separated into teams to check all the likely airports. Ian, Ostin, Taylor, and I got to the Boise Airport just as a private jet was taking off. Ian saw Tara inside the plane. She was in constraints, and it's safe to assume that a RESAT was being used; otherwise she would have disabled the pilots."

The RESAT devices were the bane of our existence. As Zeus once said, the RESAT is to us what Kryptonite is to Superman.

"We tried to stop the flight," I said. "But the woman at the airport wasn't helpful. Fortunately, Taylor was able to find the information we needed in her mind. She knew that the plane was headed to Puerto Maldonado."

"Was the woman at the airport one of them?" Zeus asked.

"No," Taylor said, still angry. "I could see into her little mind. She was just an unhappy jerk who was putting her position over my sister's life."

My father said, "We're now confident that it's the Chasqui we're dealing with, since Puerto Maldonado is near their headquarters in the old Starxource plant."

"The Chasqui had an HQ there before the plant," Quentin said.

"Tell us about it," my father said.

"When I was fourteen, Hatch, Torstyn, Nichelle, and I met with the Chasqui leaders in Puerto Maldonado. They had come in from the jungle for the meeting. They looked like soldiers. You remember that, Nichelle?"

"Of course," she said. "They had an office in Puerto, but their headquarters was in a cave in the Amazon jungle. I don't even know if Hatch knew exactly where it was."

"Why would they have a separate headquarters?" McKenna asked.

"They had it before the Starxource plant was built," Tessa said. "Remember, they existed before the Elgen."

"Tessa is right," my father said. "They always kept their autonomy—even after the plant was built. They moved into the plant after the Elgen abandoned it. They're like hermit crabs, moving into a larger abandoned shell. You destroyed the rat bowl, but the MEIs, the laboratories, and the rest of the facilities were still fully functional. They would need those to electrify the bats."

"What bats?" Zeus asked.

"I'll tell you about them later," I said.

"That doesn't mean they've abandoned their cave," my father said. "They still might be operating from it. And no one knows where it is."

"I've been there," Tessa said.

We all looked at her.

"Torstyn and I weren't like the rest of the Glows," she said. "We didn't have AmEx black cards and diamond jewelry. Hatch took us to the jungle and left us there. We had to work for our living."

"It's true," Quentin said. "It wasn't fair."

"Do you remember where their cave was?" my father asked.

"No. I was pretty young. But it wasn't that far from the Starxource plant. Maybe a few miles. And there was a waterfall near it."

"That will help," my father said.

"Hidden caves in the Amazon jungle," McKenna said. "Talk about a needle in a haystack."

"I find needles in haystacks all the time," Ian said. "Metaphorically speaking, at least."

My dad lifted a remote. "I mentioned that the Chasqui were using the old MEIs and laboratory. Let me show you what they've been up to."

He pulled up the same video he'd shown us of the bats. Everyone watched in silence.

Tessa was the first to speak. "Are those bats?"

"Yes. A few weeks ago, we discovered that someone has been releasing electrified bats into the VRAEM region of Peru."

"You mean, like electrified rats?" Zeus asked.

"Yes, except flying rats," Ostin said. "And wherever they roost, they set on fire."

"That's insane," Zeus said. "They could burn the whole country down."

"Theoretically," my father said. "We think that's their goal."

"What's this VRAEM place?" Zeus asked.

Ostin cleared his throat. "'VRAEM' is an acronym for 'Valle de los Ríos Apurímac, Ene, y Mantaro.' In English, that means 'Valley of the Rivers Apurímac, Ene, and Mantaro.' It's also called 'Cocaine Valley.' It's an extremely poor, mountainous area with fertile soil. It's where most of the world's coca plants are grown.

"Not coincidentally, it's also the hiding place of the Shining Path terrorist group. They force the locals to grow coca and process it; then they sell the paste to the drug cartels. They use the money to fund their war against the Peruvian government."

"The VRAEM is about five hundred kilometers west of Puerto Maldonado," my father said. "We believe the Chasqui are behind this all, experimenting with the MEIs.

"Since they lost the Starxource plants, they're going to be in need of another way to fund their operation. They are either cooperating with the cartels or preparing to take them over. If that's the case, they've grown more powerful than we realized."

"So what do they want with us?" McKenna asked.

"We don't know. If I were to guess, I'd say they probably still believe that you are a threat."

"But why kick the bear?" Quentin asked. "If they'd left us alone, we probably wouldn't have even known they existed."

"That's a good question," my father said. "One of many. The biggest question right now is how do we rescue our friends without becoming victims ourselves, especially since it appears more obvious now that this is a trap." He looked around the room. "I'd like to hear your thoughts."

It was quiet for a moment. Then McKenna said, "I think we should first go to Texas and see what we can find out about Abi. We might be able to find clues about what we're up against. And who."

"I agree," Taylor said.

"I disagree," Quentin said. "We already know it's the Chasqui. The more time we give them, the more time they have to prepare for us. I say we go right at them. Now."

"They're already prepared for us," Tessa said.

I turned to Ostin. "What do you think?"

Ostin was looking down at the table. He looked lost in thought. "Ostin?"

He looked up. "What?"

"What do you think we should do?"

He was quiet for a moment, then said, "I don't know."

His reply surprised everyone.

"I don't think I've ever heard him say that," Zeus said.

After a moment I asked Ostin, "What are you thinking?"

"I just don't get it. Why would they even want Jack? He's not electric. . . ."

"But he's still part of the Electroclan," Nichelle said. "They could use him as bait."

"Yeah." He rubbed his forehead. "But why? Like Quentin said, 'Why kick the bear?'" He breathed out. "There's more to this. I just can't make it work."

"Give us your best guess," Quentin said.

"I don't guess."

"Hypothesize," I said.

He nodded. "Maybe the Chasqui weren't after Jack. He was just another guy the company sent down. Wrong place, wrong time."

"Then why did they take Tara?"

"Maybe it's what Nichelle said, she's bait."

"Bait for what?" Tessa asked.

Ostin looked at her. "The rest of us."

"Then you think Abi is bait too?" I asked.

"Maybe," Ostin said. "But not necessarily."

"What do you mean?"

"Abi's disappearance could just be a coincidence."

"What are the odds of that?" Quentin said. "After years of nothing, three of us go missing in the same week."

"I can't give you precise odds of that," Ostin said.

"It was a rhetorical question," Quentin said.

"Not really," Ostin said. "It's actually a good question. But that's why they call them odds. Odds are meant to be broken. We can't rule out that there are other people who would be interested in Abigail."

"Like who?" Taylor asked.

Ostin looked at her. "Who stole the comb?"

"What?"

"Who stole the comb?"

"I don't get where you're going with this."

"Tell us," I said. "Who stole the comb?"

"Someone with hair," Ostin said.

Taylor shook her head.

"I get it," I said. "You're saying that whoever kidnapped Abi was someone who needed her specific powers. Someone in pain."

"Exactly."

"Why didn't you just say that?" Taylor asked.

"Elaborate on that," my father said.

"People will pay anything for pain relief," Ostin said. "The world spends more than a trillion dollars on pain pills every year. You could say that Abi's street value is higher than all of us combined."

"I've never thought of that," I said.

"Great," Nichelle said. "That narrows our search down to a few hundred million people. Pain is the one thing the world will never have a shortage of."

"Well, not exactly," Ostin said. "There might be hundreds of millions who need her power, but there are only a few people who knew what she could do. We need to focus our search on that."

"You mean us," Zeus said. "We're the only ones who knew."

"No. The Elgen knew," I said. "And there were a lot of them." I looked at Ostin. "There's another reason they would go after Abi. Threatening her would be the best way to get Jack to cooperate."

"Again," Ostin said. "Cooperate with what? Jack's strong, but why would they put so much effort into getting him?"

"Jack is the assistant head of global security," my father said. "If their endgame is to take back the corporation, he would be a good place to start."

"And we still don't know for sure that they wanted Tara," Ostin said.

I turned to him. "What do you mean?"

"Grace's text said to save Jack and Taylor, and Taylor's right here. What if the guards who kidnapped Tara thought she was Taylor? It seems like a stupid mistake, but we can barely tell the difference. How would they know?"

"You've got a point," I said. "That would explain Grace's text. If she's intercepting their messages, she would know that it was Taylor the Chasqui were after. She would assume they knew what they were doing."

"That still doesn't answer the question of what we're supposed to do," Taylor said. "And don't tell me to wait."

"That time is past," Quentin said. "Right now the most dangerous course of action would be no action. Otherwise we're letting the Chasqui set the agenda."

"They're already setting the agenda," Cassy said.

I looked around the room. "I think McKenna and Quentin are both right," I said. "As much as I hate separating, I think we need to split up into two teams. One team goes to Texas to see what they can learn; the other team goes to Puerto Maldonado to look for our friends. When the first team finishes, they join us in Peru."

Everyone was quiet for a moment. Then Taylor said, "Okay. What are the teams?"

"The teams should match the objectives," I said. I walked up to the whiteboard at the front of the room, and on the left side wrote:

TEAM 1

"Team one is more about fact-finding than fighting, though we can't rule that out. Team two is about fighting and rescue. This is how I would divide us."

I wrote under team one:

Taylor
Ostin
McKenna
Nichelle
Cassy

Cassy gave me a furtive, unhappy glance.

"That leaves Ian, Zeus, Quentin, Tessa, and me." I wrote on the other side of the board:

TEAM 2
Ian
Zeus
Quentin
Tessa
Michael

I turned back to the table. "What do you think?"

Everyone was quiet. I sensed Cassy wanted to speak, but she didn't. Finally Ostin said, "I think that's about right."

My father said, "Alpha Team is already in Peru. I'll have them meet you in Puerto Maldonado. They're well trained and well armed. They'll be helpful if the Chasqui are using RESATs, which I have no doubt they will."

I looked back over at Taylor. "What do you think, Taylor?"

She frowned. "I think it's probably right. It's just, I want to look for my sister, but this makes more sense."

"I think it's a good plan," Quentin said.

"Then, is everyone in agreement?" I asked.

Everyone nodded.

"Corbin won't be," Nichelle said, shrugging. "He hates it when I leave him to go to Pilates."

"What are you going to tell him?" Taylor said. "You can't tell him where we're going."

"Taylor makes a good point," my father said. "You can't tell anyone where you're going. We don't know who is listening. You could put everyone's lives in danger."

"Loose lips sink ships," Ostin said.

"My loose lips will tell Corbin that I have unfinished business," Nichelle said. "That's all he needs to know."

Cassy still looked unhappy. "After Texas, will we meet up again in Peru?"

"That's the plan," I said. I turned to my father. "When can we leave?"

"It will take time to get everything ready. I'll have the Gulfstream prepared. You can fly out tomorrow at six a.m. We'll drop team one off in Dallas, then fly direct to Puerto Maldonado."

"How long is that flight?" I asked.

"It's about four and a half hours to Dallas, then another eight hours to Puerto. With refueling and takeoff, it will be about fourteen hours in all."

"So we'll arrive in Peru after dark," Quentin said.

My father nodded. "Alpha Team will pick you up at the airport and take you to a safe house." He looked around the room. "Does anyone have any more questions?"

No one said anything.

"Then we'll see you tomorrow morning at six a.m. If anyone needs a ride, let me know. If you're taking an Uber, there's a card with our hangar's address on that shelf." He took a deep breath. "Get some rest. And please, stick together."

Everyone stood from the table. I had just stepped back when Cassy walked up to me.

"Can I talk to you alone?"

"Out here," I said. We stepped out into the hall.

"Why am I not going with the second team? You know I'm the most powerful member of this group. Besides you."

"That's why I want you with team one," I said. "You're the only real muscle they'll have. And if we end up walking into an ambush, we're going to need a powerful backup."

She looked unconvinced. "Are you sure it's not personal?"

"Why would this be personal?"

"Taylor wouldn't want me to be alone with you."

"No. It's not personal."

Cassy still looked like she didn't believe me.

"Don't make this harder than it already is."

"Why shouldn't I?" She looked into my eyes. "You know you're the only reason I dragged myself all the way over here."

"What am I supposed to say to that?"

"I don't know, what are you supposed to say to that?"

I took a deep breath. "Cass . . . who knows. In another time and place . . ."

"I'm sorry, but this is the only time and place I have." She looked at me for a moment; then her expression softened. "Anyway, I just thought you should know. I'll see you in the morning." She turned and walked away.

My father walked out to me. "Before we leave, I need to talk to you in my office."

"All right."

I went to Taylor. "You should go on home without me. My father needs to talk to me."

"What did Cassy want?"

"She didn't like where we put her."

"Of course not. She wanted to be with you."

"She wanted to be where she would be of the most value."

"Right," she said. "With you."

I sighed. "Call me when you get home."

I walked back over to my father.

"Let's go to my office," he said.

"Just one second." I looked back at everyone. "I'll see you all in the morning. Get some rest."

"Like that's going to happen," Zeus said.

As I was walking out of the room, I heard McKenna ask Ostin, "'*Puerto*' means 'port,' but what does '*Maldonado*' mean?"

"It's a name of an eighteenth-century explorer," Ostin replied. "But it means 'ill-favored.'"

"That's not a good omen," she said.

25

RESATs and RADDs

My father shut the door behind us. "Have a seat. I just wanted to go over a few things with you before it got too late."

I sat down in one of the chairs in front of my father's desk. He leaned against the front edge of his desk.

"Alpha Team has detailed maps of the region. Hiking through the jungle is slow and we don't know what surveillance systems the Chasqui have in place, but you know how the Elgen love their cameras, so expect you'll be watched.

"To get into the jungle, you're going to have to take a boat up the river, the Río de Madre de Dios. There are several tourist lodges in the area, and tourist boats travel up the river all the time, so your presence won't necessarily draw undue attention, but you will be vulnerable.

"If they're still in their cave, the most difficult challenge you'll

151

face may be finding them. Based on what Tessa said, we have a rough idea of where their headquarters might be, at least within a five-mile radius. But in jungle that thick, it's going to seem more like fifty miles. Fortunately, we have something that will help."

He walked behind his desk and lifted a black case. He opened the case and brought out a slim black device about six inches long, roughly the shape of a shoe sole. It had a green-tinted display screen with a series of LED lights at its base. It was slimmer in the middle, with a ribbed corrugated rubber edge. He pushed a button on the device, and it lit up. The LEDs flashed once, then went dark.

"What's that?" I asked.

"It's an RRDD," he said. "That stands for 'RESAT Radiation Detection Device.' We just call it 'the RADD.'"

I took the instrument from my father.

"We had completed it about a week before you took down Hatch, so we never put it to use, but this is going to help you find the Chasqui.

"Like I said, we have a rough idea of where they are. That's where the RADD will come in. If they're holding Tara and Abi, they're going to have to have the RESATs engaged twenty-four seven. This works to our advantage. RESATs release a low-level gamma radiation, about point-oh-two millisieverts a day—about double the amount of radiation from a dental X-ray. The RADD can pick up that radiation from two miles away—about thirty-two hundred meters. I wish it were more powerful, but that's still three times more sensitive than the most powerful Geiger counters. Let me show you how it works."

I handed the RADD back to him. He held it in front of me so I could see the screen.

"It's directional, so, depending on where you point it, the radiation levels will change. To use it, you just hold down this side button and scan it in front of you. If it detects radiation, it will register here, on this monitor." He pointed to the screen. "The number it gives is the approximate distance in meters." He handed it back to me.

"It seems simple enough." I waved the device around in front of me. "Do the Chasqui know we have this?"

"It's not likely."

"Is this the only one we have?"

"No, we have three of them." He gestured to two other cases on the floor. One of the cases was much larger than the others.

"Why is that one so much bigger?"

"That one is attached to a drone. This way you can fly it out over the jungle canopy. You can cover more ground and not expose yourself to danger."

"Will other radiation interfere with this?"

"Not enough to concern yourself with. There's not going to be much radiation in the jungle. If this detects something, you can be sure there's something human nearby."

"Will this detect handheld RESATs?"

"Yes, but only when they're activated."

"What if the RESAT is moving?"

"If you're stationary and the monitor shows steady change in radiation levels, then the source of the radiation is moving. Why do you ask?"

"They'll probably have Tara wearing a RESAT vest."

"Probably." He looked down at the machines. "I'll have all three of these placed in the jet. I want you to deliver one to Alpha Team." He scratched the side of his head. "I have something at home I need to give you as well. But this is enough for now. You should get some sleep."

"I doubt I'll get much sleep."

"I know." He put his hand on my shoulder. "But it's past midnight. And you still need to pack."

26

Saying Goodbye

By the time my father and I got back to the conference room, everyone except my mother and Taylor's father were gone.

"I'm headed to the hangar," Mr. Ridley said to my father. "Do you need anything before I go?"

"Yes. I need you to take the three RADDs with you to the airport. They're in my office, on the floor behind my desk."

"You got it. Anything else?"

"No. Thank you. I'll see you in the morning."

As we walked out to the elevator, my mother said, "Chuck isn't going home?"

"No. We need extra security at the hangar tonight. He'll pick up his family in the morning."

It was nearly one in the morning when we arrived home. I said good night to my parents, then went up to my room to pack. My parents looked like they still had things to talk about.

I brought the backpack I'd bought last summer out of my closet, then began to pack. I laid out a week of clothing, but ended up putting half of it back. The last time I was in the jungle, I'd worn the same clothing for more than a month.

I gathered a few toiletries, then set my pack next to my door and climbed into bed. I thought of calling Taylor but, considering the hour, decided against it. I lay back and tried to sleep. My mind was crowded with thoughts of the Elgen and the last time I'd been in the Amazon jungle. It wasn't a good memory, the Elgen hunting me in helicopters equipped with flamethrowers and native tribespeople with poisonous blow darts.

Somehow, in all that chaos, I fell asleep. I dreamed of the tree again. Only this time, one of the three tendrils had wrapped itself around my ankle. As hard as I tried to pull away from it, I couldn't get free.

I woke a little after four the next morning. I checked my backpack again just to make sure I hadn't forgotten anything. I added a bar of soap and a few more clothes, thinking I could always just leave them in the jungle if they got too heavy.

My heart felt as heavy as my pack. I hadn't felt dread like that for years. It's funny how quickly we can forget pain once we're out of it. Maybe "funny" isn't the right word. Maybe I should say "tragic."

I checked my phone. There was a text from Taylor.

You up?

I called her.

"Hi." Taylor's voice was soft. Vulnerable.

"Are you ready for this?" I asked.

"How can you be ready for this? I'm scared. As scared as I was when we went to Tuvalu."

I sighed. "I know. It's been a while. I'm afraid I've gotten soft. I had the tree dream again last night. This time one of the tendrils wrapped itself around my leg."

"The Chasqui tendril," Taylor said. "I had a dream last night too."

"What kind of dream?"

"One of those," she said.

I was afraid to ask. "Was it good or bad?"

"I don't know."

"Tell me about it."

"Bryan and Kylee were in it."

"Where were they?"

"We were at a college campus."

I shook my head. "Which is where you're heading this morning. Were they alone?"

"No. There were other people."

"Elgen?"

"I don't know."

"What did they look like?"

"They were about our age, maybe a little younger. Hispanic. The weird part, they were glowing, like us, except they glowed red. And their eyes glowed red. Do you think there could be more electrics?"

"I don't know. If there were, I think we would have known about them by now. The part of your dream about Bryan and Kylee, it makes sense with what Ostin was saying. They knew what Abi could do."

"Do you think they've joined the Chasqui?"

"Where else would they go? I'm glad Nichelle's with you. If there are more electrics, you'll need her."

"I'm sorry to get you worked up over another stupid dream."

"Your 'stupid' dreams haven't been wrong yet."

"But they're not exactly helpful either. I never understand them until after they happen in real life. What good is that?" She exhaled loudly. "Why am I having these?"

"I think it's just part of your gift that's still developing."

"It doesn't feel like a gift," she said softly. "And I'm not worried about Kylee and Bryan. I can handle them. And Cassy can handle anything."

Up to that point, she hadn't said anything about Cassy going with her. I hoped they'd get along all right. She breathed out heavily. "I'd better go. I'm not even done packing. I'll see you at the airport. I love you, Mr. Vey."

"Me too," I said.

I took a hot shower, dressed, then went downstairs. I could smell bacon cooking from the top of the stairs.

My mother was in the kitchen. She glanced over as I walked into the dining area.

"Good morning, Michael."

"Morning," I said.

My mother set down the tongs she was holding and came over and hugged me. She had clearly been up for a long time, as she had made breakfast: waffles with strawberries and whipped cream, bacon, scrambled eggs with cheddar cheese, coffee, and orange juice.

"You got up early," I said.

"No, I never went to sleep." She forced a smile. "I wanted to make you a nice breakfast. It might be a while before you have another one."

"Sounds like you're making me my last meal."

She stopped what she was doing. "Please don't say that. I'm worried enough about you leaving."

"I'm sorry."

My father walked into the kitchen. "How are you feeling?" he asked.

"Anxious."

"Pregame jitters." He glanced down at his phone. "The jet's ready."

"So is breakfast," my mother said. "Sit down, please."

My father and I sat down at the table as my mother brought over my plate with a bowl of strawberries. The whipped cream was already on the table.

I spooned the whipped cream over my waffle, then covered it with strawberries.

"I have a few things I still need to give you," my father said. "In addition to the three RADDs, I'm sending you down with two satellite phones, one for each team, so you can call us from anywhere. Even the jungle."

"That's not just a suggestion," my mother said. "I want you to check in. Please."

"I will."

"There are a few more things I'll tell you about at the airport."

"All right." I figured they were things my father didn't want my mother to worry about.

He glanced down at his phone, then sent a text message.

"Alpha Team will meet you in Puerto. I told them to position near the airport and keep an eye on things."

We finished eating. Then I carried my pack out to my father's car and we headed off to the airport. Meridian is almost twenty miles from the Boise Airport. The drive seemed interminable. We really didn't talk much. My mother asked if I'd remembered bug spray for the jungle. I reminded her that I didn't need it since I was a human bug zapper. That, at least, got her to smile.

It felt like I was being driven to my execution. I hadn't been through a departure this intense since Christmas Ranch. Life could be worse, though. It could always be worse. Hatch could have won and I could be back in Cell 25. Or on a platter.

It was still dark when we reached the airport. We drove north alongside the runway until we came to the corporate hangar, less than a quarter mile from where we'd last seen Tara. It already felt like it had been days instead of hours.

The Veytric Corporation owned three jets and had its own hanger at the Boise Airport. I'd been inside the hangar a dozen times or so. It had a large space for the jets and maintenance equipment but also some side rooms—a kitchen and rec room for the crew and passengers.

As my father pulled up, the chain-link gate opened for us, letting us onto the tarmac. The cement grounds were lit by large overhead lights, the kind they have at soccer fields.

The jet was on the tarmac, its door open and its stairway down. It was the largest of the corporate fleet, a Gulfstream G650E. It was white with a gold stripe and a black nose cone. Taylor had affectionately nicknamed it the Pug because the aircraft's black nose reminded her of the dog.

My father parked our car near the jet, and we all got out. There was a light breeze, and the rich Idaho air felt cool and moist. The thin squeal of the aircraft's engine reverberated in the predawn silence.

Nichelle and Corbin were already there, standing outside a white BMW. Nichelle was dressed the way she used to dress. She was clothed all in black, with a leather corset and midthigh leather pants, exposing the tattoo of an intertwined snake and roses running down her leg. She was wearing a black collar with a silver chain. I suppose it was her battle uniform. To her side was a small travel roller bag.

When she saw me, the two of them kissed. Then Corbin got back into the car while Nichelle dragged her bag toward me. Something seemed a little off about her. Then I remembered that Nichelle was the only one of us that didn't glow.

When she was close, I said, "Good morning."

"Not really."

"You look . . ."

". . . Like Nichelle?"

"I was going to say 'the old Nichelle.'"

"The old Nichelle would have gone more extreme, but it didn't really go with the jungle. The piercing chains would just snag on things."

"You're going to wear that in the jungle?" I asked.

"Maybe. I have boring clothes too."

"How did Corbin take your leaving?"

"Not great, but he's pretty chill. He has to be to hang around me."

"I don't know if I've ever met a chill dentist."

"You have now."

She walked to the back of the plane, where a crew member was waiting to load bags.

I got my pack out of the back of the car as a Maserati SUV squealed onto the tarmac. It pulled up alongside our car, and Zeus stuck his head out the window. "Where should I park this beast?"

"Inside the hangar," my father said. "There's automobile parking stalls on the right."

Zeus saluted him. "Excellent." He turned to the back. "Everybody, out. Take your bags."

Quentin, Tessa, and Ian climbed out of the car. The car's rear hatch opened, and Quentin and Ian started grabbing bags. They pulled everything out of the car, then shut the hatch. Zeus squealed off to the hangar.

A few minutes later, the Lisses pulled up in their minivan. Even from a distance I could see that Dorothy was losing it. Mr. Liss was his usual stoic self. Ostin just looked embarrassed.

The side door slid open, and McKenna hopped out of the van almost before it had come to a full stop. I'm sure she'd had all of Dorothy she could take.

An Uber driver in a silver Toyota Camry pulled up near the jet, and Cassy got out of the car. She wore a beige leather jacket and had a silk scarf wrapped around her neck. A Louis Vuitton bag hung from her shoulder.

The driver handed her a suitcase from the trunk, then drove off. She was the only one of us who had come alone. She furtively glanced over at me, then walked to the airplane.

"Michael," my father said. He was standing next to the car, holding a small black case about the size of a lunch box. "I wanted to give you these. More toys."

He opened the case's lid. Secured in the interior's black foam were two metallic devices that looked like cell phones. Next to them were a dozen round disks about the size and tone of a nickel. Each one was marked with a different capital letter.

"They look like nickels."

"They're made of nickel," he said.

"What are they?"

"We call them buttons. They're extremely powerful global tracking devices. We can pinpoint one of these anywhere in the world within five meters. There are twelve, one for each of you, and two more just in case you need them. They each have a different digital ID and tracking, so you'll need to log in which one belongs to who."

He extracted one from the polyester foam that filled the case. Before he handed it to me, he said, "Don't squeeze it."

"Okay." I took the disk, wondering, of course, what would happen if I squeezed it. It probably weighed less than a nickel.

"They're magnetic on one side; the other has a super powerful adhesive strip. It's like superglue. If you remove the backing and stick it to flesh, it won't come off without some kind of solvent, like turpentine or nail polish remover. Those with long hair should probably wear it on their necks at the base of their skull, so it's concealed by their hair. Otherwise, find a place to conceal it on your body, so if you're captured, they won't take it from you. You could even swallow it if you had to, but obviously that would only be temporary."

"Are they already activated?"

"They're always activated."

"What's the battery life?"

"On you, indefinite. It will draw energy from any of the electrics."

"Even Nichelle?"

He thought a moment. "I don't know. We didn't have the chance to test it on her. Without supplementary electricity, the battery life is about three weeks. So, you might want to charge hers up like the rest of the Nonels. Just in case."

"How do I do that?"

"You can put them on any wireless charger, or just put it back into this case. The top of the button is a lithium battery. It takes about an hour for a full charge."

"Too bad we don't have Ostin's jellyfish cell batteries."

My dad grinned. "I told him, he has a job waiting for him here."

I pointed to the two cell-phone-like devices in the case. "What are those?"

My father pulled one of the devices out of the case and handed it to me. "This is how you track the devices. It's a standard GPS. It's pretty easy to use."

I looked over the device, then put it back. "Thanks."

"There's one more very important thing. Go ahead and squeeze the button twice."

I did as he said. The disk emitted a soft, melodic chirp.

"If you squeeze the button quickly five times, it will send out a distress signal to the handheld and our HQ. If you squeeze it ten times slowly, it will send out a different signal after a fifteen-minute delay. You'll know it's activated because you'll immediately hear a series of five short beeps."

"Why the delay?"

"The button is a homing device. If we receive that signal, a guided missile will be sent directly to where it is. Whatever you do, don't push it ten times if you can't find shelter at least a hundred yards away from the disk in fifteen minutes."

"A personal self-destruct button."

"I hope not. Now repeat to me how it works."

"Magnet on one side, superglue on the other. Squeeze it five times, it sends a distress signal. Squeeze it slowly ten or more times, it will send a missile to itself."

"Exactly. Most important, this way we will always know where you are. Always. Losing another one of you is not an option."

I returned the disk to the foam, and my father closed the box.

"Does Alpha Team have them?"

"Yes."

"Does Jack?"

"Unfortunately, no. Otherwise we'd know where he is. That was our failure. We didn't anticipate another attack."

My father handed the case to me. "Hand them out to everyone before you separate; then let us know which one goes to who."

"Okay," I said. "What about the RADDs?"

"They're in the cargo bay with your luggage."

"Is there anything else I should know about the Chasqui?"

"The leadership is mostly European or Middle Eastern, but the actual soldiers are almost all Peruvian. Most of them were recruited from the Shining Path guerrillas. The foot soldiers speak Spanish; the leadership speak multiple languages. They may be living in the jungle, but they're not savages. Do not underestimate them."

I nodded. "Okay. Then I guess that's everything."

My father looked at me for a moment, then said, "You have no idea how much your mother and I wanted to avoid this."

"I have an idea," I said.

"We're more proud of you than you could possibly know. I

honestly didn't want you to go again, but I knew that once your friends were taken, I wouldn't be able to stop you. You're the most loyal man I have ever known. I wish I could say you got it from me, but you didn't. Just be safe."

"Thanks, Dad." We embraced.

"You'd better go say goodbye to your mother. This is killing her."

My mother wiped her eyes as I walked toward her. Even though she was acting brave, I could still see the pain in her eyes. She put her arms around me. Only then did I hear a sniffle. She leaned back and looked into my eyes. "You're going to be okay," she said. "If I had to bet on someone, I'd bet on you."

"Thanks."

Just then the Ridleys' Land Rover pulled up near the plane.

"How is Taylor doing?" she asked.

"Not great. But she's a warrior."

"She's a special woman. You're a lucky man."

"Like Dad," I said.

She smiled and hugged me again. "You'd better go. Take good care of everyone. Then come back safe."

"Don't worry. I'll be home soon."

I walked off toward the Ridleys' car. Mr. and Mrs. Ridley were both turned toward the back seat, talking to Taylor. As I neared the car, they all got out. Mrs. Ridley looked like she'd been crying all night, which was likely the case. She put her arms around Taylor, then turned to me. "You keep her safe, Michael. And yourself."

"I'll do my best."

She forced a smile. "I know you will."

Mr. Ridley pulled Taylor into him, kissing the top of her head. "We'll see you in a week or so."

That sounded optimistic to me, which is maybe exactly what we all needed to hear. He looked at me. "Good luck, Michael. Remember, you're the storm."

"Thank you, sir." I turned to Taylor. "Are you ready?"

She wiped her eyes. "As I'll ever be."

Taylor hugged and kissed her mother and father once more; then

I grabbed her suitcase and we started toward the plane. Ostin and McKenna met us halfway. They had already stowed their luggage and were just waiting for us.

"How's Dorothy?" I asked.

"An ocean of emotion," McKenna said.

"I think we're all here," I said. "There are ten of us." I looked around, pointing at each person as I said their name. "Taylor, McKenna, Ostin, Zeus, Cassy, Ian, Quentin, Nichelle, and Tessa. That's only nine. Who are we missing?"

"You didn't count yourself," McKenna said.

"Of course." I had been gulping a lot, and I exhaled to help clear my nerves. "Let's do this."

We all walked toward the jet.

After I gave the crew Taylor's bag, she took my hand. "I'm glad we're taking the Pug. I love the Pug."

I turned to her. "Are you okay?"

"I'll be okay. I just forgot what this was like."

"What *what* was like?"

"Wondering if I'll ever see my home again."

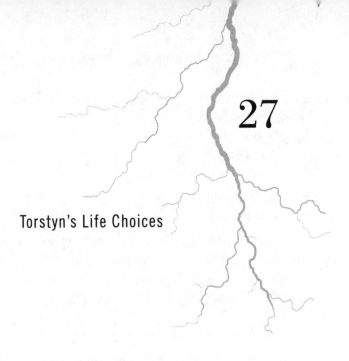

27

Torstyn's Life Choices

The best thing about private jets, besides basically everything, is that you don't have all the hassle of being told when you can stand, walk around, or even go to the bathroom. On one of our flights, Quentin and Torstyn played hockey in the aisle.

I stowed the case of buttons in the overhead, then sat with Taylor next to a window on the port side of the plane so we could see everyone outside. Everyone waved goodbye as the jet taxied off toward the runway. I saw my mother bury her face in my father's chest.

Taylor laid her head against my shoulder, and I just held her. After a moment she said, "Thank you."

I looked down. "For what?"

"For loving me."

Within a few minutes we were airborne. Most of the group hadn't eaten, so Zeus raided the kitchen and played flight attendant, tossing out snacks and cans of juice and soda. Neither Taylor nor I wanted anything. Other than Ostin, McKenna, and Cassy, the rest of the group was pretty loud. I finally said to Taylor, "Let's go lie down in back."

"That would be good."

There were two leather couches in the back of the plane. I got Taylor a blanket from an overhead bin; then we lay down on the opposing couches. She fell asleep quickly, which made me glad. She needed sleep more than I did, since she'd hit the ground running in just a few hours. I would have time to sleep on the flight to Peru.

A few minutes after Taylor was out, I went back up to the front of the plane.

"So you missed us after all," Tessa said as I walked by her in the aisle.

"I always miss the clan," I said.

She smiled. "It's good to be missed."

Cassy was reading a book as I passed her. She glanced over at me with a slight smile. I smiled back, and she returned to her book. She really was alone, which made me a little sad. I would have sat by her, but it would have caused problems. She wasn't especially secretive about her feelings toward me.

I went to the front of the plane, knocked on the cockpit door, and then opened it. Our two pilots, Captains Scott and Boyd, were seated before a massive dock of flight controls, switches, monitors, and screens.

"Hey, Michael," Captain Boyd said.

"Hey, guys. Could you let us know about an hour before landing in Dallas? We have some things we need to cover, but I want to let everyone sleep as long as possible."

"Sure thing. I'll make an announcement when we're close."

"Thank you."

I walked back out to the cabin and sat down in a forward-facing seat near Ostin and McKenna, who were both asleep. Quentin came over and sat in the seat next to mine.

"We should probably brainstorm before we land in Texas," he said.

"Yeah. I just asked the pilots to let us know when we're an hour out. Taylor, Ostin, and McKenna need rest. An hour should give us enough time to go over team one's game plan. We can go over ours after we take off again."

"We're on the same page," he said. "How are you doing?"

"I'm okay. My tics are active."

"These are stressful times. Do you think the Chasqui know we're coming?"

"I'm sure that they're expecting us. They wouldn't have taken Tara if they weren't certain we'd come after her."

"If only we weren't so loyal," he said, grinning.

"Then we'd be them," I said.

"You know, I think Ostin had an interesting idea. What if they weren't after Tara but got her mixed up with Taylor?"

"I've been thinking about that. But why would they want Taylor?"

"No idea. But it's an interesting thought."

"So, what's the deal with Torstyn?"

Quentin shook his head slowly. "It's bad, man. He just lost it. You know how it's been since Tuvalu. It's like soldiers coming back from combat. They go from the constant adrenaline rush of gunfire and bombs blowing up around them, to comparing prices on hot dog buns, with Muzak playing in the background. Torstyn got bored. When he got tired of extreme sports, he started hanging out with some bad types. Then he met some drug traffickers."

"Was he using drugs?"

"No. He's too smart for that. But too dumb to know that hanging with the wrong crowd can be just as bad."

"It couldn't have been for the money," I said. "He's got plenty."

"No, it's not about the money. Torstyn's always been a thrill-seeker. You know he used to hunt jaguar in the jungle without a weapon. It was the sport of the thing. I guess he just missed the danger. But when you live dangerously, it always catches up to you.

"One day an undercover cop pulled a gun on him. Torstyn dropped him. That's where it began. When he realized he'd killed a cop, he changed. It's like it psychologically moved him to the dark side. Like Vader. He started getting more into the drug world. Eventually, word of his powers reached the top of a drug cartel. They recruited him."

"Torstyn works for a drug lord?"

"That's what he told me. The way he tells it, they lured him to a meeting in Mexico. The drug lord made him an offer to come work for them. Torstyn said he'd think about it. The main hit man told Torstyn it wasn't a request—that he could either join them or die. Torstyn started laughing. Then he sent microwaves into the hit man's eyes, blinding him. He said, 'No one tells me what to do. I could kill you all right now with a thought.'"

"What did the drug lord do?"

"According to Torstyn, he applauded, then asked him to be his new number one. Torstyn accepted."

"Are you still in contact with him?"

"Sometimes. Which means I get occasional visits from the Feds. He's not able to carry a normal cell phone, since the DEA would track it, but now and then he reaches out. It's getting less frequent, though. He knows I don't like what he's doing."

I shook my head. "How do you get that deep into something like that?"

"I don't judge him, man. When you think about it, it's really not any different from the Elgen life he was raised in. His life isn't like yours. Or even mine, for that matter. I was right there with Hatch, was his golden boy, but, for the most part, my abilities don't hurt people, just machines. Torstyn has one gift, if you can call it that, and it's a horrible one. He kills things. And Hatch made the most of that.

"When you get right down to it, Torstyn did worse things with Hatch than he's doing now. Hatch was as sadistic and cruel as any drug lord. He was just peddling electricity instead of dope. People are addicted to both."

"When is the last time you saw him?"

"Last summer, he dropped by my place. He was in town and wanted to hang out. We went out dancing. As we were coming back, he said, 'See that car? It's DEA. We're being followed.' It was like a game to him. He said, 'Slow down, let them get close so I can melt them.' I killed their cars so he didn't kill them. He was pretty pissed at me for doing that. We haven't talked since."

"Think we'll ever see him again?"

"I don't know. It's a rough world. And, unlike you, he's not bullet-proof. Someday, someone's going to get the drop on him. I'm afraid it's just a matter of time."

"We need to rescue him, too."

"You can't rescue someone who doesn't want to be rescued. He'll just go back."

"Sometimes you can. It's worth a try."

Quentin smiled. "You're a good man, Vey." He sat back in his seat.

I lay back and closed my eyes. Even with all the horrible things he'd done, I felt heartsick for Torstyn. He was still my brother.

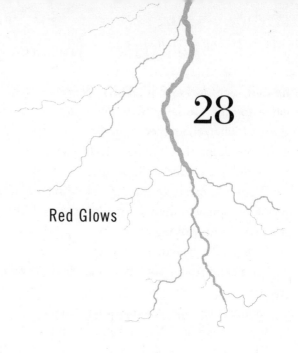

28

Red Glows

It seems like I'd just barely closed my eyes when Captain Scott came over the PA system.

"Attention, ladies and gentlemen. We are starting our descent into the Dallas Love airport. We'll be touching down in around seventy minutes."

I opened my eyes and exhaled slowly. "Rock and roll," I said softly.

"Ready?" Quentin asked, setting down the tablet he was playing a video game on.

"Yeah." I leaned forward and shook Ostin's knee. "Ostin."

"Yeah?" he said groggily.

"Time to wake up. We're going to be meeting in a few minutes."

McKenna lightly groaned, then opened her eyes. "I heard that," she said.

I walked to the back of the plane and knelt next to Taylor. "Time to get up."

Her eyes fluttered open. "Are we already there?"

"No. We've still got an hour. But we need to go over some things before we land."

She breathed in deeply, then sat up, pulling her hair from her face. "I'll be right there." She pushed her blanket aside, then went to the bathroom while I returned to the front of the cabin. I took out the black case of buttons my father had given me before take-off.

By the time Taylor was back, everyone else had assembled. Cassy had turned her seat to face us. I stood at the front of the plane.

"We'll be in Dallas in an hour. There will be a van waiting for you. You'll check in at your hotel in Fort Worth, grab some lunch at the hotel, then go from there. Taylor will be leading team one. Are you all okay with that?"

Everyone was. Even Cassy nodded.

"The objective of your mission is to find Abigail and rescue her. We don't believe that she's still in Texas, but we need to be prepared if she is. That's our objective."

"What's the plan?" Nichelle asked.

Ostin looked around. Then, when no one else spoke, he said, "I say we handle it like any police investigation. We interview anyone she was with, check all the campus video footage, and create a time-line of events and likely abductors."

"What do we know so far?" Cassy asked.

Taylor said, "Abi has four roommates. Three of them were around when Abi left. Allyson, Annie, and Lucy. Annie was the one who told me she saw Abi leave."

"There's something else you should know," I said. "Last night Tay-lor had another dream. And we're learning that her dreams tend to be true visions of what's to come." I turned to Taylor. "Would you tell them about it?"

Taylor nodded. "We were at a university. There were students all around us; the buildings were all brick. I think we were in front of a dorm or something."

"What did the building look like?" McKenna asked.

"It was newer, tall, four or five stories. It was between a few other buildings that looked the same. It had a hotel-style entrance. It also was made of yellow brick."

"You just described Hays Hall," McKenna said. "Abi's dorm."

"What happened in your dream?" Quentin asked.

"We were looking for Abi, when we saw two people glowing. It was Bryan and Kylee."

"If I see Bryan again, I'm going to fry him," Zeus said. "We've got history."

"I'll help you," Tessa said.

"You two aren't even going to be with us," Ostin said.

"I am," Nichelle said. "I'll help."

We sometimes forgot that Nichelle could amp up our powers as well. Maybe only a third as much as Tessa did, but it was significant all the same.

I continued. "Taylor saw Abi surrounded by people. They were about our age and Hispanic, like the Chasqui. These people glowed like us, only red."

"Are you saying there's more of us?" Zeus asked.

Cassy spoke for the first time. "It's possible."

We all turned toward her.

"What do you mean?" I asked.

"Back in the Elgen days, we were following reports that there were other electrics. After the Elgen pulled their MEI machine from Pasadena, they were sitting on a two-billion-dollar investment. It's not like they were going to just put it in a closet somewhere.

"What we learned from Grace is that after the Pasadena debacle, Hatch secretly shipped the MEI to South America. We don't know to what extent, since he didn't keep records, but we believe that he was conducting experiments down there, using poor illiterate farmers as guinea pigs. He was far out in the countryside, where he would be free from lawsuits."

"You're saying that there are more Glows?" Tessa said.

"It's very likely," Cassy said.

"Why didn't anyone tell us this?" Tessa asked.

"Because," Cassy said, "at the time, it was irrelevant. And you didn't need more to worry about."

"Then can we assume these other Glows have joined the Chasqui?" McKenna asked.

"I don't think we can assume anything right now," I said. "Even that there are other electrics. We just wanted to warn you to be aware. Just in case."

"So, after the hotel, we go to the campus," Taylor said. "We interview the roommates and see if there's video footage."

"There will definitely be video footage," Ostin said. "It's a college campus. There's more surveillance on campuses than there is at Fort Knox. Big Brother is everywhere. The challenge will be getting someone to let us view it without a warrant."

"We have ways," Cassy said.

"Yeah, we do," I said. "Just keep a low profile."

"What do we do after we complete the mission?" McKenna asked.

"After they drop us off in Peru, we'll send the jet back for you. We'll meet up in Puerto Maldonado."

"How will we communicate?" Ostin asked. "It's not like we'll have cell coverage in the jungle."

"My father sent two satellite phones. One for each team. They're back in the cargo area. I'll get them out when we land. Which reminds me." I lifted the case my father had given me before boarding. "He also sent these." I opened the case, exposing the array of silver disks. "Everyone gets one."

"What are they?" Nichelle asked.

"They're tracking devices." I lifted one out. "They're made to be worn on our bodies, someplace where they won't be found. He suggested that those of you with longer hair, like Taylor or McKenna, put it on the back of your neck."

"It will stick to our skin?"

"Like superglue. So sticking won't be a problem, but getting it off might be."

"Now we're just like the Borg," Ostin said. "Part machine, part organic matter."

"What about us short hairs?" Quentin asked. "Where should we hide it?"

"Find a place on your body that's not uncomfortable."

"Like what?"

"I'm thinking my underarm," I said.

"Or behind your ear," McKenna said. "It wouldn't be any more invasive than glasses."

"That's a good idea," I said. "And it won't require me to shave my armpits, so that's a plus."

"Then you'd know what we women go through," Taylor said under her breath.

"What's the point of these things?" Cassy said.

"The point is that with these, we won't lose any more of us. We'll always know where to find you."

"Even if we're dead?"

I looked at her. "If it comes to that."

"All right. Let's hand them out."

"Before I do, you need to know, there's more that these things will do. Everyone, please pay very close attention." I held up the disk. "If you press this quickly five times, it will send out a distress signal." I looked over at everyone. "Got it?"

"Yeah," Zeus said.

"How many times?" I asked.

"Five times," Nichelle said.

"Right. Okay, here's the scary part. Everyone, pay super-close attention."

"We already are," Tessa said.

"Then pay closer attention," I said. "This is a matter of life and death."

"We got you," Zeus said.

"If you push this thing ten times slowly, it will send out a signal to launch a guided missile. It will home in on the disk and destroy anything in the immediate vicinity."

"Which would include us," Cassy said. "You're talking suicide."

"It will be if you don't get rid of it. But the signal it sends out has a fifteen-minute delay. So, you'd have fifteen minutes to put as much distance between you and the button as you can."

"Button?" Tessa said.

"That's what the corporation calls these things. Buttons."

Tessa said, "So you're saying, if we set off the bomb thing, we'll have to tear the button off our body?"

"Yes."

"That sounds painful."

"If you're in a situation where you need to set off a guided missile, I think ripping this thing off your body is probably the least of your worries."

"Good point," she said.

"Do these have batteries?" Cassy asked.

"Yes. But they're designed to run off our bodies' electricity. That won't apply to Ostin and maybe Nichelle." I looked at Nichelle. "Sorry. We're not sure."

"No worries. I'm used to being the odd girl out."

"All right, everyone take one." I turned to Ostin. "Will you keep track of what letter everyone takes and text them to my father? Taylor and I will be *A* and *B*."

"No problem. I'll put you down as *A* and Taylor as *B*. Who's next?"

Everyone lined up to take a button. Zeus, unable to resist, pushed the button. It beeped.

"Stop!" Tessa shouted. "What part of 'guided missiles' and 'sudden death' did you not understand?"

"I heard him," Zeus said. "He said don't press it five or ten times. I only pressed it once to get a feel for it."

Quentin held his button in the air. "So, if I pressed this right now, slowly, ten times, a missile would blow up this jet."

"That's how it works," I said.

"That's cool," he said. "Totally cool."

"Look," Zeus said. "It really does stick to flesh." The button was stuck to his finger. He shook it, but it wouldn't come off. "It won't come off."

Quentin laughed. "You're such an idiot, dude."

"All right," I said. "Don't do what Zeus just did. Take your time and put it on carefully. And, do not touch the adhesive back to any part of your body you don't want it to permanently adhere to."

"No, serious, guys," Zeus said. "How do I get this off?"

Tessa grinned. "Maybe you should press it ten times now, hot-shot."

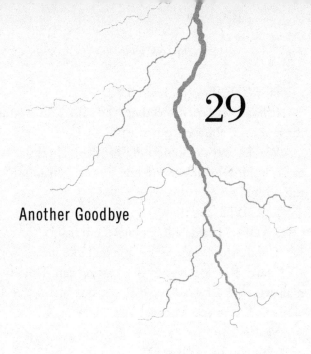

29

Another Goodbye

Fortunately, Taylor had some nail polish remover in her bag, and after soaking the button for a couple of minutes, Zeus was able to pry it off, though not without some blood. He was much more careful the next time he stuck it on. Secretly, I was glad he'd done that, so everyone else would take it a little more seriously before they stuck it onto their face or whatever.

We landed at the Dallas Love Field Airport just a little after eleven o'clock. The plane taxied over to a private terminal and stopped. Captain Boyd lowered the stairs; then everyone from both teams got out.

"Man, it's warm here," Ostin said.

"It's warmer than usual," Captain Boyd said. "Summer came early."

The shuttle van the corporation had reserved was waiting on the tarmac. Zeus walked up next to me as I waited for Taylor to get her bag.

"How's the finger?" I asked.

"It finally stopped bleeding," he said. "You weren't kidding about those things' adhesive qualities."

"Would you do something for me? There are three cases in the cargo hold, two small, one big. Would you mind taking them up to the cabin?"

"Sure. What are they?"

"RADDs," I said. "I'll explain them inside."

"Good. More toys. Makes me feel like James Bond."

I walked Taylor over to the waiting van. The driver, a silver-haired man wearing a tweed ivy cap, got out of the car. He was holding a clipboard. "Are you Michael Vey?"

"Yes, sir."

"Will you be in charge?"

"No. Taylor will."

Taylor raised her hand to her chest. "I'm Taylor."

"Fine and dandy, Ms. Taylor. If you'll please sign here. That's just to prove to the boss that I showed up for work."

She signed the form.

"Your company paid for full-time service, so I'll be at your beck and call for the next few days. If you need to extend, you just need to give me twenty-four hours' notice."

"I hope we're not here that long," she said.

"Better to be safe," I said. "And I forgot your satellite phone. I'll be right back."

I walked back to the jet. Cassy was leaving the cargo hold with her bag as I walked up.

"Michael," she said, walking up to me. "I'm sorry about all my drama. We don't need that right now. I just want you to know that you can count on me to do the right thing."

"I know. And thank you for keeping this team safe."

"I'll keep them safe. Especially Taylor. You stay safe too, okay?" She smiled lightly. "Remember, it's a jungle out there."

I hugged her. After we separated, she said, "See you soon." She walked off to the van.

Captain Boyd was still up in the cargo hold.

"Boyd, will you hand me those satellite phones? They're in those cases by your leg."

"You got it, boss."

I took both cases, handed one to Quentin, and then took the other one to Taylor.

"That's bigger than I expected," she said. "How big is this phone?"

"It's just the case. The phone itself is about the size of a normal cell phone. It's just got all the charging equipment inside."

"Will I know how to use it?"

"It's basically the same as your cell phone. The instructions are inside the case. If you have problems with it, you've got Ostin."

"Our resident genius."

"Are you talking about me?" Ostin said, walking up behind Taylor.

"How did you guess?" I said. We man hugged. "Good luck."

"We'll figure this out. Just a little old-fashioned detective work."

McKenna sidled up to me. She kissed me on the cheek. "Bye, Michael. We'll see you soon."

"I'm counting on it. Be safe. Keep everyone safe."

"I always do."

I turned back to Taylor. "Call me after you figure it out, just so we know they work."

"I'll probably do it in the next few hours. Can I reach you on the jet?"

"You can reach me anywhere with this."

"Even a cave?"

Her reference was obvious. "That probably depends how deep it goes."

She looked at me. "I wish we were doing this together."

"Me too. But it's best this way. Let me know as soon as you know what happened to Abi."

"I will. The same with you. If you hear anything about Tara . . ."

"Of course."

Taylor's eyes welled up.

"We'll find her," I said. "We always do. Don't forget to put on your button."

"I won't. I'm going to put it under my hair when we get to the hotel." Taylor looked deeply into my eyes. "I can't believe that three days ago my biggest worry was if we'd have enough pastries for our party. Keep safe, please. Promise me."

"I promise. And we have Alpha Team with us. They're tough."

"You're pretty tough yourself," she said. She put her arms around me, and we kissed. "I'll see you soon, boyfriend."

I hoped so.

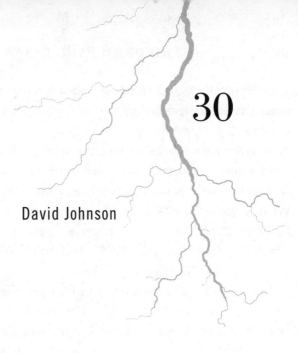

30

David Johnson

Despite my general game-day anxiety, I was glad to be working with Alpha Team. We didn't have their discipline or training, but then, they didn't have our electricity. And, after all we'd been through, we were hardly inexperienced. We had seen real battle. Maybe more than they had.

Alpha Team was a new concept in the Veytric Corporation. The fall and dissolution of the Elgen guard organization that Hatch had created had left a hole in the company's security forces. There was still a need for security, of course, and the Starxource plants all had some form of it. It was just that right now it more resembled a shopping mall security team than the Elgen army that Hatch had built.

Under Hatch's leadership, all Elgen guard prospects had undergone an intense training and indoctrination program—the one he'd held at the jungle Starxource plant in Peru. Since the Elgen hadn't had to answer to any country or government, the training had sometimes been lethal. Hatch actually encouraged the death of failed prospects. He believed it "thinned out the herd" and made the others tougher.

It was Jack's job to rebuild the security force. Jack wanted to build something better and more powerful than what Hatch had created but without the brainwashing. It was the perfect job for Jack. Warrior was in his blood. Had he not been hired by the corporation, he likely would have joined a special operations force, such as the Green Berets or Navy SEALs. He had even looked into joining the Sayeret Matkal, Israel's special forces.

Because of the immediate need to get the Starxource plants operational and under control, the first security forces the corporation hired were from private security companies stationed in the country of the plant. Jack brought them all onto weekly online meetings. They had to employ more than a dozen translators to meet all their different groups' language needs.

After every plant was staffed, Jack moved to phase two of his plans—building a mobile army of elite forces to protect the company. He had planned to name the elite squads using the NATO phonetic alphabet, i.e., Alpha Team, Bravo Team, Charlie Team, though he had already decided to name the seventh unit "Gervaso"—instead of the standard name "Golf"—after our friend we'd lost in the battle of Hades. I had no doubt Jack would be using Wade's name as well.

Alpha Team was composed of a squad of six men. There were two Navy SEALs, a Polish JW GROM, and two Army Rangers. Captain David Johnson, the team leader, had been a Green Beret. I had met Captain Johnson a little more than a year ago when he and Jack had come to Idaho to meet with my father. Johnson had just retired from the military after a tour in Nigeria, where his team had been ambushed. He was the lone survivor and had still been struggling with that.

Johnson looked the way you would imagine a Green Beret to look. He was African American, powerfully built, about six inches taller than me. He had movie-star good looks. His head was shaved, and he had a strong jaw and dark piercing eyes.

He came by tough naturally. For most of his life, he'd been raised, with his older sisters, by his mother in Emeryville, the most crime-ridden and dangerous small town in California. On David's seventh birthday, his father was killed in a convenience store robbery gone bad.

Johnson dropped out of school at fifteen to work at an auto parts warehouse, then joined the army two years later. The day he turned twenty he applied for the Special Forces Preparation Course, an intense assessment program for special forces and Green Beret training. He excelled in all levels of the training and was admitted into the program. For the next seven years he flew around the world and engaged in intense special ops in cities, deserts, and—mostly—jungles.

As soon as he could afford it, he moved his mother out of Emeryville, to Waco, Texas. Only seven months later, she was diagnosed with stage four breast cancer. He took a leave from the military to take care of his mother and was at her side when she passed. That's where he was when he answered an advertisement that Jack had posted in *Soldier of Fortune* magazine. It wasn't lost on Jack that Hatch had used the same publication to find his Elgen guards.

Johnson and I became fast friends, I suspect largely due to all the things Jack had told him about me before we even met. He was a true warrior and could quote a hundred lines from the ancient book *The Art of War*. Before he left, he paid me the greatest compliment I think he could share. "I'd be proud to fight by your side," he said.

It had been inspiring to hear. I just had never thought it would ever actually happen. Especially not today.

PART THREE

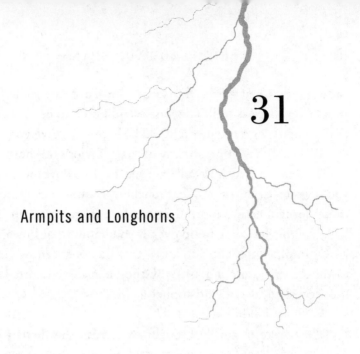

31

Armpits and Longhorns

"My name is Clarence," the driver said, speaking into the rearview mirror. "I know what you're thinking. 'Clarence' as in Clarence Darrow . . ."

"Whoever that is," Nichelle said under her breath. She pointed her finger at Ostin. "Don't tell me."

". . . I'd like to be the first to give you a warm welcome to Fort Worth, but the sun's beat me to it. It's a bit unseasonably warm right now. I see you're staying at the Hyatt. That's a real nice place. If you've got a little downtime, there are some things our town has to offer that I think you might really enjoy. Our zoo is something we're really proud of. One of those national magazines rated it the number one zoo in North America. There are all sorts of creatures to see there.

"And speaking of creatures, I know you won't want to miss the Texas longhorn cattle drive over near the Stockyards. They run the cattle every day at eleven thirty and four. There are some fine places to eat over there as well. The missus and I used to head over there on Friday nights for our date night. I'd be happy to drive you over."

"We won't have time for any of that," Taylor said shortly.

The man was a little taken back by her directness. "I'm sorry you're going to miss that. That longhorn is quite a creature. Some of those horns measure more than ten feet from tip to tip. The cattle look like they're going to tip over, if you know what I mean."

Ostin piped in. "Did you know that the longhorn was introduced to the Americas around 1493 by the Spanish conquistadors during the second voyage of Christopher Columbus?"

"Well, no, I didn't know that."

"They were originally brought over from the Iberian Peninsula. They're considered an excellent example of survival evolution, since some of the cattle escaped and became feral, producing a new breed of tougher, drought-tolerant livestock unique to America, which we know today as the Texas longhorn."

"Well," the man said. "I didn't know that either. It sounds like you've been preparing for your little visit."

"No," Nichelle said. "He just knows everything."

The Hyatt was less than six miles from the university. Clarence dropped them off at the hotel's front entry, then parked in the hotel's lot to wait for them. After everyone had their room number, Taylor gathered the group in the hotel's lobby.

"I was thinking we'd take a few minutes to take our things up to our rooms, have a planning lunch here in the hotel, then head over to Abi's dorm. We'll meet back down here in a half hour." She checked her watch. "About two o'clock. Anything else?"

Ostin looked up from the GPS tracker that Michael had left them. "Remember your buttons."

"That's right," Taylor said. "Don't forget to attach your buttons."

"I could use help getting mine on," Nichelle said.

"I'll help you," Taylor said. "Give me a few minutes to settle, then come to my room. I'm in 807."

Everyone had started to walk away when Taylor said, "Cassy."

Cassy turned around. "Yes."

Taylor walked up to her. "I want to be sure that we're on the same team."

Cassy's brow furrowed. "Of course we are." She looked at Taylor. "You must be glad that I'm here."

"I'm glad to have someone on my team as powerful as you."

"You're not just glad that I'm not out there with Michael?"

Taylor lightly sighed. "One of the curses of being a mind reader is that people can't hide anything from me. I know how you feel about Michael."

"You didn't need to read my mind to know that. I told you back in Tuvalu."

". . . And I know that Michael thinks you're beautiful."

Cassy didn't say anything.

"I didn't have to be a mind reader for that either. I mean, why wouldn't he? Just look at you. You're pretty much perfect."

"No one's perfect."

"Close enough," Taylor said. "I admit, I'm jealous. And I'm not real proud of that. But right now, my sister and two of my friends are in serious trouble. We need you. I need you. Please, for their sake, let's just put this aside for now."

Cassy thought for a moment, then said, "No, not just for their sake. I'm sorry, Taylor. The heart just has a mind of its own. I should have stayed in Switzerland."

"I'm glad you didn't."

Cassy lightly smiled. "Thanks."

"Truce?"

"Truce," Cassy said, putting out her hand.

Taylor hesitated. "You know that if I shake your hand, I'll see what you're thinking."

Cassy nodded. "I know. I want you to know that I'm sincere. And even though it may not seem like it, I do respect you." Cassy set down her bag, and they shook. Then they spontaneously hugged.

After they parted, Taylor asked, "Do you need help with your button? On your neck?"

"No. I can get it. Are you going up?"

"In a second. I'm going to see if the concierge has a map of the campus."

"Then I'll see you in a few minutes." Cassy swung her bag back over her shoulder, then walked off toward the bank of elevators.

Taylor walked over to the concierge stand. A middle-aged woman wearing a hotel uniform and a crimson scarf looked up from the counter and smiled. "May I help you?"

"Do you have a map of the TCU campus?"

"I think I do," she said. She leaned over and shuffled through a file drawer. "Here we are." She lifted a brochure. "It's an enrollment brochure, but it has a map."

"Thank you."

Taylor put the map into her bag, then went up to her room. She set the satellite phone case on her bed and opened it. The phone itself wasn't much larger than her own cell phone. She took the phone out of the case and turned it on. The screen lit with options. One said "DIRECTORY." Three entries came up:

> Phone 2
> Veytric
> Jack Vranes

She hadn't known that Jack had a phone too. No doubt that whoever had captured him now had possession of it. It was a peculiar feeling knowing that with the push of a button she could call her enemy. She pushed the button for phone two. It rang twice; then Michael answered.

"Hey, you figured it out."

"Wasn't much to figure out."

"How's it going?"

"We're meeting downstairs for lunch, then heading over to Abi's dorm."

"Is everyone okay?"

"Yes. Cassy and I had a talk."

"How did that go?"

"Good. We'll be good."

Michael was quiet a moment, then said, "I'm not sure what to say."

"You don't have to say anything. It is what it is. I'm glad we have her here."

"Me too. It makes me less worried."

Taylor sighed. "Well, I'd better get ready. I just wanted to make sure this thing worked. Did you notice that Jack's phone is programmed in here?"

"I saw that."

"It's just weird that I could push a button and a Chasqui would probably answer."

"Don't do it."

"I won't." Taylor sighed. "So close, but so far."

"Call after you go to the campus, okay?"

"I will."

"I love you."

"Me too."

Taylor hung up the phone, setting it on the room's dresser. She walked into the bathroom and washed her face, then checked her watch. She still had fifteen minutes before she needed to be downstairs, so she lay back on the bed and closed her eyes. Her head had barely hit the pillow when there was a knock on her door. She groaned, then sat back up.

Looking through the door's peephole, she saw McKenna. She was holding a razor and a can of shaving cream. Taylor opened the door.

"Am I too early?" McKenna asked.

"No. You're good. Come in."

"I brought a razor and cream."

"I'll get a towel." She walked to the bathroom and returned with a couple of towels. "You can sit on the bed."

McKenna set the razor and shaving cream on the bed, next to the button, then wrapped the towel around her head, leaving the back of her neck exposed.

Taylor daubed shaving cream around the nape of McKenna's neck.

"I'm going to put it as high on your neck as I can."

She took the razor and made short, slow strokes that left a quarter-sized bald spot at the base of McKenna's hairline; then she rubbed the spot with the towel until it was dry.

"All right. The moment of truth."

"Just don't get it stuck to your fingers like Zeus did."

"Zeus had it coming," Taylor said. She removed the strip, carefully positioned the button, and then pressed it into place. The disk beeped.

McKenna let her hair down. "Want me to do you now?"

"Yes, please," Taylor said, pulling up her hair.

A couple of minutes later McKenna stepped back. "Done. You are now trackable."

"I could have used one of these when I was a kid," Taylor said. "I was always getting lost."

"I did have one," McKenna said. "Hatch put those RFIDs in us. I kept getting in trouble for melting mine."

"Where is Ostin putting his?"

"Under his arm. He said 'No real man would ever look in another man's pit.'"

Taylor laughed. "He's got a point."

"He always does. But it still sounds funny."

There was another knock on the door.

"That's probably Nichelle," Taylor said. "I told her I'd help her put her button on."

"I already helped her," McKenna said. She looked out the peephole. "It's Ostin." She opened the door. "Hey, sweetie."

"You guys ready to eat? I'm starving."

"You're always starving," Taylor said.

"Not always," Ostin said. "Sometimes I'm just hungry."

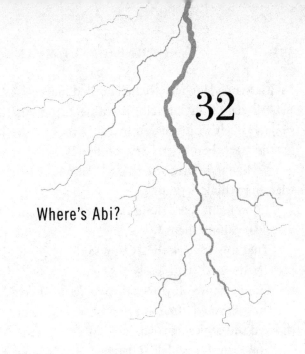

32

Where's Abi?

$\mathbf{C}$assy and Nichelle were already in the restaurant when the others arrived. The restaurant was called the Toro Toro steak house. It wasn't crowded, and Taylor had the hostess seat them in a corner of the restaurant where they could meet in private.

After they had ordered, Taylor brought out the map of the campus the concierge had given her and spread it out on the table. Ostin brought out an even larger map, spread it out on the empty table next to them, and then pulled the table over next to theirs.

"Where did you get that?" Taylor asked.

"I printed it back home."

"Always thinking ahead," she said.

"Those who fail to plan, plan to fail."

"You sound like Yoda," Nichelle said.

"Take that as a compliment, I will."

McKenna laughed. Nichelle rolled her eyes.

"All right," Taylor said, pointing to her map. "Abi lives here in Hays Hall. It's on the southwest corner of the campus. I think we should start there with her roommates."

"I'd like to interrogate them," Ostin said. "They might know more than they think they do."

"I don't think we should *interrogate* anyone," Cassy said. "Maybe just, like, talk to them."

"That might work too," Ostin said.

"Then what?" Cassy asked.

"I don't know," Taylor said. "We'll see where it leads us."

They finished their meals, then walked out to the van. Taylor showed the driver her map.

"You want Hays Hall," Clarence said. "It's fenced along West Berry Street, so I'll drop you off over here," he said, pointing to the map. "Then I'll find a place to park. You can call me when you're ready to be picked up." He handed Taylor a business card. "That's my cell number."

As Taylor took the card from him, their hands touched. She was immediately filled with sadness. Clarence had lost his wife to cancer only five weeks earlier, and he was deeply grieving. She saw him kneeling next to his wife's grave, sobbing. She felt bad that she had been so curt with him.

"I'm so sorry," she said.

Clarence looked up at her. "Excuse me?"

Taylor caught herself. "I mean, I'm just sorry for the inconvenience."

"It's no inconvenience, young lady," he said. "Glad to help."

McKenna was the only one of them familiar with the campus. She had flown in a week before Abigail had started school to help Abi get settled in. They'd spent their time finding the local hot spots, buying Abi a car, and setting up her room, which mostly had entailed buying and assembling furniture from Ikea.

Clarence drove through the center of the university, then pulled off West Berry Street into a fenced-in area. There were students all around them, coming to and from campus.

"You can let us off anywhere along here," McKenna said.

"I can get you a little closer," Clarence said.

"Is that Hays Hall?" Taylor asked.

"No, that's Marion," Clarence said. "Hays is the dorm just past it."

"You are familiar with the campus."

"Oh yes. My wife went to TCU a hundred years ago. That's where we met. Are you thinking of going to school here?"

"No," Ostin said. "I go to Caltech."

"Where's that?"

Ostin frowned. "It's in California."

"Love the beach," Clarence said. A minute later he turned on his emergency flashers and pulled up to the curb, then put the van in park. "Unless you tell me otherwise, I'll pick you up here when you call."

"Thank you," Taylor said.

They all got out.

"I like that driver," McKenna said. "He's corny, but he's nice."

"He's in a lot of pain," Taylor said. "His wife just died."

"He told you that?"

"Not intentionally."

They walked west across the grass until they came to a section of sidewalk that divided off to different buildings.

"The front of the dorm is over here," McKenna said. "Abi probably would have come out on this side. The walk here leads to the parking garage."

"Hays Hall," Ostin said. "Named for the university benefactors Marlene and Spencer Hays."

Cassy said, "He is like a walking—"

"Encyclopedia?" Taylor said.

"I was going to say 'Trivial Pursuit game,' but that works too."

Ostin's brow furrowed. "Why do people talk about me like I'm not here?"

McKenna took his hand. "Because you're special."

"What kind of special?"

"Good special," she said.

Nichelle said, "I wonder how much you have to give for them to name a building after you."

"In this case, about a hundred million," Ostin said.

"Sheesh," Nichelle said.

They entered the building through the front portico.

"Abi's dorm is on the second floor," McKenna said.

"Why is all the furniture purple?" Nichelle asked.

"It's the school color," McKenna said.

"That would do it."

They walked upstairs, then halfway down the corridor.

"This is it," McKenna said.

Taylor knocked on the door. A half minute later a young woman opened it. She wore TCU purple sweats and a Horned Frog T-shirt. Her dark brown hair was pulled back in a ponytail. "Hi," she said brightly.

"Hi. My name is Taylor. I'm a friend of Abigail's."

The young woman looked over the group quizzically. "Abi's not here."

"I know. Are you Annie?"

"I'm Lucy."

"I spoke with Annie yesterday. Abi was supposed to be at our party, but she never came. So we came to see if we could find her."

"Wasn't her party in Idaho?"

"We flew in from Idaho this morning," Ostin said.

"You flew all the way from Idaho to see why she didn't come to your party?"

"We were worried," McKenna said.

"I need to upgrade my friends," Lucy said.

"Is Annie here?" Taylor asked.

"Yeah. Just a minute. You can come in." She pointed at Ostin. "Except you. Ally's not dressed."

Ostin looked dejected. "Okay."

The women followed Lucy into the main room. There was a charcoal-gray, contemporary-style sofa with a matching chaise and a round, oak-veneer coffee table in front of a flat-screen television.

Translucent plastic butterflies had been glued to the wall behind the sofa, and strings of lights were hung across the ceiling.

"Yeah, just sit or whatever," Lucy said. "Hey, Annie," she shouted. "Abi's friends are here."

A tall, dishwater-blond woman emerged from one of the doors. She looked surprised to see them. "Hi. There's four of you."

"Five. We left the guy in the hall," Taylor said.

"I'm in my underwear," a voice said from a bedroom.

"She's always in her underwear," Annie said.

Taylor stepped forward. "Annie, I'm Taylor. We talked yesterday."

"Oh, right. Have you heard from Abi yet?"

"No. That's why we came. She's not answering her phone."

"Yeah, I kept calling her. I just figured she was dead."

Taylor blanched. "Dead?"

"I mean her phone. Or, maybe since she was having trouble with her boyfriend, she just bailed on the party, unplugged, and went home instead."

"She doesn't have a home," Nichelle said.

"I meant her parents' place."

"So did I."

Annie looked over Nichelle, as if noticing her for the first time. "You're Goth."

"You're preppy," Nichelle returned.

McKenna said, "We knew she was having trouble with Jack. But it wasn't that. Jack wasn't even going to be at the party."

"We're just really worried about her," Taylor said. "It's not like her to go dark like that. You said that you saw her car."

"Yeah. I mean, it's the only pink BMW I've ever seen, so it's kind of hard to miss."

"Could she have taken an Uber to the airport?" Cassy asked.

"She could have, but it wouldn't make sense. I offered her a ride to the airport, but she told me that it was a private hangar and there was a place she could leave her car. I mean, why would she call an Uber after saying that?"

"Not likely," Taylor said. "And you saw her leave?"

"Yeah. You know how affectionate Abi is. She's, like, hugging everyone, saying goodbye."

"Then what?"

"Then nothing. Later that night I went to meet some friends at Torchy's, and that's when I noticed her car. I thought it was weird. Then you called."

"What's Torchy's?" Nichelle asked.

"It's a taco place. You should try it while you're here."

"I saw Abi," Allyson said walking out of her room.

"When?" Taylor asked.

"Just out front, when she was leaving. She had her little roller suitcase."

"Was she alone?"

"No. There were some guys with her."

The words sent a chill down Taylor's spine. "Someone from school?"

"Maybe. I mean, I've never seen them before, but it's a big school. She probably had a class with them or something."

"What did they look like?" Taylor asked.

"They were our age. Hispanic."

"Hispanic. Like, Mexican?"

"No. I'm pretty sure they were Peruvian."

"How do you know they were Peruvian?" Cassy asked.

"Peruvians look different, and I heard them talking. I'm from Brownsville, so I grew up speaking Spanish. Then I did a summer study abroad in Lima. Peruvians have their own dialect. Just like people from Brooklyn speak different English than someone from Alabama."

"You mean they have an accent," Taylor said.

"Right," Allyson said.

"But Abi doesn't speak Spanish," McKenna said.

"They were speaking English with her. They spoke Spanish with each other."

"Did you hear what they were saying?"

"No. I was just walking by, so I didn't really pay attention."

"Did she look stressed?"

"Not that I noticed. But you know how chill she is. She was just talking to them."

Taylor thought a moment, then said, "Could we let our guy in? He's helping us find her."

"Sure. I'll get a robe." Allyson walked back into her room. McKenna went to get Ostin.

A moment later, Ostin followed McKenna into the dorm room, looking around as he walked. "This is nicer than my dorm."

"Where do you go to school?" Annie asked.

"Caltech. It's in California."

"I know Caltech. So, you're a brain."

"He's a brain," Taylor said. "Ostin, this is Annie. She's one of Abi's roommates."

"Nice to meet you, Annie," Ostin said.

"Sure," she replied.

Cassy said, "One of Abi's dormmates saw her out front with some men."

"Were they Hispanic?"

"That sounded racist," Lucy said as she walked to the kitchen.

"It wasn't," Ostin said. "Were they?"

"Yes," Nichelle said.

Ostin turned to Taylor. "Just like in your dream."

Annie's brow furrowed. "Dream?"

"It's nothing," Taylor said.

"What time was it when she left?" Ostin asked.

"I don't know. A little after noon?"

"It was about one o'clock," Allyson said from her bedroom. "I just got out of class."

"Could we look in her room?" McKenna asked.

"Sure," Annie said. "I guess she wouldn't mind. It's probably locked."

"Do you have a key?"

"Yeah. Hold on." She went over and opened the cabinet door and brought out a key. It was attached to a TCU Horned Frog key chain.

She unlocked the door across from the bathroom, and everyone crowded in. Abigail had hung inspirational sayings on the wall.

Chocolate is God's
apology for broccoli.

It is in the darkest skies
that stars are best seen.

To fly you must first accept
the possibility of falling.

Believe in yourself as if your life
depended on it. Because it does.

"Definitely Abi's room," McKenna said.

There were pictures of Abigail and Jack on one wall, also the group photograph of the Electroclan that was taken at the dedication of the memorial in Tuvalu.

"Hey," Annie said. "That's you guys. Where was that taken? Hawaii?"

"Tuvalu," Nichelle said.

"Where's Tuvalu?"

"In the ocean."

McKenna looked inside Abigail's closet, then through her dresser drawers.

"What are you looking for?" Annie asked.

"Abi had a little sloth stuffed animal. She never went anywhere without it. It's not here."

"Where is her car?" Ostin asked.

"In the parking garage. It's on the second level, east side. Near the end."

"Okay," Taylor said. "Let's go check out her car." She turned back to Annie. "Thank you for your help."

"Don't mention it. You don't think, like, something bad has happened to her, do you?"

Ostin said, "Practically speaking, there's an eighty-five percent—"

"No," Taylor said, cutting him off. "I'm sure there's a reasonable explanation."

"Oh good. She's such a nice girl. When you see her, tell her to call."

"We will. Thank you for your help."

They walked outside the dorm.

"That was interesting," Nichelle said. "Peruvian abductors."

"Back to Peru," Taylor said. "It's hard to believe that before the Elgen kidnapped me, I couldn't find Peru on a map."

Nichelle looked over. "I'm sorry."

"About what?"

"For kidnapping you."

"That wasn't you," Taylor said.

"The parking garage is over there," McKenna said. "Wait. Where's Ostin?"

"He's there," Cassy said, pointing.

Ostin was still back near the dorm, looking around.

"Are you coming?" McKenna shouted.

"In a minute."

She walked back to him. "What are you doing?"

"I'm looking for the CCCs."

"What's that?"

"Closed-circuit cameras." After another minute he said, "Okay." He put his hands into his pockets. "We can go."

When they were back with the group, McKenna said, "He was looking for the campus cameras."

"Did you find any?" Nichelle asked.

"Six," he said. "Heavy redundancy."

"Big Brother," she said.

"Did you know there's an estimated one billion surveillance cameras in the world? And two-thirds of those are in Asia."

"No," Nichelle said. "Didn't know that. Didn't especially want to either."

They walked across the lawn to the parking garage and climbed the stairs to the second level.

"There's her car," McKenna said. As Annie had said, it was hard to miss. Abi had bought the pink BMW Z4 convertible a few days after arriving in Texas. It was parked at the far end of the parking garage. They walked to it. McKenna checked the doors.

"It's locked."

"Did she leave anything inside?" Taylor asked.

"Not that I can see. If she had her suitcase, she would have put it in her trunk."

"We could use Ian right now," Taylor said.

"There are cameras all around here too," Ostin said. "I wonder where they feed." He looked around. "Probably at the entrance booth."

They took the stairs back down to the first level. Near the garage opening was a wide two-sided toll booth. "There we are."

They all walked over to the booth. At the rear window, a young man with tight, curly brown hair sat before a series of screens. Across from him was another man, a little older and wearing a stocking cap. He was sitting on the other side of the counter, counting money.

"Good evening," Ostin said.

The young man looked up, startled. "What do you want?"

"I have a question. Can you see everything in the parking garage from your monitors?"

"Yep."

"No blind spots?"

"Nope. There are multiple cameras on every floor."

"Could you show us some of your video from yesterday?"

"No can do, amigo. That's above my pay grade. You might even need a police warrant."

Nichelle stepped forward. "Could we bribe you to see them?" She took a hundred-dollar bill from her pocket and held it up. "I'll give you a hundred dollars right now. You can take your girlfriend out."

"Don't have one," he said. "But I'll take you out. I'm into Goth too. I'm thinking of getting a tat right here of a red skull with octopus tentacles."

"Good for you," Nichelle said. "How about it?"

He looked over to the other guy. "We're always open to a bribe, right, Tim?"

The guy on the other side of the booth didn't even look up. "We don't keep the recordings. That's handled elsewhere."

"Do you know where?" Taylor asked.

"Everything on campus feeds into the control center at the campus police."

"I didn't know that," the first guy said. "How do you know that?"

"Two months ago we had a car stolen during my shift. The police had to send me the video to go through so I could write my report."

"Where's the campus police station?" Ostin asked.

"East end of the campus, about six blocks from here on Berry and Lubbock. It's just east of the DIS building. There are signs; you can't miss it."

"Thanks," Ostin said. "Is there a place around here where we could buy some TCU swag? Like, sports shirts, the nicer stuff."

"The campus store," the first guy said. "It's on the corner of Berry and . . ."

"South University Drive," the other guy said.

"Yeah, University. If you're walking to the police station, you won't miss it. It's about halfway between us and the station."

"Thanks for your help," Taylor said.

"No problem."

They all walked out of the garage.

"That wasn't good," Taylor said as they reached the sidewalk.

"Did he say we needed a warrant?" McKenna asked.

Taylor nodded. "How are we going to get the police to show us the video?"

"No worries," Ostin said. "I have a plan."

"After we stop and buy our souvenir TCU shirts?" Nichelle asked sarcastically.

"Exactly," Ostin said. "That's part of the plan."

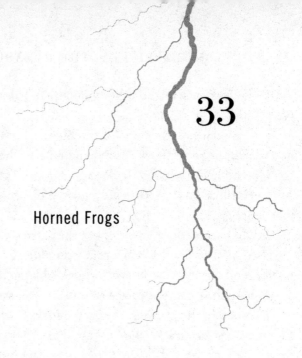

33

Horned Frogs

Leaving the parking garage, they headed back toward the dorm and West Berry Street, where they'd been let off.

McKenna said, "Abi told me they used to call this street 'Scary Berry.'"

"Why?" Taylor asked.

McKenna cocked her head. "I don't know."

After a few minutes of walking, they came to a sign that read:

MARY WRIGHT ADMISSION CENTER

"I need to make a stop in the admissions building," Ostin said, then ran off.

"Where is he going?" Nichelle asked.

"Probably the bathroom," Cassy said.

"I wish he'd tell us what he's up to," Taylor said.

"You know Ostin," McKenna said. "Information is on a need-to-know basis."

"No, I get a lot of info from him that I don't need to know," Nichelle said.

They stopped to wait for Ostin.

"What's taking him so long?" Cassy asked.

"There he is," McKenna said.

Ostin was running toward them. When he got to them, he stopped to catch his breath.

"Get what you need?" Taylor asked.

"Yes," he said. "Now on to the campus store."

The campus store was only a few blocks farther east. It was crowded with students.

"What are we here for?" Taylor asked.

"Shirts," he said.

"I like this one," Nichelle said, holding up a purple-and-gray tee.

Baylor Sucks.
Go Frogs.

"Or this one."

Horned Frogs Do It Better

"I just need to burn a few holes in it."

"Not what we're looking for," Ostin said. He stopped at a row of purple polo shirts. "Here we are. Everyone, find one in your size."

"I'm not wearing one of those," Nichelle said. "I don't even want a TCU shirt. I'm a Gonzaga fan."

"We all need a shirt," Ostin said. He grabbed a TCU clipboard and notebook. "And these."

"What are we doing?" Taylor asked.

"I have an idea for how to get the police to show us the video footage."

"That's a good enough reason for me," Taylor said. "Everyone, get a shirt."

"You need to put them on," Ostin said, pulling off his shirt.

"I think I'll find a dressing room," Cassy said.

"We all will," McKenna said. "Give us a moment."

A few minutes later they all returned wearing the purple shirts.

"We look like we work here," Nichelle said.

"That's what I was going for," Ostin replied.

Taylor paid for the shirts. As they walked out of the store, Ostin took out his phone, then said, "Hold on just a few minutes."

"What now?" Taylor asked.

"I need to learn how a CCTV system works." Less than five minutes later he put down his phone. "That should do it."

"You learned how to use their system that fast?" Cassy asked.

"Not all of it." He turned to Taylor. "Just be ready to reboot them if I screw up."

34

Don't Call Him Horseface

A few minutes later, the group walked through the front doors of the TCU campus police station, which, oddly, was located in a strip mall next to a tanning salon and a pizza parlor. The walls were covered with DATE SAFE posters and TCU sports calendars and paraphernalia. An officer sat behind a counter in front of a narrow waiting room. He had a long, narrow face and thick black hair.

"He looks like a horse," Nichelle said to Cassy.

"I see it," she replied.

The officer looked back and forth between them all. "May I help you?"

Ostin glanced down at the officer's badge, then said, "Yes, thank you, Officer McCarthy. We're from campus IT. We're here to conduct a surprise inspection of the CCTV system."

He looked them over. "Where's your badges?"

For a minute Ostin was stumped; then he lightly groaned as he shook his head. "I knew I forgot something." He leaned in close to the officer. "Look, this is embarrassing. I forgot mine. These guys don't have badges; they're interns. The Asian woman, she's from our sister campus in Taiwan. It's kind of a big deal that she's here. . . ."

Ostin held out the business card he'd grabbed when he'd stopped at the admissions building. "I've got my card right here. You can call the admin office if you need approval, but, guy to guy, I could use a break today. My boss is already on my case. He has it in for me. I think he's afraid I'm going to take his job, you know?"

The officer glanced at the others, then back to Ostin. "All right. Just this once."

"I really appreciate it, Officer McCarthy."

"All right. Follow me." He led them past the counter and down the corridor to the last room on the hall. He opened the door. A man was sitting before a bank of six flat-screen monitors. Each monitor had sixteen images.

"Hey, Mark," the officer said. "These guys are here from campus IT. They say they're doing a surprise inspection of the CCTV system."

The officer swiveled back in his chair. "No one told me about this."

"If they had, it wouldn't have been a surprise, would it?" Ostin said, walking up next to the man. For the next few minutes Ostin just stood there, looking over the screens.

Finally, Officer McCarthy said, "I'll leave you to it."

After he was gone, Ostin said to the officer, "Mark, huh? How do you like this Bosch system?"

"I've no complaints."

"I think the university made a good choice." He stopped. "Now, that's interesting."

"What's interesting?"

"These garage images," he said, pointing at the screens. "What is the lux rating on those cameras?"

"I have no idea."

"We discussed this in a staff meeting the other day. We were concerned that the cameras we installed in the garages weren't the right lux. You know last February when that car was stolen in the Worth Hills Parking Garage?"

"Yes. I worked that."

"Were you satisfied with how the system performed?"

"I mean, it worked."

"No doubt due to your skills overcompensating for a lackluster technical performance."

The officer smiled at the compliment.

"Frankly, I'd prefer a higher lux rating with better color definition."

Ostin turned back to the others. "Remember this, team. These cameras with a lux rating of point two or less are considered low-light cameras. But what we gain in exposure we lose in color definition." Ostin leaned forward as if confiding in the man. "Between us, I'd like to see them just change them all out for infrared."

Ostin took a step back from the console. "Yesterday afternoon, there was a reported power outage near Hays Hall and the Greek Village. Some frat kid stuck a butter knife into an outlet. We're not sure if it affected the cameras or not. Our biggest concern was Hays Hall. Do you have the DVR handy? I'd like to compare time stamps."

"I have access here. What side of the dorm do you need?" Officer Mark asked. "North or south?"

"Let's begin with the south side of the building. We should start at one and shuttle through it."

"One it is."

The screen in front of them now showed the front of Abi's dorm. Ostin watched the increasing time stamp.

"There's Abi," Taylor said. "Stop the video."

Officer Mark stopped the playback and turned to Ostin. He suddenly looked skeptical. "I thought we were just checking the time stamp."

"We are," Ostin said. "She just recognized a friend, that's all."

"How do I know you're not looking for someone?"

Taylor rebooted him. He looked around the room, then said, "What just happened?"

Cassy said, "I think you just fainted."

"Or had a stroke," Nichelle said.

Officer Mark looked confused. "Who are you again?"

"We're with campus IT," Cassy said. "You were helping us track down a missing student. Don't you remember?"

Officer Mark looked even more confused. "I'm sorry. I . . ."

"You really look pale," Cassy said. "Would you like some water or something?"

He took a deep breath. "No, I'm fine. Let's just keep at it. Remind me where we were."

Ostin said, "You just found her."

"Good job," Taylor said.

"Uh, thank you."

Abigail was in the center of the screen, pulling her suitcase behind her.

"Keep shuttling," Ostin said.

Officer Mark started the video again. Abigail looked happy. Suddenly she stopped and looked around as if she had just heard something.

"Stop the video," Ostin said. "Did you see that?"

"Did I see what?" Taylor asked.

"Abi's hair."

"She's been growing it out," McKenna said.

"It's not the length I'm talking about. Her hair was blowing."

"Yeah, it's weird, but hair moves when the wind blows it," Nichelle said.

"It's not windy," Ostin said, ignoring her sarcasm. "Look at the trees and bushes. If there's so much wind, why is nothing else moving?"

"He's right," Taylor said. "Wait, wait. Stop there."

"What?" the officer asked.

"Go back five seconds; then shuttle forward one frame at a time," Ostin said.

"All right." The officer bent over the console and began slowly turning the large, ribbed nob.

"Stop," Ostin said.

"What is that?" Taylor asked.

"That blur," Ostin said, touching the screen. "Can you zoom in?"

"A little," the officer said.

The size of the blur increased.

"How many fps is this camera running?"

"Thirty."

"What's 'fps'?" Taylor asked.

"Frames per second," Ostin said. "Advance to the next frame, please."

The blur moved from one side of the screen to the other in just one frame.

"It must be a glitch," the guard said. "That's a thirtieth of a second. Nothing can move that fast."

"Whatever it is," Ostin said, "it's a freaking missile." Ostin scratched his chin. "There's about forty-five feet between those two points. Forty-five feet in one frame that's approximately thirteen hundred and fifty feet a second. There are five thousand two hundred and eighty feet in a mile, so each mile takes three point nine seconds. . . . There are thirty-six hundred seconds in an hour, so it's traveling nine hundred twenty-three miles per hour."

"That's Mach 1," Cassy said. "Supersonic."

"Faster," Ostin said. "Mach 1 is seven hundred and sixty-seven miles per hour. He's definitely supersonic."

Taylor looked at Ostin. "You said 'he'?"

Ostin nodded. "Or she. It's a person. See, the front of that blur is clearly a hand."

"It looks like a ghost," Nichelle said.

"Ghosts aren't that fast," Ostin said. No one questioned how he knew this. Ostin continued staring at the screen. Then he said, "There's more. Look closer." He pointed to the right side of the screen with a pencil. "Back there. In the shadows."

"It looks like there's someone standing there," Taylor said.

"I see two people," McKenna said.

"Can we zoom in again?" Ostin asked.

"Yeah. Just a minute."

There were clearly two silhouettes, both partially obscured behind a row of sycamore trees.

"Notice anything strange about that?" Ostin asked.

"Other than two people lurking in the shadows?" Taylor said.

"They're both wearing long sleeves in the middle of a heat wave here," Cassy said.

"Maybe they just like the heat," Nichelle said.

Ostin shook his head. "Look more closely. Look at their hands."

"That's weird," Officer Mark said. "It's like . . . they're glowing."

Ostin nodded. "They're electrics. Can you zoom in closer?"

The officer looked over. "What's an electric?"

"Zoom in," Ostin said, ignoring his question.

"I can capture a frame, then zoom in." He hit a few buttons. "All right. There you go."

Ostin examined the image, then turned back. "Look at the guy on the right. Look at his face."

"Oh no," McKenna said.

"You know him?" Officer Mark asked.

"His name is Bryan. He's a fugitive."

35

Finding Bryan and Kylee

"What's the time stamp?" Ostin asked.

"Thirteen, oh seven, seventeen," the officer said.

Two students walked by. One of them glanced over at Abigail.

"That girl, that's her roommate," Cassy said.

McKenna said, "That's Allyson. It's just like she said."

"What other cameras might have caught this?"

"There's the camera on Marion Hall. It's about fifty yards away. It will give us a different angle."

"Let's check it," Ostin said. "Go to the thirteen, oh one, zero time stamp. Let's see what's happening."

The officer switched screens to another camera. They could see the two figures walking up behind the trees.

"That's definitely Bryan and Kylee," Nichelle said. "I'd recognize Bryan's stupid walk anywhere."

"It's my dream," Taylor said. "It's exactly what I saw."

There was another blur; then suddenly there was another person in the frame, as if he'd just appeared out of nowhere. He was leaning over, his hands on his knees, vomiting.

"Where did he come from?" Taylor asked.

"He just magically appeared," Cassy said.

"Not magic," Ostin said. "That's our supersonic phantom. And look at his skin."

"He's glowing too. But . . . he's red," Cassy said. "Really red."

"Then there is another kind of Glow," Nichelle said. "We're not alone."

The officer suddenly spoke up. "What's going on here? What am I looking at? Who are you people?" Up to that point he had been so focused on the screens that he hadn't noticed the pale glow of their skin. "You're all glowing. Except you," he said to Ostin.

"And me," Nichelle said.

The officer looked afraid. "What are you, aliens?"

"Mutants," Ostin said.

"We're not mutants," Taylor said. "I told you not to call us that."

"Why are you glowing?" he asked.

Taylor looked into the man's eyes. "It's what we do." He suddenly jerked back in his seat. He had the strange look in his eyes of someone who had just woken from sleep.

"Welcome back," Cassy said.

Officer Mark looked around. "What just happened?" He looked at Taylor. "Why are you glowing?"

"Not again," Nichelle said.

Just then Officer McCarthy walked back into the room. He had two other officers with him, and he had his Taser drawn. "No one move."

"What's up?" Cassy asked calmly.

"I just called Adrienne at campus IT."

"Who's Adrienne?" Taylor asked.

"Ask your friend," he said, glaring at Ostin. "It's the name on the card he handed me."

"Sorry for the subterfuge," Ostin said. "It may seem morally ambiguous, but considering the circumstances, it was the right thing to do at the moment. Like stealing medicine to save a dying child."

The officers just looked at him.

"You're holding that thing like a gun," Nichelle said. "I assume that means you're going to Tase us?" Nichelle took a step toward the officer. "You have no idea how ironic that is."

"The only thing ironic is you being arrested."

"That literally made no sense at all," Nichelle said. "Do you even know the meaning of the word 'ironic'?"

The officer just looked at her.

"While we're on the topic of Tasers," Ostin said, "here's a fun fact. Do you know where the word 'Taser' came from? It's inventor, Jack Cover, created the acronym from the title of a book he loved as a kid: *Tom Swift and His Electric Rifle*. Pretty interesting, don't you think?"

"That was really random," Cassy said softly.

None of the officers said anything, though several of them looked like they were thinking about it.

"I think it's interesting," Nichelle said. "And, for the record, you're not really going to be arresting us. Not today. Not ever." She took a step toward the officer. "Go ahead, Tase me. I dare you."

"Don't test me," McCarthy said. "Take another step like that, and I will."

"No, you won't."

"Nichelle, don't," Taylor said.

"I want to see if he'll really do what he says." She took another step forward. "Come on, horseface, show me your stuff."

Officer McCarthy's face turned red with embarrassment. "What did you call me?"

"Neigh . . ."

He fired the Taser. The barbs stuck on Nichelle's clothing, lightly piercing her skin. "Ow," she said. She pulled the barbs off. "And?"

The officers just stared. "What the . . . ?"

"Not what you expected?" Nichelle asked.

"You're all under ar—" Officer McCarthy stopped midword, as still as a statue. All the police were frozen except for Officer Mark.

"You were saying?" Cassy said.

"What did you do to them?" Officer Mark asked. His hand started moving toward his gun.

"I wouldn't do that," Cassy said. "Not unless you want me to stop your lungs."

He stopped moving.

"Aliens," Cassy said, shaking her head.

"We should leave," Taylor said.

"We're going to want these images," Ostin said. "And whatever other images they have. Give me a minute to capture them. Freeze this guy too."

Officer Mark's eyes widened, then froze that way.

"Cassy, how long can you hold them?" Taylor asked.

"Just four guys, an hour easy."

"I can help too," Nichelle said.

"I'm good," Cassy said.

"We don't have an hour," Taylor said. "Ostin, you've got ten minutes."

Ostin rolled the frozen officer back from the screen and got in front of the computer. He began shuttling through all the different camera views, capturing pictures and sending them to his own email account. After five minutes, Ostin said. "All right. We've got everything. We can leave."

"What did you do?" Taylor asked Nichelle, who was grinning and looking guilty.

McKenna laughed, but caught herself when she saw Taylor's angry expression. Nichelle had found a marker and drawn a mustache on Officer McCarthy.

Nichelle laughed. "Oh, come on, it's funny. Even McKenna laughed."

"I apologize," McKenna said.

"It's disrespectful," Taylor said. "What did he do to you?"

"He shot me with a Taser," Nichelle said. "*That's* disrespectful."

"You called him 'horseface,'" Taylor said. "You provoked him."

"Okay. I'm bad. And I'm sorry. I forgot your dad was a cop."

"Let's go," Taylor said. "I'm doing a heavy reboot." She turned to Officer Mark. "Don't worry, you won't remember any of this."

As they walked out of the room, Nichelle kissed Officer McCarthy on the cheek. "Bye, Officer. Have a good day protecting and serving."

36

The Speed of Electricity

"This is going to be a day they don't forget," McKenna said when they were out of the police station.

"They've already forgotten it," Taylor told her. "But we won't. I can't believe Bryan and Kylee were here."

"I can," Ostin said. "It makes sense that they joined up with the Chasqui. It's like moving in with your aunt and uncle after your parents die."

"That's a bizarre comparison," Cassy said.

"Yet so accurate," Ostin said.

"If that was the Chasqui," Cassy said, "I'm more concerned about those other Glows. What if the Chasqui were doing their own experiments with the MEIs and created their own force of electrics?"

"There could be hundreds of them," McKenna said.

Ostin nodded. "Or more. Only twenty-eight point eight percent survived the initial procedure in Pasadena, but if the Chasqui are working in a third world country, they could open a free clinic in the jungle and bring in thousands of pregnant women. Which means, theoretically, there could be hundreds of electrics."

"Which is theoretically terrifying," Cassy said.

"What if the electrics two-point-oh are more powerful than us?" Nichelle asked.

"You said *if* it was the Chasqui," Taylor said. "You're still not sure."

"You don't know until you know," Ostin replied. "It's probable, but we can't be sure until we meet them."

"If it wasn't the Chasqui, who else would it be?" McKenna asked.

Ostin shrugged. "I don't know."

McKenna frowned. "I hate it when you don't know something."

Taylor took out her phone and called the driver. "Clarence, please meet us at the campus bookstore at the corner of University and West Berry. Thank you." She put away her phone. "He'll be there in three minutes."

"Hey, baby, baby, baby," a guy said to Cassy. He was holding a cup of coffee.

"Keep walking," she said.

"Skank," he said.

He tripped and fell, spilling his coffee all over himself.

"Did you do that?" McKenna asked Cassy.

"Does it matter?" Nichelle said.

"We should change out of these shirts," Cassy said. "We're drawing too much attention to ourselves."

"I feel freakish," Nichelle said. "Which is something, coming from me."

"I still can't believe you drew a mustache on that guy," Cassy said.

"It was funny, though, right?"

Cassy grinned. "Yeah."

Taylor said, "I wonder how long his coworkers will let him walk around with it without telling him. My dad said they did pranks like that at the police station all the time."

"Now that we know Abi's been taken, what do we do?" Nichelle asked.

"We find her," Taylor said.

"Where?" Cassy said. "She could be anywhere."

"If I were the Chasqui," Taylor said, "I would take her back to my stronghold with the others."

"Back to collecting electrics again," Nichelle said. "Nothing ever changes."

"It's like Elgen two-point-oh," Cassy said. "Only, this time, they know where everyone is."

"And this time we know we're being collected," Taylor said.

"They took Abi before they got Tara," McKenna said. "She's probably already in Puerto Maldonado."

"I need to call Michael and tell him what we found."

The van was waiting for them in a no-parking zone next to the curb. Clarence jumped out of the car and opened all the doors. After everyone was in, he said, "Welcome back, everyone. Did everything go all right?"

"Yes," Taylor said.

"But if the police start chasing us—don't stop," Nichelle said.

Clarence glanced back. "Really?"

Nichelle nodded. "Really."

Clarence still wasn't sure if Nichelle was joking, but he quickly pulled away from the curb.

"Is the plane coming back tonight?" McKenna asked.

"I don't know," Taylor said. "They didn't say when they'd be back. We need to let them know we're done here."

"The pilots are going to need to sleep," Ostin said. "They'll probably stay in Puerto tonight and leave early in the morning. Which means they'd be here around two o'clock tomorrow afternoon. We could be in Puerto by tomorrow night."

"So you're saying that we have tonight off," Nichelle said.

"Nothing more we can do here," Taylor said.

"Is anyone in the mood to go dancing?" Nichelle asked.

"How could you be in the mood to go dancing?" McKenna said. "Abi was kidnapped."

"*Three* of our friends were kidnapped," Cassy said.

"Keep it down," Taylor said. "We don't need Clarence hearing any of this."

"After what Nichelle said about the police chasing us, I think he's ignoring us."

"Dancing is how I cope with painful things," Nichelle said. "Or should I just go back to my room and sulk?"

"I'm sorry," McKenna said. "I'm just upset."

"I'll go dancing with you," Cassy said.

"As for me," Ostin said, even though no one asked, "I'm going back to my room to study these videos some more. There's got to be something we're missing."

"Just let me know where you're going," Taylor said. "In case something happens."

"Isn't that what the buttons are for?" Cassy asked.

"What are you doing tonight?" McKenna asked Taylor.

"I need to call Michael, then take a long hot bath. Or maybe get a massage."

"A massage sounds nice," McKenna said. "Really nice."

"I'll check with the concierge when we get back," Taylor said.

"Ostin, I have a question," Cassy said. "Who do you think that guy was who moved like the wind?"

"Not wind," Ostin said. "Light. Or lightning. Electricity and light are both forms of electromagnetic radiation. Waves of electricity travel at 670,616,629 miles per hour, or 186,000 miles per second, about ninety percent the speed of light."

"I thought Einstein said it was impossible to travel at the speed of light," Cassy said.

"Einstein never said that. It was James Maxwell who postulated that." Ostin scratched his head. "Traveling at the speed of lightning must be that Glow's electric gift."

"Why was he throwing up?" McKenna asked.

"Probably because the human body can't stand much more than nine g's."

"What's a g?" Nichelle asked.

"One g-force is equal to the gravity you are feeling right now. Have you ever been on a roller coaster?"

"Of course."

"You know that feeling when you suddenly make a steep drop and it pushes you back in the seat? You're pulling between three to five g's for a few seconds. So, nine g's would make you feel nine times heavier than you do now."

"Like I weighed a thousand pounds?" Cassy said.

"Yes. Only worse. Because g-forces affect every cell of your body, and your heart wasn't made to pump blood that heavy. Fighter jets like the F-16 can pull nine g's. The pilots can hold it for a while, but not too long. That's why they wear antigravity suits. The same is true of astronauts. The suit inflates to prevent blood from pooling in their feet and legs."

"So jumping to light speed is a problem," Nichelle said.

Ostin laughed. "Every time someone's being chased in space, they jump to light speed. The thing is, if you were really to accelerate that fast, you'd be crushed in your chair. It would feel like a train fell on you. Moving at the speed of electricity would create nearly thirty million g's. That's millions of times more than enough to kill you."

"Then how does that guy do it?"

"There's only one way I can see. When he travels, he must actually turn into electricity—the way Michael did on the tower. Einstein's theory of relativity proves that mass and energy are interconvertible, so his mass must convert to energy. Then, as he stops moving, he rematerializes back into mass.

"It's during that transition back that he must feel the g-forces. Even minimal g-forces can make you vomit. That's why there are barf bags on airplanes."

"I don't like the idea of an enemy moving that fast," Taylor said. "He'd be invincible."

"No one is invincible," McKenna said. "Even Superman has his Kryptonite."

"Superman isn't real," Nichelle said. "We are."

"I wonder how many other electrics there are," Cassy said.

"I hope we never find out," Taylor said. "But I'm glad we have Nichelle with us just in case."

Nichelle smiled. "It's nice to be needed."

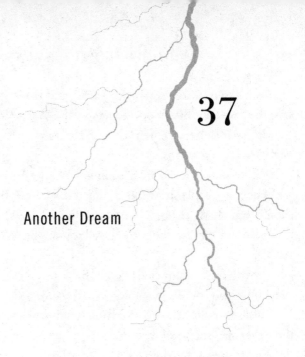

37

Another Dream

Taylor called Michael the moment she got back to her room. "Are you there yet?" she asked.

"We're still about thirty minutes out. Did you find anything?"

"Yes. We talked to Abi's roommates. One of them saw Abi, with her suitcase, talking to a couple of Peruvian men."

"How did she know they're Peruvian?"

"She lived in Lima, so she knew the dialect. Then we went to the police station to see the recordings from their cameras."

"The police let you see them?"

"No, we posed as university IT staff. The recordings confirmed what Abi's roommate said about Abi and the Peruvian men. We think they're electrics."

"Why?"

"They glowed red. And one of them could move like lightning."

"Like your dream," Michael said.

"Just like my dream," Taylor said. "And there's more. We're pretty sure that we saw Bryan and Kylee on the video."

Michael sighed. "Then they have her. When are you coming down?"

"We can leave now. How soon will the jet be back?"

"They were planning on flying out of here before sunrise. That should put them back in Texas around one."

"Then we can be there by tomorrow night. Will you wait for us?"

"Of course."

"I love you," Taylor said. "Say it back."

"I love you too."

Taylor hung up the phone, then went downstairs to meet up with the others in the hotel restaurant.

"Did you talk to Michael?" Ostin asked.

"We just hung up. They were about to land."

"What did he think about what we saw?"

"The same as us."

"Scared," Nichelle said.

After dinner, Nichelle and Cassy went out to find a club, while Ostin went to his room to study the videos, and McKenna and Taylor booked a massage and pedicure in the hotel spa.

That night Taylor had another dream, one that scared her more than any other dream she had had. She saw an entire town on fire. The flames were as high as the buildings and fanned by torrential winds. Everywhere people were screaming and dying. And there was nothing anyone could do to save them.

PART FOUR

38

An Unexpected Admirer

"**S**hall I remove the head bag from the captive, Your Eminence?"

"Please, Mr. Torrez."

Abductions were a routine event with the Chasqui, and the bag was especially designed for its use—fabricated from a heavy, canvas-like material that restricted all vision but allowed its occupant to breathe as long as he or she didn't overexert themselves. It was fastened around the neck by a three-inch-wide, double-thick leather collar that was riveted firmly with two heavy metal grommets on each end, connected by a heavy brass lock.

They had put the bag over Jack's head when he'd been captured at the Starxource plant outside the Peruvian mountain village of Acaray. Once Jack had been in the cell, they'd taken off his handcuffs but had left the bag on his head to keep him disoriented and vulnerable.

When he asked for something to drink, the guard threw a bottle of water into the cell, which Jack only knew because he heard it bounce on the stone floor.

"How am I supposed to drink with a bag over my head?" he shouted.

The guard replied in a thick Peruvian accent, "When you are thirsty enough, amigo, you will *figure* it out."

Jack lay on his back, pushed the bag into his mouth, and poured the water into the indentation he'd created. *It's like I'm waterboarding myself,* he thought. He choked at first, but eventually he got the hang of it. The water pooled in the bag, then slowly seeped through the fabric into his mouth. Even though the water tasted like the bag, it was still water.

Jack closed his eyes now as the bag was taken off his head, giving his eyes time to adjust to the room's bright lights.

Even with the bag over his head, Jack had known he was in a cave. The air was damp, and the stone walls of his cell had been cool, even in the jungle tropics, dripping with condensation.

The room he was now in was surprisingly luxurious and as sophisticated as his own office in the Veytric building. The walls were covered with screens and monitors, the wiring run through steel conduit drilled through the thick cave walls. It was at least triple the size of his cell, which he'd measured by walking the circumference with his hand on the wall.

Jack rubbed his eyes, then looked forward. The man in front of him was not Peruvian like his guards. Jack guessed he was from the Middle East. He was surprisingly handsome and well groomed, his beard neatly trimmed. He just gazed at Jack silently and intensely.

After a minute Jack asked, "What do you want?"

The man said softly, in perfect English, "Welcome, Jack Vranes."

"Where is my team?"

"They are fine, just fine. Even well cared for."

"Like I was?"

The man frowned. "I'm sorry for your inconvenience. We survive by reason of our stealth. As do you and your friends. Do you know who I am?"

"You're Elgen."

"No. We wore the Elgen uniform for a short while. But that was only a costume, one of many we have worn through the centuries. In the end, it is not the uniform that matters; it is the heart and mind of the one who wears it." He leaned forward. "But first, you must be hungry. It is difficult to think of lofty matters when our baser needs are unmet." He turned to one of the guards. "Please bring Mr. Vranes food worthy of his status."

"My status," Jack repeated. "What's that? Worms?"

The man looked at Jack with surprising empathy. "Oh, no, Mr. Vranes. You are admired here. In truth, I have admired you for some time. You see, the Chasqui—I will use that name since it is the one most familiar to you—the Chasqui admire, above all, valor and courage. In your fight against the Elgen, indeed, in your fight against your very upbringing, you have demonstrated both of those.

"I think you will agree that no matter what side of the battlefield you stand on, valor is valor and courage is courage. Even on his knees, the true warrior admires a worthy opponent, and you, my friend, are a worthy opponent."

A large wooden platter of food was brought in. There was fried rice with beer sausage, quinoa, and potatoes with cheese sauce on a bed of lettuce and fried onions. As hungry as he was, Jack didn't touch it.

"We would not poison you," he said. "If that is your fear. That would be cowardice. Not to mention pointless. Why would we go to the trouble to bring you all the way here, only to kill you?"

It's a fair question, Jack thought. Still, he didn't eat.

"Let me prove it to you. Point to something on your plate. Anything."

Jack pointed to the potatoes with cheese sauce. The man took the fork and stabbed it into the food and ate it, then set the fork back down. "Not bad. Papa a la Huancaína, a delicacy in my adopted country. Surprisingly, lettuce is not easily come by in the jungle. Please eat, Jack. I know you're hungry."

Jack couldn't remember how many days it had been since he'd eaten. He suddenly began to wolf down the food.

The man smiled. "Very good."

After Jack had eaten everything on the platter, the man said, "It is our way to be sure that all our guests have what they need."

"Don't you mean 'prisoners'?" Jack said.

"I leave the definition up to you," he said. "May we bring you more food?"

Jack wasn't sure what to make of this hospitality. Finally he nodded.

"Good. I would hate for you to still be hungry." The man said to one of the guards, "Bring our friend a new platter. And a chilled cerveza to soften his pain."

"Yes, Your Eminence."

The guard took the platter from before Jack.

"I can guess what you must be thinking. It is a peculiar thing to meet your enemy, is it not? To see them, not as the caricature you make of them but as the breathing, moving human they truly are. I have found myself in your place many, many times. And I still find it fascinating.

"There is a book . . ." His brow furrowed. "What is that book? I know, you do not like to read, not like your friend, the one they call Ostin, but it's a profound book. There is a chapter in the book where the man, a soldier of the First World War, finds himself in a foxhole with his enemy, watching him die, watching his humanity flowing from him as blood.

"After the man is dead, he takes the man's wallet and looks through the photographs of the man's family and his girl." His eyes narrowed. "You have a girl, Jack. One who matters to you. Her name is a pretty name. Abigail."

Jack's eyes flashed at the mention of her name. "You stay away from her."

"Jack. You don't understand. Not yet, but you will. You will." He breathed out. "Your girl is in no danger from us. We are not beasts.

"But back to my point. These two men in the foxhole together. Are they not, beneath the uniform, both men? Is not the color of their blood the same? In the final moment of his enemy's life, he realizes the truth, that they are not enemies, but chess pieces. It is the chess players who turn the pieces on each other. As the great Napoleon once said, 'We are kings or pawns. Kings or pawns.' Chess pieces.

"If these two men had met off the battlefield, not as soldiers but as men, they might have shared a fine meal together, lifted a drink together, maybe even shared a story or two.

"And in that moment, the man in the foxhole, not the soldier but the *man*, understands the truth, that, by a stroke of fate, he might have been the man dying next to him."

He shook his head. "Is this not us, Jack? Is this not how it is? I speak to you now not as a soldier, not as the Chasqui, or Elgen or whatever you will call me, but as a man.

"That is why I am confident in our eventual friendship, as you come to understand that we, our clan, are not pawns to be used and played by kings and tyrants. No. We are the masters of our fate. Which is why we are still here after centuries, while the kings and tyrants and empires have all come and gone."

At that moment the guards returned with more food and a stein of beer. The man nodded, and they set the food on the table in front of Jack.

"Keep eating, Jack. Please, and drink."

"Thank you," Jack said.

"You are welcome. I'm sorry it is not the fine food you have, no doubt, grown accustomed to in Italy. The Italians, they are magicians with their food, but we are in the jungle. We do what we can. I hope it is good enough for you."

Jack looked up at him. "How do you know so much about me?"

"Successful warriors study their opponent. If you know your enemy and yourself, you need not fear the result of a hundred battles."

"Why are you being so nice to me?" Jack asked.

"That is a good question. But I have a better one. Why would I not? Especially to one I admire."

"Why do you keep saying that?"

"Because it is true, Jack. Men like you are so hard to find. The discipline and loyalty and strength—the valor. Had you served in your country's military, I have no doubt that you would have been awarded the Medal of Honor. And what word is inscribed on that treasured medal? Just one. 'Valor.'"

The man's words had a powerful impact on Jack. It was the highest compliment he had ever been given.

The sovereign leaned forward and said softly, "Jack, I would take ten of you for a hundred of these mercenaries. These men who kill for money, which they exchange for base pleasures." He shook his head. "No, you and I, we are not such men." He lifted his forefinger in thought. "Which reminds me of a very serious matter, Jack. One of the gravest importance. Please, forgive me for reopening this painful wound. But you must know that we, the Chasqui, did not kill your friend Wade."

Jack stopped eating.

"No. I was very sorry for your loss. I can't imagine the pain that caused you. To the child, the parent may be the whole of his life, but it still will never match the love the parent has for the child. No. Wade loved you, admired you, almost worshipped you as a father. All he wanted in life was your approval and love. But you, Jack. Wade was like your child. You suffered more than he ever could, even in death. I am sincerely sorry for your loss."

"How do you know about Wade?"

"This is our land. We came here before the Elgen trespassed; we will be here long after the last remnants of the Elgen have gone. The Elgen were here by our permission, and part of our agreement was that any mortal action they took was reported to us." He shook his head. "I was not happy with the news I received of Wade's death.

"I only broach this painful episode to assure you that we did not take your friend from you. That would be unconscionable. We may have been on the opposite side of the chessboard, but we were not your enemies."

"What do you want from me?"

He looked at Jack for a moment, then smiled. "Straight to the point. I like that." He sat back. "I like that, my friend. I will answer in kind. I want three things from you, Jack. I have just three simple requests."

Jack looked at him. "What three things."

"First, I desire your respect."

"Why would you want my respect?"

"From a man as principled as you, it would be an honor."

"What's the second?"

"Your understanding. Of course, this is the path to my first desire. Once you understand us, I have no doubt that you will respect us. At the very least, you will respect our principles and mission."

Jack just looked at him. "And the third?"

"I know that this will seem much to ask, especially considering how you've been treated of late." He looked into Jack's eyes. "But even more than your respect, I desire your love. And, with it, your devotion."

The words echoed in the silence of the stone room. Then the sovereign stood. "I have looked forward to meeting you, Jack. There is another one of your tribe on her way to us. The one you call 'Taylor.'"

"You kidnapped Taylor?"

"No, no. We invited Taylor to our home. And soon the whole of your tribe will come to us. We hope to bring all of them into our tribe. And I sincerely hope that you will help us help them understand."

"I would never help you capture my friends."

"Jack, 'capture' is a hard word. But let's be honest. You already have helped us. By being captured, you made yourself bait. Your friends are already planning your rescue.

"But Taylor, we didn't bring her here as bait. We brought her here because of her special gift."

"Because she can reboot minds?"

The sovereign shook his head. "No. That trick of hers is a mere novelty. Her true gift is much greater. And one you might not even know she has. Your friend Taylor can see the future."

Jack just looked at him.

"Ah, you didn't know," he said, stroking his beard. "I'm not

completely surprised that you didn't know. It's a gift she's just coming to understand herself." He gestured to the guards. "That's enough
for now. Please return Mr. Vranes to his cell. Not that I prefer it, but
reason must dictate. There is still too much of the outside world in
you, Jack, to allow you to wander free. Am I not right? Would you
not try to escape? I would be disappointed if you said no."

Jack nodded. "I would."

"Of course you would. As would I. It is in our nature. But you
will be well taken care of. And this thing . . ." He lifted the hood.
"You will not wear it again. It is my sincere hope that in time, you
will walk free among us as a brother." He smiled. "Have a good night,
Jack."

He said to the guard, "Take Mr. Vranes back to his room. Bring
him in a real mattress and a fine alpaca blanket. Make sure he has
whatever he needs to be comfortable."

"Yes, Your Eminence."

The guard took Jack's arm. "Let's go."

"Oh, Jack."

Jack turned back to look at the man.

"I just remembered. The book I referenced earlier was called *All
Quiet on the Western Front*. I'll find you a copy. As a warrior, I think
you'll find it an interesting read."

"Thank you."

The guards didn't even handcuff him as they took him away.

PART FIVE

39

Remembering the Future

"**A** doubloon for your thoughts," Ian said, holding up a gold coin.

I looked up from the maps I'd been studying. "Do you always have those on you?"

"I always have at least one for good luck."

"I'd share my thoughts for free, but I'll take the coin, if you're really offering it."

"It's yours, my friend." He flipped me the coin. I caught it. "Like I said, it's lucky."

"Then I hope you brought a lot of them."

I hadn't really talked to Ian since we'd taken off in Fort Worth. I had been lying on the couch in the back of the plane looking over the maps of the Amazon jungle that my father had thrown in with the RADDs. Ian had been in the front of the plane reading reports of ancient shipwrecks while everyone else played cards.

No one would play cards with him. I can't blame them. It was kind of pointless, since he could read everyone's hands. Earlier, I overheard Quentin trying to convince Ian to give up hunting shipwrecks to play professional poker. Their conversation went something like this:

"Dude, you could make millions."

"I make millions."

"You would be famous."

"Why would I want to be famous? So I can pretend to be loved by people I don't know?"

"All right, then; you would be a legend. You would be known for all times as the greatest poker player in history."

"I'd rather uncover *real* legends from real history. Taking money from people isn't something I'd like to be known for."

Quentin exhaled. "I give up. You're too good-hearted. I guess that's why Hatch put you in Purgatory and not me."

So it went.

"Another rumble in the jungle?" Ian said to me.

I put down a map. "I'm afraid so."

"Remember the last time?"

"I wish I could forget. I was sure we were going to die."

"And now?"

"No idea. I'm not clairvoyant like Taylor."

"Tell me about that," Ian said. "You think these dreams she's having have something to do with her electricity?"

"I do. So does Ostin. He says that electricity, time, and space are all interconnected."

Ian nodded. "Someone once asked the great physicist Stephen Hawking what in life most baffled him. He said, 'Other than my wife, I don't understand why we can't remember the future.' Maybe it's as simple as that and Taylor does remember it." He frowned. "Does it ever scare you?"

"Sometimes." I exhaled. "It seems like the dreams that come to her are always frightening. I wish that sometime she'd just have a dream where we're sitting around laughing."

"Maybe she only dreams of intense things because that's what stands out. It's like a movie trailer. They pick the most dramatic clips to pique your interest. Maybe that's how her mind works as well."

"Maybe," I said. "Maybe."

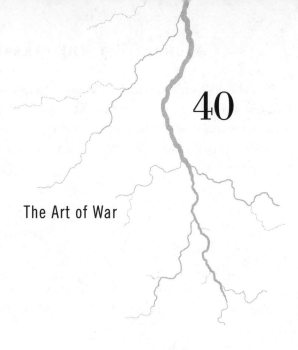

40

The Art of War

The skies above Puerto Maldonado and the neighboring jungle were covered with clouds for as far as I could see, like a great foam lake above the world.

"Prepare for landing," Captain Scott said over the jet's PA system.

"Showtime," Zeus said.

I said to Ian, "Keep your eyes open."

It was already several hours after sunset when we touched down on the airport's runway. The small airstrip was lit by a few lights off the side of the fenced field, which separated the tarmac from the jungle. It was the tail end of the rainy season, and the concrete landing strip was spotted with puddles of water.

We taxied for only a couple of minutes before coming to a stop in front of the airport's metal-walled terminal building. Across the top of the building were the words:

AEROPUERTO INTERNACIONAL PADRE ALDAMIZ PUERTO MALDONADO

A bright green flag with a yellow diagonal line flew over the building.

"Anything, Ian?" I asked.

"Just some motorcycle taxis," he said. "A coca leaf merchant."

"What about the jungle?"

"Jungle creatures," he said. "No humans."

As the jet powered down, Captain Boyd emerged from the cockpit.

"We're here, folks. I'll lower the stairs, then meet you outside with your luggage." He opened the door. A rush of the jungle's warm, moist air filled the plane.

"Welcome back to the jungle," Tessa said.

I had forgotten that Tessa had been living in the jungle when I found her. Or vice versa.

"Bring back memories?" she asked.

"A few I'd rather not have."

As I looked out over the tarmac, a bright yellow-orange object fluttered by like a massive lightning bug.

"Did you see that?"

"I'm not sure what I saw," Tessa said. "What was it?"

"I think it was an electric bat."

"It was," Ian said. "Fascinating."

At the top of the airstair Zeus said, "*Internacional*. If this is an international airport, then I'm a god."

I turned to him. "Aren't you?"

Zeus laughed. "I love you, man."

Just then two white utility vans with tinted windows pulled up to a closed gate near the side of the terminal. The gate began lifting.

"Ian? Who is that?"

"Five men—three in the front van, two in the back. Heavily armed. Automatic weapons."

"But are they ours?"

"They're not Peruvian. They've got American and Israeli weapons."

When the gate was vertical, the vans started toward us.

"Zeus, Quentin, get ready."

"On it, boss," Quentin said. "I can stop them from here."

"Not yet. Tessa, back us up."

"You're Tessa powered," she said.

I held up my hands like a preacher and prepared to pulse. The vans abruptly stopped.

"Was that you?" I asked Quentin.

"Nope."

The first vehicle flashed its lights three times. Then the passenger-side door opened and a Black man, wearing a stocking cap, stepped out. He was smiling and holding his hands up, as if surrendering. "Michael. Don't shoot."

I dropped my hands. "David." I turned back to my people. "We're good. It's Alpha Team." I walked down the airstair to the field as Johnson walked toward me. We shook hands, then embraced.

"How long have you been here?" I asked.

"We got in last night. We staked out the airfield about four hours ago."

"How are things?"

"Quiet. No sign of Chasqui." He looked around. "But we're vulnerable here. Let's get your things and get out of here."

He signaled to the vans, and both pulled up to the plane. The men got out of the van and helped us unload, taking everything from the plane to the vans.

"You got the RADDs?" Johnson asked.

"Yeah. They're in those three cases, one big, two small."

Captain Boyd stuck his head out from the cargo hold. "Looks like you got everything."

"Thanks. We'll see you tomorrow night."

Johnson said, "This is Luther. He'll be guarding the jet tonight."

Luther was short and muscular, with red hair and sharp facial features. He had an AR-15 hanging from his shoulder. He waved to Johnson, then climbed into the jet. After he was inside, the airstair folded back up into the plane and the jet taxied off toward a small, red-tin-roofed hangar on the side of the airfield.

Ian and I climbed into the first van with Johnson and one other member of his team. As we drove off, Johnson said to his man, "Jax, this is Michael and Ian. Men, this is Jax."

We shook hands.

Johnson continued. "Michael's the team leader, and Ian . . . has good vision." He turned to Ian. "Keep an eye out. The Chasqui know we're here."

"How do you know?" Ian asked.

"They know everything that happens in this town. They've learned from the drug lords to take care of the locals. They pay for the hospital and the church, and most of the police are on their payroll. At Christmas they distribute tons of free food and American toys in the plaza—they've bought and paid for the town's loyalty. They've got a thousand pairs of eyes watching out for them."

"It must be nice to be loved," I said.

Johnson grinned. "I'm just saying watch your back."

"That's my job," Ian said.

Three miles from the airport, the van turned down a long mud-and-dirt road. Every few yards there were huge potholes filled with water. Some of them were almost as wide as the van.

"You could swim in some of those," I said.

"Yeah," Johnson said. "The locals aren't big on road maintenance during the rainy season."

We drove for more than twenty minutes, past old buildings and tin sheds, most of them abandoned. At one point we passed a flock of vultures devouring something by the side of the road.

"Where are we going?" I asked.

"We've got a safe house just outside town. It's not the Four Seasons, but the Chasqui don't know about it."

"How long have we had a safe house here?"

"Longer than you think. The Amazon Starxource plant wasn't just the first one built by the Elgen; it was also the central training point for the Elgen guard. Back then you couldn't walk through the airport without running into Elgen. The resistance wanted to keep an eye on their activities, so they took over an old warehouse and made it into a safe house."

"You mean, you were down here when we attacked the Starxource plant?"

"A few of us were. Where do you think Jaime came from?"

"It's been a while since I've heard that name. I wonder what he's up to."

"You can ask him yourself when you see him."

"Jaime's here?"

"This is where he's from."

The safe house was actually several large metal buildings disguised as a warehouse and shipping office for a castaña nut wholesaler. The buildings had several lookout places and were surrounded by a brick-and-stucco wall topped with razor wire. It reminded me of the place we'd stayed at in Kaohsiung, Taiwan, after rescuing Jade Dragon. It was far enough away from the town that any vehicle in the area would raise suspicion.

"This was government-owned land until about ten years ago," Johnson said. "When it was forcibly seized by the people. There are a lot of illicit activities going on around here."

An automatic gate opened, and both vans pulled in. After we were inside the yard, the gates shut and the overhead doors of the warehouse opened in front of us. The vans pulled in. No one got out until all the doors had shut behind us.

"Welcome to Chez Vey," Johnson said, grinning. *"Mi casa su casa."*

"Gracias," I said.

As we got out, Johnson asked, "You guys hungry?"

"Not really," I said. "There was a lot of food on the plane."

"You gotta love the Gulfstream. That's traveling in style," he said. "Here, not so much. The beds are barrack style. But there's a private room for you."

"I'll stay with the others," I said.

Johnson nodded in approval. "'Treat your men as you would your own beloved sons. And they will follow you into the deepest valley.'"

"Is that from Sun Tzu?"

"Yes."

"Jack said you loved quoting him." I grabbed my bag. Then, as I began to walk toward the house entrance, a familiar face greeted me.

"Michael Vey, the legend."

"Jaime," I said.

"What trouble you have caused since I saw you last."

We embraced. "It's good to see you too," I said.

"Come in. When I heard you were coming, I prepared my famous *piña leche*. Or was it Inca Kola you liked?"

"I'll take both," I said.

We took our things to our rooms; then everyone gathered in the large rec room next to the kitchen. It had a foosball table and a large television with cabinets filled with DVDs.

"So this is where you live," I said to Jaime.

"Since the beginning. Even before I met the voice."

"You knew who the voice was all along?"

"No. They were too smart to tell me."

"Jaime cooks for us when we're here," Johnson said. "Otherwise he keeps an eye on the place."

"And I grow a garden," Jaime said. He brought over a bowl of ceviche and set it on the table next to the drinks he'd already brought in.

"All right," Johnson said. "Let's get down to business. We were boots on the ground in Acaray four days ago. The Peruvian military had sent in forces to restore the power grid, so we weren't surprised that the Chasqui were gone. We looked around for clues but didn't find anything. Since we suspected the Chasqui, we decided to head down here to see if we could find our people. We were near Arequipa when we got word that Abigail and Tara had been abducted."

"So awful," Jaime said, shaking his head.

"We hoped to intercept them before they got into the jungle. We had Jaime and some of his men stake out the airport and the mouth of the river, but they didn't see any movement from the Chasqui.

"Once we arrived, we spelled off his team. We have a man on the river right now. Gunnar. He's got night-vision capability, so if the Chasqui try to smuggle them in the dark, he'll see them."

"No word from him so far?" I asked.

"No. It's been quiet."

"What about the Chasqui? Any sign of them in town?"

"No, but we might not know it if we saw them. They don't wear uniforms into town. They're not even permitted to say who they are. The Chasqui are, as the natives say, *fantasmas*. Ghosts. They've survived as ghosts for centuries. If it wasn't for their charitable endeavors, the people in Puerto probably wouldn't even know they're here. Hatch didn't know half the things they know."

"You've done your research on the Chasqui," I said.

"It's the first law of war." Johnson took a drink of pineapple milk. "What do you hear from the rest in your group? I understand they went to Texas."

"They've completed their mission," I said. "They secured video of Abi's abductors. They were Peruvian. And they appear to be electrics."

Johnson's brow fell. "Peruvian electrics?"

"We recognized two of them as Hatch's Glows Kylee and Bryan. The others we didn't know existed."

"Interesting," Johnson said. "How did they determine they're electric?"

"They glowed like us. Taylor said that one of them moved like lightning."

"Fascinating. The Chasqui never had much interest in the Glows. It was Hatch and the Domguard who were obsessed with them. More Glows could be a problem."

"Fortunately, Nichelle's in the next group. She'll be valuable if the Glows are here."

"She's the one with RESAT powers?"

"Yes."

He rubbed his chin. "When are they coming?"

"As soon as they can get here. The pilots will pick them up tomorrow afternoon and head back down. They'll probably arrive close to the same time we did tonight."

"According to the dossier your father sent me, there's some serious firepower in that group."

"There is. Taylor can reboot people's minds. McKenna can heat herself to more than three thousand kelvins. Cassy is the most powerful. She can freeze people. In Taiwan she froze an entire schoolyard and an Elgen platoon for about ten minutes."

"I met Cassy once," Johnson said. "In Switzerland. I was told there were five in Dallas. That's only four. Who am I missing?"

"Ostin."

"Ostin. What's his power?"

"He's not electric. He's just crazy smart."

"He's the one Jack told me about. Smart and a touch socially awkward."

"That's him," Tessa said.

"He's gotten us out of more scrapes than I can remember," I said.

"It's better to think your way to a victory than to fight your way to one."

"Sun Tzu again?" I asked.

Johnson smiled. "No. That one's mine."

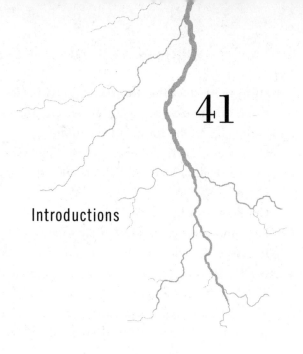

41

Introductions

"It's important that everyone here knows who they're working with. With your permission, Michael, I'll start the introductions."

I nodded. "Go ahead."

"Alpha Team is made up of six men, all former special forces. You saw Luther at the airport. He's the one we left with the jet. He's a former Navy SEAL, as is Gunnar. You haven't met Gunnar yet; he's currently in the jungle keeping an eye on the river.

"The other three besides me are Jax, Bentrude, and Cibor." He pointed to a thick-chested African American man who had been in the van with us. "This is Jax from Waco, Texas. Jax is a decorated Army Ranger and someone you want by your side in a firefight."

Jax nodded humbly.

"To his left, that tall drink of water is Bentrude. He's also an Army Ranger and one very tough hombre."

"Hi, all."

"And this scary man here," Johnson said, pointing to the soldier seated directly across from him, "is Cibor."

Cibor was as tall as Bentrude, but more slightly built. His head was shaved, and he had thick dark brows and a cleft chin.

"Hello," Cibor said.

"You might guess from his accent that he's not from around these parts. He's from Kraków, Poland. He served with the elite Jednostka Wojskowa 2305, better known as the JW GROM."

"And for those I haven't met, I'm David Johnson, commander of Alpha Team. I'm a former Green Beret." He looked around at his men. "This is a strong team, one I'm proud of. All of us have been tested by fire." I could tell there was more to that simple statement than he let on. He slowly breathed out. "Speaking of tested by fire, Michael, tell us about your team."

"First, we're honored to be working with you," I said. "I'm Michael. This is Quentin, Ian, Tessa, and Zeus.

"Quentin can create powerful EMPs, which means he can shut down pretty much any electronic device."

"I break things," Quentin said. "That's my gift."

"Ian has incredible vision. He can see through walls, jungle, you name it. He can see more than two miles away."

"Pleasure," Ian said.

"Tessa, our lone woman for now, has the ability to amplify our electric powers."

"I just bring out the best in these boys," she said.

"Zeus, like his namesake, has the power to shoot lightning."

"I'd like to see that," Cibor said. "If you don't mind."

"Happy to oblige," Zeus said. He pointed toward the door. With a loud crack, electricity shot from his hand to the doorknob.

Even though they had heard about his power, it's not the same as actually seeing it.

"Wow," Cibor said. "That is amazing."

"How far can you shoot that?" Bentrude asked.

"About fifty yards," Zeus said.

"Zeus once shot a bullet out of the air," I said. "He saved my life."

"What is your power, Michael?" Bentrude asked.

"I'm kind of a jack-of-all-trades," I said. "I do what I call 'pulse.' It's like sending out an electric shock wave."

"Not to be confused with what I do," Quentin said. "My pulse hurts machines; Michael's hurts everything."

Jax said, "I heard that you once pulsed so hard that you wiped out an entire island."

"That was a bit more than me," I said. "I channeled a lightning strike."

"Good to know," he said. "I'll stay away from you in a lightning storm."

I grinned. "I'll introduce the rest of our team when they arrive."

Johnson said, "I believe we should always go at the enemy with as much firepower as we can muster. That being said, I think we should wait for the rest of your team before we move into the jungle. Do you agree, Michael?"

"I agree," I said. "This is primarily a rescue mission. For many of us, it's personal as well. We've been sent down here to find and liberate Jack, Tara, and Abigail, as well as the other captives from our northern Starxource plant. Jack is a good friend of mine, as well as yours. We've also been assigned to gather intelligence. We want to know why the Chasqui are suddenly on the move again and what they're up to.

"In accomplishing our objectives, we are facing two major obstacles. The most obvious being, we don't know where the captives are. We have zero intelligence on their movement. For that matter, we're not even one hundred percent sure that it is the Chasqui who have abducted them. Still, it is the logical assumption. If it was the Chasqui, it is likely that they will take our friends back to the abandoned Starxource plant. But even that might not be the case."

"Where else would they take them?" Tessa asked.

"Caves," Quentin said.

Johnson looked at him. "Yes. The Chasqui have a headquarters in the jungle. We believe that it is in a cave. Or a network of them."

"Finding them in a cave will be like finding a needle in a haystack," Bentrude said.

"No," Johnson said. "It will be more like finding a needle in a hay-field. The Amazon jungle is almost seven million square kilometers, with millions of acres of uncharted territory. These are caves that have remained concealed for thousands of years. Up until a few decades ago, explorers didn't even know there were caves in the Amazon. If the Chasqui have the captives there, the RADDs may be our only hope in finding them."

"Tessa has been to their cave," I said.

Johnson looked at her. "You know where their cave headquarters are?"

"No. I was too young to remember. It was all just more jungle to me. But it was less than an hour on foot from the plant."

"That is helpful," Johnson said. He glanced down at his watch. "It's late. We should get some rest. We need to spell off Gunnar in the morning." He turned to me. "While we wait for your friends, we'll take a scouting trip up the river to see what we can find. Now that we have a better idea of their cave's whereabouts, we can send up the RADD drone. We might get lucky."

"Won't they see us?" Quentin asked.

"They might, but hopefully they won't know it's us. We have a craft disguised as a tourist boat, and there are enough tourists moving up and down the river that the Chasqui don't pay much attention to them. The Madre de Dios is a thoroughfare, and there's more traffic along the river than you might think. Besides tourism, there's farm-ing, logging, and gold mining. Not to mention drug running.

"We'll take just a few of us—perhaps two of us and three of you." He asked me, "Who would you recommend, Michael?"

"If it's just reconnaissance, Tessa and Ian."

"Very well." He stood. "For now, everyone sleep well. The next few days will be busy, so rest while you can. Have a good night."

We all went to our rooms. I took the bunk beneath Zeus.

I had just closed my eyes when Zeus asked, "Do you think they're being held at the plant?"

"I don't know."

"Do you think we'll find them?"

"I'm sure we will. I just hope the Chasqui don't find us first."

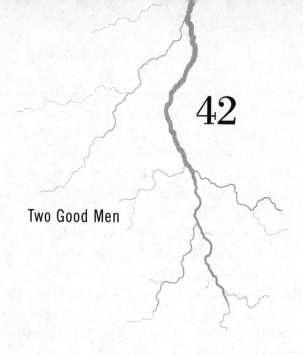

42

Two Good Men

I woke around five thirty to hushed talking outside my door. I pulled on some pants, then walked out to investigate. Johnson, his men, and Jaime were in the kitchen. All but Bentrude and Jaime were dressed for combat.

"What's going on?" I asked.

Johnson looked over at me. "Ten minutes ago, we got distress signals from both Luther and Gunnar. We're going out to find them."

"Do they have buttons too?"

"We all have buttons."

"I'll come with you," I said. I went back to the room and quickly dressed. When I returned, Johnson handed me a bulletproof vest. "You'll want this."

"I don't need it," I said.

"Don't be cavalier."

"I'm not. I'm electric."

"I'll take it," Ian said, walking into the kitchen. "I'm not bullet-proof."

"There's already four of us," Johnson said.

"He'll be useful," I said to Johnson.

He handed Ian the vest. "We'll leave everyone else here to protect the place."

I woke Quentin to let him know that he was in charge; then five of us climbed into the same van we'd come in. Jax took the wheel.

"Go to the airport first," Johnson said. "We need to make sure the jet got off okay. We'll grab Luther, then head up the river for Gunnar."

The men were quiet as we drove through the predawn twilight back across town to the airport. Everything was dark, including the airport. As we neared the airport, I said, "Ian, do you see anyone?"

"Just a lot of monkeys."

The gate opened, and Jax pulled the van onto the tarmac and parked it next to the hangar. Johnson grabbed his rifle. "Let's go in."

"There's no one inside," Ian said.

"The plane?"

"It's gone."

The hangar door was locked, so Jax kicked it in. Then he reached in and turned on the lights. As Ian had said, the jet was gone. So was Luther.

"Luther!" Johnson shouted. There was no reply. "Something's not right. The GPS says he's still here." He panned the handheld around the room while the rest of us walked through, inspecting the place.

On the far side of the hangar a table was knocked over and there were several broken bottles on the cement floor, next to a pool of blood. The blood was streaked across the floor as if someone had been dragged through it.

Jax crouched down and lifted something from the floor. "It's a button."

He examined it more closely. "There's blood on it . . . and flesh."

"They cut it off his arm," Johnson said fiercely. He took the button from Jax, wiped the blood off with his sleeve, and then put the button into his shirt pocket.

"Look at this, sir," Cibor said, lifting a pistol from the floor. "It was Luther's."

"Has it been fired?"

Cibor popped the cartridge from the gun. "Once."

Johnson's expression was hard. "Let's go find Gunnar."

Gunnar had been dropped off on the north bank of the river, about a mile east of Puerto Maldonado. Then he'd hiked deeper into the jungle. Following the GPS, we drove about three miles past where Johnson said the drop-off point was.

"Be alert," Johnson said. "This could be an ambush."

"It's hard to ambush Ian," I said.

Ian nodded. "I'm watching."

We drove east along an increasingly muddy road until it dead-ended at a wall of jungle about a kilometer past what Johnson said was the Kawsay Biological Station. We got out of the van. The jungle was a deafening cacophony of insect life—loud enough that it was almost hard to hear each other. Johnson held the GPS out in front of him.

"He's close."

"Gunnar must have hiked about seven kilometers past the drop-off," Jax said. "He was in deep."

"I don't like this," Johnson said. He turned to Ian. "Anything?"

"No."

"Be aware."

We hiked farther into the jungle, pushing back the vegetation. Bugs burned off me, leaving a pungent trail of smoke.

"Bugs catch on fire on you," Cibor whispered.

"I know."

"And you glow."

"I know that, too."

Johnson suddenly crouched down and whispered, "The readout says he's just thirty meters ahead of us. You sure there's no one?"

"There's no one," Ian said. "And no body. I'm sure of it." He cocked his head. "But there's something on the ground."

"What is it?"

He squinted. "Maybe a dead animal. There's a lot of blood."

We pressed forward, Johnson, Jax, and Cibor holding their guns in front of them. We came to a slight clearing where the vegetation was crushed down and there were footprints in the mud. Johnson held out his flashlight. On the edge of the grass indentation was what Ian had seen—a grotesque mass surrounded by a black pool of blood. Whatever it was, it was still wet, glistening beneath the glow of the moon. I could smell the stringent odor of death. Johnson and I both got down on our knees to better examine the spot. Near the center of the gore was a blood-covered button.

"That is a human stomach," Ian said.

Johnson looked up at him. "How can you tell?"

"I know what stomach tissue looks like. That grayish matter is membrane. It's the stomach's inner lining. He must have swallowed the button, so they wouldn't find it."

"But they did," Johnson said. "They cut it out of his stomach."

"They cut out his whole stomach," Jax said.

We were all silent as the revelation of Gunnar's death settled on us.

"I can track these footprints," Ian said.

"They'll just lead to the river. They would have come by boat." Johnson looked around. "No matter, we should get back to the others."

I stared out into the jungle. The yowl of howler monkeys echoed through the humid air, like a prehistoric moan. The jungle was frightening to me again. It was a gladiator's arena—a perpetual battle of life and death, predators and prey. Even for us.

Johnson kept his head down as we walked back to the van. I heard him say, "They've been one step ahead of us the entire way."

43

Losing

We drove back to the compound in silence as the sun began to rise above the jungle. I could feel the heaviness Johnson was holding. He had just lost two men under his command. But Luther and Gunnar weren't just fellow soldiers; they were his friends. Add to that the pervasive sense of doom we now felt, and our mood was as dark as the heart of the jungle. We knew the score. The Chasqui were winning.

It was nearly seven thirty when we got back to the compound. Everyone was in the kitchen and dining area except for Quentin. The mood in the room darkened with our return, like a curtain being drawn.

"You didn't bring anyone back," Zeus said.

"No," I said. "Where's Q?"

"He's in the exercise room. What's going on, brother?"

"Just get Q. Meeting in the rec hall in five minutes."

Zeus ran off. Less than a minute later Zeus returned with

Quentin. He was wearing exercise shorts and a sleeveless tee. He looked upset.

"What happened, Michael?"

"We're about to tell you," Johnson said. "Take a seat."

Johnson and I stood at the front of the room.

"We lost two men this morning," Johnson said. "Luther and Gunnar."

There was an audible gasp.

"We received a distress signal from both of their buttons at around five thirty a.m. We went to the airport. Luther was gone. Then we went to the jungle to find Gunnar. He was gone too."

"Are they alive?" Quentin asked.

"We don't know. The Chasqui don't leave bodies. But it's not likely. There was a lot of blood. We found both of their buttons. Luther's had been cut off his skin. Gunnar's was cut from his stomach." He knit his fingers together. "They cut out his whole stomach."

Tessa looked like she wanted to throw up.

"What about the pilots?" Tessa asked.

". . . And the jet," Quentin added.

Bentrude said, "We've been in contact with the pilots. They radioed in about an hour ago. Everything was normal."

"The Chasqui must have attacked right after the jet took off," Johnson said.

"Thank goodness they got away," Tessa said.

"At least we've had one bit of luck," Bentrude said.

The room fell into the silence of despair.

"Now what?" I asked.

Johnson rubbed his eyes, then looked at me. "We shouldn't go up the river today. It's too dangerous." I could tell he was in deep pain. "I need to think about this. I'm going back to my room. Bentrude, keep an eye out."

"Roger that."

No one spoke as he disappeared down the hall.

I was glad that the pilots had gotten off safe and were headed back to Texas. But now I didn't want them to bring Taylor and the others back. Somehow this felt more dangerous than even the Elgen. With the Elgen we'd known what we were fighting. And why.

44

Troubling Thoughts

For the next several hours I just lay on my bunk. I had had less than four hours of sleep the night before, and not much the night before that, but I still couldn't sleep. The horrific images we'd seen that morning kept replaying through my mind like a broken DVD.

Finally I gave up. I got out of bed and went to Johnson's room. I lightly rapped on his door. "Johnson?"

"Come in." His voice was hoarse.

I opened the door. Johnson was sitting cross-legged on his bed, his eyes closed as if he were meditating. On the bed next to him was a Bible.

"David?"

He opened his eyes. They were filled with sadness.

"I'm sorry to bother you."

"It's okay." He motioned to the chair near his desk. "Take a seat."

I pulled the chair out and sat down.

"Are you okay?" I asked. The words sounded as stupid as they were.

"It's like Niger again," he said softly. He slowly shook his head. "This is insane. We're trying to defeat an enemy who knows everything we're going to do before we do it. This is a suicide mission."

"You're right," I said.

"No, man, nothing's right."

I breathed out slowly. "Like you said, the Chasqui know everything we're going to do before we do it. I don't think it was luck that our plane got away. I think they let it go."

"Why would they do that?"

"It was serving their purpose."

He looked at me quizzically. "What's that?"

"Bringing down the rest of the Electroclan."

He slowly nodded. "That's possible.

"But if that's true, it raises an even bigger question. How did they know that we weren't all on that first flight?"

Johnson looked puzzled. "I didn't think of that."

"And the buttons . . . it doesn't make sense, especially Gunnar's button."

"Gunnar swallowed his button because he's a warrior. He knew he would be captured, so he swallowed the button to lead us to them."

"But how did the Chasqui know he swallowed the button?"

"They must have seen him do it."

"How? He wouldn't have let them see him, would he? He would have at least tried to hide it, right?"

Johnson nodded. "He would have concealed his action."

"And even if they did see him swallow something, they wouldn't have known what it was. It was as if they knew what they were looking for. And after they found it, they just left it." I looked at him. "If you had found a device like that, would you have thrown it away? Especially after seeing your enemy try to hide it?"

"No. I would have taken it back to examine."

"The only reason they would have thrown away something that their target tried to hide would be if they already knew it was a tracking device."

Johnson looked at me, his eyes wide. "They knew about the buttons."

I nodded. "I think it's more than that. The jungle's a big place. Gunnar was skilled in jungle warfare. How did they find him?"

"I don't know. We didn't even know exactly where he was."

"I don't think the Chasqui just know about the buttons. I think they're tracking us with them. That would explain everything, including how they knew we weren't all on the plane."

"How could they have access to them?"

"They would have to have someone inside the company. That's how they've been ahead of us the whole time. If someone has infiltrated Veytric, our phones are probably bugged too."

"Which phones?"

"The satellite phones. Maybe my father's cell phone."

"If they know where we are right now, why haven't they already attacked?"

"The same reason they let the plane leave. They want all of us."

"Then they're waiting for the rest of your team."

I nodded. "We need to send them back." I reached behind my ear and tore the button from my skin. It stung. I set it on the desk in front of me.

"I need to ask my father about these," I said. As I lifted the satellite phone, Johnson shook his head. I set it back down. "You're right. I can't use this. Do you have regular cell phone service here?"

"It's a little spotty but it usually works."

I went to my room to get my own cell phone. I called my mother. She answered on the first ring.

"Michael. Why are you calling from your cell phone?"

"Our satellite phones might have been bugged. I think Dad's cell phone is bugged too. Is he home?"

"No, he's at the office."

"I need you to go there and get him out of the office. Don't trust anyone. Don't talk to anyone. No one. Just say you're taking him to lunch or something personal, and then call me from your phone."

"Michael, what's going on?"

"Two members of Alpha Team were killed this morning. The Chasqui know everything we're doing."

"I'll go right now."

About a half hour later my phone rang.

"Michael?" It was my father. "What's going on?"

"Just a moment," I said. "Let me get Johnson." I walked back to Johnson's room. "It's my father."

I put the phone on speaker. "We lost two men this morning," I said.
"Who?"

"Luther and Gunnar," Johnson said.

"They're both dead?"

"It's likely. We know Gunnar is dead, but we're not sure about Luther. The Chasqui don't leave bodies."

"What happened?"

"Luther was at the hangar guarding the plane and Gunnar was in the jungle. The Chasqui knew exactly where they were." I breathed out heavily. "The buttons you gave us, is there any way to track them other than the handhelds? Is there a way to hack into them?"

"No. They're tied directly to the handhelds. Each button has a special code only recognized by the handheld."

"Are there more trackers than the three you gave Johnson and me?"

"No, the lab just created the three." He hesitated. "Wait. There were two prototypes. But they're locked in my safe."

"Are you sure?"

"Not now. Let me go back to my office. I'll call you back."

Ten minutes later my phone rang.

"They've been stolen."

"Then we have been compromised," I said. "Who could have taken them from your safe?"

"I don't know. But you've got to get rid of the buttons before the Chasqui find you."

"It's too late for that. They've been tracking us since we landed. What about team one? Can their buttons be tracked on the jet?"

"The buttons can be tracked anywhere on the planet."

"Then the Chasqui will be waiting for the rest of our team to land. We need to change team one's flight."

"Where are they now?" my father asked.

"Taylor texted that they left Dallas around two our time. They should land around ten p.m." I checked my watch. "That's about five hours from now. How much farther can the jet go without refueling?"

"Not enough to turn back. They're going to have to refuel in Peru."

I turned to Johnson. "Hand me that map." He handed me a map. I spread it out on his desk. "Could they reach La Paz?"

"Bolivia? They could do that. Should I radio Scott?"

"Not yet," I said. "We don't know who the leak inside the company is. For all we know, it could be the pilots."

"That would explain why the Chasqui let them escape," Johnson said.

"I'm going to make sure my satellite phone hasn't been bugged. Then I'll call Taylor when they're an hour out of Puerto and have them change the flight just before landing, to throw the Chasqui off. Is there a way to temporarily block the buttons?"

"I'd take a hammer to all of them," my father said. "But if you just want to temporarily block them, you'll need a Faraday cage or some kind of lead box."

"Would a lead pipe work?" I asked.

"That would work."

"All right. And don't forget to check all your phones for bugs. Including this one."

"I'll do that right now," my father said. "Keep me updated on your plans."

"I will. Bye." I hung up the phone.

"Do you still plan to meet up with the others tonight?" Johnson asked.

"Yes."

"Then La Paz is too far. It's nearly fourteen hours by car. And if the Chasqui catch wind of your plan, it would be easy for them to lay a trap on the road."

"What other options do we have?"

"There's an old dirt airstrip near Sudadero. It was used by drug smugglers. It's only thirty kilometers from Puerto. The buttons don't show altitude, so it would take the Chasqui a few minutes to realize that the jet had already landed, then at least another forty minutes to reach us. By then, the pilots could have landed and taken off again. And we would be long gone."

"Gone where?"

"I know a place we can go. There's a woman who lives on the outskirts of Puerto Maldonado. She has a private zoo with animals she has saved from the jungle. Her zoo is fenced in. It's far from the town, and it's on a hill, so we could see anyone approaching for miles."

"We can trust her?"

"Yes. She hates the Elgen. Maybe more than we do."

"We'll need to give the pilots the exact coordinates of the airstrip. But only at the last possible moment. One more thing. Do you know how to check the satellite phone for a bug?"

"Cibor can. He's an expert at tech."

"Let's see what he can find."

45

Coconut Oil and Buttons

As I suspected, there had been a spy chip implanted in the satellite phone.

Cibor handed me the small bronze chip. "Whoever did this had access to your phone."

"We could check it for fingerprints," I said. "Ian can see them."

"It's not worth your time. If someone's smart enough to install this, they're smart enough to wear gloves."

"You can bet Taylor's satellite phone is bugged as well. I'm sure Ostin could remove it. The trick is, how do I tell them their phone is bugged on a bugged phone, without the Chasqui knowing it?"

As I pondered the dilemma, I decided to call my mother's phone to tell her that we had found a bug.

"We found them on our end too," she said. "Your father just picked up a new cell phone. I have the number if you want to call him."

"He picked it up himself, or did someone else?"

"I think he had Marius pick it up."

"We can't trust anyone. Not even Marius. Would you take your phone back to him?"

"Whatever you need. It will take me a half hour."

"I'll wait. Have him take the new phone to his techs to check for a bug."

"You can't think Marius is the spy?"

"I hope not, but who else has that kind of access?"

"You're right. We'll call you as soon as we know."

While I waited for my father's call, Johnson and I again gathered everyone together.

"The Chasqui have been ahead of us the whole time," I said. "We've just found out why. There was a bug in my satellite phone. We think they've bugged the satellite phones. In addition, they've also been tracking us through the buttons. That's how they found Luther and Gunnar."

At the mention of their names, Jaime made the sign of the cross on his chest.

"You mean they're tracking our buttons right now?" Quentin said.

"Yes. I've already taken mine off."

Everyone started reaching for their buttons.

"If you stuck it to your skin, like I did, we've got some coconut oil to help dissolve the glue on back. And remember, do not press the buttons. They're still active."

"I have oil here," Cibor said, holding up two bottles.

"I'll take one," Quentin said. "We'll do you first," he said to Tessa.

Tessa pulled up her hair, and Quentin poured some oil around the disk, then removed it.

"I'll help you with yours," Tessa said.

Quentin grinned. "No you won't. It's not real . . . accessible." He took off his belt as he walked out of the room. He returned a minute later holding the button. "What should we do with them?"

"Burn them," Tessa said.

"Not yet," I said. "Put them in here." I pointed to a woven basket sitting on the end table. "The Chasqui already know where we are, so having the buttons can't do any more damage than they already have. We might be able to use them to our advantage."

"Are they tracking the others?" Tessa asked.

"We should assume so. We think that's why the Chasqui haven't already attacked. They're waiting for everyone else to get here."

"Then they need to turn back," Tessa said.

"We've come up with an alternative plan," Johnson said.

"Do tell," Quentin said.

"We have a little more than two hours until they land. This is what we're going to do."

46

Trust No One

I called Taylor on the satellite phone.

"I'm glad you called," she said. "We're about two hours out."

"I know. I need to talk to Ostin."

"He's sleeping."

"I need you to wake him."

"What's going on?"

"Just get him, please."

A moment later Ostin came to the phone. "Hey, Michael." He sounded groggy.

"Do you remember the first summer I moved in and we were playing bank robber behind the school and you saw those kids with walkie-talkies?"

"That's a pretty random thing to wake me for," he said.

"Do you remember what you said to me?"

"That the kid had a head shaped like a pineapple?"

"The other thing."

"That it would be easy to—"

"Stop," I said. "Think about it."

"Dude, you're being so cryptic."

"Think about it, Ostin. Think it through."

Ostin was quiet a moment, then said, "Let me call you back." Less than five minutes later the phone rang.

"We can talk," he said. "You were right, the phone was bugged."

"Mine was bugged too. And there's more. The Chasqui have access to the GPS system that's tracking the buttons. They know where we all are."

"Then we're about to fly into an ambush."

"Exactly. Except they don't know that we know, so we now have the advantage. This is what we're going to do. At the last minute you need to change your flight to land on an airstrip in the jungle. This is the problem: we know we've been infiltrated, but we don't know the extent of it or by whom."

"You're saying that you don't know if the pilots are working for the Chasqui."

"Yes. Could you land that jet if you had to?"

He thought a moment. "I've done it in a simulator. I could do that."

"Hopefully it won't come to that. I want you and Taylor to go into the cockpit and have Taylor read their minds. Have Cassy with you as your backup. If Scott and Boyd are with the Chasqui, we don't know what they'll do."

"Will do."

"Put me back on with Taylor."

A moment later Taylor came on. "Michael, the phone was bugged?"

"Yes. We've been infiltrated. All of the satellite phones were bugged. So was my father's personal phone. They've also been tracking us with the GPS system. We lost two men this morning."

"Lost?"

"We think they were killed."

"I'm so sorry."

"Right now we don't know if the pilots are with us or the Chasqui."

"You mean Scott and Boyd? They've been with us forever. They're friends."

"Here's our dilemma. Right now we don't know who our friends are. I need you to go into the cockpit and find out if they're Chasqui."

"You want me to just ask them?"

"Just ask what they know about the Chasqui. You'll know from their thoughts. If they are, have Cassy freeze them."

"If they're frozen, who will fly the jet?"

"Ostin."

She paused. "Can he do that?"

"He took flying lessons last summer."

"But this is a jet."

"Have you ever seen Ostin fail at anything he put his mind to?"

"No."

"Have faith in him. Hopefully it won't come to that. But if they're with the Chasqui, they're flying you into an ambush. I'm sending you the coordinates for a jungle airstrip. We're going to have you make an emergency landing there, and we'll pull everyone off. So be ready. As soon as the Chasqui figure out that we've tricked them, they'll head to the buttons' last coordinates."

"All right. Ostin knows the plan?"

"Yes. Call me as soon as you know if the pilots are clean. And make sure that they keep radio silence. Don't let them talk to anyone. If they reach for the radio, reboot them."

"Okay. I'll call you back."

While we waited, we packed the vans with weapons, ammunition, and food—everything we thought we might need for the next week. We didn't know how long we would be gone, but for now we were abandoning the compound.

Taylor called as we were finishing packing.

"They're clean," she said. "Scott and Boyd are clean."

"You told them that we're changing the landing site?"

"Yes. They're just waiting for the coordinates."

"Okay. Get Ostin, I'll put him on with Johnson."

When Ostin answered, I said, "I'm putting you on with Captain Johnson. He has the coordinates for the airstrip. Make sure the pilots stay on course to the Puerto Maldonado airport until the last possible moment."

"Brilliant," Ostin said. "The buttons don't show altitude, so the Chasqui won't know we've landed for at least fifteen minutes."

"Exactly. Also, before you land, collect everyone's buttons. As soon as you land, we'll put them in lead. Hopefully the Chasqui will just think there's a technical glitch and it will buy us time."

"Got it."

"Here's Johnson."

Johnson read Ostin the coordinates, then handed the phone back to me.

"Thanks, buddy," I said. "I'll see you in an hour. Put those buttons in your pocket. I want to collect them first thing."

"On it, chief."

I had just hung up when the phone rang. It was my father on my mother's phone.

"You were right, Michael. There was a spy chip in the new phone. Marius is gone."

"He's probably already on a plane to South America," I said.

"No doubt. Good luck, son. Keep us informed of what's going on."

Knowing that the Chasqui would be tracking us, we sent Quentin, Ian, Bentrude, and Jax as a decoy to the Puerto Maldonado airport. Only Bentrude and Jax carried their buttons. We didn't want the Chasqui to know that they had Ian's and Quentin's capabilities with them. As Johnson quoted, "'When you are strong, appear weak. When you are weak, appear strong.'"

"Be careful," I said to the men. "We know it's a trap. We don't know how many soldiers there will be."

"I will," Ian said. "No worries."

"And, if they give chase, I'll shut them down," Quentin said.

"Not before I take them out," Jax said.

"Not yet," I said. "We still need them."

After they drove off, the rest of us climbed into the other three vans, leaving the compound deserted.

"I hope this works," Zeus said.

I grinned darkly. "What could possibly go wrong?"

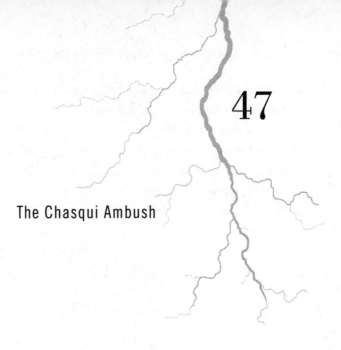

47

The Chasqui Ambush

It was dark when we arrived at the secluded landing strip. Johnson, Jaime, and Cibor drove around the field, placing kerosene torches along the edges of the runway. Except for a sloth, a dozen monkeys, and a few million insects, we seemed to be alone.

"How far out are they?" Johnson asked.

"About twenty minutes."

"We'll light the torches."

They simultaneously drove down both sides of the runway, stopping every fifty yards to light the torches.

"Too bad McKenna isn't here," Zeus said. "She'd be good at that." He turned to me. "Wouldn't it be funny if some narcos tried to land right now?"

I looked at him. "No."

Quentin came over the radio. "Michael."

"Yes."

"We're about a quarter mile from the airport."

"Anyone show up yet?"

"Oh yeah. They've got a whole party planned. There are five trucks with about twenty Chasqui soldiers and lots of toys. They've got an antiaircraft gun, RESAT vests, and one of those big RESAT broadcaster things."

"Where are they?"

"Right now, just east of the airport. They're hiding behind one of the hangars."

"Do they know you're there?"

"We think so. Ian saw one of the guys with a handheld pointing toward us, like he was showing someone where we were."

"Good. It's working. So, here's a question for you, can your EMP shut down one of those RESAT broadcasters?"

"I've never tried. It probably depends on who fires first."

"That makes sense. I'll call as soon as we have everyone. See you at the rendezvous." I hung up the phone.

"Ian?" Zeus asked.

"Quentin. The Chasqui are there."

"For once we know something they don't. I like this way better."

"Me too."

A few minutes later Johnson and his men returned with the vans and parked them off to the side of the runway.

"We're ready," Johnson said. "As soon as they land, we get everyone out and the pilots take back off."

"I just heard from Quentin. The Chasqui are there."

"No surprise. How many?"

"About twenty soldiers. Heavily armed."

"I wish I were there with a machine gun."

I could see the fire in his eyes. "You'll have your chance." I looked back up at the sky. I could see the silhouette of a large bird circling above us.

"I told Taylor to call me when they could see the runway. How's our new safe house?"

"She's ready."

"What's your friend's name?"

"Jacinta. It means 'hyacinth.' Like the flower."

"Jacinta." I looked at him. "What's your relationship with her?"

He thought a moment, then said, "Friends."

Fifteen minutes later my phone rang. It was Taylor. "We're getting ready to land. Are we safe?"

"Yes. The Chasqui are at the Puerto airport, planning their ambush."

"Okay. See you soon."

A few minutes later we could see the lights of the approaching plane.

"There they are," I said.

Johnson lifted his radio. "Alpha Team, be alert."

"Roger that."

I was glad to see my friends. But, in my heart, I wished they were all a thousand miles away.

48

Another Reunion

The jet touched down, loudly powering up its thrusters to brake on the short runway. By the time the jet reached us, it had already slowed to a taxi.

I handed the lead pipe to Johnson. "First thing, we collect the buttons."

"I'll do it myself." He turned to the other vans and waved. "Go! Go! Go!"

The vans pulled up to the side of the jet. The door on the jet opened and the airstair dropped. Johnson and Jaime ran up the stairs. Taylor was the first one out, carrying her suitcase. Jaime grabbed the bag from her and tossed it down to Cibor, and Zeus put it into the van.

I hugged Taylor. She looked around. "Where's Ian and Quentin?"

"They're in Puerto. Get into the first van; I'll explain on the way."

Jaime hurried everyone out of the plane. Cassy was the last of us

275

to come out. Captain Boyd appeared at the doorway behind her. He shouted to me, "Michael, are we done?"

"Yes. Get out of here. The Chasqui have antiaircraft, so don't take any chances."

"*Con Dios,*" he said.

He took up the airstair. The moment the door shut, the jet's engines began to rev. The jet made a 180-degree turn, then moved forward for takeoff.

Johnson was standing outside the first van. "We're all here."

I climbed into the first van next to Taylor. I dialed Quentin.

"Boss?"

"We're on our way," I said. "What's going on there?"

"Not much. They're still just patiently waiting to kill all of us."

"Good. It worked. In five minutes, drive toward the airport so they think you're coming; then shield your buttons and get out of there. We'll meet you at the rendezvous."

"See you at the zoo."

I turned to Johnson. "We're good. Let's get out of here."

49

A Night at the Zoo

Everything Johnson had said about the zoo's location was true. It was about thirty minutes from the city and was surrounded on all sides by thick jungle. I held Taylor the whole way. She was lightly shaking. I could tell that she was reading my mind, so I kept sending her positive messages. Each time I did, she just held on to me tighter.

As we neared the zoo, Johnson called Jacinta from his phone. She met us at the zoo's entrance—a heavy metal gate that she unlocked and pulled open. We all drove in, and she shut the gate behind us.

"What about the others?" Taylor asked.

"They're about twenty minutes behind us," Johnson said. "If they're not being followed, she'll open the gate when they get here."

"And if they are?"

"We'll have some work to do."

At the front of the compound was a large, primitive-looking

house with a thatched roof and a large front porch, the overhang held up by wide bamboo poles.

Jacinta pointed to where she wanted us to park. We pulled up next to the house, and everyone got out.

Past the house there was another gate and a wall with a window for ticket sales. Immediately behind it was a massive, dirt-floored cage with thick metal bars. The cage had a concrete foundation about a meter high that had once been painted in a cheerful baby blue but was now faded and peeling. The concrete was cracked and chipped in places, revealing heavy rebar.

The cage had been partitioned into two smaller cages by a wall of iron bars. Individually, the spaces were at least thirty by thirty feet, the outer bars fifteen feet high, with chain-link fencing wired across the top. Both cages had large tree trunks laid across the ground in the center for the animals to climb on.

In the section of the cage nearest the house a large jaguar paced back and forth. The powerful animal was beautifully marked, its pale green eyes reflective in the zoo's dim lighting. In one corner of the cage there was a large, galvanized tank filled with water, and next to it was the stripped rib cage of a cow.

The second cage was empty, and its front gate was open. A sign above the door read PUMA, but other than the birds that could fly through the bars, there was no animal of any kind to be seen.

Johnson and Jacinta embraced. Then he took her hand and led her over to us.

"This is Michael," he said. "And his friend Taylor."

"*Mucho gusto,*" Jacinta said.

"*Mucho gusto,*" I said back. "I don't speak Spanish."

"You spoke that very well," she said in clear English. "Do not worry, I speak English. Welcome."

"Thank you for letting us stay here." I almost felt stupid saying that. We weren't just an inconvenience; we were threatening her life and property.

"I am glad to help my friends. Especially those who are fighting the Elgen *demonios.*"

Jaime walked up to us. "Jacinta."

"Jaime." They embraced.

"Jaime introduced us," Johnson said. "They were friends even before we came to Peru."

We quickly emptied the vans; then Jacinta led us through the small zoo to a metal-sided warehouse. There were a couple dozen cages at most. The animals were rescues and all native to the region. There were tapirs; javelinas; many species of birds, including a couple of toucans and a harpy eagle; tortoises; and several cages filled with screeching monkeys—capuchin, and makisapa.

"Look at those gnarly pigs," Nichelle said.

"They're not pigs," Ostin said. "They're javelinas."

"Whatever. If it looks like a pig, it's a pig."

As we carried our bags to the back, Cassy walked up to Taylor and me.

"How are you?" I asked.

"I'm doing well, thank you."

"You're going to be the main event tonight."

"So I hear."

"Are you ready?"

"I'm always ready."

We walked into the warehouse. There were mats spread out across the floor.

"I'm sorry," Jacinta said. "This is not nice. And there is only one bathroom to share."

"We're just grateful for your help," Taylor said. "We're not princesses."

"Speak for yourself," Tessa said, grinning. "And we are grateful."

Taylor, McKenna, Ostin, and I claimed an area near the back and put down our bags. Johnson and Jacinta walked up to me.

"I just heard from Bentrude. They're five minutes out. They're not being followed yet."

"I'm going up front to meet them," I said to Taylor. "I'll be right back."

"I'll help everyone get ready here."

As we walked out of the warehouse, Johnson said to me, "You sure you want to lead the Chasqui here?"

"I think it's our only choice. Once they're back in the jungle, we've lost them."

"You're right. At least here the battle's on our turf."

The three of us stopped next to the front gate to wait.

"Why does your skin glow?" Jacinta asked.

"I don't know. It's how I was born."

"You know, Peruvian scientists just discovered a new species of glow worm in the Amazon jungle."

"Maybe we're related," I said.

She covered her mouth and laughed.

Within a few minutes we could see the approaching headlamps of the other van.

"They look like they're alone," Jacinta said. "It would be impossible to drive this road without lights."

"They could with night-vision goggles," Johnson said.

"Ian would know if they were being followed," I said.

"I wish we had trackers on the Chasqui," Johnson said. "So we knew if they were coming."

"They'll come," I said. "You can be sure of that."

We opened the gate, and Bentrude pulled the van into the compound. He stopped and rolled down the window. "Where should I put it?"

"Park next to the others," Johnson said.

He pulled over to the side of the house. The doors opened, and Ian and Quentin climbed out. They didn't have any luggage since we'd brought their things from the compound with us.

"How did it go?" I asked.

"Like clockwork," Quentin said. "They fell for it."

"One of the cars started to follow us," Ian said. "The one with the antiaircraft gun. Quentin took it out."

"Just the one?"

"Just the one. We figured that we'd thin the herd a little."

Bentrude handed a lead pipe to Johnson. "There's our souls."

Johnson took the cap off the pipe and spilled the buttons into his hand. "Come and get us, Chasqui scum," he said.

He put the buttons into his pants pocket, then handed me the pipe.

"Bentrude, take Jax and plan a defensive line in case they break through."

"Yes, sir," he said.

"They won't break through," I said.

"I hope not. Are you ready?"

"I'm ready. Time to get this party started."

The three of us—Johnson, Jacinta, and I—walked into the main home. We took the rest of the buttons from the other pipe and spread them around the house.

"What do these do?" Jacinta asked. She pressed it, and it beeped.

"Don't press those," Johnson said.

"Sorry. They make pretty music."

"Press too many times, and you'll hear harps," I said.

She looked at me quizzically. "Harps? *Arpas?*"

"I'm just kidding. Don't do it."

"The buttons are bait for *las ratas*," Johnson said.

"*Sí*. Rats they are."

After we had distributed the buttons, Johnson carried a chair into the front room.

"That's for interrogations," he said.

"Where is the best place for Ian?" I asked.

"There's a ladder that leads to the top of the warehouse. It will give the best view."

"It would be a good spot for a sniper," Jacinta added.

I turned to Johnson. "She's hard-core."

"Like I said."

It made me wonder even more what the Chasqui had done to her.

We all walked back to the warehouse. The lights were mostly off, and the room was illuminated by the faint glow of kerosene lanterns and the electrics.

We gathered everyone together.

"We've put the buttons out," I said. "So we expect the Chasqui to be on their way soon. Nichelle, I'd like you to help amp Ian."

"Will do," she said.

"Quentin, I want you up there too. It's your job to take out any drones. Zeus, you're with me on backup. Tessa, you're with Cassy."

I turned to Cassy. "Ian will let us know when they're all in range. On my signal, you freeze them like Popsicles."

"Gladly. Where do you want Tessa and me?"

"By us," I said. "Up near the front. Alpha Team will bring them in for interrogations with Taylor. Everyone clear?"

"What about me and McKenna?" Ostin said.

"You two stick with Alpha Team."

"What if they don't all come in at once?" Zeus asked.

"Cassy?"

"It doesn't matter. With Tessa's help, I can freeze them all within a quarter mile."

"All right." I handed Nichelle a radio. "Test it when you're on top. Channel seven."

"Channel seven."

"What if they don't come?"

"They'll come," I said. "It's like throwing a chicken to a crocodile."

Zeus's brow furrowed. "Are we the chicken in this scenario?"

"Sorry. I'll pick a better metaphor next time."

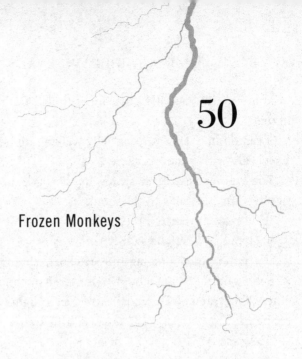

50

Frozen Monkeys

It was less than forty minutes before there was a squelch on my radio, followed by Nichelle's voice. "Michael, Ian just spotted four trucks about a half mile out. They've stopped by the side of the road."

"Are they the same trucks from the airport?"

"I'll ask. Yes, he thinks so."

"I'll alert Alpha Team."

Taylor and I walked to the front of the complex. Jacinta was sitting alone at the far end of the jaguar cage. Her hands were through the bars, and she was scratching the large cat's neck like it was a kitten. In front of her, Johnson, Cibor, Bentrude, and Jax were crouched down behind a cinder-block wall next to the cage. Jaime was on the opposite side of the path, next to a pen with a massive black caiman.

"There are four trucks about a kilometer out," I said.

Johnson lifted his rifle, checking its bolt. "You're sure your girl can do this?"

"I can do it," Cassy said, casually walking up behind us with Tessa. "Especially with vitamin E here."

The women had been sitting in the dark next to the makisapa cage, feeding plantains to the monkeys.

Tessa said, "Is that *E* for 'electric' or 'energy'?"

"Pick one," Cassy said. "Or both."

My radio squelched again. "Michael, the trucks are moving," Nichelle said. "They're about a hundred meters out. Seventy-five meters. Fifty meters. They just turned their lights off. They're pulling off the road again. The soldiers are getting out."

"How many?"

"Less than twenty. I'll give this to Ian."

"Looks like there are eighteen, Michael. They're the same guys from the airport. The leader has a GPS handheld. Now they're off the road and moving through the jungle. They're throwing up rope ladders. It looks like they're planning on going over the far wall."

"All of them?"

"They're all going over." A minute later he said, "Leader-dude is pointing to the house. He's making hand gestures for them to spread out."

"They're following the buttons," I said.

Johnson looked out through his night-vision binoculars. "I have them in sight."

I turned to Cassy. "Ready?"

She nodded.

"They've reached the driveway," Johnson said.

"Now, Cassy."

Cassy reached out her hands. Everyone froze.

"They are all snowmen," Ian said. "There is no movement. I repeat, there is no movement."

"Are you sure?" I asked.

"Not a creature is stirring. Not even a louse."

"That was funny," Cassy said.

Johnson stood and turned to his men. "Let's go."

Zeus walked around from the side of the house. "What a sight this is. Eighteen ugly Chasqui statues."

"Take their weapons, communications, and shoes," Johnson said.

"Where do you want the prisoners?" Bentrude asked.

Jacinta walked up from behind the zoo entrance. "We can put them in the puma cage."

"Does it lock?" Johnson asked.

"Yes, of course it locks. But I also have more chains and padlocks in the warehouse."

"We'll do that," Johnson said. "Strip the prisoners to their underwear, to be sure they're not hiding anything, then lock them up. Bentrude and Cibor, take guard."

"I will get the locks and chain," Jacinta said. She walked back to the warehouse.

"Check this out," Zeus said. "It's like cow tipping." He pushed one of the soldiers, and the man fell back, as solid as a plank.

"We used to do that on the farm," Bentrude said. "That's what you do when you don't have cable."

Zeus laughed. "How else are we going to get their boots off, right?"

Cibor, Bentrude, and Zeus walked through the platoon of soldiers, stripping them of their weapons and boots, throwing them into a large pile on one side of the yard. Like Zeus said, it was like walking through a garden of statues. Or mannequins.

Jacinta brought the chains back in a hay-filled wagon. She left the chains near the cage, then brought the wagon out front. "You can put their weapons in here."

"Much obliged," Bentrude said.

Johnson and Jax walked up to the Chasqui's frozen leader, who was still holding the handheld out in front of him, his eyes looking down at the screen. Johnson took the handheld from him. "This isn't yours." He looked over the man's uniform. "You look important. We'll start with you."

Jax dropped to one knee, then lifted the man over his shoulders in a fireman's carry.

"Let's take him inside," Johnson said. "Jaime, come with us. We might need your Spanish."

"Yes, sir."

"And you'll need Taylor," I said.

We followed them all into the house. The Chasqui officer was a stocky, broad-faced man with pocked skin and a thick mustache. He had a patch on his shoulder with the Chasqui emblem, a torch. On his other shoulder was the hammer and sickle of the Shining Path Communist movement. The word "*CAPITÁN*" was embroidered above his pocket.

Johnson and Jax sat him in a chair, then tied him to it, even though he was still frozen.

"Tell Cassy she can let him go," Johnson said to Jax.

"Yes, sir."

A minute later the man sat up. He strained against his bonds.

"Do you speak English?" Johnson asked.

He glared at Johnson defiantly. "I won't tell you anything."

"So you do. You'll tell us *everything*."

Taylor walked up to the man's side. The man in the chair looked confused. "It's you."

"Whatever that means," Taylor said. She put her hand on the man's shoulder, then looked up at Johnson. "Go ahead."

Johnson looked fiercely into the man's eyes. "Where have you taken our people?"

The Chasqui leader just looked ahead. "What people?"

"Where are Tara and Abigail?"

After a moment Taylor said, "He doesn't know either of those names."

Johnson pressed. "Where are the young American women you kidnapped a few days ago?"

Taylor said, "He's thinking 'She's right here.' He thinks I'm her."

Johnson looked into the captain's eyes. "What about the other girl? The blond."

"He doesn't know who you're talking about."

"Peculiar. Where is Tara being held? The one who looks like her."

"He doesn't know there are two of us," Taylor said.

Johnson said, "This girl is a twin."

Taylor said, "She's being held at the Starxource plant."

"Where in the plant?"

"He doesn't know."

"Where is Jack Vranes?"

"He doesn't know who that is."

"Where is the young American man you kidnapped four days ago in Acaray?"

"He just thought something about a cave."

"Where is the cave?"

After a moment Taylor said, "He's not giving me anything I understand." She thought a moment, then said, "I have an idea. Do we have a map of the jungle?"

"I can get one on my phone." Johnson looked up the Amazon map. When he had it, he held the screen up in front of them.

"Where's the Starxource facility?" Taylor asked Johnson.

He touched his finger to the screen. "The plant would be about here."

"Move your finger around, like you're looking for the cave."

Johnson slowly moved his finger around the screen.

"There," Taylor said. "It's right there. Pull in closer."

"Where is the entrance?" Johnson asked.

"There's a lot of them." She looked up. "It's facing the river but not near the river. He doesn't know it that well. Only high-ranking officers are allowed there."

Johnson held out the GPS handheld. "Where did you get this?"

Taylor said, "One of his superiors. He doesn't know where they got it."

"You're not much help," Johnson said.

"I need to ask him some things," Taylor said.

"Go ahead."

Taylor walked around the chair to face the man, her hand still on his shoulder.

"Where are the Glows Bryan and Kylee?"

"What did he think?" I asked.

"He doesn't know who they are," she said. She turned back to him. "Why are you looking for all of us?"

After a moment, Taylor looked over at me, her eyes wide. "They're not looking for *us*. They're looking for me."

"Then why did they take Jack, Abi, and Tara?" I asked.

"Jack was in the way, he doesn't know anything about Abi, and they took Tara because they thought she was me." She turned back to the man. "What do you want with me?"

I could see from her expression that the answer was frightening her.

"What is it?" I asked.

"He said their sovereign says I can see the future."

I put my arm around her.

"That's enough," Johnson said.

"There's one more thing," Taylor said. "I don't know if I should tell you."

"Tell me what?" Johnson asked.

Taylor looked at him. "This is the man who killed your friend at the river." She hesitated, then said, "They dumped his body in the river for the piranha and caimans."

Johnson grabbed the man by his chin. "You killed Gunnar?"

The Chasqui tried to turn away, but Johnson pulled his head back. "Look at me!" he screamed. "You killed my friend!" Johnson hit him in the face so hard that it knocked the chair back. Then he said to Jax, "Get him out of here. Lock him up."

"With the others?"

"No. Put him in the cage with the jaguar."

Taylor and I looked at each other, but neither of us said anything.

"Please, no," the man said. *"Por piedad!"*

"He's asking for mercy," Jaime said.

"Mercy? Like you showed Gunnar?" Johnson turned to Jax. "Just do it."

"Yes, sir."

Jax dragged the man out.

After he was gone, Bentrude brought in another soldier. Then another. And another. In all, Johnson and Taylor interrogated five soldiers but basically got the same information. Not one of them knew anything about Abigail.

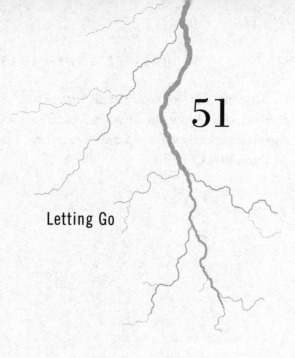

51

Letting Go

It was past midnight when we finished the interrogations and the last of the Chasqui were locked up in the cage. I was about to leave the house with Taylor when Johnson said, "Michael. Can we talk?"

"Yeah." I squeezed Taylor's hand. "I'll meet you back at the warehouse."

She kissed me on the cheek, then walked out, leaving just me, Johnson, and Jacinta in the house.

Johnson handed me the lead pipe with the buttons. "I'm giving this to you. I'll let you decide what to do with them. I have Jax on the lookout. Cibor is guarding the prisoners."

He glanced over at Jacinta. "Our first victory. They didn't kill or capture us as they planned, and we've got their weapons and some intel. But we've got a tiger by the tail. It's just a matter of time before they send more men to hunt us down."

"Do you have a plan?" I asked.

"Not yet. As you know, there is only one way to the Starxource plant. It's up the river."

"We could take their uniforms and take their boats back up."

"These men didn't come in boats. The Chasqui have a base on the river near the old port. That is where they came from." He turned to Jacinta. "When the reinforcements come, they will destroy your zoo."

"I know."

"We will take care of you," I said. "The company will buy your property."

"I'm more concerned about her," Johnson said. "We need to get her out of here."

She crossed her arms. "I'm not leaving Puerto."

"It's not safe here," Johnson said.

"I don't care."

The moment fell into silence. I turned to Johnson. "How long do you think we have until reinforcements get here?"

"It would take them at least four hours to assemble and come up the river. But they won't move until morning."

"Why not?"

"We tricked them," Johnson said. "Jaime spoke to them on their radio. They still think everything is going well, so they have no reason to respond. Not yet. But they'll figure it out soon enough. Before they do, we need to go someplace where they won't find us."

"I know a place where they won't find us," I said.

"Where?" Johnson asked.

"The Chasqui Puerto Maldonado military base."

"You want to move into their base?" Jacinta asked.

"Just until we launch our attack."

"That's either brilliant or crazy," Johnson said.

"Sometimes that's a fine line," I said.

"I want to think more about it," Johnson said. He rubbed his eyes. "Regardless, we move out early. So let's get some rest. We have some very long days ahead of us. Tonight Alpha Team will keep watch on the prisoners and the grounds."

He glanced down at his watch. "It's zero hundred one-fife. Let's meet here at zero six hundred."

"I'll go back and tell everyone," I said. "You two get some rest."

Jacinta looked sad. "In the morning, I will have to let my animals go. Otherwise, they will die in their cages."

"I'm sorry," I said.

She nodded lightly. "Good night, Michael." Jacinta disappeared into one of the rooms.

After the door shut, I said, "She's sacrificed so much."

Johnson nodded. "Too much. And now her zoo."

"Why does she hate the Elgen so much?"

I could see that the question pained him. "Six years ago, Jacinta lived here with her husband and eight-year-old son. She got a degree as a veterinarian, but most of her income came from working with foreign companies, providing animals for zoos and pet store companies. Not big animals, mostly small reptiles and amphibians.

"Her husband was an accountant, but he'd help her out sometimes to bring in a little extra. One day her husband and son went down the river looking for Amazon poison dart frogs. They ventured too close to the Starxource plant and were never seen again."

"How does she know it was the Elgen?"

"Jacinta traveled up and down the river for the next few months looking for them, talking to everyone she crossed on the river. An old tribal fisherman told her that he had seen the Elgen kill her husband, then throw him into the river. He didn't know what they did with her son.

"She went to the police for help, but they wouldn't do anything against the Elgen. They blamed her husband for trespassing on Elgen property. The next day her house was burned down.

"She was living in the streets when she met Jaime. He gave her a place to stay, then helped her get established here."

"The reason she won't leave Puerto is because of her son?" I asked.

Johnson nodded. "While we were interrogating, she was doing her own. She asked all the prisoners if they'd seen her son." His face fell. "Honestly, knowing the Elgen like I do, I don't think he's still alive. I think, in her heart of hearts, she knows that, but she'll never stop looking.

"That's why she doesn't care if she lives or dies." He exhaled slowly. "All she has is her animals. And now they have to go."

"Maybe letting her animals go will help her leave Puerto," I said.

"Maybe."

I thought for a moment then, lifting the lead pipe, said, "At least now I know what to do with our buttons."

52

Cristiano

I walked alone out onto the porch, the screen door springing shut behind me. The moon was high in the sky, bright above the compound. The thrum and buzzing of insects were almost deafening. Ostin once told me that a single Amazon tree cricket, the cicada, could be heard from nearly a mile away. Multiply that by a million, and you'll understand what I was listening to. Just another reminder that I was a long way from Boise.

I looked out over the dark scenery and yawned. With all the adrenaline of battle, I had forgotten how tired I was.

I walked past the brick wall to the jaguar cage where the *capitán* was being held. He had taken refuge in a small holding pen near the back of the cage, where the jaguar couldn't get to him. Even though it looked like pure vengeance, there was wisdom to Johnson's putting him in with the jaguar. The holding pen the *capitán* was holed up in was on the far side of the cage, so he couldn't talk to his men without shouting, and the jaguar was a better guard than we were.

Cibor was about ten yards in front of me, sitting on a bench that he'd turned backward to face the prisoners. There was an AR-15 rifle in his lap. He looked bored, swatting at mosquitoes. The prisoners he was watching were scattered around the cage, lying down or sitting on the moist dirt ground.

"Yo, Michael," Cibor said.

"How's it going?"

"Just minding the *więzień*."

"Whatever that is, the prisoners seem quiet."

"There's a reason for that," he said. "See that door separating their cage from the jaguar cage? I told them that if they didn't shut up, I'd open it."

"Looks like it worked."

"It did," he said with a light grin. "Could I trouble you to get me some water?"

"No trouble. I'll get some from the warehouse."

As I was walking past the cage, someone said, "Michael Vey, sir. May I have a moment of your time, please?"

I looked over. The petition had come from one of the Chasqui, a young man, not much older than me, dressed only in his underwear like the rest of the prisoners. He was all alone, leaning against the bars in the corner of the cage.

I stopped walking. "How do you speak English so well?"

"I went to college in Phoenix, Arizona."

"ASU?" I asked.

"Yes, sir, Mr. Vey."

ASU. Taylor's school. "How do you know my name?"

"The others spoke of you. They said you are the leader of the famous Electroclan. I can help you, sir. I can tell you things that even the *capitán* doesn't know."

"What would you know that your leaders don't?"

"I was a servant to the sovereign's planning table. I heard things from Sovereign Amash's own mouth. I know things others don't know."

". . . Or you just want to get out."

He looked as desperate as he sounded. "Yes, of course I want to get out. I was recruited into the Chasqui with lies. These men in here will kill me just for talking to you. See how they look at me now? I risk my life right now, you know?"

I looked at him for a moment, then shook my head. "Sorry, but I can't trust you." I started to walk away.

"They say your girlfriend can read minds. If this is true, she will know I speak the truth. Please, I know the horrible plan they have."

"Everything the Elgen do is horrible."

"But do you know about their horrible plan for the bats?"

I stopped. "You know about the bats?"

"Yes, of course. Do you know their plan? It is beyond horrible. So many innocent people will die."

I took a step back toward the cage. "What is your name?"

"Cristiano. Cristiano Velasquez."

"You'd better be telling the truth. I'll get my girlfriend."

I walked the short dirt trail back to the warehouse. The metal warehouse door squeaked as it opened. It was dark inside, lit with only a few small candles. Most of our group was lying down asleep. I grabbed a couple of bottles of water, then went to Taylor, who was lying on the ground next to Ostin and McKenna.

"Taylor, can you come with me for a minute?"

She sat up. "What's up?"

"I need you to tell me if someone is telling the truth." I looked at Ostin and McKenna. "I could use you too, Ostin."

"No problem," Ostin said. "I couldn't sleep anyway. Too much stimulation."

"I'll come with you," McKenna asked.

"Do any of you have any bug spray?" I asked. "Cibor's getting eaten out there."

"I'll get it," Taylor said. She grabbed a bottle of DEET, and the four of us walked back to the cage. As we approached, we could hear shouting. When we got there, Cristiano was lying on the ground, sur- rounded by three men who were savagely kicking and beating him, while other prisoners shouted. *"Tú eres un traidor! Chivato. Soplón."*

Cibor was shouting at them to stop.

"Get away from him!" I said.

Two of the men stopped, but the third continued kicking. I reached out and pulsed, knocking the man to the ground. The other two raised their hands above their heads and stepped back. Cristiano lay on the ground, still. I couldn't tell if he was alive or not.

"Cristiano," I said.

He slowly looked up at me. Even in the darkness I could see that his face was badly bruised. He was covered with blood and mud and manure.

"Let's talk," I said.

I took the bottles of water to Cibor.

"Thanks, brother," he said. "You left me with a little excitement."

I shook my head. "It follows me."

"Here's this," Taylor said, handing him the bug spray. "Michael said the bugs are eating you."

"You're an angel," Cibor said.

"I want to talk to that guy over there," I said.

"The one they just beat up?"

"Yes."

Cibor set the water and spray down and pointed to Cristiano. "Yo. *Vete aquí!*" Cibor took a key from a chain around his neck and unlocked the gate, then the chain lock. Several of the other men started to stand as well.

"*Quedarse,*" he shouted to them. Then he pointed his pistol at a group of them. "Just give me a reason." The men all sat back down.

Cristiano struggled to his feet, then limped slowly over to the gate.

"Come on out," I said.

"Thank you," he said softly. He was in a lot of pain.

Cibor unhooked the chain around the gate, unlocked the gate's dead bolt, and then opened the gate a few inches, just enough for Cristiano to slide out. Cibor shut the gate behind him and locked it. "Are you going to be a while?" he asked.

"I don't know. Maybe."

"Roger that." He wrapped the chain back around the gate and secured it again with the padlock.

I grabbed Cristiano by the arm. "Just to be clear, if you try anything, anything at all, I will electrocute you on the spot. No warning, no stun, no funeral. Do you understand?"

"Yes, sir," he said, his voice gravelly from the beating he'd just received. "Set phasers to kill."

Despite the circumstances, it was kind of funny. "You watched *Star Trek* in the States?"

"Yes. We have it here too."

"Or we could just put him back in the cage with those guys," Ostin said. "Same difference."

"I understand," he said. "If I lie, I die."

It wasn't true, but I was okay with him believing it.

The five of us walked back into the house where we had interrogated the others. Johnson and Jacinta had both gone to their rooms, and the lamps in the house had all been turned off.

"McKenna, could you help?"

"Sure." She immediately lit up her hand, bathing the room in a soft glow.

Cristiano looked at her in wonder. "How does she do that?"

"We're not human," she said.

"You must be the one?" he said.

"The one?" I said.

"The one the sovereign is looking for." Cristiano looked around at the rest of us. "Why do you all glow except for this one?" he said, pointing to Ostin.

"He's more human than us," McKenna said.

I lifted a pair of handcuffs from the counter. "I'm going to put these on you."

"I understand." He looked at Taylor. "Is it true that you can read minds?"

"Yes."

"This is good. You will know I speak the truth. You will know I'm not one of them."

"The beating was pretty good evidence of that," Ostin said.

Taylor put her hand on his shoulder and closed her eyes. After a minute she said to me, "He's telling the truth. He hates and fears the Chasqui. And he went to ASU." She looked at him. "I'm going to ASU right now."

"Go, Sun Devils," he said. Considering the circumstances, it was kind of surreal.

"That doesn't mean he won't kill," I said, looking at him.

"He's not one of them."

"Let's see where this goes." I looked into Cristiano's eyes. "Taylor is going to read your thoughts. She'll know immediately if you're lying. If you are, you go back into the cage with the others."

"I won't lie," he said. "I promise."

"What do the Chasqui want with us?"

"They're looking for one they call *la profetisa*."

"The prophetess," Ostin said.

"Yes. Sovereign Amash believes that she can see the future."

I looked at Taylor. She looked scared.

"Why is that so important to them?" I asked.

"They believe in prophecies. They believe it is their destiny to rule the world. Sovereign Amash believes the *profetisa* will help guide them."

"Who is this Sovereign Amash?"

"Eli Amash is the sovereign leader of the Chasqui. He is a very clever man. He speaks honey. He is the one who brought me and my brother into the Chasqui."

"Where is he from?"

"He is from the Middle East. I don't know where. The Chasqui have come to Peru, but they are not Peruvian."

"Where are our friends they have kidnapped?"

"They have kidnapped many from the Peruvian plant. Some are at the plant. I believe some are at the cave."

"Do you know where the cave is?"

"*Sí*. I mean, yes. I lived there for more than a year."

"Do you know how to get into it?"

"The cave is very, very large. There are many ways to get into the cave. Some they don't use anymore. So they are locked but not protected."

"What do you know about our friends?"

"I do not know who your friends are."

"They are American. Two females, one male."

His brow fell. "Only two Americans have been taken. One man and one woman." He turned to Taylor. "The woman looks like you."

"You've seen her?" Taylor asked.

"Yes. I saw her when they brought her through Puerto Maldonado a day ago. The other they've taken is a strong man who is not electric."

"That's Jack and Tara," McKenna said. "So where is Abigail?"

"I do not know this Abigail."

"She's a little taller than me. She's blond. She glows."

"Like I said, there is no other girl."

"That's what the others told us," I said. "Is it possible that they have her and you don't know about it?"

"It is not likely."

"Why is that?" I asked.

"The Chasqui guards always boast about their prisoners. Especially important ones."

"Where is Tara? My sister."

"She is in the jail at the plant. They are keeping her with bats."

"And what about Jack?" I asked.

"He is with Sovereign Amash."

"You mean, he's being held prisoner by Amash?"

"That is not what I mean. Your Jack is with Eli Amash. The sovereign is . . . teaching him."

"He's *grooming* him," Ostin said.

Cristiano turned to him. "I do not know that word."

"He'll never turn Jack," Taylor said. "He's way too smart."

"Never say never," Ostin said. "It is usually the smart who embrace ideologies. Especially the ancient ideologies."

"You said you know what the Chasqui are up to," I said. "Tell us."

"*Sí.* The Chasqui are, as this one says, ancient. They have been around for a very, very long time. Maybe a thousand years or more. They have always believed it is their destiny that they will rule the world. Eli Amash believes that day is now."

"How long have you been with the Chasqui?"

"Almost four years. Four terrible years."

"Then you know about the Elgen."

"*Sí*. But Sovereign Amash never believed in the Elgen cause and the man they called 'Hatch.' The Chasqui were using the Elgen to help them rise to power.

"But now that Hatch is gone, they have changed their way. Their plan now is to take over the drug world. They are starting with the cocaine trafficking in Peru."

"That's explains the VRAEM," Ostin said.

Cristiano looked over. "You know the VRAEM?"

"Yes." Ostin walked over to a map of Peru that Jacinta had on the wall. "Now it makes sense." Ostin drew a big ring on the map between Lima and Cuzco. "Michael's dad talked a little about this in America. This area here is called the VRAEM. It's where the Shining Path rebels hide and where they grow the coca leaves for cocaine." He touched his finger to the map. "This area here was the site of a Peruvian military base the government had set up to hunt the rebels. That's where the Chasqui first attacked with their bats, destroying the base.

"The next attack was a month later, here, near the Ene River. This time the Chasqui burned hundreds of acres of coca fields."

"That is right," Cristiano said. "How do you know this?"

"I don't get it," Taylor said. "Why would they attack both sides?"

"Basic psychology," Ostin said. "They're using the carrot and the stick. When the Chasqui first came to South America, they aligned themselves with the Shining Path army. The Shining Path funded their army through the drug money they made by growing coca plants. The peasants grow and pick the leaves, and make the paste. Then the soldiers take it.

"When the Elgen came along, the Chasqui found an easier revenue source, one without the risk." He looked at me. "In a way, you could say that we're responsible for what the Chasqui are doing right now."

"How is that?" I said.

"When the money from the Elgen Starxource plants dried up, the Chasqui needed another source of income. So they've gone back to the Shining Path. Or, at least, to their drug trade.

"They were offering the Shining Path the carrot by taking out a military base, showing how the Chasqui could benefit them. Presumably, when the rebels still didn't accept their offer, the Chasqui used the stick and turned their power against the rebels, showing how easily they could destroy the Shining Path crops. They say an army runs on gold. In the case of the Shining Path, it's cocaine. If the Chasqui burned all their coca fields, the Shining Path would be defeated without the Chasqui firing a shot."

"But taking on the cartels and their armies isn't a small thing," I said. "Not even the country's marines can take them out. The Chasqui must have a bigger army than we thought."

"Not necessarily," Ostin said. "There are two ways to win a war. You can win by destroying your enemy, or you can win by becoming your enemy. The Chasqui don't win wars by fighting battles. They win by integration. The Chasqui infiltrate their enemy. One enemy within the walls is more powerful than a legion outside."

"What this one says is all true," Cristiano said. "This is their plan."

"You said the Chasqui are after the entire drug trade," I said.

"Yes, it is the Chasqui goal to create a . . . *monopolio* . . ."

"A monopoly," Ostin said.

"But Peru is only a portion of that," I said.

"After they have all the coca fields in Peru, they plan to destroy all the other fields in the world."

"How will they do that?" McKenna asked. "Not even the army has been able to do that."

"That is why they have the bats. The bats will burn the fields. The cartel armies cannot fight a million bats."

"Why would the bats burn the fields?" I asked. "Bats don't roost in fields."

Cristiano said, "Some of the bats in the plant are being fed coca leaves every day. They are addicted to the coca leaves."

"Can animals get addicted to drugs?" McKenna asked.

"Just like humans," Ostin said. "That's why scientists test drugs on rats."

"But coca leaves aren't cocaine," I said. "They have to be processed."

"No," Ostin said, "but it's close enough. It's like caffeine. And people get addicted to caffeine all the time. That's why there's a million coffee shops."

"This is true," Cristiano said. "The Chasqui plan to fly the addicted bats over the Colombian fields in large planes and release them. They have tested this. They have already destroyed twenty-five thousand hectares."

Ostin said, "Last month there was a news story that the Colombian government had recently burned almost twenty-five thousand hectares of coca fields. The government took credit for that."

"Yes. The politicians took the credit, that is what they do, but they had nothing to do with it. It was the Chasqui bats. And that was only the beginning.

"And there is more. They have turned the Starxource plant into a drug-processing plant."

"Of course they would," I said. "It's already a laboratory. It's secure and hidden. It's on the river. It's perfect for that."

"They are also using the labs to create . . . what is the word . . . when you make something from chemicals . . ."

"Synthetic," Ostin said.

"Yes. Synthetic drugs. Like the drug fentanyl. Then they plan to flood America with cheap drugs so that many more people are addicted. Especially Americans."

"About twenty million Americans already have some form of drug addiction," Ostin said. "Just imagine if you doubled or tripled that. It would be an epidemic."

"But if the Chasqui move all their drug production to one place, doesn't that just make it easier to stop them?" Taylor said. "Especially once they pose such a threat."

"Yes," Cristiano said. "And the sovereign is prepared for that. That is why he developed the most horrific plan of all. He calls it MAD. That stands for 'mutually assured destruction.'"

"Like the nuclear Cold War," Ostin said.

"Yes. If anyone attempts to attack him, or the Chasqui, he will destroy their largest cities."

"How will he do that?"

"He will set fire to them using the bats. He plans to burn down the city of Arequipa as a demonstration to the world. It will be horrible. Thousands of people will die."

Taylor suddenly flushed. "Just like my dream."

"It could be Dresden again," Ostin said. "Only worse."

"What's Dresden?" McKenna asked.

Ostin said, "Near the end of World War II, the Allies decided to firebomb the German city of Dresden. It was a controversial decision because Dresden was mostly civilian and not a major military target.

"The British and American forces sent thirteen hundred heavy bombers to drop almost eight million pounds of bombs and incendiary devices onto the city, starting a massive fire. The more the city burned, the more oxygen it sucked in, creating a firestorm that was so intense that it melted concrete." He looked at McKenna. "Not as hot as you can get, but close."

McKenna frowned.

"The fires sucked the oxygen out of the air, and thousands of people died from suffocation. Twenty-five thousand people were immediately killed, and hundreds of thousands of people were made homeless.

"Arequipa has double the number of people Dresden had. And there are miles of wooden shelters and hotels. If the Chasqui were to set the city on fire, there could be a hundred thousand deaths. It would be the greatest single man-made tragedy in history."

"The Chasqui have a weapon of mass destruction, and no one knows it," I said.

"They will soon," Cristiano said. "That is the point of burning down Arequipa. Arequipa is only thirteen hours from Puerto

Maldonado by highway. The Chasqui plan is to drive the bats in regular cargo containers and release them near the city."

"Why don't they fly them over the city and release them?"

"A plane could perhaps be tracked by radar. But a simple truck will not draw any suspicion. This is a test. If it works, they will do the same thing by boat. They can put the bats in shipping containers and then release them while the boats are still far out at sea."

"At any time there are millions of shipping containers at sea," Ostin said. "No one would ever find it."

"How far can a bat fly?" Taylor asked.

"Some bats can fly as far as two hundred miles in a night," Ostin said. "It's a brilliant plan."

"If the Chasqui are attacked by American forces, they will release bats near every major American coastal city, such as Los Angeles, New York, Miami, Seattle, Boston, Portland, and Houston."

"It's brilliant," Ostin said again.

"Quit calling it that," Taylor said. "It's horrific."

"Then, diabolical," he said. "There's still something that doesn't make sense. Where are the Chasqui getting all these electrified bats? They're not like rats; they reproduce too slowly. It would take decades for them to breed that many."

"They do not breed them. They *make* them."

"What do you mean 'make'?"

"They point a machine at them, and they become electric. I cannot explain it. The machine they use is like an X-ray. It changes them."

Ostin groaned. "The Chasqui have figured out how to alter the MEI to make electrics postpartum."

"Postpartum?" Cristiano said.

"Yes. All of my friends were made electric before they were born. The Chasqui have figured out how to do it *after* they're born."

Cristiano shook his head. "It wasn't the Chasqui who invented this machine. It was the Elgen. It was invented during the time of Hatch."

"Then why didn't they use it to make rats?" McKenna asked.

"They didn't need to," Ostin replied. "They had to breed the rats anyway, so electrifying them before or after made no difference. Bats breed too slowly. But if they can electrify living bats, that's a game changer."

"Why didn't Hatch use his machine on humans?" Taylor said. "That was his entire sick dream, to rid the world of Nonels."

Cristiano's expression grew even more sad. "He tried it on many, many humans. He called them *cuyes*. Guinea pigs."

"GPs," I said. "We're familiar with them."

"But it didn't work. Everyone he experimented on blistered, then got cancer and died. It was like a radiation bomb. That is how I lost my brother and my two friends who came into the Chasqui with me." His chin quivered. "They died very slowly and painfully." Even though he was handcuffed, Cristiano still managed to wipe his eyes on his shoulder.

"The scientists tried the machine with rats and other animals, but it didn't work on them, either. It only worked on the bats."

"Why do you think it only worked on bats?" I asked Ostin.

Ostin scratched his chin. "Probably because bats are genetic superstars. They adapt quickly to externals. They don't get cancer, and they can carry dangerous viruses, like rabies, that would kill other animals. They even resist ageing, which is why they live twenty times longer than rats. If bats bred as fast as rats, they would have already overrun the world."

"How many bats are there in the world?" Taylor asked.

"It is estimated close to a billion," Ostin said. "There are bats on almost every continent. We don't see them, because they only come out at night and they are naturally stealthy, living in hidden places like caves, or belfries, or even abandoned mine shafts. But they are almost as plentiful as the common sparrow. There can be millions of them in a single colony. In Bracken Cave near San Antonio, Texas, there's an estimated fifteen million bats alone. If you electrified them all at once, just imagine the damage they could do."

"I don't want to imagine," Cristiano said. "Especially here. These are my people, my country. I have family in Arequipa." He looked into my eyes. "I know that you are trying to save your friends, but if you don't stop the Chasqui from taking their bats to Arequipa, millions of people will suffer."

"The classic trolley problem," Ostin said.

"We can't let that happen," Taylor said.

"We have to stop it," McKenna said.

"These electrified bats. How do they handle water?" I asked.

"They cannot be in water. The first time they dropped the bats, there was a rainstorm. They were all electrocuted."

"Just like the rats," Ostin said. "That's probably why the Chasqui have been waiting for the rainy season to end."

"Yes, and it's almost over," Cristiano said.

I breathed out heavily. "When do these bats go to Arequipa?"

"When there is no chance of rain in the region. It will take time for the Chasqui to transport all those bats into Puerto and then transfer them onto the trucks. I suspect it will take several days to move the large crates upriver."

"That will give us time." I looked around the room. Everyone looked exhausted. "But for now we'd better get some sleep."

"What do we do with him?" Ostin asked.

"We can't put him back in with the others," Taylor said. "They'll kill him."

"But we can't let him go," Ostin said. "He might get us killed."

"I understand your difficult situation," Cristiano said. "I have a possible solution. Just ten meters past the big cage there is a smaller cage where there are toucan birds. You can lock me in there. If you would be so kind, I would appreciate a blanket and some water."

I glanced at Taylor, and she put her hand back on Cristiano's shoulder.

"Do you plan to escape?" I asked.

Taylor said, "No. In fact, he would like to join our team and be one of us."

I took off his handcuffs and set them back on the counter. "I'll put you in the birdcage with a blanket and water. We'll be leaving early in the morning."

"Thank you for rescuing me, Mr. Vey. I am still in a cage, but for the first time in many years, I feel hope that I may be free again."

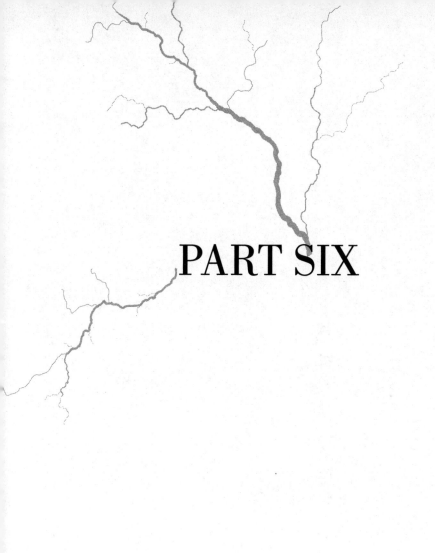

PART SIX

53

The Wrong Twin

Two Days Earlier,
Puerto Maldonado Starxource Plant

Tara pressed herself tightly against the wall near the back of her cell, balled up in a fetal position. The RESAT vest was turned high enough to make her nauseous and dizzy and burn her skin every time she moved.

The cell she was in stank of animal feces. Thousands of black bat droppings covered her cell floor as well as her blanket and mattress, which she hadn't used since she had been locked away.

She forced herself not to look up at the hundreds of bats that hung from the ceiling above her. Occasionally, one would fly by or crawl across the ground, which was especially terrifying. She didn't know what kind of bats they were, but one of the guards had told her that a few of them were vampire bats and hadn't had blood for a while.

There was no natural light in her cell, so she didn't know what time of day or night it was. That's why she had no idea what time it was when Sovereign Amash walked into her cell. He shut the door after him so the bats wouldn't escape.

"Good morning, Taylor."

Tara didn't correct him or even look up at him.

"These bats are marvelous creatures, don't you think?"

"By marvelous do you mean 'demonic'?"

He grinned. "These droppings on the ground are known around the world as guano. It's valued as a fertilizer. It is interesting to note that the word 'guano' comes from the Quechuan word 'wanu,' which means it has its origins right here in the Peruvian Andes, a dying culture's contribution to the world's language.

"This particular species of bat is called the Mexican free-tailed. It is quite abundant throughout the world and is the fastest flier of all bats. I have grown quite fond of them. I've read that just one roost can consume up to two hundred fifty tons of insects every night."

"You sound like Ostin," Tara said.

"Believe it or not, I understand the reference. I have heard much about this Ostin character. I genuinely look forward to meeting him." He stepped closer. "Are you as miserable as you look?"

"No. This is a party."

"I like that, Taylor. Defiance in a hopeless situation shows true character. You win points for that."

"Can I buy a clean blanket with them?"

He just smiled. "It might surprise you that Pablo Escobar, the once great Colombian drug lord, had many interesting sayings. One I especially enjoy is, 'Life is full of surprises, some good, some not so good.' I've wondered if he thought that just before the DEA agents shot him.

"There is another quote of his that I liked so much, I had it framed and put on my office wall. 'All empires are created of blood and fire.' That one is very apropos to my world. There is one other quote, perhaps his most famous one, that is very apropos to yours. 'Plata o plomo.' Silver or lead. What it means, of course, is that you can profit from our arrangement, or you can take a bullet."

"What do you want?" Tara said.

"I want your gift. Your ability to read the future."

"I don't have that gift."

"No, not with this painful machine hooked up to you, but there is no reason to hide your light under a bushel, Taylor. I know the truth."

"Life is full of surprises," Tara said. "You've mistaken me for my twin sister."

Amash looked at her for a moment, then said, "Prove it."

"How would I do that?"

"A simple quiz will suffice. Tara was raised Elgen. Taylor wasn't." He thought a moment, then said, "Answer me this. For the Glows collective twelfth birthday celebration, where did Dr. Hatch take them?"

"Tokyo," Tara said. "Then Taiwan."

The sovereign's brow furrowed. "What happened while you were in Taiwan?"

"There was a typhoon."

Amash spun back to the guard. "You brought me the wrong girl!"

"Your Eminence, we had the picture in the dossier. We didn't know there were twins."

"Idiots," he said. After he had calmed some, he said, "I suppose it's not all loss. Yours is a loyal brood. Having you will assuredly bring your sister to us."

"She won't come."

"She's already on her way. In the meantime"—he looked up to the ceiling—"enjoy the company." He walked to the gate, then said to the guard, "Increase the RESAT one click."

"No!" Tara shouted.

The echo of the heavy steel door clinking shut was drowned out by Tara's screams.

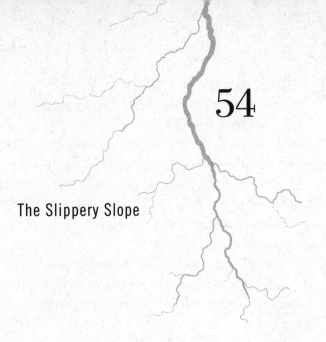

54

The Slippery Slope

The Next Morning

"Good morning, Jack." Jack looked over from his cot. Amash was standing outside his cell holding a tray. "I brought you some brunch." The guard opened the door, and the sovereign stepped inside. He wasn't armed; nor did he seem the least bit apprehensive. Jack considered attacking him but, with the armed guard so close, decided against it.

"Things have been a little better for you, I trust." He spoke as unctuously as a hotel concierge.

"I'm being held against my will."

"I know." He set the tray of food down on the small wooden table. There was even a small flower vase with a brilliant yellow-and-orange flower. "And I'm aggrieved by that. Maybe with time we can embrace the civility we both desire."

314

"Where are my men?"

"As before, I assure you, they are well. You might be surprised to learn this, but three of them have already joined our ranks. Happily, I might add. It took very little persuasion."

Jack didn't believe him. "Which ones?"

"I'll try to get their names right. Edmundo, Emilio, and the one from Italy, Lorenzo. He was most enthusiastic, but you know how Italians are."

Jack just looked at him.

"No doubt you're wondering if I'm lying, but I assure you, I'm not. People lie, generally, because they are afraid to tell the truth. I harbor no fear." He motioned to the tray. "Go ahead, Jack. Eat. The food is delicious. My chef makes a rather exquisite frittata. You'd almost forget we're in the middle of a jungle. And the passion fruit smoothie is my favorite. I find myself craving it."

Jack got up and sat down at the table. Amash sat down at the foot of the cot. After Jack had taken a few bites, Amash said, "Have you had a chance to consider my proposal? My three simple requests."

"No."

"Disappointing. May I ask why?"

"I don't need to. You're just Hatch two-point-oh."

To Jack's surprise, the sovereign erupted in laughter. "That's very funny, Jack. Not true, but very funny." He breathed in deeply. "Oh, Hatch. I almost miss the twisted loon. The thing is, Hatch had a god complex. His freakish philosophy was all about the triumph of the 'Glows,' as he called them. He wanted to repopulate the world with these mutants and forever be known as its creator—the new God of Genesis. What good that would do him, I'll never know. There is no life after death, Jack. So why waste precious breath of life to create a legacy you will never even know existed? The only earthly certainty, my friend, is oblivion.

"The fool, Hatch, believed that a world populated by Glows would look back at him as the creator of a new species. No offense to your friends, but we don't care about these electric people. They're a curiosity, to be sure, but nothing more. Even the electric rats and bats, while interesting, are but a means to an end.

"We're not about populating the world with a new order, Jack. We are about populating the world with *our* order. And so far as the Starxource plants, it was never our intention to draw our power from a monthly electric bill. We would much rather use that electricity to burn down the world and build a new one. A better one. One where people are free and happy."

"If you're so big on freedom, why do you keep me locked up?"

"Yes, ironic, isn't it? That's what happens when an idealist crosses a realist."

"And your drug smuggling. You're destroying lives."

"Again, just a means to an end. If people are stupid enough to use drugs, they must already hate their lives. That they are weak, do not blame us." He tilted his head. "How is the frittata? Is it as good as I promised?"

Jack looked up at his captor. "Why are you so interested in me?"

Amash looked at him for a moment, then said, "I'm almost afraid to answer."

"Why?"

"Because I'm not sure you would respect a sentimental man."

"Sentimental?"

"There is that side of me, Jack. Just as there is in you. Wade is proof of that. Like you, I have my fierce loyalties. And, like you, I too have had my heartbreaks."

Jack stopped eating to look at him.

Amash's voice fell softly. Reflectively. "I had a son, once. He was strong and brave and smart. In short, you remind me of him. You even look a little like him."

"You have a son?" Jack asked.

"*Had*," Amash said, the tone of his voice falling. "He's gone now. He was protesting on a college campus. The police called it a riot. He was shot and killed.

"The police and judges—the *system*—ruled it an accident, and my son's death was passed off as an unfortunate incident. The police officer was let off with a month's paid suspension." His eyes narrowed.

"He murdered my son, and they essentially gave him a month's vacation." He stopped speaking for a moment, then exhaled loudly. "I know loss too, Jack. Just like you."

Jack said, "I'm sorry."

"Thank you," Amash said. He leaned forward. "I'd like to share an observation with you. It's about the current state of the world we live in. All great cultures follow the same pattern—the Romans, the Mayans, now the Americans. They start with a vision of a better life. A dream, they call it. They grow through hard work and this shared dream. Then, once they've achieved the fruits of that dream, it is almost as if mass amnesia sets in.

"It's like the generations of the wealthy: The first generation works and sacrifices to create a better situation for themselves and their posterity. The second generation enjoys the benefits of the first generation's hard work. Then the third generation thinks nothing of their predecessors' sacrifice and just believe themselves entitled to their privilege. More times than not, they blame their benefactors for not giving them more. It is an awful weakness of humanity, Jack. People do not value what they do not work for.

"American culture has peaked. Americans today are entitled, paranoid, selfish, and shallow creatures who overvalue their own opinions." He looked into Jack's eyes. "Or am I wrong?"

"I don't know," Jack said softly.

"You don't know, or you don't want to admit it?" Amash sighed. "We're not bringing down a society; it's doing that on its own. We're just giving it a shove.

"So, before you judge us, I ask that you take just a moment to truly consider what we are about. I will make you a promise. After I teach you our way, if you can honestly tell me that you disagree, I will let you walk away from here, back to that cultural cesspool you call home."

Jack looked at him skeptically. "You'll let me go?"

"If that's what you want. I'll even give you a ride home. I only ask that you give me a fair hearing. Does that sound fair?"

"Fair enough," Jack said.

"All right, then," Amash said, nodding. "Let's begin with our current situation. Last night one of the guards told me that you called the Chasqui a parasite."

Jack started to speak, but the sovereign raised his hand.

"It's okay, Jack. No need to explain yourself. Some might have taken offense to that, but I don't. In the ancient tongue, the word 'parasite' comes from the word '*parasitos*,' meaning 'one who eats from the table of another.' What is a parasite? It's an organism that lives on a host and benefits by deriving nutrients at the host's expense." He leaned forward. "In short, it's a victor. To be a parasite, one must be smarter, more cunning, and more powerful than one's host. Am I wrong?"

Jack shook his head.

"As I said earlier, we are not the Chasqui. Our true name is one I cannot reveal to you because it is a secret to the world—a secret I hope to someday share with you. That will be a very special moment, because our true and ancient name is holy, and I speak it only with great reverence. But, for our discussion's sake, I'll refer to us as *the Cause*.

"Thirty-six years ago, the Cause came to South America, seeking a new host. We initially went after the drug cartels, but we found them too unstable. They were constantly at war with each other and under constant government scrutiny.

"But the source of the cartels' drugs was a different matter. That's when we found the Shining Path movement. The Shining Path espoused a Maoist Communist philosophy, claiming that they were the champion of the working class." Amash sighed. "The usual hogwash, of course. When in history has a Communist rebellion really been about anything except increasing their own power and privilege?

"Not surprisingly, the Shining Path soldiers raped, murdered, and plundered the peasants in the countryside, forcing them into the servitude of growing coca leaves at slave-labor wages. What irony, enslaving the very people they claimed to be liberating.

"That's about the time that we came along. The Shining Path

were always looking for soldiers and mercenaries, so we filled their ranks.

"After several years three things happened. First, Peruvian president Fujimori began in earnest to crack down on Peru's terrorists." He suddenly smiled. "I believe you and your friends are still on that Most-Wanted Terrorists list."

Jack nodded. "We still are."

"Well done," he said. "Anyway, hundreds of rebels were killed, including some of ours.

"Second, thanks to the multitude of Shining Path atrocities, the people themselves turned against the group. The government simply supplied guns to the locals, and they created their own patrols and began, with success, to hunt down the rebels. Imagine that, civilians killing soldiers for a change. What a twist.

"Then, third, the founder of the Shining Path himself was captured. It was a time when we could have easily taken over the organization, but, by then, there was not much left to take over.

"Fatefully, this was the same time that Hatch came to town recruiting his Elgen guard. I recognized the potential the opportunity presented, and we, as you say, signed up. Our guards provided labor and protection as Hatch built the first Starxource plant in the jungle—the same one you and your friends destroyed. I must say, that's when I first became a fan of yours, Jack. That's when I knew you were something special."

Jack didn't know what to say to that.

"We, the *Cause*, adopted the name 'Chasqui' in much the same way that an author adopts a pen name. It identified us, but it wasn't our true identity. We grew with the Elgen, but always with the intent that we would one day take it over and further our cause."

Amash's voice grew still more passionate. "Think of the long game, Jack. Governments, tyrants, and empires rise and fall. But after more than a thousand years, we, the *Cause*, are still here, sitting patiently behind the curtain, awaiting the final act. *We* are the final act."

The sovereign's face animated, and he raised his arms. "Can you appreciate what I'm offering you? You could be a part of history, Jack, or, you can be blown away in its dust.

"If you choose the former, you will be given power and wealth you never dreamed of—the power to protect and provide for all those you care about. You will usher in a new world order and bring the peace of one world government to the stupid masses. Think of it, Jack. No more wars. No more hunger. No more want. Order from chaos."

He breathed out slowly. "America is sinking. The whole world is sinking. I'm offering you a life raft." He smiled. "No, I'm offering you a throne." He looked deeply into Jack's eyes. "Is what you left at home really worth all that?"

PART SEVEN

55

A Change of Plans

I woke around five the next morning. I looked around the warehouse at my slumbering companions. Next to me Taylor was lightly snoring. She had woken in the middle of the night with a short scream. I wondered if she was having another dream. I hoped not.

I pulled on my clothes and walked out of the warehouse to the main house. It was still dark outside, and the jungle seemed just as alive as when I'd gone to bed. The jungle doesn't sleep.

Sometime in the night, Johnson had taken over Cibor's watch, and he was sitting outside the cage with his gun in his lap.

"Did you sleep at all?" I asked.

I startled him. "Morning, Michael. I got a few hours." He turned toward me. "Who was that you were talking to last night after we went to bed?"

"One of the prisoners."

"The guy in the birdcage?"

"Yes. We had to move him. They would have killed him if we'd put him back in with the others. They tried once already."

"Did he tell you anything useful?"

"He told us everything."

"Let's catch up over breakfast. Jacinta's cooking for everyone."

"That's unexpected," I said. "Considering we're leaving so soon."

"We've got to eat. At least she won't have to do the dishes."

"I'll see you in a minute," I said. I walked into the main house. The smell of Jacinta's cooking filled the room.

"*Buenos días,*" Jacinta said from across the room.

"Good morning," I replied.

"How did you sleep?" she asked.

"About as well as expected. It smells good. What are you making?"

"Scrambled eggs, sausages, and jungle pancakes."

"What are jungle pancakes?"

"They have bananas in them. I was told that bananas are good for the electric ones. Or was Johnson, what is the saying, pulling my leg?"

I smiled. "No, it's true. The potassium strengthens our electricity. Would you like some help?"

"Everything is about ready. Could you tell everyone to come?"

"Sure. I'll round up the herd."

I walked back to the warehouse, passing the toucan cage on the way. Cristiano was standing near the front of the cage.

"Mr. Vey, sir. *Buenos días.*"

He looked worse than he had earlier, his face purple and black from the beating he'd received. One of his eyes was nearly closed.

"How did you sleep?" I asked.

"In a bird's cage," he said. "I think the toucan tried to bite off my nose."

"It is big," I said.

"The bird's beak is very big," he said.

"I meant your beak."

I could still detect a slight smile.

"Are you leaving this morning?" he asked.

"Yes. Soon."

"Please take me with you. I will fight with you."

"I'll think about it," I said.

"Thank you for your consideration," he said.

Before I got to the warehouse, Taylor walked out. "Good morning," she said. "How did you sleep?"

"Next to you," I said. "It was nice."

"It *was* nice." She looked down. "Except for the dream I had."

"I heard you scream. What was it?"

She shook her head. "I saw Jack. He was free."

"Finally, a good dream."

"He was wearing a Chasqui uniform."

"I don't know what to say to that." I exhaled slowly. "Something else, Cristiano asked me if he could join us. What do you think?"

"I don't see why not. At the least we should let him go. He's not going to help these guys. He's more afraid of them than he is of us."

"I'll put it to a vote after we eat. I told Jacinta I'd round up the troops. Is everyone up?"

"Yes. They're getting ready."

"We're meeting after breakfast. But before we do, I need to ask you to do something for me."

She smiled at me. "I'll do anything for you."

"Good." I looked into her eyes. "I want you to go home."

She blinked. "What?"

"You heard what the Chasqui said. They don't care about us; they only want you. You need to go home."

"I'm not going home without Tara. Besides, I'm safer here. They got Tara in Boise. Here, we got them."

"Going after them in the jungle is a whole different thing. I can't risk losing you."

"But I'm supposed to be okay risking you? It doesn't work that way. I can't leave her here. And I'm not leaving you again. We need each other." She leaned forward. "It will be okay, Michael. I promise." She kissed me. "Now let's round everyone up. We've got a lot to do."

We let everyone know that breakfast was ready; then Taylor and I went back to the kitchen while the rest of our group made their way to the house, groggy and carrying their luggage and packs. Nichelle looked like she hadn't slept in days.

Jax and Cassy walked in together, which made me happy. I was glad she wasn't alone.

Taylor and I helped serve breakfast. I poured papaya and mango juice while Taylor served the sausage and eggs and Jacinta flipped pancakes. After everyone was served, Taylor and I took a plate out to Johnson and ate with him. We told him about our interrogation of Cristiano; then we went back into the house to start the meeting.

"Gather in," Johnson shouted. "Time to meet."

Everyone came together.

"Who's watching the cage?" Cibor asked.

"It doesn't matter much," Jacinta said. "They cannot get out."

"You mean I lost all that sleep for nothing?" Cibor said.

"Better safe than dead," Johnson said.

I walked up to the front of the room with Johnson.

"Congratulations, everyone," Johnson said. "Yesterday was a well-executed operation. Instead of them capturing us, we captured them. A special thanks to Cassy. I can't tell you how many times I could have used you in Afghanistan."

Jax and Cassy were sitting on the floor next to each other. He gave her five.

"Glad to help," she said.

"Last night we interrogated the prisoners and got valuable information. As we thought, they were tracking us by the buttons. No more. We have confiscated the GPS handheld from them, and the buttons are currently shielded in a lead pipe.

"They confirmed that Tara is being held at the Starxource plant, which is also being used by the Chasqui to create electrified bats as well as to process drugs.

"We also learned that Jack is being held at the Chasqui cave complex, about four kilometers southwest of the Starxource plant. Right now, attacking the cave is not an option. The jungle around it is nearly impenetrable and full of hidden cameras and automatic-machine-gun nests. Michael, you and Tessa know about those."

"Too well," Tessa said.

"To our surprise, not one of them knew anything about Abigail. It's possible that she wasn't kidnapped by the Chasqui after all."

McKenna elbowed Ostin. "You were right."

I wasn't sure if this was good news or not. Now we had almost nothing to go on.

"Perhaps the most surprising thing we learned is that the Chasqui weren't looking for all of you. They were only looking for Taylor. They kidnapped Tara by mistake, thinking that she was Taylor."

"That's a relief," Zeus said.

Taylor looked at him. "Speak for yourself."

"What do they want with Taylor?" Cassy asked.

"They want my dreams," Taylor said.

Johnson nodded. "The Chasqui leader believes that Taylor can see the future."

"She can," I said. "It's part of her gift."

"It's not a gift," Taylor said. "Not one I want."

"But it's one that the Chasqui want," Johnson said. "So we need to be careful of Taylor's safety." He looked over at Jacinta. "On a personal note, I'd like to thank Jacinta. She has sacrificed everything for us to be here."

We started to clap for her, but Jacinta held up her hand to stop us.

"No, please. You'll embarrass me. I sacrificed little. I lost all that really mattered to me a long time ago." She sighed. "Unfortunately, this morning I will have to release all my animals. There are many cages, so I would appreciate some help."

"I'll help," McKenna said.

"So will I," Tessa and Nichelle said almost simultaneously.

"Thank you."

"Speaking of animals," Zeus said. "What are we going to do with the prisoners?"

"We'll leave them here," Johnson said. "We'll let the Chasqui release them."

"What if they don't?" McKenna asked.

"Then it's on them," Johnson said. "We don't have many options. We can shoot them, or we can detain them. But if we let them out, they'll just hunt us again."

"What about the dude in the toucan cage?" Quentin asked. "What's his story?"

"Yeah, who is that?" Nichelle asked. "It looks like the birds beat him up or something."

"It wasn't the birds," McKenna said. "It was the other Chasqui."

"His name is Cristiano," I said. "We interrogated him last night and got a lot of important information from him."

"He's a good guy," Taylor said.

"How can he be a good guy?" Quentin said. "He's a Chasqui."

"You were an Elgen once too," Taylor said.

"Whoa," Quentin said, lifting his hands. "That was harsh."

"She didn't mean it that way," I said.

"Actually, I did," Taylor said. "Look at Quentin now. He's a good man. Sometimes people choose evil because they like evil, and sometimes they choose evil because they don't know better. It's not the same thing. Last night I saw into Cristiano's mind. He's a victim of the Chasqui just like Quentin and Zeus and Tara were victims of Hatch. Cristiano risked his life to help us. I say we let him join us."

McKenna spoke up. "I'm not a mind reader, but I believe he's good too. The other prisoners almost beat him to death because he talked to us. They might have if Michael hadn't stopped them."

I looked out over the room. "There's more to Cristiano's story. He was a server for the Chasqui leader, Eli Amash. He spent more than a year at his side. He could be an asset to us. He knows everything they're planning.

"He told us that in the last year the Chasqui have taken over the coca production in Peru and are now using electrified bats to destroy the coca crops outside the country. They've already destroyed thousands of acres of Colombian crops. Their goal is to create a monopoly on cocaine.

"But the drugs are only a means to an end. Their endgame is something much bigger—the destruction of civilization as we know it. The Chasqui drug trafficking is weakening countries while providing the Chasqui with the money they need to grow their empire and build an army bigger than Hatch ever dreamed of.

"But it gets worse. The Chasqui have developed a weapon of mass destruction by weaponizing bats. They have the potential to destroy entire cities. They already destroyed a military base in the VRAEM using only a few dozen bats.

"Cristiano says that the Chasqui are about to release a million bats in the city of Arequipa, the second-largest city in Peru. Over a million people live there. If they succeed, it could cause tens of thousands of deaths and destroy hundreds of thousands of homes."

"We need to warn them," Jacinta said.

"Warn who?" I said. "Who are we going to tell that a swarm of electrified bats are going to burn down their city? They would laugh." I looked out over the group. "Arequipa is just the beginning. They're using the destruction of the city as a threat, but it's much more than that. It's the first shot in their war. They already have the potential to launch terrorist attacks on almost every major city in the world— New York, Los Angeles, London, Tokyo, Paris, Rome—any city within a hundred miles of an ocean.

"Once they have a big enough army, they will start to tear apart the world, one country at a time. The resulting chaos will destroy the world economy and break the system."

I took a deep breath. "We came here to save our friends—three people we care about. But now that we're here, Jack is unreachable, we have no idea where Abi is, and Tara's our only real possibility for rescue. In the meantime, we're the only ones in the world who know what the Chasqui are planning. Thousands will die if we do nothing. I say we stop them."

I looked over at Johnson. "What about Alpha Team?"

"We're in," Johnson said.

"Roger that," Bentrude said.

I looked back out to my group. "Electroclan?"

"I can't speak for anyone else," Cassy said, "but I don't think we have a choice."

"Anyone not in?" Quentin asked.

Everyone shook their heads. Zeus arced lightning between his hands. "All in."

"We're doing this," Quentin said. "So, we stop the destruction of the city, then go after Tara?"

"We should act simultaneously," Ostin said. "The Chasqui's attack on Arequipa will distract them. That gives us a better opportunity to save Tara."

"So we split up again," Taylor said, frowning.

"Who goes where?" Tessa asked.

"We can't plan our tactics until we have a strategy," Johnson said. "And we can't make our strategy until we know more about what we're facing."

"What's our timing?" Quentin asked.

"The bats are vulnerable to water," I said. "Cristiano said the Elgen are waiting for the end of the rainy season before they strike."

"We're near the end of it right now," Jacinta said.

"Which means they could strike at any time. Up until now, they have been releasing bats from planes, dropping only a few hundred at a time. For this new attack, they plan to transport the bats in cargo containers to Arequipa. That means they'll have to bring the bats upriver to load them onto the trucks. That will take several days. They won't be able to do that without us seeing them."

"So we stake out the river," Ian said. "Then what?"

"I don't recommend trying to take them out in Puerto," Johnson said. "That's where they'll be at their strongest. We need to hit them in transit, either on the boats or the trucks."

"We could sink their boats," Quentin said. "That would kill all the bats."

"Again," Johnson said, "we need more information before we can plan our attack. But for now we've got to get out of here."

"Where are we going?" Tessa asked.

"We're not sure yet. Last night Michael came up with a bold plan." Johnson turned to me. "Michael?"

"I was thinking we could move into the Chasqui's base in Puerto."

"That is definitely bold," Zeus said. "Crazy, maybe. But bold."

"They'd never think to look for us there," Cassy said.

"I think it's too risky," Ostin said. "I'd rather hide in the jungle."

Johnson said, "This morning, Jacinta came up with another idea. Jacinta?"

Jacinta stood. "A friend of mine owns a jungle lodge about two miles down the river. Right now he's hosting a Save the Rain Forest fundraiser. Foreigners are attending from all around the world. We could blend in with them and no one will know.

"It will also take us closer to the Starxource plant, and since the lodge is on the river, it will give us a place to watch the river's traffic. When those cargo containers come floating by, we will see them."

"Do they have room for us?" Nichelle asked.

"I've spoken to my friend," Jacinta said. "We will have to share rooms, but he has enough bungalows for all of us."

"Brilliant," Ostin said.

"I agree," I said. "It's a better option."

"All right," Johnson said. "If we're agreed, then let's pack up and go."

Jacinta said, ". . . The animals."

"Yes . . . after we release the animals."

"There's one more thing," I said. "Cristiano has asked to come with us to fight the Chasqui. I questioned him for more than an hour. Taylor was inside his mind most of that time. We believe he is sincere. Like Jacinta, he has reason to hate the Chasqui. They murdered his brother and two of his friends. He's also the only one we interrogated who knows where the cave is and how to get into it. He is willing to lead us to it."

"He is either very brave or is planning to lead us to our death," Bentrude said.

"That's why I'm asking for a vote," I said. "How many of you think we should take him with us?"

Everyone raised their hand except for Quentin and Bentrude. Then Quentin shrugged and lifted his hand. "All right. I'll roll the dice."

"Are any opposed?"

No one raised their hand.

I looked at Bentrude. "You didn't vote."

"Yeah, I don't know. I've seen things like this go both ways. I've seen mercy cost a man his life." He looked over at Taylor. "But we didn't have someone who could read people's minds then either. So, I'll go along with whatever the group decides."

"All right, then," I said. "We'll bring him. One more thing. Cassy, can you freeze monkeys?"

Cassy grinned. "That's not something a girl gets asked every day," she said. "I've made squirrels fall out of trees, so I'm sure I could. Muscle is muscle."

"We're pretty sure that the Chasqui have another GPS tracker for the buttons. If it's okay with Jacinta, before we let the animals out, I'd like to attach the buttons to the monkeys and give the Chasqui something else to chase."

Everyone laughed.

"I'm fine with that," Jacinta said.

"That's brilliant," Ostin said. "I wish I'd thought of that."

"You would have," I said. "I just beat you to it."

56

An Unexpected Phone Call

It took us more than an hour to pack up the vans and release the animals, which ended up taking longer than we expected. The anaconda took six of us to get it out of its tank, and the ill-natured javelinas, the ones that Nichelle had called pigs, charged Ostin as he opened the gate. Fortunately, Zeus was nearby and Tased them. They squealed like pigs.

The most difficult animal to release was the caiman. It was sixteen feet long and looked like a dinosaur but moved like a statue. If I hadn't known better, I would have thought it was dead. We finally just opened the pen's door, put a dead chicken next to the gate, and left it to find its own way out.

The last animals we released were the monkeys. Cassy froze them one at a time, and Jacinta attached the buttons to their backs before releasing them into the jungle.

Cristiano was released along with the toucans. He was so grateful for our decision that he almost cried. He said, "You won't be sorry. I will defend you with my life."

"I hope you mean it," I said. "Because we might take you up on it."

"I would rather die free than live Chasqui," he said.

We gave him back his Chasqui boots and uniform. He didn't want to wear them, but we figured that keeping him in uniform could come in handy. Besides, we didn't have anything else for him to wear.

As Taylor and I were getting into the van to leave, my satellite phone rang.

"Who is it?" Taylor asked.

"It's probably my father." I glanced down at the ID then back up, the surprise apparently evident on my face.

"Who is it?" Taylor asked again.

"It's Jack."

I pushed the receive button. "Jack?"

"Michael, brother. It's so good to hear your voice."

He sounded strangely calm. "It's good to hear yours. We've been so worried. Where are you?"

"I'm fine," he said.

"That's not what I asked," I said. "Where are you?"

"Not far. Which is convenient, since I need to talk to you. You and Taylor."

"The Chasqui are looking for Taylor."

"The Chasqui don't exist anymore," Jack said. "But if we can meet up in the jungle, I'll explain everything."

"We're not going into the jungle."

"Of course you are. You're planning your visit to us right now. You came here to rescue Tara, didn't you?"

"We came down to rescue you."

"There's no need for that, so I'll make things easier for you. We'll make you a swap. Tara for Taylor."

"Who's 'we'?"

"My new friend, Sovereign Amash."

My heart froze. It was Taylor's dream. "You've joined the Chasqui?"

"Well, again, the Chasqui don't exist anymore. But if that's what you're calling them, yes. I have."

"What happened to you, Jack?"

"Good things, Michael. You don't need to worry about me. These are exciting times. My eyes have been opened."

"Opened to a lie," I said. "Whatever your new friend is telling you isn't real."

"Oh, it's real, all right. Real enough that I'd bet my life on it. Anyway, that's the deal. Bring Taylor to us, or go back to Idaho without Tara."

"Neither of those are going to happen," I said.

"Be smart, Michael. What's happening here is way bigger than you and me. It's bigger than the Electroclan. It's bigger than Hatch and the Elgen ever dreamed of being. These are historic moments, and, unfortunately, you're on the wrong side of history, my friend. You have no place here. This isn't your war."

"You're wrong, Jack. You're holding Tara captive, so that makes it my war. And, if I have to, I'll bring it to you."

"Then I look forward to seeing you, my friend," Jack said. "We'll be waiting."

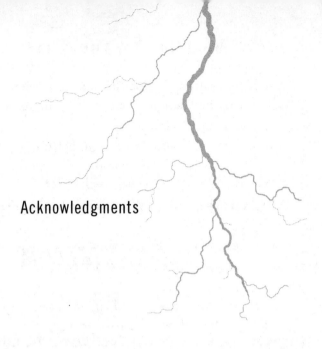

Acknowledgments

Thank you to Jonathan Karp and Jon Anderson, who encouraged me to bring Michael back and then gave me a wonderful team to work with: Valerie Garfield and Kristin Gilson. It really has been a pleasure working with you.

Thank you, Owen Richardson, for the electric cover design.

Keri and Jangles. So fresh.

Laurie Liss, bff. Thank you to Tyler Cardon and Mercury Ink for all your support. Diane, glad once again for the assist.

Most of all, a sincere thanks to Veyniacs around the world, who have kept Michael and the Electroclan alive. Shock on, my friends.

Join the Veyniac Nation!

For Michael Vey trivia, sneak peeks, and events in your area,
follow Michael and the rest of the Electroclan at:

MICHAELVEY.COM

Facebook.com/MichaelVeyOfficialFanPage

Twitter.com/MichaelVey

Instagram.com/RichardPaulEvansAuthor

RICHARD PAUL EVANS

is the #1 *New York Times* and *USA Today* bestselling author of more than forty novels. There are currently more than thirty-five million copies of his books in print worldwide, translated into more than twenty-four languages. Richard has won the American Mothers Book Award, two first-place Storytelling World Awards, the Romantic Times Best Women's Novel of the Year Award, and the German Leserpreis Gold Award for Romance, and is a five-time recipient of the Religion Communicators Council's Wilbur Award. Seven of Richard's books have been produced as television movies. In 2011, Richard began writing Michael Vey, a #1 *New York Times* bestselling young adult series that has won more than a dozen awards. Richard is the founder of The Christmas Box International, an organization devoted to maintaining emergency shelters for children and providing services and resources for abused, neglected, or homeless children and young adults. To date, more than 125,000 youths have been helped by the charity. For his humanitarian work, Richard has received the Washington Times Humanitarian of the Century Award and the Volunteers of America National Empathy Award. Richard lives in Salt Lake City with his wife, Keri, and their five children and two grandchildren. You can learn more about Richard on his website RichardPaulEvans.com.